T. MacVeagh Thompson

C

MR. CREWE'S CAREER

THE MACMILLAN COMPANY
NEW YORK · BOSTON · CHICAGO
ATLANTA · SAN FRANCISCO

MACMILLAN & CO., Limited
LONDON · BOMBAY · CALCUTTA
MELBOURNE

THE MACMILLAN CO. OF CANADA, Ltd.
TORONTO

"I can make you governor of this State."

MR. CREWE'S CAREER

BY

WINSTON CHURCHILL

AUTHOR OF "RICHARD CARVEL," "THE CRISIS,"
"THE CROSSING," "CONISTON," ETC.

ILLUSTRATED

New York
THE MACMILLAN COMPANY
1908

Norwood Press
J. S. Cushing Co. — Berwick & Smith Co.
Norwood, Mass., U.S.A.

To

THE MEN WHO

IN EVERY STATE OF THE UNION

ARE ENGAGED IN THE STRUGGLE FOR

PURER POLITICS

THIS BOOK

IS DEDICATED

CONTENTS

CONTENTS

LIST OF ILLUSTRATIONS

MR. CREWE'S CAREER

CHAPTER I

THE HONOURABLE HILARY VANE SITS FOR HIS PORTRAIT

I MAY as well begin this story with Mr. Hilary Vane, more frequently addressed as the Honourable Hilary Vane, although it was the gentleman's proud boast that he had never held an office in his life. He belonged to the Vanes of Camden Street, — a beautiful village in the hills near Ripton, — and was, in common with some other great men who had made a noise in New York and the nation, a graduate of Camden Wentworth Academy. But Mr. Vane, when he was at home, lived on a wide, maple-shaded street in the "city" of Ripton, cared for by an elderly housekeeper who had more edges than a new-fangled mowing machine. The house was a porticoed one which had belonged to the Austens for a hundred years or more, for Hilary Vane had married, towards middle age, Miss Sarah Austen. In two years he was a widower, and he never tried it again; he had the Austens' house, and that many-edged woman, Euphrasia Cotton, the Austens' housekeeper.

The house was of wood, and was painted white as regularly as leap year. From the street front to the vegetable garden in the extreme rear it was exceedingly long, and — perhaps for propriety's sake — Hilary Vane lived at one end of it and Euphrasia at the other. Hilary was sixty-five, Euphrasia seventy, which is not old for frugal people, — though it is just as well to add that there had never been a breath of scandal about either of them, in Ripton or elsewhere. For the Honourable Hilary's modest needs one

room sufficed, and the front parlour had not been used since
poor Sarah Austen's demise, thirty years before this story
opens.

In those thirty years, by a sane and steady growth,
Hilary Vane had achieved his present eminent position in
the State. He was trustee for I know not how many
people and institutions, a deacon in the first church, a
lawyer of such ability that he sometimes was accorded the
courtesy-title of "Judge." His only vice — if it could
be called such — was in occasionally placing a piece, the
size of a pea, of a particular kind of plug tobacco under
his tongue,—and this was not known to many people.
Euphrasia could not be called a wasteful person, and Hilary
had accumulated no small portion of this world's goods, and
placed them as propriety demanded, where they were not
visible to the naked eye : and be it added in his favour
that he gave as secretly, to institutions and hospitals the
finances and methods of which were known to him.

As concrete evidence of the Honourable Hilary Vane's
importance, when he travelled he had only to withdraw
from his hip pocket a book in which many coloured cards
were neatly inserted, an open-sesame which permitted
him to sit without payment even in those wheeled palaces
of luxury known as Pullman cars. Within the limits of
the State he did not even have to open the book, but
merely say, with a twinkle of his eyes to the conductor,
"Good morning, John," and John would reply with a
bow and a genial and usually witty remark, and point him
out to a nobody who sat in the back of the car. So far
had Mr. Hilary Vane's talents carried him.

The beginning of this eminence dated back to the days
before the Empire, when there were many little principalities of railroads fighting among themselves. For we
are come to a changed America. There was a time,
in the days of the sixth Edward of England, when the
great landowners found it more profitable to consolidate
the farms, seize the common lands, and acquire riches
hitherto undreamed of. Hence the rising of tailor Ket
and others, and the levelling of fences and barriers, and

the eating of many sheep. It may have been that Mr.
Vane had come across this passage in English history,
but he drew no parallels. His first position of trust
had been as counsel for that principality known in the
old days as the Central Railroad, of which a certain Mr.
Duncan had been president, and Hilary Vane had fought
the Central's battles with such telling effect that when it
was merged into the one Imperial Railroad, its stockholders — to the admiration of financiers — were guaran-
teed ten per cent. It was, indeed, rumoured that Hilary
drew the Act of Consolidation itself. At any rate, he
was too valuable an opponent to neglect, and after a certain interval of time Mr. Vane became chief counsel in the
State for the Imperial Railroad, on which dizzy height
we now behold him. And he found, by degrees, that he
had no longer time for private practice.

It is perhaps gratuitous to add that the Honourable
Hilary Vane was a man of convictions. In politics he
would have told you — with some vehemence, if you
seemed to doubt — that he was a Republican. Treason
to party he regarded with a deep-seated abhorrence, as
an act for which a man should be justly outlawed. If he
were in a mellow mood, with the right quantity of Honey
Dew tobacco under his tongue, he would perhaps tell you
why he was a Republican, if he thought you worthy of
his confidence. He believed in the gold standard, for one
thing; in the tariff (left unimpaired in its glory) for
another, and with a wave of his hand would indicate the
prosperity of the nation which surrounded him, — a prosperity too sacred to tamper with.

One article of his belief, and in reality the chief article,
Mr. Vane would not mention to you. It was perhaps
because he had never formulated the article for himself.
It might be called a faith in the divine right of Imperial
Railroads to rule, but it was left out of the verbal creed.
This is far from implying hypocrisy to Mr. Vane. It
was his foundation-rock and too sacred for light conversation. When he allowed himself to be bitter against
various "young men with missions" who had sprung up

in various States of the Union, so-called purifiers of politics, he would call them the unsuccessful with a grievance, and recommend to them the practice of charity, forbearance, and other Christian virtues. Thank God, his State was not troubled with such.

In person Mr. Hilary Vane was tall, with a slight stoop to his shoulders, and he wore the conventional double-breasted black coat, which reached to his knees, and square-toed congress boots. He had a Puritan beard, the hawk-like Vane nose, and a twinkling eye that spoke of a sense of humour and a knowledge of the world. In short, he was no man's fool, and on occasions had been more than a match for certain New York lawyers with national reputations.

It is rare, in this world of trouble, that such an apparently ideal and happy state of existence is without a canker. And I have left the revelation of the canker to the last. Ripton knew it was there, Camden Street knew it, and Mr. Vane's acquaintances throughout the State; but nobody ever spoke of it. Euphrasia shed over it the only tears she had known since Sarah Austen died, and some of these blotted the only letters she wrote. Hilary Vane did not shed tears, but his friends suspected that his heart-strings were torn, and pitied him. Hilary Vane fiercely resented pity, and that was why they did not speak of it. This trouble of his was the common point on which he and Euphrasia touched, and they touched only to quarrel. Let us out with it — Hilary Vane had a wild son, whose name was Austen.

Euphrasia knew that in his secret soul Mr. Vane attributed this wildness, and what he was pleased to designate as profligacy, to the Austen blood. And Euphrasia resented it bitterly. Sarah Austen had been a young, elfish thing when he married her, — a dryad, the elderly and learned Mrs. Tredway had called her. Mr. Vane had understood her about as well as he would have understood Mary, Queen of Scots, if he had been married to that lady. Sarah Austen had a wild, shy beauty, startled, alert eyes like an animal, and rebellious black hair that curled about her ears and gave her a faunlike appearance. With a pipe and the costume of Rosalind she would have been perfect. She had had a habit of running off for the day into the hills with her son, and the conventions of Ripton had been to her as so many defunct blue laws. During her brief married life there had been periods of defiance from her lasting a week, when she would not speak to Hilary or look at him, and these periods would be followed by violent spells of weeping in Euphrasia's arms, when the house was no place for Hilary. He possessed by matrimony an intricate mechanism of which his really admirable brain could not grasp the first principles; he felt for her a real if unaccountable affection, but when she died he heaved a sigh of relief, at which he was immediately horrified.

Austen he understood little better, but his affection for the child may be likened to the force of a great river rushing through a narrow gorge, and he vied with Euphrasia in spoiling him. Neither knew what they were doing, and the spoiling process was interspersed with occasional and (to Austen) unmeaning intervals of severe discipline. The boy loved the streets and the woods and his fellow-beings; his punishments were a series of afternoons in the house, during one of which he wrecked the bedroom where he was confined, and was soundly whaled with an old slipper that broke under the process. Euphrasia kept the slipper, and once showed it to Hilary during a quarrel they had when the boy was grown up and gone and the house was silent, and Hilary had turned away, choking, and left the room. Such was his cross.

To make it worse, the boy had loved his father. Nay, still loved him. As a little fellow, after a scolding for some wayward prank, he would throw himself into Hilary's arms and cling to him, and never knew how near he came to unmanning him. As Austen grew up, they saw the world in different colours: blue to Hilary was red to Austen, and white, black; essentials to one were nonessentials to the other; boys and girls, men and women, abhorred by one were boon companions to the other.

Austen made fun of the minister, and was compelled to go to church twice on Sundays and to prayer-meeting on Wednesdays. Then he went to Camden Street, to live with his grandparents in the old Vane house and attend Camden Wentworth Academy. His letters, such as they were, were inimitable if crude, but contained not the kind of humour Hilary Vane knew. Camden Wentworth, principal and teachers, was painted to the life; and the lad could hardly wait for vacation time to see his father, only to begin quarrelling with him again.

I pass over escapades in Ripton that shocked one half of the population and convulsed the other half. Austen went to the college which his father had attended, — a college of splendid American traditions, — and his career there might well have puzzled a father of far greater tolerance and catholicity. Hilary Vane was a trustee, and journeyed more than once to talk the matter over with the president, who had been his classmate there.

"I love that boy, Hilary," the president had said at length, when pressed for a frank opinion, — "there isn't a soul in the place, I believe, that doesn't, — undergraduates and faculty, — but he has given me more anxious thought than any scholar I have ever had."

"Trouble," corrected Mr. Vane, sententiously.

"Well, yes, trouble," answered the president, smiling, "but upon my soul, I think it is all animal spirits."

"A euphemism for the devil," said Hilary, grimly; "he is the animal part of us, I have been brought up to believe."

The president was a wise man, and took another tack.

"He has a really remarkable mind, when he chooses to use it. Every once in a while he takes your breath away —but he has to become interested. A few weeks ago Hays came to me direct from his lecture room to tell me about a discussion of Austen's in constitutional law. Hays, you know, is not easily enthused, but he declares your son has as fine a legal brain as he has come across in his experience. But since then, I am bound to admit," added the president, sadly, "Austen seems not to have looked at a lesson."

"'Unstable as water, thou shalt not excel,'" replied Hilary.

"He'll sober down," said the president, stretching his conviction a little, "he has two great handicaps: he learns too easily, and he is too popular." The president looked out of his study window across the common, surrounded by the great elms which had been planted when Indian lads played among the stumps and the red flag of England had flown from the tall pine staff. The green was covered now with students of a conquering race, skylarking to and fro as they looked on at a desultory baseball game. "I verily believe," said the president, "at a word from your son, most of them would put on their coats and follow him on any mad expedition that came into his mind."

Hilary Vane groaned more than once in the train back to Ripton. It meant nothing to him to be the father of the most popular man in college.

The "mad expedition" came at length in the shape of a fight with the townspeople, in which Austen, of course, was the ringleader. If he had inherited his mother's eccentricities, he had height and physique from the Vanes, and one result was a week in bed for the son of the local plumber and a damage suit against the Honourable Hilary. Another result was that Austen and a Tom Gaylord came back to Ripton on a long suspension, which, rumour said, would have been expulsion if Hilary were not a trustee. Tom Gaylord was proud of suspension in such company. More of him later. He was the son of old Tom Gaylord, who owned more lumber than any man in the State, and whom Hilary Vane believed to be the receptacle of all the vices.

Eventually Austen went back and graduated — not *summa cum laude*, honesty compels me to add. Then came the inevitable discussion, and to please his father he went to the Harvard Law School — for two years. At the end of that time, instead of returning to Ripton, a letter had come from him with the postmark of a Western State, where he had fled with a classmate who owned a ranch. Evidently the worldly consideration to be derived from conformity counted little with Austen Vane. Money was a medium only — not an end. He was in the saddle all day, with nothing but the horizon to limit him; he loved his father, and did not doubt his father's love for him, and he loved Euphrasia. He could support himself, but he must see life. The succeeding years brought letters and quaint, useless presents to both the occupants of the lonely house, — Navajo blankets and Indian jewellery and basket-work, — and Austen little knew how carefully these were packed away and surreptitiously gazed at from time to time. But to Hilary the Western career was a disgrace, and such meagre reports of it as came from other sources than Austen tended only to confirm him in this opinion.

It was commonly said of Mr. Paul Pardriff that not a newspaper fell from the press that he did not have a knowledge of its contents. Certain it was that Mr. Pardriff made a specialty of many kinds of knowledge, political and otherwise, and the information he could give — if he chose — about State and national affairs was of a recondite and cynical nature that made one wish to forget about the American flag. Mr. Pardriff was under forty, and with these gifts many innocent citizens of Ripton naturally wondered why the columns of his newspaper, the *Ripton Record*, did not more closely resemble the spiciness of his talk in the office of Gales' Hotel. The columns contained, instead, such efforts as essays on a national flower and the abnormal size of the hats of certain great men, notably Andrew Jackson; yes, and the gold standard; and in times of political stress they were devoted to a somewhat fulsome praise of regular and orthodox Republican candidates, — and praise of any one was not in character with the editor. Ill-natured people said that the matter in his paper might possibly be accounted for by the gratitude of the candidates, and the fact that Mr. Pardriff and his wife and his maid-servant and his hired man travelled on pink mileage books, which could only be had for love — not money. On the other hand, reputable witnesses had had it often from Mr. Pardriff that he was a reformer, and not at all in sympathy with certain practices which undoubtedly existed.

Some years before—to be exact, the year Austen Vane left the law school—Mr. Pardriff had proposed to exchange the *Ripton Record* with the editor of the *Pepper County Plainsman* in a far Western State. The exchange was effected, and Mr. Pardriff glanced over the *Plainsman* regularly once a week, though I doubt whether the Western editor ever read the *Record* after the first copy. One day in June Mr. Pardriff was seated in his sanctum above Merrill's drug store when his keen green eyes fell upon the following:—

"The *Plainsman* considers it safe to say that the sympathy of the people of Pepper County at large is with Mr. Austen Vane, whose personal difficulty with Jim Blodgett resulted so disastrously for Mr. Blodgett. The latter gentleman has long made himself obnoxious to local ranch owners by his persistent disregard of property lines and property, and it will be recalled that he is at present in hot water with the energetic Secretary of the Interior for fencing government lands. Vane, who was recently made manager of Ready Money Ranch, is one of the most popular young men in the county. He was unwillingly assisted over the State line by his friends. Although he has never been a citizen of the State, the *Plainsman* trusts that he may soon be back and become one of us. At last report Mr. Blodgett was resting easily."

This article obtained circulation in Ripton, although it was not copied into the *Record* out of deference to the feelings of the Honourable Hilary Vane. In addition to the personal regard Mr. Pardriff professed to have for the Honourable Hilary, it may be well to remember that Austen's father was, among other things, chairman of the State Committee. Mr. Tredway (largest railroad stockholder in Ripton) pursed his lips that were already pursed. Tom Gaylord roared with laughter. Two or three days later the Honourable Hilary, still in blissful ignorance, received a letter that agitated him sorely.

"DEAR FATHER: I hope you don't object to receiving a little visit from a prodigal, wayward son. To tell the truth, I have found it convenient to leave the Ready Money Ranch for a while, although Bob Tyner is good enough to say I may have the place when I come back. You know I often think of you and Phrasie back in Ripton, and I long to see the dear old town again. Expect me when you see me.

"Your aff. son,
"AUSTEN."

CHAPTER II

ON THE TREATMENT OF PRODIGALS

WHILE Euphrasia, in a frenzy of anticipation, garnished and swept the room which held for her so many memories of Austen's boyhood, even beating the carpet with her own hands, Hilary Vane went about his business with no apparent lack of diligence. But he was meditating. He had many times listened to the Reverend Mr. Weightman read the parable from the pulpit, but he had never reflected how it would be to be the father of a real prodigal. What was to be done about the calf? Was there to be a calf, or was there not? To tell the truth, Hilary wanted a calf, and yet to have one (in spite of Holy Writ) would seem to set a premium on disobedience and riotous living.

Again, Austen had reached thirty, an age when it was not likely he would settle down and live an orderly and godly life among civilized beings, and therefore a fatted calf was likely to be the first of many follies which he (Hilary) would live to regret. No, he would deal with justice. How he dealt will be seen presently, but when he finally reached this conclusion, the clipping from the *Pepper County Plainsman* had not yet come before his eyes.

It is worth relating how the clipping did come before his eyes, for no one in Ripton had the temerity to speak of it. Primarily, it was because Miss Victoria Flint had lost a terrier, and secondarily, because she was a person of strong likes and dislikes. In pursuit of the terrier she drove madly through Leith, which, as everybody knows, is a famous colony of rich summer residents. Victoria probably stopped at every house in Leith, and searched them with characteristic vigour and lack of ceremony, sometimes entering by the side door, and sometimes by the front, and

11

caring very little whether the owners were at home or not. Mr. Humphrey Crewe discovered her in a box-stall at Wedderburn, — as his place was called, — for it made little difference to Victoria that Mr. Crewe was a bachelor of marriageable age and millions. Full, as ever, of practical suggestions, Mr. Crewe proposed to telephone to Ripton and put an advertisement in the *Record*, which — as he happened to know — went to press the next day. Victoria would not trust to the telephone, whereupon Mr. Crewe offered to drive down with her.

" You'd bore me, Humphrey," said she, as she climbed into her runabout with the father and grandfather of the absentee. Mr. Crewe laughed as she drove away. He had a chemical quality of turning invidious remarks into compliments, and he took this one as Victoria's manner of saying that she did not wish to disturb so important a man.

Arriving in the hot main street of Ripton, her sharp eyes descried the *Record* sign over the drug store, and in an astonishingly short time she was in the empty office. Mr. Pardriff was at dinner. She sat down in the editorial chair and read a great deal of uninteresting matter, but at last found something on the floor (where the wind had blown it) which made her laugh. It was the account of Austen Vane's difficulty with Mr. Blodgett. Victoria did not know Austen, but she knew that the Honourable Hilary had a son of that name who had gone West, and this was what tickled her. She thrust the clipping in the pocket of her linen coat just as Mr. Pardriff came in.

Her conversation with the editor of the *Record* proved so entertaining that she forgot all about the clipping until she had reached Fairview, and had satisfied a somewhat imperious appetite by a combination of lunch and afternoon tea. Fairview was the "summer place" of Mr. Augustus P. Flint, her father, on a shelf of the hills in the town of Tunbridge, equidistant from Leith and Ripton. And Mr. Flint was the president of the Imperial Railroad, no less.

Yes, he had once been plain Gus Flint, many years ago, when he used to fetch the pocket-handkerchiefs of Mr.

Isaac D. Worthington of Brampton, and he was still "Gus" to his friends.   Mr. Flint's had been the brain which had largely conceived and executed the consolidation of principalities of which the Imperial Railroad was the result; and, as surely as tough metal prevails, Mr. Flint, after many other trials and errors of weaker stuff, had been elected to the place for which he was so supremely fitted. We are so used in America to these tremendous rises that a paragraph will suffice to place Mr. Flint in his Aladdin's palace.   To do him justice, he cared not a fig for the palace, and he would have been content with the farmhouse under the hill where his gardener lived.   You could not fool Mr. Flint on a horse or a farm, and he knew to a dot what a railroad was worth by travelling over it.   Like his governor-general and dependent, Mr. Hilary Vane, he had married a wife who had upset all his calculations. The lady discovered Mr. Flint's balance in the bank, and had proceeded to use it for her own glorification, and the irony of it all was that he could defend it from everybody else.   Mrs. Flint spent, and Mr. Flint paid the bills; for the first ten years protestingly, and after that he gave it up and let her go her own gait.

She had come from the town of Sharon, in another State, through which Mr. Flint's railroad also ran, and she had been known as the Rose of that place.   She had begun to rise immediately, with the kite-like adaptability of the American woman for high altitudes, and the leaden weight of the husband at the end of the tail was as nothing to her. She had begun it all by the study of people in hotels while Mr. Flint was closeted with officials and directors.   By dint of minute observation and reasoning powers and unflagging determination she passed rapidly through several strata, and had made a country place out of her husband's farm in Tunbridge, so happily and conveniently situated near Leith.   In winter they lived on Fifth Avenue.

One daughter alone had halted, for a minute period, this progress, and this daughter was Victoria — named by her mother.   Victoria was now twenty-one, and was not only of another generation, but might almost have been

judged of another race than her parents. The things for
which her mother had striven she took for granted, and
thought of them not at all, and she had by nature that
simplicity and astonishing frankness of manner and speech
which was once believed to be an exclusive privilege of
duchesses.

To return to Fairview. Victoria, after sharing her five
o'clock luncheon with her dogs, went to seek her father,
for the purpose (if it must be told) of asking him for a
cheque. Mr. Flint was at Fairview on the average of
two days out of the week during the summer, and then
he was nearly always closeted with a secretary and two
stenographers and a long-distance telephone in two plain
little rooms at the back of the house. And Mr. Hilary
Vane was often in consultation with him, as he was
on the present occasion when Victoria flung open the
door. At sight of Mr. Vane she halted suddenly on the
threshold, and a gleam of mischief came into her eye as
she thrust her hand into her coat pocket. The two
regarded her with the detached air of men whose thread
of thought has been broken.

"Well, Victoria," said her father, kindly if resignedly,
"what is it now?"

"Money," replied Victoria, promptly; "I went to Avalon
this morning and bought that horse you said I might have."

"What horse?" asked Mr. Flint, vaguely. "But never
mind. Tell Mr. Freeman to make out the cheque."

Mr. Vane glanced at Mr. Flint, and his eyes twinkled.
Victoria, who had long ago discovered the secret of the
Honey Dew, knew that he was rolling it under his tongue
and thinking her father a fool for his indulgence.

"How do you do, Mr. Vane?" she said; "Austen's coming home, isn't he?" She had got this by feminine arts
out of Mr. Paul Pardriff, to whom she had not confided
the fact of her possession of the clipping.

The Honourable Hilary gave a grunt, as he always did
when he was surprised and displeased, as though some
one had prodded him with a stick in a sensitive spot.

"Your son? Why, Vane, you never told me that,"

said Mr. Flint. "I didn't know that you knew him, Victoria."

"I don't," answered Victoria, "but I'd like to. What did he do to Mr. Blodgett?" she demanded of Hilary.

"Mr. Blodgett!" exclaimed that gentleman. "I never heard of him. What's happened to him?"

"He will probably recover," she assured him.

The Honourable Hilary, trying in vain to suppress his agitation, rose to his feet.

"I don't know what you're talking about, Victoria," he said, but his glance was fixed on the clipping in her hand.

"Haven't you seen it?" she asked, giving it to him.

He read it in silence, groaned, and handed it to Mr. Flint, who had been drumming on the table and glancing at Victoria with vague disapproval. Mr. Flint read it and gave it back to the Honourable Hilary, who groaned again and looked out of the window.

"Why do you feel badly about it?" asked Victoria. "I'd be proud of him, if I were you."

"Proud of him!" echoed Mr. Vane, grimly. "Proud of him!"

"Victoria, what do you mean?" said Mr. Flint.

"Why not?" said Victoria. "He's done nothing to make you ashamed. According to that clipping, he's punished a man who richly deserved to be punished, and he has the sympathy of an entire county."

Hilary Vane was not a man to discuss his domestic affliction with anybody, so he merely grunted and gazed persistently out of the window, and was not aware of the fact that Victoria made a little face at him as she left the room. The young are not always impartial judges of the old, and Victoria had never forgiven him for carrying to her father the news of an escapade of hers in Ripton.

As he drove through the silent forest roads on his way homeward that afternoon, the Honourable Hilary revolved the new and intensely disagreeable fact in his mind as to how he should treat a prodigal who had attempted man-slaughter and was a fugitive from justice. In the mean-time a tall and spare young man of a red-bronze colour

alighted from the five o'clock express at Ripton and
grinned delightedly at the gentlemen who made the station their headquarters about train time. They were
privately disappointed that the gray felt hat, although
broad-brimmed, was not a sombrero, and the respectable,
loose-fitting suit of clothes was not of buckskin with
tassels on the trousers; and likewise that he came without
the cartridge-belt and holster which they had pictured in
anticipatory sessions on the baggage-trucks. There could
be no doubt of the warmth of their greeting as they sidled
up and seized a hand somewhat larger than theirs, but the
welcome had in it an ingredient of awe that puzzled the
newcomer, who did not hesitate to inquire : —

"What's the matter, Ed? Why so ceremonious,
Perley?"

But his eagerness did not permit him to wait for explanations. Grasping his bag, the only baggage he
possessed, he started off at a swinging stride for Hanover
Street, pausing only to shake the hands of the few who
recognized him, unconscious of the wild-fire at his back.
Hanover Street was empty that drowsy summer afternoon,
and he stopped under the well-remembered maples before
the house and gazed at it long and tenderly; even at the
windows of that room — open now for the first time in
years — where he had served so many sentences of im-
prisonment. Then he went cautiously around by the side
and looked in at the kitchen door. To other eyes than his
Euphrasia might not have seemed a safe person to embrace,
but in a moment he had her locked in his arms and weeping. She knew nothing as yet of Mr. Blodgett's misfor-
tunes, but if Austen Vane had depopulated a county it
would have made no difference in her affection.

"My, but you're a man," exclaimed Euphrasia, backing
away at last and staring at him with the only complete
approval she had ever accorded to any human being save
one.

"What did you expect, Phrasie?"

"Come, and I'll show you your room," she said, in a
flutter she could not hide; "it's got all the same pictures

in, your mother's pictures, and the chair you broke that
time when Hilary locked you in.   It's mended."

"Hold on, Phrasie," said Austen, seizing her by the
apron-strings, "how about the Judge?"   It was by this
title he usually designated his father.

"What about him?" demanded Euphrasia, sharply.

"Well, it's his house, for one thing," answered Austen,
"and he may prefer to have that room — empty."

"Empty!   Turn you out?   I'd like to see him," cried
Euphrasia.   "It wouldn't take me long to leave him
high and dry."

She paused at the sound of wheels, and there was the
Honourable Hilary, across the garden patch, in the act of
slipping out of his buggy at the stable door.   In the
absence of Luke, the hired man, the chief counsel for the
railroad was wont to put up the horse himself, and he
already had the reins festooned from the bit rings when
he felt a heavy hand on his shoulder and heard a voice
say : —

"How are you, Judge?"

If the truth be told, that voice and that touch threw
the Honourable Hilary's heart out of beat.   Many days
he had been schooling himself for this occasion : this very
afternoon he had determined his course of action, which
emphatically did not include a fatted calf.   And now
surged up a dryad-like memory which had troubled
him many a wakeful night, of startled, appealing eyes that
sought his in vain, and of the son she had left him flinging himself into his arms in the face of chastisement.
For the moment Hilary Vane, under this traitorous influence, was unable to speak.   But he let the hand rest
on his shoulder, and at length was able to pronounce, in a
shamefully shaky voice, the name of his son.   Whereupon
Austen seized him by the other shoulder and turned him
round and looked into his face.

"The same old Judge," he said.

But Hilary was startled, even as Euphrasia had been.
Was this strange, bronzed, quietly humorous young man
his son?   Hilary even had to raise his eyes a little; he

c

had forgotten how tall Austen was. Strange emotions, unbidden and unwelcome, ran riot in his breast ; and Hilary Vane, who made no slips before legislative committees or supreme courts, actually found himself saying : —

"Euphrasia's got your room ready."

"It's good of you to take me in, Judge," said Austen, patting his shoulder. And then he began, quite naturally to unbuckle the breechings and loose the traces, which he did with such deftness and celerity that he had the horse unharnessed and in the stall in a twinkling, and had hauled the buggy through the stable door, the Honourable Hilary watching him the while. He was troubled, but for the life of him could find no adequate words, who usually had the dictionary at his disposal.

"Didn't write me why you came home," said the Honourable Hilary, as his son washed his hands at the spigot.

"Didn't I? Well, the truth was I wanted to see you again, Judge."

His father grunted, not with absolute displeasure, but suspiciously.

"How about Blodgett?" he asked.

"Blodgett! Have you heard about that? Who told you?"

"Never mind. You didn't. Nothing in your letter about it."

"It wasn't worth mentioning," replied Austen. "Tyner and the boys liked it pretty well, but I didn't think you'd be interested. It was a local affair."

"Not interested! Not worth mentioning!" exclaimed the Honourable Hilary, outraged to discover that his son was modestly deprecating an achievement instead of defending a crime. "Godfrey! murder ain't worth mentioning, I presume."

"Not when it isn't successful," said Austen. "If Blodgett had succeeded, I guess you'd have heard of it before you did."

"Do you mean to say this Blodgett tried to kill you?" demanded the Honourable Hilary.

" Yes," said his son, " and I've never understood why he didn't.   He's a good deal better shot than I am."

The Honourable Hilary grunted, and sat down on a bucket and carefully prepared a piece of Honey Dew.   He was surprised and agitated.

" Then why are you a fugitive from justice if you were acting in self-defence ? " he inquired.

" Well, you see there were no witnesses, except a Mexican of Blodgett's, and Blodgett runs the Pepper County machine for the railroad out there.   I'd been wanting to come East and have a look at you for some time, and I thought I might as well come now."

" How did this — this affair start ? " asked Mr. Vane.

" Blodgett was driving in some of Tyner's calves, and I caught him.   I told him what I thought of him, and he shot at me through his pocket.   That was all."

" All !   You shot him, didn't you ? "

" I was lucky enough to hit him first," said Austen.

Extraordinary as it may seem, the Honourable Hilary experienced a sense of pride.

" Where did you hit him ? " he asked.

It was Euphrasia who took matters in her own hands and killed the fatted calf, and the meal to which they presently sat down was very different from the frugal suppers Mr. Vane usually had.   But he made no comment. It is perhaps not too much to say that he would have been distinctly disappointed had it been otherwise.   There was Austen's favourite pie, and Austen's favourite cake, all inherited from the Austens, who had thought more of the fleshpots than people should.   And the prodigal did full justice to the occasion.

CHAPTER III

So instinctively do we hark back to the primeval man that there was a tendency to lionize the prodigal in Ripton, which proves the finished civilization of the East not to be so far removed from that land of outlaws, Pepper County. Mr. Paul Pardriff, who had a guilty conscience about the clipping, and vividly bearing in mind Mr. Blodgett's mishap, alone avoided young Mr. Vane; and escaped through the type-setting room and down an outside stairway in the rear when that gentleman called. It gave an ironical turn to the incident that Mr. Pardriff was at the moment engaged in a " Welcome Home " paragraph meant to be propitiatory.

Austen cared very little for lionizing. He spent most of his time with young Tom Gaylord, now his father's right-hand man in a tremendous lumber business. And Tom, albeit he had become so important, habitually fell once more under the domination of the hero of his youthful days. Together these two visited haunts of their boyhood, camping and fishing and scaling mountains, Tom with an eye to lumbering prospects the while.

After a matter of two or three months had passed away in this pleasant though unprofitable manner, the Honourable Hilary requested the presence of his son one morning at his office. This office was in what had once been a large residence, and from its ample windows you could look out through the elms on to the square. Old-fashioned bookcases lined with musty books filled the walls, except where a steel engraving of a legal light or a railroad map of the State was hung, and the Honourable Hilary sat in a Windsor chair at a mahogany table in the middle.

The anteroom next door, where the clerks sat, was also a waiting-room for various individuals from the different parts of the State who continually sought the counsel's presence.

"Haven't seen much of you since you've be'n home, Austen," his father remarked as an opening.

"Your — legal business compels you to travel a great deal," answered Austen, turning from the window and smiling.

"Somewhat," said the Honourable Hilary, on whom this pleasantry was not lost. "You've be'n travelling on the lumber business, I take it."

"I know more about it than I did," his son admitted.

The Honourable Hilary grunted.

"Caught a good many fish, haven't you?"

Austen crossed the room and sat on the edge of the desk beside his father's chair.

"See here, Judge," he said, "what are you driving at? Out with it."

"When are you — going back West?" asked Mr. Vane.

Austen did not answer at once, but looked down into his father's inscrutable face.

"Do you want to get rid of me?" he said.

"Sowed enough wild oats, haven't you?" inquired the father.

"I've sowed a good many," Austen admitted.

"Why not settle down?"

"I haven't yet met the lady, Judge," replied his son.

"Couldn't support her if you had," said Mr. Vane.

"Then it's fortunate," said Austen, resolved not to be the necessary second in a quarrel. He knew his father, and perceived that these preliminary and caustic openings of his were really olive branches.

"Sometimes I think you might as well be in that outlandish country, for all I see of you," said the Honourable Hilary.

"You ought to retire from business and try fishing," his son suggested.

The Honourable Hilary sometimes smiled.

" You've got a good brain, Austen, and what's the use of wasting it chasing cattle and practising with a pistol on your fellow-beings ? You won't have much trouble in getting admitted to the bar. Come into the office."

Austen did not answer at once. He suspected that it had cost his father not a little to make these advances.

" Do you believe you and I could get along, Judge ? How long do you think it would last ? "

" I've considered that some," answered the Honourable Hilary, " but I won't last a great while longer myself."

" You're as sound as a bronco," declared Austen, patting him.

" I never was what you might call dissipated," agreed Mr. Vane, " but men don't go on forever. I've worked hard all my life, and got where I am, and I've always thought I'd like to hand it on to you. It's a position of honour and trust, Austen, and one of which any lawyer might be proud."

" My ambition hasn't run in exactly that channel," said his son.

" Didn't know as you had any precise ambition," responded the Honourable Hilary, " but I never heard of a man refusing to be chief counsel for a great railroad. I don't say you can be, mind, but I say with work and brains it's as easy for the son of Hilary Vane as for anybody else."

" I don't know much about the duties of such a position," said Austen, laughing, " but at all events I shall have time to make up my mind how to answer Mr. Flint when he comes to me with the proposal. To speak frankly, Judge, I hadn't thought of spending the whole of what might otherwise prove a brilliant life in Ripton."

The Honourable Hilary smiled again, and then he grunted.

" I tell you what I'll do," he said; " you come in with me and agree to stay five years. If you've done well for yourself, and want to go to New York or some large place at the end of that time, I won't hinder you. But I feel it my duty to say, if you don't accept my offer, no son of mine shall inherit what I've laid up by hard labour. It's against American doctrine, and it's against my principles. You can go back to Pepper County and get put in jail, but you can't say I haven't warned you fairly."

"You ought to leave your fortune to the railroad, Judge," said Austen. "Generations to come would bless your name if you put up a new station in Ripton and built bridges over Bunker Hill grade crossing and the other one on Heath Street where Nic Adams was killed last month. I shouldn't begrudge a cent of the money."

"I suppose I was a fool to talk to you," said the Honourable Hilary, getting up.

But his son pushed him down again into the Windsor chair.

"Hold on, Judge," he said, "that was just my way of saying if I accepted your offer, it wouldn't be because I yearned after the money. Thinking of it has never kept me awake nights. Now if you'll allow me to take a few days once in a while to let off steam, I'll make a counter proposal, in the nature of a compromise."

"What's that?" the Honourable Hilary demanded suspiciously.

"Provided I get admitted to the bar I will take a room in another part of this building and pick up what crumbs of practice I can by myself. Of course, sir, I realize that these, if they come at all, will be owing to the lustre of your name. But I should, before I become Mr. Flint's right-hand man, like to learn to walk with my own legs."

The speech pleased the Honourable Hilary, and he put out his hand.

"It's a bargain, Austen," he said.

"I don't mind telling you now, Judge, that when I left the West I left it for good, provided you and I could live within a decent proximity. And I ought to add that I always intended going into the law after I'd had a fling. It isn't fair to leave you with the impression that this is a sudden determination. Prodigals don't become good as quick as all that."

Ripton caught its breath a second time the day Austen hired a law office, nor did the surprise wholly cease when, in one season, he was admitted to the bar, for the proceeding was not in keeping with the habits and customs of prodigals. Needless to say, the practice did not immediately begin to pour in, but the little office rarely lacked a visitor, and sometimes had as many as five or six. There was an irresistible attraction about that room, and apparently very little law read there, though sometimes its occupant arose and pushed the visitors into the hall and locked the door, and opened the window at the top to let the smoke out. Many of the Honourable Hilary's callers preferred the little room in the far corridor to the great man's own office.

These visitors of the elder Mr. Vane's, as has been before hinted, were not all clients. Without burdening the reader too early with a treatise on the fabric of a system, suffice it to say that something was continually going on that was not law; and gentlemen came and went — fat and thin, sharp-eyed and red-faced — who were neither clients nor lawyers. These were really secretive gentlemen, though most of them had a hail-fellow-well-met manner and a hearty greeting, but when they talked to the Honourable Hilary it was with doors shut, and even then they sat very close to his ear. Many of them preferred now to wait in Austen's office instead of the anteroom, and some of them were not so cautious with the son of Hilary Vane that they did not let drop certain observations to set him thinking. He had a fanciful if somewhat facetious way of calling them by feudal titles which made them grin.

"How is the Duke of Putnam this morning?" he would ask of the gentleman of whom the *Ripton Record* would frequently make the following announcement: "Among the prominent residents of Putnam County in town this week was the Honourable Brush Bascom."

The Honourable Brush and many of his associates, barons and earls, albeit the shrewdest of men, did not know exactly how to take the son of Hilary Vane. This was true also of the Honourable Hilary himself, who did not wholly appreciate the humour in Austen's parallel of the feudal system. Although Austen had set up for himself, there were many ways — not legal — in which the son might have been helpful to the father, but the Honourable Hilary hesitated, for some unformulated reason, to make use of him; and the consequence was that Mr. Hamilton Tooting and other young men of a hustling nature in the Honourable Hilary's office found that Austen's advent did not tend greatly to lighten a certain class of their labours. In fact, father and son were not much nearer in spirit than when one had been in Pepper County and the other in Ripton. Caution and an instinct which senses obstacles are characteristics of gentlemen in Mr. Vane's business.

So two years passed, — years liberally interspersed with expeditions into the mountains and elsewhere, and nights spent in the company of Tom Gaylord and others. During this period Austen was more than once assailed by the temptation to return to the free life of Pepper County, Mr. Blodgett having completely recovered now, and only desiring vengeance of a corporal nature. But a bargain was a bargain, and Austen Vane stuck to his end of it, although he had now begun to realize many aspects of a situation which he had not before suspected. He had long foreseen, however, that the time was coming when a serious disagreement with his father was inevitable. In addition to the difference in temperament, Hilary Vane belonged to one generation and Austen to another.

It happened, as do so many incidents which tend to shape a life, by a seeming chance. It was a June evening, and there had been a church sociable and basket picnic during the day in a grove in the town of Mercer, some ten miles south of Ripton. The grove was bounded on one side by the railroad track, and merged into a thick clump of second growth and alders where there was a diagonal grade crossing. The picnic was over and the people preparing to go home when they were startled by a crash, followed by the screaming of brakes as a big

engine flew past the grove and brought a heavy train to
a halt some distance down the grade.   The women shrieked
and dropped the dishes they were washing, and the men
left their horses standing and ran to the crossing and
then stood for the moment helpless, in horror at the scene
which met their eyes.   The wagon of one of their own
congregation was in splinters, a man (a farmer of the
neighbourhood) lying among the alders with what seemed
a mortal injury.   Amid the lamentations and cries for
some one to go to Mercer Village for the doctor a young
man drove up rapidly and sprang out of a buggy, trusting to some one to catch his horse, pushed through the
ring of people, and bent over the wounded farmer.   In an
instant he had whipped out a knife, cut a stick from one
of the alders, knotted his handkerchief around the man's
leg, ran the stick through the knot, and twisted the handkerchief until the blood ceased to flow.   They watched
him, paralyzed, as the helpless in this world watch the
capable, and before he had finished his task the train crew
and some passengers began to arrive.

"Have you a doctor aboard, Charley?" the young man
asked.

"No," answered the conductor, who had been addressed;
"my God, not one, Austen."

"Back up your train," said Austen, "and stop your
baggage car here.   And go to the grove," he added to
one of the picnickers, "and bring four or five carriage
cushions.   And you hold this."

The man beside him took the tourniquet, as he was bid.
Austen Vane drew a note-book from his pocket.

"I want this man's name and address," he said, "and
the names and addresses of every person here, quickly."

He did not lift his voice, but the man who had taken
charge of such a situation was not to be denied.   They
obeyed him, some eagerly, some reluctantly, and by that
time the train had backed down and the cushions had
arrived.   They laid these on the floor of the baggage car
and lifted the man on to them.   His name was Zeb
Meader, and he was still insensible.   Austen Vane, with

a peculiar set look upon his face, sat beside him all the way into Ripton. He spoke only once, and that was to tell the conductor to telegraph from Avalon to have the ambulance from St. Mary's Hospital meet the train at Ripton.

The next day Hilary Vane, returning from one of his periodical trips to the northern part of the State, invaded his son's office.

"What's this they tell me about your saving a man's life?" he asked, sinking into one of the vacant chairs and regarding Austen with his twinkling eyes.

"I don't know what they tell you," Austen answered. "I didn't do anything but get a tourniquet on his leg and have him put on the train."

The Honourable Hilary grunted, and continued to regard his son. Then he cut a piece of Honey Dew.

"Looks bad, does it?" he said.

"Well," replied Austen, "it might have been done better. It was bungled. In a death-trap as cleverly conceived as that crossing, with a down grade approaching it, they ought to have got the horse too."

The Honourable Hilary grunted again, and inserted the Honey Dew. He resolved to ignore the palpable challenge in this remark, which was in keeping with this new and serious mien in Austen.

"Get the names of witnesses?" was his next question.

"I took particular pains to do so."

"Hand 'em over to Tooting. What kind of man is this Meagre?"

'He is rather meagre now," said Austen, smiling a little. "His name's Meader."

"Is he likely to make a fuss?"

"I think he is," said Austen.

"Well," said the Honourable Hilary, "we must have Ham Tooting hurry 'round and fix it up with him as soon as he can talk, before one of these cormorant lawyers gets his claw in him."

Austen said nothing, and after some desultory conversation, in which he knew how to indulge when he wished to conceal the fact that he was baffled, the Honourable Hilary departed. That student of human nature, Mr. Hamilton Tooting, a young man of a sporting appearance and a free vocabulary, made the next attempt. It is a characteristic of Mr. Tooting's kind that, in their efforts to be genial, they often use an awkward diminutive of their friends' names.

"Hello, Aust," said Mr. Tooting, "I dropped in to get those witnesses in that Meagre accident, before I forget it."

"I think I'll keep 'em," said Austen, making a note out of the Revised Statutes.

"Oh, all right, all right," said Mr. Tooting, biting off a piece of his cigar. "Going to handle the case yourself, are you?"

"I may."

"I'm just as glad to have some of 'em off my hands, and this looks to me like a nasty one. I don't like those Mercer people. The last farmer they ran over there raised hell."

"I shouldn't blame this one if he did, if he ever gets well enough," said Austen. Young Mr. Tooting paused with a lighted match halfway to his cigar and looked at Austen shrewdly, and then sat down on the desk very close to him.

"Say, Aust, it sometimes sickens a man to have to buy these fellows off. What? Poor devils, they don't get anything like what they ought to get, do they? Wait till you see how the Railroad Commission'll whitewash that case. It makes a man want to be independent. What?"

"This sounds like virtue, Ham."

"I've often thought, too," said Mr. Tooting, "that a man could make more money if he didn't wear the collar."

"But not sleep as well, perhaps," said Austen.

"Say, Aust, you're not on the level with me."

"I hope to reach that exalted plane some day, Ham."

"What's got into you?" demanded the usually clear-headed Mr. Tooting, now a little bewildered.

"Nothing, yet," said Austen, "but I'm thinking seriously of having a sandwich and a piece of apple pie. Will you come along ? "

They crossed the square together, Mr. Tooting racking a normally fertile brain for some excuse to reopen the subject. Despairing of that, he decided that any subject would do.

" That Humphrey Crewe up at Leith is smart — smart as paint," he remarked.   " Do you know him? "

" I've seen him," said Austen.   " He's a young man, isn't he ? "

" And natty.   He knows a thing or two for a millionaire that don't have to work, and he runs that place of his right up to the handle.   You ought to hear him talk about the tariff, and national politics.   I was passing there the other day, and he was walking around among the flowerbeds.   'Ain't your name Tooting ? ' he hollered.   I almost fell out of the buggy."

" What did he want ? " asked Austen, curiously.   Mr. Tooting winked.

" Say, those millionaires are queer, and no mistake. You'd think a fellow that only had to cut coupons wouldn't be lookin' for another job, wouldn't you?   He made me hitch my horse, and had me into his study, as he called it, and gave me a big glass of whiskey and soda.   A fellow with buttons and a striped vest brought it on tiptoe. Then this Crewe gave me a long yellow cigar with a band on it and told me what the State needed, — macadam roads, farmers' institutes, forests, and God knows what. I told him all he had to do was to get permission from old man Flint, and he could have 'em."

" What did he say to that ? "

" He said Flint was an intimate friend of his.   Then he asked me a whole raft of questions about fellows in the neighbourhood I didn't know he'd ever heard of.   Say, he wants to go from Leith to the Legislature."

" He can go for all I care," said Austen, as he pushed open the door of the restaurant.

For a few days Mr. Meader hung between life and death.   But he came of a stock which had for generations thrust its roots into the crevices of granite, and was not easily killed by steam-engines. Austen Vane called twice, and then made an arrangement with young Dr. Tredway (one of the numerous Ripton Tredways whose money had founded the hospital) that he was to see Mr. Meader as soon as he was able to sustain a conversation. Dr. Tredway, by the way, was a bachelor, and had been Austen's companion on many a boisterous expedition.

When Austen, in response to the doctor's telephone message, stood over the iron bed in the spick-and-span men's ward of St. Mary's, a wave of that intense feeling he had experienced at the accident swept over him. The farmer's beard was overgrown, and the eyes looked up at him as from caverns of suffering below the bandage. They were shrewd eyes, however, and proved that Mr. Meader had possession of the five senses — nay, of the six. Austen sat down beside the bed.

"Dr. Tredway tells me you are getting along finely," he said.

"No thanks to the railrud," answered Mr. Meader; "they done their best."

"Did you hear any whistle or any bell?" Austen asked.

"Not a sound," said Mr. Meader; "they even shut off their steam on that grade."

Austen Vane, like most men who are really capable of a deep sympathy, was not an adept at expressing it verbally. Moreover, he knew enough of his fellow-men to realize that a Puritan farmer would be suspicious of sympathy. The man had been near to death himself, was compelled to spend part of the summer, his bread-earning season, in a hospital, and yet no appeal or word of complaint had crossed his lips.

"Mr. Meader," said Austen, "I came over here to tell you that in my opinion you are entitled to heavy damages from the railroad, and to advise you not to accept a compromise. They will send some one to you and offer you a sum far below that which you ought in justice to receive. You ought to fight this case."

" How am I going to pay a lawyer, with a mortgage on my farm ? " demanded Mr. Meader.

" I'm a lawyer," said Austen, "and if you'll take me, I'll defend you without charge."

" Ain't you the son of Hilary Vane ? "

" Yes."

" I've heerd of him a good many times," said Mr. Meader, as if to ask what man had not.   " You're railrud, ain't ye ? "

" No."

Mr. Meader gazed long and thoughtfully into the young man's face, and the suspicion gradually faded from the farmer's blue eyes.

"I like your looks," he said at last. "I guess you saved my life.   I'm — I'm much obliged to you."

When Mr. Tooting arrived later in the day, he found Mr. Meader willing to listen, but otherwise strangely non-committal.   With native shrewdness, the farmer asked him what office he came from, but did not confide in Mr. Tooting the fact that Mr. Vane's son had volunteered to wring more money from Mr. Vane's client than Mr. Tooting offered him.   Considerably bewildered, that gentleman left the hospital to report the affair to the Honourable Hilary, who, at intervals during the afternoon, found himself relapsing into speculation.

Inside of a somewhat unpromising shell, Mr. Zeb Meader was a human being, and no mean judge of men and motives.   As his convalescence progressed, Austen Vane fell into the habit of dropping in from time to time to chat with him, and gradually was rewarded by many vivid character sketches of Mr. Meader's neighbours in Mercer and its vicinity.   One afternoon, when Austen came into the ward, he found at Mr. Meader's bedside a basket of fruit which looked too expensive and tempting to have come from any dealer's in Ripton.

"A lady came with that," Mr. Meader explained.   "I never was popular before I was run over by the cars. She's be'n here twice.   When she fetched it to-day, I kind of thought she was up to some game, and I didn't want to take it."

" Up to some game ? " repeated Austen.

" Well, I don't know," continued Mr. Meader, thoughtfully, " the woman here tells me she comes regular in the summer time to see sick folks, but from the way she made up to me I had an idea that she wanted something. But I don't know. Thought I'd ask you. You see, she's railrud."

" Railroad ! "

"She's Flint's daughter."

Austen laughed.

" I shouldn't worry about that," he said. " If Mr. Flint sent his daughter with fruit to everybody his railroad injures, she wouldn't have time to do anything else. I doubt if Mr. Flint ever heard of your case."

Mr. Meader considered this, and calculated there was something in it.

" She was a nice, common young lady, and cussed if she didn't make me laugh, she has such a funny way of talkin'. She wanted to know all about you."

" What did she want to know ? " Austen exclaimed, not unnaturally.

" Well, she wanted to know about the accident, and I told her how you druv up and screwed that thing around my leg and backed the train down. She was a good deal took with that."

" I think you are inclined to make too much of it," said Austen.

Three days later, as he was about to enter the ward, Mr. Meader being now the only invalid there, he heard a sound which made him pause in the doorway. The sound was feminine laughter of a musical quality that struck pleasantly on Austen's ear. Miss Victoria Flint was seated beside Mr. Meader's bed, and qualified friendship had evidently been replaced by intimacy since Austen's last visit, for Mr. Meader was laughing, too.

" And now I'm quite sure you have missed your vocation, Mr. Meader," said Victoria. " You would have made a fortune on the stage."

" Me a play-actor ! " exclaimed the invalid. " How much wages do they git ? "

" Untold sums," she declared, " if they can talk like you."

" *He* kind of thought that story funny — same as you," Mr. Meader ruminated, and glanced up. " Drat me," he remarked, " if he ain't a-comin' now ! I callated he'd run acrost you sometime."

Victoria raised her eyes, sparkling with humour, and they met Austen's.

" We was just talkin' about you," cried Mr. Meader, cordially ; " come right in." He turned to Victoria. " I want to make you acquainted," he said, " with Austen Vane."

" And won't you tell him who I am, Mr. Meader ? " said Victoria.

" Well," said Mr. Meader, apologetically, " that was stupid of me — wahn't it ? But I callated he'd know. She's the daughter of the railrud president — the one that was askin' about you."

There was an instant's pause, and the colour stole into Victoria's cheeks. Then she glanced at Austen and bit her lip — and laughed. Her laughter was contagious.

" I suppose I shall have to confess that you have inspired my curiosity, Mr. Vane," she said.

Austen's face was sunburned, but it flushed a more vivid red under the tan. It is needless to pretend that a man of his appearance and qualities had reached the age of thirty-two without having listened to feminine comments of which he was the exclusive subject. In this remark of Victoria's, or rather in the manner in which she made it, he recognized a difference.

" It is a tribute, then, to the histrionic talents of Mr. Meader, of which you were speaking," he replied laughingly.

Victoria glanced at him with interest as he looked down at Mr. Meader.

" And how is it to-day, Zeb ? " he said.

" It ain't so bad as it might be — with sech folks as her and you araound," admitted Mr. Meader. " I'd almost agree to get run over again. She *was* askin' about you, and that's a fact, and I didn't slander you, neither. But I never callated to comprehend wimmen-folks."

D

"Now, Mr. Meader," said Victoria, reprovingly, but there were little creases about her eyes, "don't be a fraud."

"It's true as gospel," declared the invalid; "they always got the better of me. I had one of 'em after me once, when I was young and prosperin' some."

"And yet you have survived triumphant," she exclaimed.

"There wahn't none of 'em like you," said Mr. Meader, "or it might have be'n different."

Again her eyes irresistibly sought Austen's, — as though to share with him the humour of this remark, — and they laughed together. Her colour, so sensitive, rose again, but less perceptibly this time. Then she got up.

"That's unfair, Mr. Meader!" she protested.

"I'll leave it to Austen," said Mr. Meader, "if it ain't probable. He'd ought to know."

In spite of a somewhat natural embarrassment, Austen could not but acknowledge to himself that Mr. Meader was right. With a womanly movement which he thought infinitely graceful, Victoria leaned over the bed.

"Mr. Meader," she said, "I'm beginning to think it's dangerous for me to come here twice a week to see you, if you talk this way. And I'm not a bit surprised that that woman didn't get the better of you."

"You hain't a-goin'!" he exclaimed. "Why, I callated —"

"Good-by," she said quickly; "I'm glad to see that you are doing so well." She raised her head and looked at Austen in a curious, inscrutable way. "Good-by, Mr. Vane," she said; "I — I hope Mr. Blodgett has recovered."

Before he could reply she had vanished, and he was staring at the empty doorway. The reference to the unfortunate Mr. Blodgett, after taking his breath away, aroused in him an intense curiosity — betraying, as it did, a certain knowledge of past events in his life in the hitherto unknown daughter of Augustus Flint. What interest could she have in him? Such a question, from similar sources, has heightened the pulse of young men from time immemorial.

She raised her head and looked at Austen in a curious, inscrutable way.

CHAPTER IV

"TIMEO DANAOS"

THE proverbial little birds that carry news and prophecies through the air were evidently responsible for an official-looking letter which Austen received a few mornings later. On the letter-head was printed "The United Northeastern Railroads," and Mr. Austen Vane was informed that, by direction of the president, the enclosed was sent to him in an entirely complimentary sense. "The enclosed" was a ticket of red cardboard, and its face informed him that he might travel free for the rest of the year. Thoughtfully turning it over, he read on the back the following inscription: —

"*It is understood that this pass is accepted by its recipient as a retainer.*"

Austen stared at it and whistled. Then he pushed back his chair, with the pass in his hand, and hesitated. He seized a pen and wrote a few lines: "Dear sir, I beg to return the annual pass over the Northeastern Railroads with which you have so kindly honoured me" — when he suddenly changed his mind again, rose, and made his way through the corridors to his father's office. The Honourable Hilary was absorbed in his daily perusal of the *Guardian*.

"Judge," he asked, "is Mr. Flint up at his place this week?"

The Honourable Hilary coughed.

"He arrived yesterday on the three. Er — why?"

"I wanted to go up and thank him for this," his son answered, holding up the red piece of cardboard. "Mr. Flint is a very thoughtful man."

The Honourable Hilary tried to look unconcerned, and succeeded.

35

" Sent you an annual, has he ?   Er — I don't know as I'd bother him personally, Austen.   Just a pleasant note of acknowledgment."

" I don't flatter myself that my achievements in the law can be responsible for it," said Austen.   "The favour must be due to my relationship with his eminent chief counsel."

Hilary Vane's keen eyes rested on his son for an instant. Austen was more than ever an enigma to him.

" I guess relationship hasn't got much to do with business," he replied.   " You *have* be'n doing — er — better than I expected."

" Thank you, Judge," said Austen, quietly.   "I don't mind saying that I would rather have your approbation than — this more substantial recognition of merit."

The Honourable Hilary's business was to deal with men, and by reason of his ability in so doing he had made a success in life.   He could judge motives more than passably well, and play upon weaknesses.   But he left Austen's presence that morning vaguely uneasy, with a sense of having received from his own son an initial defeat at a game of which he was a master.   Under the excuse of looking up some precedents, he locked his doors to all comers for two hours, and paced his room.   At one moment he reproached himself for not having been frank; for not having told Austen roundly that this squeamishness about a pass was unworthy of a strong man of affairs; yes, for not having revealed to him the mysteries of railroad practice from the beginning.   But frankness was not an ingredient of the Honourable Hilary's nature, and Austen was not the kind of man who would accept a hint and a wink.   Hilary Vane had formless forebodings, and found himself for once in his life powerless to act.

The cost of living in Ripton was not so high that Austen Vane could not afford to keep a horse and buggy. The horse, which he tended himself, was appropriately called Pepper; Austen had found him in the hills, and he was easily the finest animal in Ripton: so good, in fact, that Mr. Humphrey Crewe (who believed he had an eye for horses) had peremptorily hailed Austen from a motor car and demanded the price, as was Mr. Crewe's wont when he saw a thing he desired. He had been somewhat surprised and not inconsiderably offended by the brevity and force of the answer which he had received.

On the afternoon of the summer's day in which Austen had the conversation with his father just related, Pepper was trotting at a round clip through the soft and shady wood roads toward the town of Tunbridge; the word "town" being used in the New England sense, as a piece of territory about six miles by six. The fact that automobiles full of laughing people from Leith hummed by occasionally made no apparent difference to Pepper, who knew only the master hand on the reins; the reality that the wood roads were climbing great hills the horse did not seem to feel. Pepper knew every lane and by-path within twenty miles of Ripton, and exhibited such surprise as a well-bred horse may when he was slowed down at length and turned into a hard, blue-stone driveway under a strange granite arch with the word "Fairview" cut in Gothic letters above it, and two great lamps in wrought-iron brackets at the sides. It was Austen who made a note of the gratings over the drains, and of the acres of orderly forest in a mysterious and seemingly enchanted realm. Intimacy with domains was new to him, and he began to experience an involuntary feeling of restraint which was new to him likewise, and made him chafe in spite of himself. The estate seemed to be the visible semblance of a power which troubled him.

Shortly after passing an avenue neatly labelled "Trade's Drive" the road wound upwards through a ravine the sides of which were covered with a dense shrubbery which had the air of having always been there, and yet somehow looked expensive. At the top of the ravine was a sharp curve; and Austen, drawing breath, found himself swung, as it were, into space, looking off across miles of forest-covered lowlands to an ultramarine mountain in the hazy south,— Sawanec. As if in obedience to a telepathic command of his master, Pepper stopped.

Drinking his fill of this scene, Austen forgot an errand

which was not only disagreeable, but required some fortitude for its accomplishment. The son had this in common with the Honourable Hilary — he hated heroics; and
the fact that the thing smacked of heroics was Austen's
only deterrent. And then there was a woman in this
paradise! These gradual insinuations into his revery at
length made him turn. A straight avenue of pear-shaped,
fifteen-year-old maples led to the house, a massive colonial
structure of wood that stretched across the shelf; and
he had tightened the reins and started courageously up
the avenue when he perceived that it ended in a circle
on which there was no sign of a hitching-post. And,
worse than this, on the balconied, uncovered porch which
he would have to traverse to reach the doorway he saw
the sheen and glimmer of women's gowns grouped about
wicker tables, and became aware that his approach was
the sole object of the scrutiny of an afternoon tea-
party.

As he reached the circle it was a slight relief to learn
that Pepper was the attraction. No horse knew better than
Pepper when he was being admired, and he arched his neck
and lifted his feet and danced in the sheer exhilaration of
it. A smooth-faced, red-cheeked gentleman in gray flan-
nels leaned over the balustrade and made audible comments in a penetrating voice which betrayed the fact that
he was Mr. Humphrey Crewe.

" Saw him on the street in Ripton last year. Good
hock action, hasn't he ? — that's rare in trotters around
here. Tried to buy him. Feller wouldn't sell. His
name's Vane — he's drivin' him now."

A lady of a somewhat commanding presence was beside
him. She was perhaps five and forty, her iron-gray hair
was dressed to perfection, her figure all that Parisian art
could make it, and she was regarding Austen with extreme deliberation through the glasses which she had
raised to a high-bridged nose.

" Politics is certainly your career, Humphrey," she remarked, " you have such a wonderful memory for faces.
I don't see how he does it, do you, Alice ? " she demanded

of a tall girl beside her, who was evidently her daughter,
but lacked her personality.

"I don't know," said Alice.

"It's because I've been here longer than anybody else,
Mrs. Pomfret," answered Mr. Crewe, not very graciously,
"that's all. Hello." This last to Austen.

"Hello," said Austen.

"Who do you want to see?" inquired Mr. Crewe, with
the admirable tact for which he was noted.

Austen looked at him for the first time.

"Anybody who will hold my horse," he answered
quietly.

By this time the conversation had drawn the attention of
the others at the tables, and one or two smiled at Austen's
answer. Mrs. Flint, with a "Who is it?" arose to repel
a social intrusion. She was an overdressed lady, inclining
to embonpoint, but traces of the Rose of Sharon were still
visible.

"Why don't you drive 'round to the stables?" suggested Mr. Crewe, unaware of a smile.

Austen did not answer. He was, in fact, looking towards
the doorway, and the group on the porch were surprised
to see a gleam of mirthful understanding start in his eyes.
An answering gleam was in Victoria's, who had at that
moment, by a singular coincidence, come out of the house.
She came directly down the steps and out on the gravel,
and held her hand to him in the buggy, and he flushed
with pleasure as he grasped it.

"How do you do, Mr. Vane?" she said. "I am so glad
you have called. Humphrey, just push the stable button,
will you?"

Mr. Crewe obeyed with no very good grace, while the
tea-party went back to their seats. Mrs. Flint supposed
he had come to sell Victoria the horse; while Mrs. Pomfret, who had taken him in from crown to boots, remarked
that he looked very much like a gentleman.

"I came to see your father for a few moments — on
business," Austen explained.

She lifted her face to his with a second searching look.

"I'll take you to him," she said.

By this time a nimble groom had appeared from out of a shrubbery path and seized Pepper's head. Austen alighted and followed Victoria into a great, cool hallway, and through two darkened rooms, bewilderingly furnished and laden with the scent of flowers, into a narrow passage beyond. She led the way simply, not speaking, and her silence seemed to betoken the completeness of an understanding between them, as of a long acquaintance.

In a plain whitewashed room, behind a plain oaken desk, sat Mr. Flint — a plain man. Austen thought he would have known him had he seen him on the street. The other things in the room were letter-files, a safe, a long-distance telephone, and a thin private secretary with a bend in his back. Mr. Flint looked up from his desk, and his face, previously bereft of illumination, lighted when he saw his daughter. Austen liked that in him.

"Well, Vic, what is it now?" he asked.

"Mr. Austen Vane to see you," said Victoria, and with a quick glance at Austen she left him standing on the threshold. Mr. Flint rose. His eyes were deep-set in a square, hard head, and he appeared to be taking Austen in without directly looking at him; likewise, one felt that Mr. Flint's handshake was not an absolute gift of his soul.

"How do you do, Mr. Vane? I don't remember ever to have had the pleasure of seeing you, although your father and I have been intimately connected for many years."

So the president's manner was hearty, but not the substance. It came, Austen thought, from a rarity of meeting with men on a disinterested footing; and he could not but wonder how Mr. Flint would treat the angels in heaven if he ever got there, where there were no franchises to be had. Would he suspect them of designs upon his hard-won harp and halo? Austen did not dislike Mr. Flint; the man's rise, his achievements, his affection for his daughter, he remembered. But he was also well aware that Mr. Flint had thrown upon him the onus of the first move in a game which the railroad president was used to playing every day. The dragon was on his home ground and had the choice of weapons.

" I do not wish to bother you long," said Austen.

" No bother," answered Mr. Flint, " no bother to make the acquaintance of the son of my old friend, Hilary Vane. Sit down — sit down. And while I don't believe any man should depend upon his father to launch him in the world, yet it must be a great satisfaction to you, Mr. Vane, to have such a father. Hilary Vane and I have been intimately associated for many years, and my admiration for him has increased with every year. It is to men of his type that the prosperity, the greatness, of this nation is largely due, — conservative, upright, able, content to confine himself to the difficult work for which he is so eminently fitted, without spectacular meddling in things in which he can have no concern. Therefore I welcome the opportunity to know you, sir, for I understand that you have settled down to follow in his footsteps and that you will make a name for yourself. I know the independence of young men — I was young once myself. But after all, Mr. Vane, experience is the great teacher, and perhaps there is some little advice which an old man can give you that may be of service. As your father's son, it is always at your disposal. Have a cigar."

The thin secretary continued to flit about the room, between the letter-files and the desk. Austen had found it infinitely easier to shoot Mr. Blodgett than to engage in a duel with the president of the United Railroads.

" I smoke a pipe," he said.

" Too many young men smoke cigars — and those disgusting cigarettes," said Mr. Flint, with conviction. "There are a lot of worthless young men in these days, anyhow. They come to my house and loaf and drink and smoke, and talk a lot of nonsense about games and automobiles and clubs, and cumber the earth generally. There's a young man named Crewe over at Leith, for instance — you may have seen him. Not that he's dissipated, — but he don't do anything but talk about railroads and the stock market to make you sick, and don't know any more about 'em than my farmer."

During this diatribe Austen saw his opening growing smaller and smaller. If he did not make a dash for it, it would soon be closed entirely.

" I received a letter this morning, Mr. Flint, enclosing me an annual pass — "

" Did Upjohn send you one ? " Mr. Flint cut in ; " he ought to have done so long ago. It was probably an oversight that he did not, Mr. Vane. We try to extend the courtesies of the road to persons who are looked up to in their communities. The son of Hilary Vane is at all times welcome to one."

Mr. Flint paused to light his cigar, and Austen summoned his resolution. Second by second it was becoming more and more difficult and seemingly more ungracious to return a gift so graciously given, a gift of no inconsiderable intrinsic value. Moreover, Mr. Flint had ingeniously contrived almost to make the act, in Austen's eyes, that of a picayune upstart. Who was he to fling back an annual pass in the face of the president of the Northeastern Railroads ?

" I had first thought of writing you a letter, Mr. Flint," he said, " but it seemed to me that, considering your relations with my father, the proper thing to do was to come to you and tell you why I cannot take the pass."

The thin secretary paused in his filing, and remained motionless with his body bent over the drawer.

" Why you cannot take it, Mr. Vane ? " said the railroad president. " I'm afraid I don't understand."

" I appreciate the — the kindness," said Austen, " and I will try to explain." He drew the red cardboard from his pocket and turned it over. " On the back of this is printed, in small letters, ' It is understood that this pass is accepted by the recipient as a retainer.' "

" Well," Mr. Flint interrupted, smiling somewhat blandly, " how much money do you think that pass would save an active young lawyer in a year ? Is three hundred dollars too much ? Three hundred dollars is not

an insignificant sum to a young man on the threshold of
his practice, is it?"

Austen looked at Mr. Flint.

"Any sum is insignificant when it restricts a lawyer
from the acceptance of just causes, Mr. Flint. As I understand the matter, it is the custom of your railroad to
send these passes to the young lawyers of the State the
moment they begin to give signs of ability. This pass
would prevent me from serving clients who might have
righteous claims against your railroads, and — permit me
to speak frankly — in my opinion the practice tends to
make it difficult for poor people who have been injured to
get efficient lawyers."

"Your own father is retained by the railroad," said Mr.
Flint.

"As their counsel," answered Austen. "I have a pride
in my profession, Mr. Flint, as no doubt you have in
yours. If I should ever acquire sufficient eminence to be
sought as counsel for a railroad, I should make my own
terms with it. I should not allow its management alone
to decide upon the value of my retainer, and my services in
its behalf would be confined strictly to professional ones."

Mr. Flint drummed on the table.

"What do you mean by that?" he demanded.

"I mean that I would not engage, for a fee or a pass, to
fight the political battles of a railroad, or undertake any
political manipulation in its behalf whatever."

Mr. Flint leaned forward aggressively.

"How long do you think a railroad would pay dividends
if it did not adopt some means of defending itself from
the blackmail politician of the State legislatures, Mr. Vane?
The railroads of which I have the honour to be president
pay a heavy tax in this and other States. We would pay
a much heavier one if we didn't take precautions to protect
ourselves. But I do not intend to quarrel with you, Mr.
Vane," he continued quickly, perceiving that Austen was
about to answer him, "nor do I wish to leave you with the
impression that the Northeastern Railroads meddle unduly
in politics."

Austen knew not how to answer. He had not gone there to discuss this last and really great question with Mr. Flint, but he wondered whether the president actually thought him the fledgling he proclaimed. Austen laid his pass on Mr. Flint's desk, and rose.

"I assure you, Mr. Flint, that the spirit which prompted my visit was not a contentious one. I cannot accept the pass, simply because I do not wish to be retained."

Mr. Flint eyed him. There was a mark of dignity, of silent power, on this tall scapegrace of a son of Hilary Vane that the railroad president had missed at first — probably because he had looked only for the scapegrace. Mr. Flint ardently desired to treat the matter in the trifling aspect in which he believed he saw it, to carry it off genially. But an instinct not yet formulated told the president that he was face to face with an enemy whose potential powers were not to be despised, and he bristled in spite of himself.

"There is no statute I know of by which a lawyer can be compelled to accept a retainer against his will, Mr. Vane," he replied, and overcame himself with an effort. "But I hope that you will permit me," he added in another tone, "as an old friend of your father's and as a man of some little experience in the world, to remark that intolerance is a characteristic of youth. I had it in the days of Mr. Isaac D. Worthington, whom you do not remember. I am not addicted to flattery, but I hope and believe you have a career before you. Talk to your father. Study the question on both sides, — from the point of view of men who are honestly trying, in the face of tremendous difficulties, to protect innocent stockholders as well as to conduct a corporation in the interests of the people at large, and for their general prosperity. Be charitable, young man, and judge not hastily."

Years before, when poor Sarah Austen had adorned the end of his table, Hilary Vane had raised his head after the pronouncement of grace to surprise a look in his wife's eyes which strangely threw him into a white heat of anger. That look (and he at intervals had beheld it afterwards) was the true presentment of the soul of the woman whose body was his. It was not — as Hilary Vane thought it — a contempt for the practice of thanking one's Maker for daily bread, but a contempt for cant of one who sees the humour in cant. A masculine version of that look Mr. Flint now beheld in the eyes of Austen Vane, and the enraging effect on the president of the United Railroads was much the same as it had been on his chief counsel. Who was this young man of three and thirty to agitate him so? He trembled, though not visibly, yet took Austen's hand mechanically.

"Good day, Mr. Vane," he said; "Mr. Freeman will help you to find your horse."

The thin secretary bowed, and before he reached the door into the passage Mr. Flint had opened another at the back of the room and stepped out on a close-cropped lawn flooded with afternoon sunlight. In the passage Austen perceived a chair, and in the chair was seated patiently none other than Mr. Brush Bascom — political Duke of Putnam. Mr. Bascom's little agate eyes glittered in the dim light.

"Hello, Austen," he said, "since when have you took to comin' here?"

"It's a longer trip from Putnam than from Ripton, Brush," said Austen, and passed on, leaving Mr. Bascom with a puzzled mind. Something very like a smile passed over Mr. Freeman's face as he led the way silently out of a side entrance and around the house. The circle of the drive was empty, the tea-party had gone — and Victoria. Austen assured himself that her disappearance relieved him: having virtually quarrelled with her father, conversation would have been awkward; and yet he looked for her.

They found the buggy and Pepper in the paved court-yard of the stables. As Austen took the reins the secretary looked up at him, his mild blue eyes burning with an unsuspected fire. He held out his hand.

"I want to congratulate you," he said.

"What for?" asked Austen, taking the hand in some embarrassment.

"For speaking like a man," said the secretary, and he turned on his heel and left him.

This strange action, capping, as it did, a stranger experience, gave Austen food for thought as he let Pepper take his own pace down the trade's road. Presently he got back into the main drive where it clung to a steep, forest-covered side hill, when his attention was distracted by the sight of a straight figure in white descending amidst the foliage ahead. His instinctive action was to pull Pepper down to a walk, scarcely analyzing his motives; then he had time, before reaching the spot where their paths would cross, to consider and characteristically to enjoy the unpropitious elements arrayed against a friendship with Victoria Flint.

She halted on a flagstone of the descending path some six feet above the roadway, and stood expectant. The Rose of Sharon, five and twenty years before, would have been coy — would have made believe to have done it by accident. But the Rose of Sharon, with all her beauty, would have had no attraction for Austen Vane. Victoria had much of her mother's good looks, the figure of a Diana, and her clothes were of a severity and correctness in keeping with her style; they merely added to the sum total of the effect upon Austen. Of course he stopped the buggy immediately beneath her, and her first question left him without any breath. No woman he had ever known seized the essentials as she did.

"What have you been doing to my father?" she asked.

"Why?" exclaimed Austen.

"Because he's in such a bad temper," said Victoria. "You must have put him in it. It can't be possible that you came all the way up here to quarrel with him. Nobody ever dares to quarrel with him."

"I didn't come up to quarrel with him," said Austen.

"What's the trouble?" asked Victoria.

The humour of this question was too much for him, and he laughed. Victoria's eyes laughed a little, but there was a pucker in her forehead.

"Won't you tell me?" she demanded, "or must I get it out of him?"

"I am afraid," said Austen, slowly, "that you must get it out of him — if he hasn't forgotten it."

"Forgotten it, dear old soul!" cried Victoria. "I met him just now and tried to make him look at the new Guernseys, and he must have been disturbed quite a good deal when he's cross as a bear to me. He really oughtn't to be upset like that, Mr. Vane, when he comes up here to rest. I am afraid that you are rather a terrible person, although you look so nice. Won't you tell me what you did to him?"

Austen was nonplussed.

"Nothing intentional," he answered earnestly, "but it wouldn't be fair to your father if I gave you my version of a business conversation that passed between us, — would it?"

"Perhaps not," said Victoria. She sat down on the flagstone with her elbow on her knee and her chin in her hand, and looked at him thoughtfully. He knew well enough that a wise general would have retreated — horse, foot, and baggage; but Pepper did not stir.

"Do you know," said Victoria, "I have an idea you came up here about Zeb Meader."

"Zeb Meader!"

"Yes. I told my father about him, — how you rescued him, and how you went to see him in the hospital, and what a good man he is, and how poor."

"Oh, did you!" exclaimed Austen.

"Yes. And I told him the accident wasn't Zeb's fault, that the train didn't whistle or ring, and that the crossing was a blind one."

"And what did he say?" asked Austen, curiously.

"He said that on a railroad as big as his something of the kind must happen occasionally. And he told me if Zeb didn't make a fuss and act foolishly, he would have no cause to regret it."

"And did you tell Zeb?" asked Austen.

"Yes," Victoria admitted, "but I'm sorry I did, now."

" What did Zeb say ? "

Victoria laughed in spite of herself, and gave a more
or less exact though kindly imitation of Mr. Meader's
manner.

" He said that wimmen-folks had better stick to the
needle and the duster, and not go pokin' about law business that didn't concern 'em.   But the worst of it was,"
added Victoria, with some distress, " he won't accept any
more fruit.   Isn't he silly ?   He won't get it into his head
that I give him the fruit, and not my father.   I suspect
that he actually believes my father sent me down there
to tell him that."

Austen was silent, for the true significance of this
apparently obscure damage case to the Northeastern Railroads was beginning to dawn on him.   The public was
not in the best of humours towards railroads: there was
trouble about grade crossings, and Mr. Meader's mishap
and the manner of his rescue by the son of the corporation counsel had given the accident a deplorable publicity.   Moreover, if it had dawned on Augustus Flint
that the son of Hilary Vane might prosecute the suit, it
was worth while taking a little pains with Mr. Meader —
and Mr. Austen Vane.   Certain small fires have been
known to light world-wide conflagrations.

" What are you thinking about ? " asked Victoria.   " It
isn't at all polite to forget the person you are talking to."

" I haven't forgotten you," said Austen, with a smile.
How could he — sitting under her in this manner ?

" Besides," said Victoria, mollified, " you haven't answered my question."

" Which question ? "

She scrutinized him thoughtfully, and with feminine art
made the kind of an attack that rarely fails.

" Why are you such an enigma, Mr. Vane ? " she demanded.   " Is it because you're a lawyer, or because you've
been out West and seen so much of life and shot so many
people ? "

Austen laughed, yet he had tingling symptoms because
she showed enough interest in him to pronounce him a

riddle. But he instantly became serious as the purport of the last charge came home to him.

"I suppose I am looked upon as a sort of Jesse James," he said. "As it happens, I have never shot but one man, and I didn't care very much for that."

Victoria got up and came down a step and gave him her hand. He took it, nor was he the first to relinquish the hold; and a colour rose delicately in her face as she drew her fingers away.

"I didn't mean to offend you," she said.

"You didn't offend me," he replied quickly. "I merely wished you to know that I wasn't a brigand."

Victoria smiled.

"I really didn't think so—you are much too solemn. I have to go now, and—you haven't told me anything."

She crossed the road and began to descend the path on the other side. Twice he glanced back, after he had started, and once surprised her poised lightly among the leaves, looking over her shoulder.

E

CHAPTER V

THE PARTING OF THE WAYS

THE next time Austen visited the hospital Mr. Meader had a surprise in store for him. After passing the time of day, as was his custom, the patient freely discussed the motives which had led him to refuse any more of Victoria's fruit.

"I hain't got nothing against *her*," he declared; "I tried to make that plain. She's as nice and common a young lady as I ever see, and I don't believe she had a thing to do with it. But I suspicioned they was up to somethin' when she brought them baskets. And when she give me the message from old Flint, I was sure of it."

"Miss Flint was entirely innocent, I'm sure," said Austen, emphatically.

"If I could see old Flint, I'd tell him what I thought of him usin' wimmen-folks to save 'em money," said Mr. Meader. "I knowed she wahn't that kind. And then that other thing come right on top of it."

"What other thing?"

"Say," demanded Mr. Meader, "don't you know?"

"I know nothing," said Austen.

"Didn't know Hilary Vane's be'n here?"

"My father!" Austen ejaculated.

"Gittin' after me pretty warm, so they be. Want to know what *my* price is now. But say, I didn't suppose your fayther'd come here without lettin' you know."

Austen was silent. The truth was that for a few moments he could not command himself sufficiently to speak.

"He is the chief counsel for the road," he said at length; "I am not connected with it."

"I guess you're on the right track. He's a pretty smooth talker, your fayther. Just dropped in to see how I be, since his son was interested. Talked a sight of law gibberish I didn't understand. Told me I didn't have much of a case; said the policy of the railrud was to be liberal, and wanted to know what I thought I ought to have."

"Well?" said Austen, shortly.

"Well," said Mr. Meader, "he didn't git a mite of satisfaction out of me. I've seen enough of his kind of folks to know how to deal with 'em, and I told him so. I asked him what they meant by sending that slick Mr. Tooting 'raound to offer me five hundred dollars. I said I was willin' to trust my case on that crossin' to a jury."

Austen smiled, in spite of his mingled emotions.

"What else did Mr. Vane say?" he asked.

"Not a great sight more. Said a good many folks were foolish enough to spend money and go to law when they'd done better to trust to the liberality of the railrud. Liberality! Adams' widow done well to trust their liberality, didn't she? He wanted to know one more thing, but I didn't give him any satisfaction."

"What was that?"

"I couldn't tell you how he got 'raound to it. Guess he never did, quite. He wanted to know what lawyer was to have my case. Wahn't none of his affair, and I callated if you'd wanted him to know just yet, you'd have told him."

Austen laid his hand on the farmer's, as he rose to go.

"Zeb," he said, "I never expect to have a more exemplary client."

Mr. Meader shot a glance at him.

"Mebbe I spoke a mite too free about your fayther, Austen," he said; "you and him seem kind of different."

"The Judge and I understand each other," answered Austen.

He had got as far as the door, when he stopped, swung on his heel, and came back to the bedside.

"It's my duty to tell you, Zeb, that in order to hush

this thing up they may offer you more than you can get from a jury. In that case I should have to advise you to accept."

He was aware that, while he made this statement, Zeb Meader's eyes were riveted on him, and he knew that the farmer was weighing him in the balance.

"Sell out?" exclaimed Mr. Meader. "You advise me to sell out?"

Austen did not get angry. He understood this man and the people from which he sprang.

"The question is for you to decide — whether you can get more money by a settlement."

"Money!" cried Zeb Meader, "I have found it pretty hard to git, but there's some things I won't do for it. There's a reason why they want this case hushed up, the way they've be'n actin'. I ain't lived in Mercer and Putnam County all my life for nothin'. Hain't I seen 'em run their dirty politics there under Brush Bascom for the last twenty-five years? There's no man has an office or a pass in that county but what Bascom gives it to him, and Bascom's the railrud tool." Suddenly Zeb raised himself in bed. "Hev' they be'n tamperin' with you?" he demanded.

"Yes," answered Austen, dispassionately. He had hardly heard what Zeb had said; his mind had been going onward. "Yes. They sent me an annual pass, and I took it back."

Zeb Meader did not speak for a few moments.

"I guess I was a little hasty, Austen," he said at length. "I might have known you wouldn't sell out. If you're willin' to take the risk, you tell 'em ten thousand dollars wouldn't tempt me."

"All right, Zeb," said Austen.

He left the hospital and struck out across the country towards the slopes of Sawanec, climbed them, and stood bareheaded in the evening light, gazing over the still, wide valley northward to the wooded ridges where Leith and Fairview lay hidden. He had come to the parting of the ways of life, and while he did not hesitate to choose his path, a Vane inheritance, though not dominant, could not fail at such a juncture to point out the pleasantness of conformity. Austen's affection for Hilary Vane was real; the loneliness of the elder man appealed to the son, who knew that his father loved him in his own way. He dreaded the wrench there.

And nature, persuasive in that quarter, was not to be stilled in a field more completely her own. The memory and suppliance of a minute will scarce suffice one of Austen's temperament for a lifetime; and his eyes, flying with the eagle high across the valley, searched the velvet folds of the ridges, as they lay in infinite shades of green in the level light, for the place where the enchanted realm might be. Just what the state of his feelings were at this time towards Victoria Flint is too vague accurately to be painted, but he was certainly not ready to give way to the attraction he felt for her. His sense of humour intervened if he allowed himself to dream; there was a certain folly in pursuing the acquaintance, all the greater now that he was choosing the path of opposition to the dragon. A young woman, surrounded as she was, could be expected to know little of the subtleties of business and political morality: let him take Zeb Meader's case, and her loyalty would naturally be with her father,—if she thought of Austen Vane at all.

And yet the very contradiction of her name, Victoria joined with Flint, seemed to proclaim that she did not belong to her father or to the Rose of Sharon. Austen permitted himself to dwell, as he descended the mountain in the gathering darkness, upon the fancy of the springing of a generation of ideals from a generation of commerce which boded well for the Republic. And Austen Vane, in common with that younger and travelled generation, thought largely in terms of the Republic. Pepper County and Putnam County were all one to him—pieces of his native land. And as such, redeemable.

It was long past the supper hour when he reached the house in Hanover Street; but Euphrasia, who many a time in days gone by had fared forth into the woods to find Sarah Austen, had his supper hot for him. Afterwards he lighted his pipe and went out into the darkness, and presently perceived a black figure seated meditatively on the granite doorstep.

" Is that you, Judge ? " said Austen.

The Honourable Hilary grunted in response.

" Be'n on another wild expedition, I suppose."

" I went up Sawanec to stretch my legs a little," Austen answered, sitting down beside his father.

"Funny," remarked the Honourable Hilary, " I never had this mania for stretchin' my legs after I was grown."

" Well," said Austen, " I like to go into the woods and climb the hills and get aired out once in a while."

"I heard of your gettin' aired out yesterday, up Tunbridge way," said the Honourable Hilary.

" I supposed you would hear of it," answered Austen.

" I was up there to-day. Gave Mr. Flint your pass — did you ? "

" Yes."

" Didn't see fit to mention it to me first — did you? Said you were going up to thank him for it."

Austen considered this.

" You have put me in the wrong, Judge," he replied after a little. " I made that remark ironically. I — I am afraid we cannot agree on the motive which prompted me."

" Your conscience a little finer than your father's — is it ? "

" No," said Austen, " I don't honestly think it is. I've thought a good deal in the last few years about the difference in our ways of looking at things. I believe that two men who try to be honest may conscientiously differ. But I also believe that certain customs have gradually grown up in railroad practice which are more or less to be deplored from the point of view of the honour of the profession. I think they are not perhaps — realized even by the eminent men in the law."

"Humph! " said the Honourable Hilary. But he did not press his son for the enumeration of these customs. After all the years he had disapproved of Austen's deeds it seemed strange indeed to be called to account by the prodigal for his own. Could it be that this boy whom he had so often chastised took a clearer view of practical morality than himself? It was preposterous. But why the uneasiness of the past few years? Why had he more than once during that period, for the first time in his life, questioned a hitherto absolute satisfaction in his position of chief counsel for the Northeastern Railroads? Why had he hesitated to initiate his son into many of the so-called duties of a railroad lawyer? Austen had never verbally arraigned those duties until to-night.

Contradictory as it may seem, irritating as it was to the Honourable Hilary Vane, he experienced again the certain faint tingling of pride as when Austen had given him the dispassionate account of the shooting of Mr. Blodgett; and this tingling only served to stiffen Hilary Vane more than ever. A lifelong habit of admitting nothing and a lifelong pride made the acknowledgment of possible professional lapses for the benefit of his employer not to be thought of. He therefore assumed the same attitude as had Mr. Flint, and forced the burden of explanation upon Austen, relying surely on the disinclination of his son to be specific. And Austen, considering his relationship, could not be expected to fathom these mental processes.

"See here, Judge," he said, greatly embarrassed by the real affection he felt, "I don't want to seem like a prig and appear to be sitting in judgment upon a man of your experience and position — especially since I have the honour to be your son, and have made a good deal of trouble by a not irreproachable existence. Since we have begun on the subject, however, I think I ought to tell you that I have taken the case of Zeb Meader against the Northeastern Railroads."

"Wahn't much need of telling me, was there?" remarked the Honourable Hilary, dryly. "I'd have found it out as soon as anybody else."

"There was this need of telling you," answered Austen, steadily, "although I am not in partnership with you, I bear your name. And inasmuch as I am to have a suit against your client, it has occurred to me that you would like me to move — elsewhere."

The Honourable Hilary was silent for a long time.

" Want to move — do you ?   Is that it ? "

" Only because my presence may embarrass you."

" That wahn't in the contract," said the Honourable Hilary; " you've got a right to take any fool cases you've a mind to.   Folks'll know pretty well I'm not mixed up in 'em."

Austen did not smile; he could well understand his father's animus in this matter.   As he looked up at the gable of his old home against the stars, he did not find the next sentence any easier.

" And then," he continued, " in taking a course so obviously against your wishes and judgment it occurred to me — well, that I was eating at your table and sleeping in your house."

To his son's astonishment, Hilary Vane turned on him almost truculently.

" I thought the time'd come when you'd want to go off again, — gypsying," he cried.

" I'd stay right here in Ripton, Judge.   I believe my work is in this State."

The Honourable Hilary could see through a millstone with a hole in it.   The effect of Austen's assertion on him was a declaration that the mission of the one was to tear down what the other had so laboriously built up.   And yet a growing dread of Hilary Vane's had been the loneliness of declining years in that house should Austen leave it again, never to return.

" I knew you had this Meader business in mind," he said.   " I knew you had fanciful notions about — some things.   Never told you I didn't want you here, did I ? "

" No," said Austen, " but — "

" Would have told you if I hadn't wanted you — wouldn't I ? "

" I hope so, Judge," said Austen, who understood something of the feeling which underlay this brusqueness. That knowledge made matters all the harder for him.

"It was your mother's house — you're entitled to that, anyway," said the Honourable Hilary, "but what I want to know is, why you didn't advise that eternal fool of a Meader to accept what we offered him. You'll never get a county jury to give as much."

"I did advise him to accept it," answered Austen.

"What's the matter with him?" the Honourable Hilary demanded.

"Well, Judge, if you really want my opinion, an honest farmer like Meader is suspicious of any corporation which has such zealous and loyal retainers as Ham Tooting and Brush Bascom." And Austen thought with a return of the pang which had haunted him at intervals throughout the afternoon, that he might almost have added to these names that of Hilary Vane. Certainly Zeb Meader had not spared his father.

"Life," observed the Honourable Hilary, unconsciously using a phrase from the "Book of Arguments," "is a survival of the fittest."

"How do you define 'the fittest'?" asked Austen. "Are they the men who have the not unusual and certainly not very exalted gift of getting money from their fellow-creatures by the use of any and all weapons that may be at hand? who believe the acquisition of wealth to be exempt from the practice of morality? Is Mr. Flint your example of the fittest type to exist and survive, or Gladstone or Wilberforce or Emerson or Lincoln?"

"Emerson!" cried the Honourable Hilary, the name standing out in red letters before his eyes. He had never read a line of the philosopher's writings, not even the charge to "hitch your wagon to a star" (not in the "Book of Arguments"). Sarah Austen had read Emerson in the woods, and her son's question sounded so like the unintelligible but unanswerable flashes with which the wife had on rare occasions opposed the husband's authority that Hilary Vane found his temper getting the best of him. The name of Emerson was immutably fixed in his mind as the synonym for incomprehensible, foolish habits and beliefs. "Don't talk Emerson to me," he exclaimed. "And as for Brush Bascom, I've known him for thirty years, and he's done as much for the Republican party as any man in this State."

This vindication of Mr. Bascom naturally brought to a close a conversation which had already continued too long. The Honourable Hilary retired to rest; but — if Austen had known it — not to sleep until the small hours of the morning.

It was not until the ensuing spring that the case of Mr. Zebulun Meader against the United Northeastern Railroads came up for trial in Bradford, the county-seat of Putnam County, and we do not wish to appear to give it too great a weight in the annals of the State. For one thing, the weekly newspapers did not mention it; and Mr. Paul Pardriff, when urged to give an account of the proceedings in the *Ripton Record*, said it was a matter of no importance, and spent the afternoon writing an editorial about the domestic habits of the Aztecs. Mr. Pardriff, however, had thought the matter of sufficient interest personally to attend the trial, and for the journey he made use of a piece of green cardboard which he habitually carried in his pocket. The editor of the *Bradford Champion* did not have to use his yellow cardboard, yet his columns may be searched in vain for the event.

Not that it was such a great event, — one of hundreds of railroad accidents that come to court. The son of Hilary Vane was the plaintiff's counsel; and Mr. Meader, although he had not been able to work since his release from the hospital, had been able to talk, and the interest taken in the case by the average neglected citizen in Putnam proved that the weekly newspaper is not the only disseminator of news.

The railroad's side of the case was presented by that genial and able practitioner of Putnam County, Mr. Nathaniel Billings, who travelled from his home in Williamstown by the exhibition of a red ticket. Austen Vane had to pay his own way from Ripton, but as he handed back the mileage book, the conductor leaned over and whispered something in his ear that made him smile, and

Austen thought he would rather have that little drop of encouragement than a pass. And as he left the car at Bradford, two grizzled and hard-handed individuals arose and wished him good luck.

He needed encouragement, — what young lawyer does not on his first important case? And he did not like to think of the future if he lost this. But in this matter he possessed a certain self-confidence which arose from a just and righteous anger against the forces opposing him and a knowledge of their tactics. To his mind his client was not Zeb Meader alone, but the host of victims who had been maimed and bought off because it was cheaper than to give the public a proper protection.

The court room was crowded. Mr. Zeb Meader, pale but determined, was surrounded by a knot of Mercer neighbours, many of whom were witnesses. The agate eyes of Mr. Brush Bascom flashed from the audience, and Mr. Nat Billings bustled forward to shake Austen's hand. Nat was one of those who called not infrequently upon the Honourable Hilary in Ripton, and had sat on Austen's little table.

"Glad to see you, Austen," he cried, so that the people might hear; and added, in a confidentially lower tone, "We lawyers understand that these little things make no difference, eh?"

"I'm willing to agree to that if you are, Nat," Austen answered. He looked at the lawyer's fleshy face, blue-black where it was shaven, and at Mr. Billings' shifty eyes and mouth, which its muscles could not quite keep in place. Mr. Billings also had nicked teeth. But he did his best to hide these obvious disadvantages by a Falstaffian bonhomie, — for Mr. Billings was growing stout.

"I tried it once or twice, my friend, when I was younger. It's noble, but it don't pay," said Mr. Billings, still confidential. "Brush is sour — look at him. But I understand how you feel. I'm the kind of feller that speaks out, and what I can't understand is, why the old man let you get into it."

"He knew you were going to be on the other side, Nat,

and wanted to teach me a lesson. I suppose it is folly to
contest a case where the Railroad Commission has completely exonerated your client," Austen added thoughtfully.

Mr. Billings' answer was to wink, very slowly, with one
eye; and shortly after these pleasantries were over, the
case was called. A fragrant wind blew in at the open
windows, and Nature outside was beginning to array herself in myriad hues of green. Austen studied the jury, and
wondered how many points of his argument he could remember, but when he had got to his feet the words came
to him. If we should seek an emblem for King David's
smooth, round stone which he flung at Goliath, we should
call it the truth — for the truth never fails to reach the
mark. Austen's opening was not long, his words simple
and not dramatic, but he seemed to charge them with
something of the same magnetic force that compelled
people to read and believe " Uncle Tom's Cabin " and the
"Song of the Shirt." Spectators and jury listened
intently.

Some twenty witnesses appeared for the plaintiff, all
of whom declared that they had heard neither bell nor
whistle. Most of these witnesses had been in the grove,
two or three in the train ; two, residents of the vicinity,
testified that they had complained to the Railroad Commission about that crossing, and had received evasive answers to the effect that it was the duty of citizens to look
out for themselves. On cross-examination they declared
they had no objection to grade crossings which were
properly safeguarded ; this crossing was a death-trap.
(Stricken out.) Mr. Billings made the mistake of trying
to prove that one of these farmers — a clear-eyed, full-
chested man with a deep voice — had an animus against
the railroad dating from a controversy concerning the
shipping of milk.

" I do have an animus, your Honour," said the witness,
quietly. "When the railrud is represented by the kind
of politicians we have in Putnam, it's natural I should —
hain't it ? "

This answer, although stricken out, was gleefully received.

In marked contrast to the earnestness of young Mr. Vane, who then rested, Mr. Billings treated the affair from the standpoint of a man of large practice who usually has more weighty matters to attend to. This was so comparatively trivial as not to be dignified by a serious mien. He quoted freely from the "Book of Arguments," reminding the jury of the debt of gratitude the State owed to the Northeastern Railroads for doing so much for its people; and if they were to eliminate all grade crossings, there would be no dividends for the stockholders. Besides, the law was that the State should pay half when a crossing was eliminated, and the State could not afford it. Austen had suggested, in his opening, that it was cheaper for the railroad as well as the State to kill citizens. He asked permission to inquire of the learned counsel for the defence by what authority he declared that the State could not afford to enter into a policy by which grade crossings would gradually be eliminated.

"Why," said Mr. Billings, "the fact that all bills introduced to this end never get out of committee."

"May I ask," said Austen, innocently, "who has been chairman of that particular committee in the lower House for the last five sessions?"

Mr. Billings was saved the embarrassment of answering this question by a loud voice in the rear calling out: —

"Brush Bascom!"

A roar of laughter shook the court room, and all eyes were turned on Brush, who continued to sit unconcernedly with his legs crossed and his arm over the back of the seat. The offender was put out, order was restored, and Mr. Billings declared, with an injured air, that he failed to see why the counsel for the plaintiff saw fit to impugn Mr. Bascom.

"I merely asked a question," said Austen; "far be it from me to impugn any man who has held offices in the gift of the people for the last twenty years."

Another gale of laughter followed this, during which Mr. Billings wriggled his mouth and gave a strong impression that such tactics and such levity were to be deplored.

For the defence, the engineer and fireman both swore that the bell had been rung before the crossing was reached. Austen merely inquired whether this was not when they had left the station at North Mercer, two miles away. No, it was nearer. Pressed to name the exact spot, they could only conjecture, but near enough to be heard on the crossing. Other witnesses — among them several picnickers in the grove — swore that they had heard the bell. One of these Austen asked if he was not the member from Mercer in the last Legislature, and Mr. Billings, no longer genial, sprang to his feet with an objection.

"I merely wish to show, your Honour," said Austen, "that this witness accepted a pass from the Northeastern Railroads when he went to the Legislature, and that he has had several trip passes for himself and his family since."

The objection was not sustained, and Mr. Billings noted an exception.

Another witness, upon whose appearance the audience tittered audibly, was Dave Skinner, boss of Mercer. He had lived, he said, in the town of Mercer all his life, and maintained that he was within a hundred yards of the track when the accident occurred, and heard the bell ring.

"Is it not a fact," said Austen to this witness, "that Mr. Brush Bascom has a mortgage on your farm?"

"I can show, your Honour," Austen continued, when Mr. Billings had finished his protest, "that this man was on his way to Riverside to pay his quarterly instalment."

Mr. Bascom was not present at the afternoon session. Mr. Billings' summing up was somewhat impassioned, and contained more quotations from the "Book of Arguments." He regretted, he said, the obvious appeals to prejudice against a railroad corporation that was honestly trying to do its duty — yes, and more than its duty.

Misjudged, misused, even though friendless, it would continue to serve the people. So noble, indeed, was the picture which Mr. Billings' eloquence raised up that his voice shook with emotion as he finished.

In the opinion of many of the spectators Austen Vane had yet to learn the art of oratory. He might with propriety have portrayed the suffering and loss of the poor farmer who was his client; he merely quoted from the doctor's testimony to the effect that Mr. Meader would never again be able to do physical labour of the sort by which he had supported himself, and ended up by calling the attention of the jury to the photographs and plans of the crossing he had obtained two days after the accident, requesting them to note the facts that the public highway, approaching through a dense forest and underbrush at an angle of thirty-three degrees, climbed the railroad embankment at that point, and a train could not be seen until the horse was actually on the track.

The jury was out five minutes after the judge's charge, and gave Mr. Zebulun Meader a verdict of six thousand dollars and costs, — a popular verdict, from the evident approval with which it was received in the court room. Quiet being restored, Mr. Billings requested, somewhat vehemently, that the case be transferred on the exceptions to the Supreme Court, that the stenographer write out the evidence, and that he might have three weeks in which to prepare a draft. This was granted.

Zeb Meader, true to his nature, was self-contained throughout the congratulations he received, but his joy was nevertheless intense.

"You shook 'em up good, Austen," he said, making his way to where his counsel stood. "I suspicioned you'd do it. But how about this here appeal?"

"Billings is merely trying to save the face of his railroad," Austen answered, smiling. "He hasn't the least notion of allowing this case to come up again — take my word for it."

"I guess your word's good," said Zeb. "And I want to tell you one thing, as an old man. I've been talkin' to

Putnam County folks some, and you hain't lost nothin' by this."

" How am I to get along without the friendship of Brush Bascom ? " asked Austen, soberly.

Mr. Meader, who had become used to this mild sort of humour, relaxed sufficiently to laugh.

" Brush did seem a mite disgruntled," he remarked.

Somewhat to Austen's embarrassment, Mr. Meader's friends were pushing forward. One grizzled veteran took him by the hand and looked thoughtfully into his face.

" I've lived a good many years," he said, " but I never heerd 'em talked up to like that. You're my candidate for governor."

CHAPTER VI

ENTER THE LION

It is a fact, as Shakespeare has so tersely hinted, that
fame sometimes comes in the line of duty. To be sure, if
Austen Vane had been Timothy Smith, the Meader case
might not have made quite so many ripples in the pond
with which this story is concerned. Austen did what he
thought was right. In the opinion of many of his father's
friends whom he met from time to time he had made a
good-sized stride towards ruin, and they did not hesitate
to tell him so — Mr. Chipman, president of the Ripton
National Bank; Mr. Greene, secretary and treasurer of
the Hawkeye Paper Company, who suggested with all
kindness that, however noble it may be, it doesn't pay to
tilt at windmills.

"Not unless you wreck the windmill," answered Austen.
A new and very revolutionary point of view to Mr. Greene,
who repeated it to Professor Brewer, urging that gentleman to take Austen in hand. But the professor burst
out laughing, and put the saying into circulation.

Mr. Silas Tredway, whose list of directorships is too long
to print, also undertook to remonstrate with the son of
his old friend, Hilary Vane. The young lawyer heard him
respectfully. The cashiers of some of these gentlemen, who
were younger men, ventured to say — when out of hearing
— that they admired the championship of Mr. Meader, but
it would never do. To these, likewise, Austen listened
good-naturedly enough, and did not attempt to contradict
them. Changing the angle of the sun-dial does not affect
the time of day.

It was not surprising that young Tom Gaylord, when
he came back from New York and heard of Austen's

F   65

victory, should have rushed to his office and congratulated him in a rough but hearty fashion. Even though Austen had won a suit against the Gaylord Lumber Company, young Tom would have congratulated him. Old Tom was a different matter. Old Tom, hobbling along under the maples, squinted at Austen and held up his stick.

"Damn you, you're a lawyer, ain't you?" cried the old man.

Austen, well used to this kind of greeting from Mr. Gaylord, replied that he didn't think himself much of one.

"Damn it, I say you are. Some day I may have use for you," said old Tom, and walked on.

"No," said young Tom, afterwards, in explanation of this extraordinary attitude of his father, "it isn't principle. He's had a row with the Northeastern about lumber rates, and swears he'll live till he gets even with 'em."

If Professor Brewer (Ripton's most clear-sighted citizen) had made the statement that Hilary Vane — away down in the bottom of his heart — was secretly proud of his son, the professor would probably have lost his place on the school board, the water board, and the library committee. The way the worldly-wise professor discovered the secret was this: he had gone to Bradford to hear the case, for he had been a dear friend of Sarah Austen. Two days later Hilary Vane saw the professor on his little porch, and lingered. Mr. Brewer suspected why, led carefully up to the subject, and not being discouraged — except by numerous grunts — gave the father an account of the proceedings by no means unfavourable to the son. Some people like paregoric; the Honourable Hilary took his without undue squirming, with no visible effects to Austen.

Life in the office continued, with one or two exceptions, the even tenor of its way. Apparently, so far as the Honourable Hilary was concerned, his son had never been to Bradford. But the Honourable Brush Bascom, when he came on mysterious business to call on the chief counsel, no longer sat on Austen's table; this was true of other

feudal lords and retainers : of Mr. Nat Billings, who, by
the way, did not file his draft after all. Not that Mr.
Billings wasn't polite, but he indulged no longer in slow
winks at the expense of the honourable Railroad Commission.

Perhaps the most curious result of the Meader case to
be remarked in passing, was upon Mr. Hamilton Tooting.
Austen, except when he fled to the hills, was usually the
last to leave the office, Mr. Tooting often the first. But
one evening Mr. Tooting waited until the force had gone,
and entered Austen's room with his hand outstretched.

"Put her there, Aust," he said.

Austen put her there.

"I've been exercisin' my thinker some the last few
months," observed Mr. Tooting, seating himself on the
desk.

"Aren't you afraid of nervous prostration, Ham ? "

"Say," exclaimed Mr. Tooting, with a vexed laugh,
"why are you always jollying me ? You ain't any older
than I am."

"I'm not as old, Ham. I don't begin to have your
knowledge of the world."

"Come off," said Mr. Tooting, who didn't know exactly
how to take this compliment. "I came in here to have a
serious talk. I've been thinking it over, and I don't know
but what you did right."

"Well, Ham, if you don't know, I don't know how I am
to convince you."

"Hold on. Don't go twistin' around that way — you
make me dizzy." He lowered his voice confidentially,
although there was no one within five walls of them. "I
know the difference between a gold brick and a government bond, anyhow. I believe bucking the railroad's
going to pay in a year or so. I got on to it as soon as you
did, I guess, but when a feller's worn the collar as long as
I have and has to live, it ain't easy to cut loose — you
understand."

"I understand," answered Austen, gravely.

"I thought I'd let you know I didn't take any too much

trouble with Meader last summer to get the old bird to
accept a compromise."

"That was good of you, Ham."

"I knew what you was up to," said Mr. Tooting, giving Austen a friendly poke with his cigar.

"You showed your usual acumen, Mr. Tooting," said
Austen, as he rose to put on his coat. Mr. Tooting regarded him uneasily.

"You're a deep one, Aust," he declared; "some day
you and me must get together."

Mr. Billings' desire for ultimate justice not being any
stronger than Austen suspected, in due time Mr. Meader
got his money. His counsel would have none of it, — a
decision not at all practical, and on the whole disappoint-
ing. There was, to be sure, an influx into Austen's office
of people who had been run over in the past, and it was
Austen's unhappy duty to point out to these that they
had signed (at the request of various Mr. Tootings) little
slips of paper which are technically known as releases.
But the first hint of a really material advantage to be
derived from his case against the railroad came from a
wholly unexpected source, in the shape of a letter in the
mail one August morning.

"DEAR SIR: Having remarked with some interest the
verdict for a client of yours against the United Northeastern Railroads, I wish you would call and see me at your
earliest convenience.

"Yours truly,
                              "HUMPHREY CREWE."

Although his curiosity was aroused, Austen was of two
minds whether to answer this summons, the truth being
that Mr. Crewe had not made, on the occasions on which
they had had intercourse, the most favourable of impressions. However, it is not for the struggling lawyer
to scorn any honourable brief, especially from a gentleman
of stocks and bonds and varied interests like Mr. Crewe,
with whom contentions of magnitude are inevitably asso-

ciated.   As he spun along behind Pepper on the Leith
road that climbed Willow Brook on the afternoon he had
made the appointment, Austen smiled to himself over his
anticipations, and yet — being human — let his fancy
play.

The broad acres of Wedderburn stretched across many
highways, but the manor-house (as it had been called)
stood on an eminence whence one could look for miles
down the Vale of the Blue.   It had once been a farm-
house, but gradually the tail had begun to wag the dog,
and the farmhouse became, like the original stone out of
which the Irishman made the soup, difficult to find.   Once
the edifice had been on the road, but the road had long ago
been removed to a respectful distance, and Austen entered
between two massive pillars built of granite blocks on a
musical gravel drive.

Humphrey Crewe was on the porch, his hands in his
pockets, as Austen drove up.

" Hello," he said, in a voice probably meant to be hospitable, but which had a peremptory ring, " don't stand
on ceremony.   Hitch your beast and come along in."

Having, as it were, superintended the securing of
Pepper, Mr. Crewe led the way through the house to
the study, pausing once or twice to point out to Austen
a carved ivory elephant procured at great expense in
China, and a piece of tapestry equally difficult of purchase.
The study itself was no mere lounging place of a man
of pleasure, but sober and formidable books were scattered
through the cases: Turner's " Evolution of the Railroad,"
Graham's " Practical Forestry," Eldridge's " Finance ";
while whole shelves of modern husbandry proclaimed that
Mr. Humphrey Crewe was no amateur farmer.   There
was likewise a shelf devoted to road building, several
to knotty-looking pamphlets, and half a wall of neatly
labelled pigeonholes.   For decoration, there was an oar
garnished with a ribbon, and several groups of college
undergraduates, mostly either in puffed ties or scanty
attire, and always prominent in these groups, and
always unmistakable, was Mr. Humphrey Crewe himself.

Mr. Crewe was silent awhile, that this formidable array of things might make the proper impression upon his visitor.

"It was lucky you came to-day, Vane," he said at length. "I am due in New York to-morrow for a directors' meeting, and I have a conference in Chicago with a board of trustees of which I am a member on the third. Looking at my array of pamphlets, eh? I've been years in collecting them, — ever since I left college. Those on railroads ought especially to interest you — I'm somewhat of a railroad man myself."

"I didn't know that," said Austen.

"Had two or three blocks of stock in subsidiary lines that had to be looked after. It was a nuisance at first," said Mr. Crewe, "but I didn't shirk it. I made up my mind I'd get to the bottom of the railroad problem, and I did. It's no use doing a thing at all unless you do it well." Mr. Crewe, his hands still in his pockets, faced Austen smilingly. "Now I'll bet you didn't know I was a railroad man until you came in here. To tell the truth, it was about a railroad matter that I sent for you."

Mr. Crewe lit a cigar, but he did not offer one to Austen, as he had to Mr. Tooting. "I wanted to see what you were like," he continued, with refreshing frankness. "Of course, I'd seen you on the road. But you can get more of an idea of a man by talkin' to him, you know."

"You can if he'll talk," said Austen, who was beginning to enjoy his visit.

Mr. Crewe glanced at him keenly. Few men are fools at all points of the compass, and Mr. Crewe was far from this.

"You did well in that little case you had against the Northeastern. I heard about it."

"I did my best," answered Austen, and he smiled again.

"As some great man has remarked," observed Mr. Crewe, "it isn't what we do, it's how we do it. Take pains over the smaller cases, and the larger cases will come of themselves, eh?"

"I live in hope," said Austen, wondering how soon this larger case was going to unfold itself.

"Let me see," said Mr. Crewe, "isn't your father the chief attorney in this State for the Northeastern? How do you happen to be on the other side?"

"By the happy accident of obtaining a client," said Austen.

Mr. Crewe glanced at him again. In spite of himself, respect was growing in him. He had expected to find a certain amount of eagerness and subserviency—though veiled; here was a man of different calibre than he looked for in Ripton.

"The fact is," he declared, "I have a grievance against the Northeastern Railroads, and I have made up my mind that you are the man for me."

"You may have reason to regret your choice," Austen suggested.

"I think not," replied Mr. Crewe, promptly; "I believe I know a man when I see one, and you inspire me with confidence. This matter will have a double interest for you, as I understand you are fond of horses."

"Horses?"

"Yes," Mr. Crewe continued, gaining a little heat at the word, "I bought the finest-lookin' pair you ever saw in New York this spring,—all-around action, manners, conformation, everything; I'll show 'em to you. One of 'em's all right now; this confounded railroad injured the other gettin' him up here. I've put in a claim. They say they didn't, my man says they did. He tells me the horse was thrown violently against the sides of the car several times. He's internally injured. I told 'em I'd sue 'em, and I've decided that you are the man to take the case—on conditions."

Austen's sense of humour saved him,—and Mr. Humphrey Crewe had begun to interest him. He rose and walked to the window and looked out for a few moments over the flower garden before he replied:—

"On what conditions?"

"Well," said Mr. Crewe, "frankly, I don't want to pay

more than the horse is worth, and it's business to settle on the fee in case you win. I thought — "

"You thought," said Austen, "that I might not charge as much as the next man."

"Well," said Mr. Crewe, "I knew that if you took the case, you'd fight it through, and I want to get even with 'em. Their claim agent had the impudence to suggest that the horse had been doctored by the dealer in New York. To tell me that I, who have been buying horses all my life, was fooled. The veterinary swears the animal is ruptured. I'm a citizen of Avalon County, though many people call me a summer resident; I've done business here and helped improve the neighbourhood for years. It will be my policy to employ home talent — Avalon County lawyers, for instance. I may say, without indiscretion, that I intend from now on to take even a greater interest in public affairs. The trouble is in this country that men in my position do not feel their responsibilities."

"Public spirit is a rare virtue," Austen remarked, seeing that he was expected to say something. "Avalon County appreciates the compliment, — if I may be permitted to answer for it."

"I want to do the right thing," said Mr. Crewe. "In fact, I have almost made up my mind to go to the Legislature this year. I know it would be a sacrifice of time, in a sense, and all that, but — " He paused, and looked at Austen.

"The Legislature needs leavening."

"Precisely," exclaimed Mr. Crewe, "and when I look around me and see the things crying to be done in this State, and no lawmaker with sense and foresight enough to propose them, it makes me sick. Now, for instance," he continued, and rose with an evident attempt to assault the forestry shelves. But Austen rose too.

"I'd like to go over that with you, Mr. Crewe," said he, "but I have to be back in Ripton."

"How about my case?" his host demanded, with a return to his former abruptness.

" What about it ? " asked Austen.

" Are you going to take it ? "

" Struggling lawyers don't refuse business."

" Well," said Mr. Crewe, "that's sensible. But what are you going to charge ? "

" Now," said Austen, with entire good humour, " when you get on that ground, you are dealing no longer with one voracious unit, but with a whole profession, — a profession, you will allow me to add, which in dignity is second to none. In accordance with the practice of the best men in that profession, I will charge you what I believe is fair — not what I think you are able and willing to pay. Should you dispute the bill, I will not stoop to quarrel with you, but try to live on bread and butter a while longer."

Mr. Crewe was silent for a moment. It would not be exact to say uncomfortable, for it is to be doubted whether he ever got so. But he felt dimly that the relations of patron and patronized were becoming somewhat jumbled.

" All right," said he, " I guess we can let it go at that. Hello ! What the deuce are those women doing here again ? "

This irrelevant exclamation was caused by the sight — through the open French window — of three ladies in the flower garden, two of whom were bending over the beds. The third, upon whose figure Austen's eyes were riveted, was seated on a stone bench set in a recess of pines, and looking off into the Vale of the Blue. With no great eagerness, but without apology to Austen, Mr. Crewe stepped out of the window and approached them; and as this was as good a way as any to his horse and buggy, Austen followed. One of the ladies straightened at their appearance, scrutinized them through the glasses she held in her hand, and Austen immediately recognized her as the irreproachable Mrs. Pomfret.

" We didn't mean to disturb you, Humphrey," she said. " We knew you would be engaged in business, but I told Alice as we drove by I could not resist stopping for one more look at your Canterbury bells. I knew you wouldn't mind, but you mustn't leave your — affairs, — not for an instant."

The word "affairs" was accompanied by a brief inspection of Austen Vane.

"That's all right," answered Mr. Crewe; "it doesn't cost anything to look at flowers, that's what they're for. Cost something to put 'em in. I got that little feller Ridley to lay 'em out — I believe I told you. He's just beginning. Hello, Alice."

"I think he did it very well, Humphrey," said Miss Pomfret.

"Passably," said Mr. Crewe. "I told him what I wanted and drew a rough sketch of the garden and the colour scheme."

"Then *you* did it, and not Mr. Ridley. I rather suspected it," said Mrs. Pomfret; "you have such clear and practical ideas about things, Humphrey."

"It's simple enough," said Mr. Crewe, deprecatingly, "after you've seen a few hundred gardens and get the general underlying principle."

"It's very clever," Alice murmured.

"Not at all. A little application will do wonders. A certain definite colour massed here, another definite colour there, and so forth."

Mr. Crewe spoke as though Alice's praise irritated him slightly. He waved his hand to indicate the scheme in general, and glanced at Victoria on the stone bench. From her (Austen thought) seemed to emanate a silent but mirthful criticism, although she continued to gaze persistently down the valley, apparently unaware of their voices. Mr. Crewe looked as if he would have liked to reach her, but the two ladies filled the narrow path, and Mrs. Pomfret put her fingers on his sleeve.

"Humphrey, you must explain it to us. I am so interested in gardens I'm going to have one if Electrics increase their dividend."

Mr. Crewe began, with no great ardour, to descant on the theory of planting, and Austen resolved to remain pocketed and ignored no longer. He retraced his steps and made his way rapidly by another path towards Victoria, who turned her head at his approach, and rose. He acknowledged an inward agitation with the vision in his eye of the tall, white figure against the pines, clad with the art which, in mysterious simplicity, effaces itself.

" I was wondering," she said, as she gave him her hand, " how long it would be before you spoke to me."

" You gave me no chance," said Austen, quickly.

" Do you deserve one ? " she asked.

Before he could answer, Mr. Crewe's explanation of his theories had come lamely to a halt. Austen was aware of the renewed scrutiny of Mrs. Pomfret, and then Mr. Crewe, whom no social manacles could shackle, had broken past her and made his way to them. He continued to treat the ground on which Austen was standing as unoccupied.

" Hello, Victoria," he said, " you don't know anything about gardens, do you ? "

" I don't believe you do either," was Victoria's surprising reply.

Mr. Crewe laughed at this pleasantry.

" How are you going to prove it ? " he demanded.

" By comparing what you've done with Freddie Ridley's original plan," said Victoria.

Mr. Crewe was nettled.

" Ridley has a lot to learn," he retorted. " He had no conception of what was appropriate here."

" Freddie was weak," said Victoria, " but he needed the money. Don't you know Mr. Vane ? "

" Yes," said Mr. Crewe, shortly, " I've been talking to him — on business."

" Oh," said Victoria, " I had no means of knowing. Mrs. Pomfret, I want to introduce Mr. Vane, and Miss Pomfret, Mr. Vane."

Mrs. Pomfret, who had been hovering on the outskirts of this duel, inclined her head the fraction of an inch, but Alice put out her hand with her sweetest manner.

" When did you arrive ? " she asked.

" Well, the fact is, I haven't arrived yet," said Austen.

"Not arrived!" exclaimed Alice, with a puzzled glance into Victoria's laughing eyes.

"Perhaps Humphrey will help you along," Victoria suggested, turning to him. "He might be induced to give you his celebrated grievance about his horses."

"I have given it to him," said Mr. Crewe, briefly.

"Cheer up, Mr. Vane, your fortune is made," said Victoria.

"Victoria," said Mrs. Pomfret, in her most imperial voice, "we ought to be going instantly, or we shan't have time to drop you at the Hammonds'."

"I'll take you over in the new motor car," said Mr. Crewe, with his air of conferring a special train.

"How much is gasoline by the gallon?" inquired Victoria.

"I did a favour once for the local manager, and get a special price," said Mr. Crewe.

"Humphrey," said Mrs. Pomfret, taking his hand, "don't forget you are coming to dinner to-night. Four people gave out at the last minute, and there will be just Alice and myself. I've asked old Mr. Fitzhugh."

"All right," said Mr. Crewe, "I'll have the motor car brought around."

The latter part of this remark was, needless to say, addressed to Victoria.

"It's awfully good of you, Humphrey," she answered, "but the Hammonds are on the road to Ripton, and I am going to ask Mr. Vane to drive me down there behind that adorable horse of his."

This announcement produced a varied effect upon those who heard it, although all experienced surprise. Mrs. Pomfret, in addition to an anger which she controlled only as the result of long practice, was horrified, and once more levelled her glasses at Austen.

"I think, Victoria, you had better come with us," she said. "We shall have plenty of time, if we hurry."

By this time Austen had recovered his breath.

"I'll be ready in an instant," he said, and made brief but polite adieus to the three others.

" Good-by," said Alice, vaguely.

" Let me know when anything develops," said Mr. Crewe, with his back to his attorney.

Austen found Victoria, her colour heightened a little, waiting for him by the driveway. The Pomfrets had just driven off, and Mr. Crewe was nowhere to be seen.

"I do not know what you will think of me for taking this for granted, Mr. Vane," she said as he took his seat beside her, " but I couldn't resist the chance of driving behind your horse."

" I realized," he answered smilingly, " that Pepper was the attraction, and I have more reason than ever to be grateful to him."

She glanced covertly at the Vane profile, at the sure, restraining hands on the reins which governed with so nice a touch the mettle of the horse. His silence gave her time to analyze again her interest in this man, which renewed itself at every meeting. In the garden she had been struck by the superiority of a nature which set at naught what had been, to some smaller spirits, a difficult situation. She recognized this quality as inborn, but, not knowing of Sarah Austen, she wondered where he got it. Now it was the fact that he refrained from comment that pleased her most.

" Did Humphrey actually send for you to take up the injured horse case ? " she asked.

Austen flushed.

" I'm afraid he did. You seem to know all about it," he added.

" Know all about it ! Every one within twenty miles of Leith knows about it. I'm sure the horse was doctored when he bought him."

" Take care, you may be called as a witness."

" What I want to know is, why you accepted such a silly case," said Victoria.

Austen looked quizzically into her upturned face, and she dropped her eyes.

" That's exactly what I should have asked myself, — after a while," he said.

She laughed with a delicious understanding of "after a while."

"I suppose you think me frightfully forward," she said, in a lowered voice, "inviting myself to drive and asking you such a question when I scarcely know you. But I just couldn't go on with Mrs. Pomfret, — she irritated me so, — and my front teeth are too valuable to drive with Humphrey Crewe."

Austen smiled, and secretly agreed with her.

"I should have offered, if I had dared," he said.

"Dared! I didn't know that was your failing. I don't believe you even thought of it."

"Nevertheless, the idea occurred to me, and terrified me," said Austen.

"Why?" she asked, turning upon him suddenly. "Why did it terrify you?"

"I should have been presuming upon an accidental acquaintance, which I had no means of knowing you wished to continue," he replied, staring at his horse's head.

"And I?" Victoria asked. "Presumption multiplies tenfold in a woman, doesn't it?"

"A woman confers," said Austen.

She smiled, but with a light in her eyes. This simple sentence seemed to reveal yet more of an inner man different from some of those with whom her life had been cast. It was an American point of view — this choosing to believe that the woman conferred. After offering herself as his passenger Victoria, too, had had a moment of terror : the action had been the result of an impulse which she did not care to attempt to define. She changed the subject.

"You have been winning laurels since I saw you last summer," she said. "I hear incidentally you have made our friend Zeb Meader a rich man."

"As riches go, in the town of Mercer," Austen laughed. "As for my laurels, they have not yet begun to chafe."

Here was a topic he would have avoided, and yet he was curious to discover what her attitude would be. He had antagonized her father, and the fact that he was the son of Hilary Vane had given his antagonism prominence.

" I am glad you did it for Zeb."

"I should have done it for anybody — much as I like Zeb," he replied briefly.

She glanced at him.

"It was — courageous of you," she said.

" I have never looked upon it in that light," he answered. " May I ask you how you heard of it?"

She coloured, but faced the question.

" I heard it from my father, at first, and I took an interest — on Zeb Meader's account," she added hastily.

Austen was silent.

" Of course," she continued, " I felt a little like boasting of an 'accidental acquaintance' with the man who saved Zeb Meader's life."

Austen laughed. Then he drew Pepper down to a walk, and turned to her.

" The power of making it more than an accidental acquaintance lies with you," he said quietly.

" I have always had an idea that aggression was a man's prerogative," Victoria answered lightly. " And seeing that you have not appeared at Fairview for something over a year, I can only conclude that you do not choose to exercise it in this case."

Austen was in a cruel quandary.

" I did wish to come," he answered simply, " but — the fact that I have had a disagreement with your father has — made it difficult."

"Nonsense!" exclaimed Victoria; "just because you have won a suit against his railroad. You don't know my father, Mr. Vane. He isn't the kind of man with whom that would make any difference. You ought to talk it over with him. He thinks you were foolish to take Zeb Meader's side."

"And you?" Austen demanded quickly.

" You see, I'm a woman," said Victoria, " and I'm prejudiced — for Zeb Meader. Women are always prejudiced, — that's our trouble. It seemed to me that Zeb was old, and unfortunate, and ought to be compensated, since he is unable to work. But of course I suppose I can't be expected to understand."

It was true that she could not be expected to understand. He might not tell her that his difference with Mr. Flint was not a mere matter of taking a small damage suit against his railroad, but a fundamental one. And Austen recognized that the justification of his attitude meant an arraignment of Victoria's father.

"I wish you might know my father better, Mr. Vane," she went on, "I wish you might know him as I know him, if it were possible. You see, I have been his constant companion all my life, and I think very few people understand him as I do, and realize his fine qualities. He makes no attempt to show his best side to the world. His life has been spent in fighting, and I am afraid he is apt to meet the world on that footing. He is a man of such devotion to his duty that he rarely has a day to himself, and I have known him to sit up until the small hours of the morning to settle some little matter of justice. I do not think I am betraying his confidence when I say that he is impressed with your ability, and that he liked your manner the only time he ever talked to you. He believes that you have got, in some way, a wrong idea of what he is trying to do. Why don't you come up and talk to him again?"

"I am afraid your kindness leads you to overrate my importance," Austen replied, with mingled feelings. Victoria's confidence in her father made the situation all the more hopeless.

"I'm sure I don't," she answered quickly; "ever since — ever since I first laid eyes upon you I have had a kind of belief in you."

"Belief!" he echoed.

"Yes," she said, "belief that — that you had a future. I can't describe it," she continued, the colour coming into her face again; "one feels that way about some people without being able to put the feeling into words. And I have a feeling, too, that I should like you to be friends with my father."

Neither of them, perhaps, realized the rapidity with which "accidental acquaintance" had melted into intimacy. Austen's blood ran faster, but it was characteristic of him that he tried to steady himself, for he was a Vane. He had thought of her many times during the past year, but gradually the intensity of the impression had faded until it had been so unexpectedly and vividly renewed to-day. He was not a man to lose his head, and the difficulties of the situation made him pause and choose his words, while he dared not so much as glance at her as she sat in the sunlight beside him.

"I should like to be friends with your father," he answered gravely, — the statement being so literally true as to have its pathetically humorous aspect.

"I'll tell him so, Mr. Vane," she said.

Austen turned, with a seriousness that dismayed her.

"I must ask you as a favour not to do that," he said.

"Why?" she asked.

"In the first place," he answered quietly, "I cannot afford to have Mr. Flint misunderstand my motives. And I ought not to mislead you," he went on. "In periods of public controversy, such as we are passing through at present, sometimes men's views differ so sharply as to make intercourse impossible. Your father and I might not agree — politically, let us say. For instance," he added, with evident hesitation, "my father and I disagree."

Victoria was silent. And presently they came to a wire fence overgrown with Virginia creeper, which divided the shaded road from a wide lawn.

"Here we are at the Hammonds', and — thank you," she said.

Any reply he might have made was forestalled. The insistent and intolerant horn of an automobile, followed now by the scream of the gears, broke the stillness of the country-side, and a familiar voice cried out:

"Do you want the whole road?"

Austen turned into the Hammonds' drive as the bull-dog nose of a motor forged ahead, and Mr. Crewe swung in the driver's seat.

G

"Hello, Victoria," he shouted, "you people ought to have ear-trumpets."

The car swerved, narrowly missed a watering fountain where the word "Peace" was inscribed, and shot down the hill.

"That manner," said Victoria, as she jumped out of the buggy, "is a valuable political asset."

"Does he really intend to go into politics?" Austen asked curiously.

"'Intend' is a mild word applied to Humphrey," she answered; "'determined' would suit him better. According to him, there is no game that cannot be won by dynamics. 'Get out of the way' is his motto. Mrs. Pomfret will tell you how he means to cover the State with good roads next year, and take a house in Washington the year after." She held out her hand. "Good-by, — and I am ever so much obliged to you for bringing me here."

He drove away towards Ripton with many things to think about, with a last picture of her in his mind as she paused for an instant in the flickering shadows, stroking Pepper's forehead.

CHAPTER VII

THE LEOPARD AND HIS SPOTS

It is difficult to overestimate the importance of Mr. Humphrey Crewe, of his value to the town of Leith, and to the State at large, and in these pages only a poor attempt at an appreciation of him may be expected. Mr. Crewe by no means underestimated this claim upon the community, and he had of late been declaring that he was no summer resident. Wedderburn was his home, and there he paid his taxes. Undoubtedly, they were less than city taxes.

Although a young man, Mr. Crewe was in all respects a model citizen, and a person of many activities. He had built a farmers' club, to which the farmers, in gross ingratitude, had never gone. Now it was a summer residence and distinctly rentable. He had a standing offer to erect a library in the village of Leith provided the town would furnish the ground, the books, and permit the name of Crewe to be carved in stone over the doorway. The indifference of the town pained him, and he was naturally not a little grieved at the lack of proper feeling of the country people of America towards those who would better their conditions. He had put a large memorial window in the chapel to his family.

Mr. Crewe had another standing offer to be one of five men to start a farming experiment station — which might pay dividends. He was a church warden; president of a society for turning over crops (which he had organized); a member of the State Grange; president of the embryo State Economic League (whatever that was); and chairman of the Local Improvement Board — also a creation of his own. By these tokens, and others too numerous to mention, it would seem that the inhabitants of Leith would have jumped at the chance to make such a man one of the five hundred in their State Legislature.

To Whitman is attributed the remark that genius is almost one hundred per cent directness, but whether or not this applied to Mr. Humphrey Crewe remains to be seen. " Dynamics " more surely expressed him. It would not seem to be a very difficult feat, to be sure, to get elected to a State Legislature of five hundred which met once a year: once in ten years, indeed, might have been more appropriate for the five hundred. The town of Leith with its thousand inhabitants had one representative, and Mr. Crewe had made up his mind he was to be that representative.

There was, needless to say, great excitement in Leith over Mr. Crewe's proposed venture into the unknown seas of politics. I mean, of course, that portion of Leith which recognized in Mr. Crewe an eligible bachelor and a person of social importance, for these qualities were not particularly appealing to the three hundred odd farmers whose votes were expected to send him rejoicing to the State capital.

" It is so rare with us for a gentleman to go into politics, that we ought to do everything we can to elect him," Mrs. Pomfret went about declaring. " Women do so much in England, I wonder they don't do more here. I was staying at Aylestone Court last year when the Honourable Billy Aylestone was contesting the family seat with a horrid Radical, and I assure you, my dear, I got quite excited. We did nothing from morning till night but electioneer for the Honourable Billy, and kissed all the babies in the borough. The mothers were so grateful. Now, Edith, do tell Jack instead of playing tennis and canoeing all day he ought to help. It's the duty of all young men to help. *Noblesse oblige*, you know. I can't understand Victoria. She really has influence with these country people, but she says it's all nonsense. Sometimes I think Victoria has a common streak in her — and no wonder. The other day she actually drove to the Ham-

monds' in a buggy with an unknown lawyer from Ripton.
But I told you about it. Tell your gardener and the people
that do your haying, dear, and your chicken woman. *My*
chicken woman is most apathetic, but do you wonder, with
the life they lead ? "

Mr. Humphrey Crewe might have had, with King Charles,
the watchword " Thorough." He sent to the town clerk
for a check-list, and proceeded to honour each of the two
hundred Republican voters with a personal visit. This is
a fair example of what took place in the majority of cases.

Out of a cloud of dust emerges an automobile, which
halts, with protesting brakes, in front of a neat farm-
house, guarded by great maples. Persistent knocking by
a chauffeur at last brings a woman to the door. Mrs.
Jenney has a pleasant face and an ample figure.

" Mr. Jenney live here ? " cries Mr. Crewe from the
driver's seat.

" Yes," says Mrs. Jenney, smiling.

" Tell him I want to see him."

" Guess you'll find him in the apple orchard."

" Where's that ? "

The chauffeur takes down the bars, Mr. Jenney pricks
up his ears, and presently — to his amazement — perceives
a Leviathan approaching him, careening over the ruts of his
wood road. Not being an emotional person, he continues
to pick apples until he is summarily hailed. Then he goes
leisurely towards the Leviathan.

" Are you Mr. Jenney ? "

" Callate to be," says Mr. Jenney, pleasantly.

" I'm Humphrey Crewe."

" How be you ? " says Mr. Jenney, his eyes wandering
over the Leviathan.

" How are the apples this year ? " asks Mr. Crewe,
graciously.

" Fair to middlin'," says Mr. Jenney.

" Have you ever tasted my Pippins ? " says Mr. Crewe.
" A little science in cultivation helps along. I'm going
to send you a United States government pamphlet on the
fruit we can raise here."

Mr. Jenney makes an awkward pause by keeping silent on the subject of the pamphlet until he shall see it.

"Do you take much interest in politics?"

"Not a great deal," answers Mr. Jenney.

"That's the trouble with Americans," Mr. Crewe declares, "they don't care who represents 'em, or whether their government's good or bad."

"Guess that's so," replies Mr. Jenney, politely.

"That sort of thing's got to stop," declares Mr. Crewe; "I'm a candidate for the Republican nomination for representative."

"I want to know!" ejaculates Mr. Jenney, pulling his beard. One would never suspect that this has been one of Mr. Jenney's chief topics of late.

"I'll see that the interests of this town are cared for."

"Let's see," says Mr. Jenney, "there's five hundred in the House, ain't there?"

"It's a ridiculous number," says Mr. Crewe, with truth.

"Gives everybody a chance to go," says Mr. Jenney. "I was thar in '78, and enjoyed it some."

"Who are you for?" demanded Mr. Crewe, combating the tendency of the conversation to slip into a pocket.

"Little early yet, hain't it? Hain't made up my mind. Who's the candidates?" asks Mr. Jenney, continuing to stroke his beard.

"I don't know," says Mr. Crewe, "but I do know I've done something for this town, and I hope you'll take it into consideration. Come and see me when you go to the village. I'll give you a good cigar, and that pamphlet, and we'll talk matters over."

"Never would have thought to see one of them things in my orchard!" says Mr. Jenney. "How much do they cost? Much as a locomotive, don't they?"

It would not be exact to say that, after some weeks of this sort of campaigning, Mr. Crewe was discouraged, for such was the vitality with which nature had charged him that he did not know the meaning of the word. He was merely puzzled, as a June-bug is puzzled when it bumps up against a wire window-screen. He had pledged to him his own

gardener, Mrs. Pomfret's, the hired men of three of his
neighbours, a few modest souls who habitually took off their
hats to him, and Mr. Ball, of the village, who sold gro-
ceries to Wedderburn and was a general handy man for
the summer people.   Mr. Ball was an agitator by temperament and a promoter by preference.   If you were a
summer resident of importance and needed anything from a
sewing-machine to a Holstein heifer, Mr. Ball, the grocer,
would accommodate you.   When Mrs. Pomfret's cook became inebriate and refractory, Mr. Ball was sent for, and
enticed her to the station and on board of a train; when
the Chillinghams' tank overflowed, Mr. Ball found the
proper valve and saved the house from being washed away.
And it was he who, after Mrs. Pomfret, took the keenest
interest in Mr. Crewe's campaign.   At length came one
day when Mr. Crewe pulled up in front of the grocery store
and called, as his custom was, loudly for Mr. Ball.   The
fact that Mr. Ball was waiting on customers made no difference, and presently that gentleman appeared, rubbing his
hands together.

"How do you do, Mr. Crewe?" he said, "automobile
going all right?"

"What's the matter with these fellers?" said Mr.
Crewe.   "Haven't I done enough for the town?   Didn't I
get 'em rural free delivery?   Didn't I subscribe to the
meeting-house and library, and don't I pay more taxes
than anybody else?"

"Certain," assented Mr. Ball, eagerly, "certain you
do."   It did not seem to occur to him that it was unfair to make him responsible for the scurvy ingratitude of
his townsmen.   He stepped gingerly down into the dust
and climbed up on the tool box.

"Look out," said Mr. Crewe, "don't scratch the varnish.
What is it?"

Mr. Ball shifted obediently to the rubber-covered step,
and bent his face to his patron's ear.

"It's railrud," he said.

"Railroad!" shouted Mr. Crewe, in a voice that made
the grocer clutch his arm in terror.   "Don't pinch me like

that. Railroad! This town ain't within ten miles of the railroad."

"For the love of David," said Mr. Ball, "don't talk so loud, Mr. Crewe."

"What's the railroad got to do with it?" Mr. Crewe demanded.

Mr. Ball glanced around him, to make sure that no one was within shouting distance.

"What's the railrud got to do with anything in this State?" inquired Mr. Ball, craftily.

"That's different," said Mr. Crewe, shortly, "I'm a corporation man myself. They've got to defend 'emselves."

"Certain. *I* ain't got anything again' 'em," Mr. Ball agreed quickly. "I guess they know what they're about. By the bye, Mr. Crewe," he added, coming dangerously near the varnish again, and drawing back, "you hain't happened to have seen Job Braden, have you?"

"Job Braden!" exclaimed Mr. Crewe, "Job Braden! What's all this mystery about Job Braden? Somebody whispers that name in my ear every day. If you mean that smooth-faced cuss that stutters and lives on Braden's Hill, I called on him, but he was out. If you see him, tell him to come up to Wedderburn, and I'll talk with him."

Mr. Ball made a gesture to indicate a feeling divided between respect for Mr. Crewe and despair at the hardihood of such a proposition.

"Lord bless you, sir, Job wouldn't go."

"Wouldn't go?"

"He never pays visits, — folks go to him."

"He'd come to see *me*, wouldn't he?"

"I — I'm afraid not, Mr. Crewe. Job holds his comb rather high."

"Do you mean to say this two-for-a-cent town has a boss?"

"Silas Grantley was born here," said Mr. Ball — for even the worm will turn. "This town's got a noble history."

"I don't care anything about Silas Grantley. What

I want to know is, how this rascal manages to make anything out of the political pickings of a town like Leith."

"Well, Job ain't exactly a rascal, Mr. Crewe. He's got a good many of them hill farmers in a position of — of gratitude. Enough to control the Republican caucus."

"Do you mean he buys their votes?" demanded Mr. Crewe.

"It's like this," explained Mr. Ball, "if one of 'em falls behind in his grocery bill, for example, he can always get money from Job. Job takes a mortgage, but he don't often close down on 'em. And Job has been collectin' credentials in Avalon County for upward of forty years."

"Collecting credentials?"

"Yes. Gets a man nominated to State and county conventions that can't go, and goes himself with a bunch of credentials. He's in a position to negotiate. He was in all them railrud fights with Jethro Bass, and now he does business with Hilary Vane or Brush Bascom when anything especial's goin' on. You'd ought to see him, Mr. Crewe."

"I guess I won't waste my time with any picayune boss if the United Northeastern Railroads has any hand in this matter," declared Mr. Crewe. "Wind her up."

This latter remark was addressed to a long-suffering chauffeur who looked like a Sicilian brigand.

"I didn't exactly like to suggest it," said Mr. Ball, rubbing his hands and raising his voice above the whir of the machine, "but of course I knew Mr. Flint was an intimate friend. A word to him from you —"

But by this Mr. Crewe had got in his second speed and was sweeping around a corner lined with farmers' teams, whose animals were behaving like circus horses. On his own driveway, where he arrived in incredibly brief time, he met his stenographer, farm superintendent, secretary, housekeeper, and general utility man, Mr. Raikes. Mr. Raikes was elderly, and showed signs of needing a vacation.

"Telephone Mr. Flint, Raikes, and tell him I would

like an appointment at his earliest convenience, on important business."

Mr. Raikes, who was going for his daily stroll beside the river, wheeled and made for the telephone, and brought back the news that Mr. Flint would be happy to see Mr. Crewe the next afternoon at four o'clock.

This interview, about which there has been so much controversy in the newspapers, and denials and counter-denials from the press bureaus of both gentlemen, — this now historic interview began at four o'clock precisely the next day. At that hour Mr. Crewe was ushered into that little room in which Mr. Flint worked when at Fairview. Like Frederick the Great and other famous captains, Mr. Flint believed in an iron bedstead régime. The magnate was, as usual, fortified behind his oak desk; the secretary with a bend in his back was in modest evidence; and an elderly man of comfortable proportions, with a large gold watch-charm portraying the rising sun, and who gave, somehow, the polished impression of a marble, sat near the window smoking a cigar. Mr. Crewe approached the desk with that genial and brisk manner for which he was noted and held out his hand to the railroad president.

"We are both business men, and both punctual, Mr. Flint," he said, and sat down in the empty chair beside his host, eyeing without particular favour him of the watch-charm, whose cigar was not a very good one. "I wanted to have a little private conversation with you which might be of considerable interest to us both." And Mr. Crewe laid down on the desk a somewhat formidable roll of papers.

"I trust the presence of Senator Whitredge will not deter you," answered Mr. Flint. "He is an old friend of mine."

Mr. Crewe was on his feet again with surprising alacrity, and beside the senator's chair.

"How are you, Senator?" he said. "I have never had the pleasure of meeting you, but I know you by reputation."

The senator got to his feet. They shook hands, and exchanged cordial greetings ; and during the exchange Mr. Crewe looked out of the window, and the senator's eyes were fixed on the telephone receiver on Mr. Flint's desk. As neither gentleman took hold of the other's fingers very hard, they fell apart quickly.

"I am very happy to meet you, Mr. Crewe," said the senator. Mr. Crewe sat down again, and not being hampered by those shrinking qualities so fatal to success he went on immediately : —

"There is nothing which I have to say that the senator cannot hear. I made the appointment with you, Mr. Flint, to talk over a matter which may be of considerable importance to us both. I have made up my mind to go to the Legislature."

Mr. Crewe naturally expected to find visible effects of astonishment and joy on the faces of his hearers at such not inconsiderable news. Mr. Flint, however, looked serious enough, though the senator smiled as he blew his smoke out of the window.

"Have you seen Job Braden, Mr. Crewe ? " he asked, with genial jocoseness. "They tell me that Job is still alive and kicking over in your parts."

"Thank you, Senator," said Mr. Crewe, "that brings me to the very point I wish to emphasize. Everywhere in Leith I am met with the remark, 'Have you seen Job Braden ? ' And I always answer, 'No, I haven't seen Mr. Braden, and I don't intend to see him.' "

Mr. Whitredge laughed, and blew out a ring of smoke. Mr. Flint's face remained sober.

"Now, Mr. Flint," Mr. Crewe went on, "you and I understand each other, and we're on the same side of the fence. I have inherited some interests in corporations myself, and I have acquired an interest in others. I am a director in several. I believe that it is the duty of property to protect itself, and the duty of all good men in politics, — such as the senator here," — (bow from Mr. Whitredge) " to protect property. I am a practical man, and I think I can convince you, if you don't see it already, that my determination to go to the Legislature is an advantageous thing for your railroad."

"The advent of a reputable citizen into politics is always a good thing for the railroad, Mr. Crewe," said Mr. Flint.

"Exactly," Mr. Crewe agreed, ignoring the non-committal quality of this remark, "and if you get a citizen who is a not inconsiderable property holder, a gentleman, and a college graduate, — a man who, by study and predilection, is qualified to bring about improved conditions in the State, so much the better."

"So much the better," said Mr. Flint.

"I thought you would see it that way," Mr. Crewe continued. "Now a man of your calibre must have studied to some extent the needs of the State, and it must have struck you that certain improvements go hand in hand with the prosperity of your railroad."

"Have a cigar, Mr. Crewe. Have another, Senator?" said Mr. Flint. "I think that is safe as a general proposition, Mr. Crewe."

"To specify," said Mr. Crewe, laying his hand on the roll of papers he had brought, "I have here bills which I have carefully drawn up and which I will leave for your consideration. One is to issue bonds for ten millions to build State roads."

"Ten millions!" said Mr. Flint, and the senator whistled mildly.

"Think about it," said Mr. Crewe, "the perfection of the highways through the State, instead of decreasing your earnings, would increase them tremendously. Visitors by the tens of thousands would come in automobiles, and remain and buy summer places. The State would have its money back in taxes and business in no time at all. I wonder somebody hasn't seen it before — the stupidity of the country legislator is colossal. And we want forestry laws, and laws for improving the condition of the farmers — all practical things. They are all there," Mr. Crewe declared, slapping the bundle; "read them, Mr. Flint. If you have any suggestions to make, kindly note them on the margin, and I shall be glad to go over them with you."

By this time the senator was in a rare posture for him — he was seated upright.

"As you know, I am a very busy man, Mr. Crewe," said the railroad president.

"No one appreciates that more fully than I do, Mr. Flint," said Mr. Crewe; "I haven't many idle hours myself. I think you will find the bills and my comments on them well worth your consideration from the point of view of advantage to your railroad. They are typewritten, and in concrete form. In fact, the Northeastern Railroads and myself must work together to our mutual advantage — that has become quite clear to me. I shall have need of your help in passing the measures."

"I'm afraid I don't quite understand you, Mr. Crewe," said Mr. Flint, putting down the papers.

"That is," said Mr. Crewe, "if you approve of the bills, and I am confident that I shall be able to convince you."

"What do you want me to do?" asked the railroad president.

"Well, in the first place," said Mr. Crewe, unabashed, "send word to your man Braden that you've seen me and it's all right."

"I assure you," answered Mr. Flint, giving evidence for the first time of a loss of patience, "that neither the Northeastern Railroads nor myself, have any more to do with this Braden than you have."

Mr. Crewe, being a man of the world, looked incredulous.

"Senator," Mr. Flint continued, turning to Mr. Whitredge, "you know as much about politics in this State as any man of my acquaintance, have you ever heard of any connection between this Braden and the Northeastern Railroads?"

The senator had a laugh that was particularly disarming.

"Bless your soul, no," he replied. "You will pardon me, Mr. Crewe, but you must have been listening to some farmer's tale. The railroad is the bugaboo in all these country romances. I've seen old Job Braden at conventions ever since I was a lad. He's a back number, one of the few remaining disciples and imitators of Jethro Bass: talks like him and acts like him. In the old days when there were a lot of little railroads, he and Bijah Bixby and a few others used to make something out of them, but since the consolidation, and Mr. Flint's presidency, Job stays at home. They tell me he runs Leith yet. You'd better go over and fix it up with him."

A somewhat sarcastic smile of satisfaction was playing over Mr. Flint's face as he listened to the senator's words. As a matter of fact, they were very nearly true as regarded Job Braden, but Mr. Crewe may be pardoned for thinking that Mr. Flint was not showing him quite the confidence due from one business and corporation man to another. He was by no means abashed, — Mr. Crewe had too much spirit for that. He merely became — as a man whose watchword is "thorough" will — a little more combative.

" Well, read the bills anyway, Mr. Flint, and I'll come and go over them with you. You can't fail to see my arguments, and all I ask is that you throw the weight of your organization at the State capital for them when they come up."

Mr. Flint drummed on the table.

" The men who have held office in this State," he said, "have always been willing to listen to any suggestion I may have thought proper to make to them. This is undoubtedly because I am at the head of the property which pays the largest taxes. Needless to say I am chary of making suggestions. But I am surprised that you should have jumped at a conclusion which is the result of a popular and unfortunately prevalent opinion that the Northeastern Railroads meddled in any way with the government or politics of this State. I am glad of this opportunity of assuring you that we do not," he continued, leaning forward and holding up his hand to ward off interruption, "and I know that Senator Whitredge will bear me out in this statement, too."

The senator nodded gravely. Mr. Crewe, who was anything but a fool, and just as assertive as Mr. Flint, cut in.

" Look here, Mr. Flint," he said, "I know what a lobby is. I haven't been a director in railroads myself for nothing. I have no objection to a lobby. You employ counsel before the Legislature, don't you — "

" We do," said Mr. Flint, interrupting, " the best and most honourable counsel we can find in the State. When necessary, they appear before the legislative committees. As a property holder in the State, and an admirer of its beauties, and as its well-wisher, it will give me great pleasure to look over your bills, and use whatever personal influence I may have as a citizen to forward them, should they meet my approval. And I am especially glad to do this as a neighbour, Mr. Crewe. As a neighbour," he repeated, significantly.

The president of the Northeastern Railroads rose as he spoke these words, and held out his hand to Mr. Crewe. It was perhaps a coincidence that the senator rose also.

" All right," said Mr. Crewe, " I'll call around again in about two weeks. Come and see me sometime, Senator."

" Thank you," said the senator, " I shall be happy. And if you are ever in your automobile near the town of Ramsey, stop at my little farm, Mr. Crewe. I trust to be able soon to congratulate you on a step which I am sure will be but the beginning of a long and brilliant political career."

" Thanks," said Mr. Crewe ; " by the bye, if you could see your way to drop a hint to that feller Braden, I should be much obliged."

The senator shook his head and laughed.

" Job is an independent cuss," he said, " I'm afraid he'd regard that as an unwarranted trespass on his preserves."

Mr. Crewe was ushered out by the stooping secretary, Mr. Freeman ; who, instead of seizing Mr. Crewe's hand as he had Austen Vane's, said not a word. But Mr. Crewe would have been interested if he could have heard Mr. Flint's first remark to the senator after the door was closed on his back. It did not relate to Mr. Crewe, but to the subject under discussion which he had interrupted; namely, the Republican candidates for the twenty senatorial districts of the State.

On its way back to Leith the red motor paused in front of Mr. Ball's store, and that gentleman was summoned in the usual manner.

"Do you see this Braden once in a while?" Mr. Crewe demanded.

Mr. Ball looked knowing.

"Tell him I want to have a talk with him," said Mr. Crewe. "I've been to see Mr. Flint, and I think matters can be arranged. And mind you, no word about this, Ball."

"I guess I understand a thing or two," said Mr. Ball. "Trust me to handle it."

Two days later, as Mr. Crewe was seated in his study, his man entered and stood respectfully waiting for the time when he should look up from his book.

"Well, what is it now, Waters?"

"If you please, sir," said the man, "a strange message has come over the telephone just now that you were to be in room number twelve of the Ripton House to-morrow at ten o'clock. They wouldn't give any name, sir," added the dignified Waters, who, to tell the truth, was somewhat outraged, "nor tell where they telephoned from. But it was a man's voice, sir."

"All right," said Mr. Crewe.

He spent much of the afternoon and evening debating whether or not his dignity would permit him to go. But he ordered the motor at half-past nine, and at ten o'clock precisely the clerk at the Ripton House was bowing to him and handing him, deferentially, a dripping pen.

"Where's room number twelve?" said the direct Mr. Crewe.

"Oh," said the clerk, and possessing a full share of the worldly wisdom of his calling, he smiled broadly. "I guess you'll find him up there, Mr. Crewe. Front, show the gentleman to number twelve."

The hall boy knocked on the door of number **twelve**.

" C-come in," said a voice. " Come in."

Mr. Crewe entered, the hall boy closed the door, and he found himself face to face with a comfortable, smooth-faced man seated with great placidity on a rocking-chair in the centre of the room, between the bed and the marble-topped table: a man to whom, evidently, a rich abundance of thought was sufficient company, for he had neither newspaper nor book. He rose in a leisurely fashion, and seemed the very essence of the benign as he stretched forth his hand.

" I'm Mr. Crewe," the owner of that name proclaimed, accepting the hand with no exaggeration of cordiality. The situation jarred on him a trifle.

" I know. Seed you on the road once or twice. How be you ? "

Mr. Crewe sat down.

" I suppose you are Mr. Braden," he said.

Mr. Braden sank into the rocker and fingered a waist-coat pocket full of cigars that looked like a section of a cartridge-belt.

" T-try one of mine," he said.

" I only smoke once after breakfast," said Mr. Crewe.

"Abstemious, be you ? Never could find that it did me any hurt."

This led to an awkward pause, Mr. Crewe not being a man who found profit in idle discussion. He glanced at Mr. Braden's philanthropic and beaming countenance, which would have made the fortune of a bishop. It was not usual for Mr. Crewe to find it difficult to begin a conversation, or to have a companion as self-sufficient as himself. This man Braden had all the fun, apparently, in sitting in a chair and looking into space that Stonewall Jackson had, or an ordinary man in watching a perform-ance of " A Trip to Chinatown." Let it not be inferred, again, that Mr. Crewe was abashed; but he was puzzled.

" I had an engagement in Ripton this morning," he said, " to see about some business matters. And after I received your telephone I thought I'd drop in here."

H

"Didn't telephone," said Mr. Braden, placidly.

"What!" said Mr. Crewe, "I certainly got a telephone message."

"N-never telephone," said Mr. Braden.

"I certainly got a message from you," Mr. Crewe protested.

"Didn't say it was from me — didn't say so — did they?"

"No," said Mr. Crewe, "but — "

"Told Ball you wanted to have me see you, didn't you?"

Mr. Crewe, when he had unravelled this sentence, did not fancy the way it was put.

"I told Ball I was seeing everybody in Leith," he answered, "and that I had called on you, and you weren't at home. Ball inferred that you had a somewhat singular way of seeing people."

"You don't understand," was Mr. Braden's somewhat enigmatic reply.

"I understand pretty well," said Mr. Crewe. "I'm a candidate for the Republican nomination for representative from Leith, and I want your vote and influence. You probably know what I have done for the town, and that I'm the biggest taxpayer, and an all-the-year-round resident."

"S-some in Noo York — hain't you?"

"Well, you can't expect a man in my position and with my interests to stay at home all the time. I feel that I have a right to ask the town for this nomination. I have some bills here which I'll request you to read over, and you will see that I have ideas which are of real value to the State. The State needs waking up — progressive measures. You're a farmer, ain't you?"

"Well, I have be'n."

"I can improve the condition of the farmer one hundred per cent, and if my road system is followed, he can get his goods to market for about a tenth of what it costs him now. We have infinitely valuable forests in the State which are being wasted by lumbermen, which ought to be preserved. You read those bills, and what I have written about them."

"You don't understand," said Mr. Braden, drawing a little closer and waving aside the manuscript with his cigar.

"Don't understand what?"

"Don't seem to understand," repeated Mr. Braden, confidingly laying his hand on Mr. Crewe's knee. "Candidate for representative, be you?"

"Yes," replied Mr. Crewe, who was beginning to resent the manner in which he deemed he was being played with, "I told you I was."

"M-made all them bills out before you was chose?" said Mr. Braden.

Mr. Crewe grew red in the face.

"I am interested in these questions," he said stiffly.

"Little mite hasty, wahn't it?" Mr. Braden remarked equably, "but you've got plenty of time and money to fool with such things, if you've a mind to. Them don't amount to a hill of beans in politics. Nobody pays any attention to that sort of fireworks down to the capital, and if they was to get into committee them Northeastern Railroads fellers'd bury 'em deeper than the bottom of Salem pond. They don't want no such things as them to pass."

"Pardon me," said Mr. Crewe, "but you haven't read 'em."

"I know what they be," said Mr. Braden, "I've be'n in politics more years than you've be'n livin', I guess. I don't want to read 'em," he announced, his benign manner unchanged.

"I think you have made a mistake so far as the railroad is concerned, Mr. Braden," said Mr. Crewe, "I'm a practical man myself, and I don't indulge in moonshine. I am a director in one or two railroads. I have talked this matter over with Mr. Flint, and incidentally with Senator Whitredge."

"Knowed Whitredge afore you had any teeth," said Mr. Braden, who did not seem to be greatly impressed, "know him intimate. What'd you go to Flint for?"

"We have interests in common," said Mr. Crewe, "and I am rather a close friend of his. My going to the Legislature will be, I think, to our mutual advantage."

"O-ought to have come right to *me*," said Mr. Braden, leaning over until his face was in close proximity to Mr. Crewe's. "Whitredge told you to come to me, didn't he?"

Mr. Crewe was a little taken aback.

"The senator mentioned your name," he admitted.

"He knows. Said I was the man to see if you was a candidate, didn't he? Told you to talk to Job Braden, didn't he?"

Now Mr. Crewe had no means of knowing whether Senator Whitredge had been in conference with Mr. Braden or not.

"The senator mentioned your name casually, in some connection," said Mr. Crewe.

"He knows," Mr. Braden repeated, with a finality that spoke volumes for the senator's judgment; and he bent over into Mr. Crewe's ear, with the air of conveying a mild but well-merited reproof, "You'd ought to come right to me in the first place. I could have saved you all that unnecessary trouble of seein' folks. There hasn't be'n a representative left the town of Leith for thirty years that I hain't agreed to. Whitredge knows that. If I say you kin go, you kin go. You understand," said Mr. Braden, with his fingers on Mr. Crewe's knee once more.

Five minutes later Mr. Crewe emerged into the dazzling sun of the Ripton square, climbed into his automobile, and turned its head towards Leith, strangely forgetting the main engagement which he said had brought him to town.

CHAPTER VIII

THE TRIALS OF AN HONOURABLE

IT was about this time that Mr. Humphrey Crewe was transformed, by one of those subtle and inexplicable changes which occur in American politics, into the Honourable Humphrey Crewe. And, as interesting bits of news about important people are bound to leak out, it became known in Leith that he had subscribed to what is known as a Clipping Bureau. Two weeks after the day he left Mr. Braden's presence in the Ripton House the principal newspapers of the country contained the startling announcement that the well-known summer colony of Leith was to be represented in the State Legislature by a millionaire. The Republican nomination, which Mr. Crewe had secured, was equivalent to an election.

For a little time after that Mr. Crewe, although naturally an important and busy man, scarcely had time to nod to his friends on the road.

"Poor dear Humphrey," said Mrs. Pomfret, "who was so used to dropping in to dinner, hasn't had a moment to write me a line to thank me for the statesman's diary I bought for him in London this spring. They're in that new red leather, and Aylestone says he finds his so useful. I dropped in at Wedderburn to-day to see if I could be of any help, and the poor man was buttonholed by two reporters who had come all the way from New York to see him. I hope he won't overdo it."

It was true. Mr. Crewe was to appear in the Sunday supplements. "Are our Millionaires entering Politics?" Mr. Crewe, with his usual gracious hospitality, showed the reporters over the place, and gave them suggestions as to the best vantage-points in which to plant their cameras. He himself was at length prevailed upon to be taken in a rough homespun suit, and with a walking-stick in his hand, appraising with a knowing eye a flock of his own sheep. Pressed a little, he consented to relate something of the systematic manner in which he had gone about to secure this nomination : how he had visited in person the homes of his fellow-townsmen. "I knew them all, anyway," he is quoted as saying; "we have had the pleasantest of relationships during the many years I have been a resident of Leith."

"Beloved of his townspeople," this part of the article was headed. No, these were not Mr. Crewe's words — he was too modest for that. When urged to give the name of one of his townsmen who might deal with this and other embarrassing topics, Mr. Ball was mentioned. "Beloved of his townspeople" was Mr. Ball's phrase. "Although a multi-millionaire, no man is more considerate of the feelings and the rights of his more humble neighbours. Send him to the Legislature ! We'd send him to the United States Senate if we could. He'll land there, anyway." Such was a random estimate (Mr. Ball's) the reporters gathered on their way to Ripton. Mr. Crewe did not hesitate to say that the prosperity of the farmers had risen as a result of his labours at Wedderburn where the most improved machinery and methods were adopted. His efforts to raise the agricultural, as well as the moral and intellectual, tone of the community had been unceasing.

Then followed an intelligent abstract of the bills he was to introduce — "the results of a progressive and statesmanlike brain." There was an account of him as a methodical and painstaking business man whose suggestions to the boards of directors of which he was a member had been invaluable. The article ended with a list of the clubs to which he belonged, of the societies which he had organized and of those of which he was a member, — and it might have been remarked by a discerning reader that most of these societies were State affairs. Finally there was a pen portrait of an Apollo Belvidere who wore the rough garb of a farmer (on the days when the press was present).

Mr. Crewe's incessant trials, which would have taxed a less rugged nature, did not end here. About five o'clock one afternoon a pleasant-appearing gentleman with a mellifluous voice turned up who introduced himself as ex (State) Senator Grady. The senator was from Newcastle, that city out of the mysterious depths of which so many political stars have arisen. Mr. Crewe cancelled a long-deferred engagement with Mrs. Pomfret, and invited the senator to stay to dinner; the senator hesitated, explained that he was just passing through Ripton, and, as it was a pleasant afternoon, had called to " pay his respects "; but Mr. Crewe's well-known hospitality would accept no excuses. Mr. Crewe opened a box of cigars which he had bought especially for the taste of State senators and a particular grade of Scotch whiskey.

They talked politics for four hours. Who would be governor? The senator thought Asa Gray would. The railroad was behind him, Mr. Crewe observed knowingly. The senator remarked that Mr. Crewe was no gosling. Mr. Crewe, as political geniuses will, asked as many questions as the emperor of Germany — pertinent questions about State politics. Senator Grady was tremendously impressed with his host's programme of bills, and went over them so painstakingly that Mr. Crewe became more and more struck with Senator Grady's intelligence. The senator told Mr. Crewe that just such a man as he was needed to pull the State out of the rut into which she had fallen. Mr. Crewe said that he hoped to find such enlightened men in the Legislature as the senator. The senator let it be known that he had read the newspaper articles, and had remarked that Mr. Crewe was close to the president of the Northeastern Railroads.

" Such a man as you," said the senator, looking at the remainder of the Scotch whiskey, " will have the railroad behind you, sure."

" One more drink," said Mr. Crewe.

" I must go," said Mr. Grady, pouring it out, " but that

reminds me. It comes over me sudden-like, as I sit here, that you certainly ought to be in the new encyclopeedie of the prominent men of the State. But sure you have received an application."

"It is probable that my secretary has one," said Mr. Crewe, "but he hasn't called it to my attention."

"You must get in that book, Mr. Crewe," said the senator, with an intense earnestness which gave the impression of alarm; "after what you've told me to-night I'll see to it myself that you get in. It may be that I've got some of the sample pages here, if I haven't left them at home," said Mr. Grady, fumbling in an ample inside pocket, and drawing forth a bundle. "Sure, here they are. Ain't that luck for you? Listen! 'Asa P. Gray was born on the third of August, eighteen forty-seven, the seventh son of a farmer.' See, there's a space in the end they left to fill up when he's elicted governor! Here's another. 'The Honourable Hilary Vane comes from one of the oldest Puritan families in the State, the Vanes of Camden Street—' Here's another. 'The Honourable Brush Bascom of Putnam County is the son of poor but honourable parents—' Look at the picture of him. Ain't that a handsome steel-engravin' of the gentleman?"

Mr. Crewe gazed contemplatively at the proof, but was too busy with his own thoughts to reflect that there was evidently not much poor or honourable about Mr. Bascom now.

"Who's publishing this?" he asked.

"Fogarty and Company; sure they're the best publishers in the State, as you know, Mr. Crewe. They have the State printing. Wasn't it fortunate I had the proofs with me? Tim Fogarty slipped them into me pocket when I was leavin' Newcastle. 'The book is goin' to press the day after eliction,' says he; 'John,' says he, 'you know I always rely on your judgment, and if you happen to think of anybody between now and then who ought to go in, you'll notify me,' says he. When I read the bills to-night, and saw the scope of your work, it came over me in a flash that Humphrey Crewe was the man they left out. You'll get a good man to write your life, and what you done for the town and State, and all them societies and bills, won't you? 'Twould be a thousand pities not to have it right."

" How much does it cost?" Mr. Crewe inquired.

" Sure I forgot to ask Tim Fogarty. Mebbe he has it here. I signed one myself, but I couldn't afford the steel-engravin'. Yes, he slipped one in. Two hundred dollars for a two-page biography, and three hundred for the steel-engravin'. Five hundred dollars. I didn't know it was so cheap as that," exclaimed the senator, " and everybody in the State havin' to own one in self-protection. You don't happen to have a pen about you?"

Mr. Crewe waved the senator towards his own desk, and Mr. Grady filled out the blank.

" It's lucky we are that I didn't drop in after eliction, and the book in press," he remarked; " and I hope you'll give him a good photograph. This's for you, I'll take this to Tim myself," and he handed the pen for Mr. Crewe to sign with.

Mr. Crewe read over the agreement carefully, as a business man should, before putting his signature to it. And then the senator, with renewed invitations for Mr. Crewe to call on him when he came to Newcastle, took his departure. Afterwards Mr. Crewe remained so long in reflection that his man Waters became alarmed, and sought him out and interrupted his revery.

The next morning Mrs. Pomfret, who was merely " driving by " with her daughter Alice and Beatrice Chillingham, spied Mr. Crewe walking about among the young trees he was growing near the road, and occasionally tapping them with his stout stick. She poked her coachman in the back and cried : —

" Humphrey, you're such an important man now that I despair of ever seeing you again. What was the matter last night ?"

" A politician from Newcastle," answered Mr. Crewe, continuing to tap the trees, and without so much as a glance at Alice.

"Well, if you're as important as this before you're elected, I can't think what it will be afterwards," Mrs. Pomfret lamented. "Poor dear Humphrey is so conscientious. When can you come, Humphrey?"

"Don't know," said Mr. Crewe; "I'll try to come tonight, but I may be stopped again. Here's Waters now."

The three people in Mrs. Pomfret's victoria were considerably impressed to see the dignified Waters hurrying down the slope from the house towards them. Mr. Crewe continued to tap the trees, but drew a little nearer the carriage.

"If you please, sir," said Waters, "there's a telephone call for you from Newcastle. It's urgent, sir."

"Who is it?"

"They won't give their names, sir."

"All right," said Mr. Crewe, and with a grin which spoke volumes for the manner in which he was harassed he started towards the house — in no great hurry, however. Reaching the instrument, and saying "Hello" in his usually gracious manner, he was greeted by a voice with a decided Hibernian-American accent.

"Am I talkin' to Mr. Crewe?"

"Yes."

"Mr. Humphrey Crewe?"

"Yes — yes, of course you are. Who are you?"

"I'm the president of the Paradise Benevolent and Military Association, Mr. Crewe. Boys that work in the mills, you know," continued the voice, caressingly. "Sure you've heard of us. We're five hundred strong, and all of us good Republicans as the president. We're to have our annual fall outing the first of October in Finney Grove, and we'd like to have you come down."

"The first of October?" said Mr. Crewe. "I'll consult my engagement book."

"We'd like to have a good picture of you in our programme, Mr. Crewe. We hope you'll oblige us. You're such an important figure in State politics now you'd ought to have a full page."

There was a short silence.

"What does it cost?" Mr. Crewe demanded.

"Sure," said the caressing voice of the president, "whatever you like."

"I'll send you a check for five dollars, and a picture," said Mr. Crewe.

The answer to this was a hearty laugh, which the telephone reproduced admirably. The voice now lost a little of its caressing note and partook of a harder quality.

"You're a splendid humorist, Mr. Crewe. Five dollars wouldn't pay for the plate and the paper. A gentleman like you could give us twenty-five, and never know it was gone. You won't be wanting to stop in the Legislature, Mr. Crewe, and we remember our friends in Newcastle."

"Very well, I'll see what I can do. Good-by, I've got an engagement," said Mr. Crewe, and slammed down the telephone. He seated himself in his chair, and the pensive mood so characteristic (we are told) of statesmen came over him once more.

While these and other conferences and duties too numerous to mention were absorbing Mr. Crewe, he was not too busy to bear in mind the pleasure of those around him who had not received such an abundance of the world's blessings as he. The townspeople of Leith were about to bestow on him their greatest gift. What could he do to show his appreciation? Wrestling with this knotty problem, a brilliant idea occurred to him, — he would have a garden-party : invite everybody in town, and admit them to the sanctities of Wedderburn; yes, even of Wedderburn house, that they might behold with their own eyes the carved ivory elephants and other contents of glass cabinets which reeked of the Sunday afternoons of youth. Being a man of action, Mr. Pardriff was summoned at once from Leith and asked for his lowest price on eight hundred and fifty invitations and a notice of the party in the *Ripton Record*.

"Goin' to invite Democrats, too?" demanded Mr. Pardriff, glancing at the check-list.

"Everybody," said Mr. Crewe, with unparalleled generosity. "I won't draw any distinction between friends and enemies. They're all neighbours."

"And some of 'em might, by accident, vote the Republican ticket," Mr. Pardriff retorted, narrowing his eyes a little.

Mr. Crewe evidently thought this a negligible suggestion, for he did not reply to it, but presently asked for the political news in Ripton.

"Well," said Mr. Pardriff, "you know they tried to get Austen Vane to run for State senator, don't you ?"

"Vane ! Why, he ain't a full-fledged lawyer yet. I've hired him in an unimportant case. Who asked him to run ?"

"Young Tom Gaylord and a delegation."

"He couldn't have got it," said Mr. Crewe.

"I don't know," said Mr. Pardriff, "he might have given Billings a hustle for the nomination."

"You supported Billings, I noticed," said Mr. Crewe.

Mr. Pardriff winked an eye.

"I'm not ready to walk the ties when I go to Newcastle," he remarked, "and Nat ain't quite bankrupt yet. The Gaylords," continued Mr. Pardriff, who always took the cynical view of a man of the world, "have had some row with the Northeastern over lumber shipments. I understand they're goin' to buck 'em for a franchise in the next Legislature, just to make it lively. The Gaylords ain't exactly poverty-stricken, but they might as well try to move Sawanec Mountain as the Northeastern."

It was a fact that young Tom Gaylord had approached Austen Vane "with a delegation" to request him to be a candidate for the Republican nomination for the State senate in his district against the railroad candidate and Austen's late opponent, the Honourable Nat Billings. It was a fact also that Austen had invited the delegation to sit down, although there were only two chairs, and that a wrestling match had ensued with young Tom, in the progress of which one chair had been broken. Young Tom thought it was time to fight the railroad, and perceived in Austen the elements of a rebel leader. Austen had undertaken to throw young Tom out of a front window,— which was a large, old-fashioned one,— and after Herculean efforts had actually got him on the ledge, when something in the street caught his eye and made him desist abruptly. The something was the vision of a young woman in a brown linen suit seated in a runabout and driving a horse almost as handsome as Pepper.

When the delegation, after exhausting their mental and physical powers of persuasion, had at length taken their departure in disgust, Austen opened mechanically a letter which had very much the appearance of an advertisement, and bearing a one-cent stamp. It announced that a garden-party would take place at Wedderburn, the home of the Honourable Humphrey Crewe, at a not very distant date, and the honour of the bearer's presence was requested. Refreshments would be served, and the Ripton Band would dispense music. Below, in small print, were minute directions where to enter, where to hitch your team, and where to go out.

Austen was at a loss to know what fairy godmother had prompted Mr. Crewe to send him an invitation, the case of the injured horse not having advanced with noticeable rapidity. Nevertheless, the prospect of the garden-party dawned radiantly for him above what had hitherto been a rather gloomy horizon. Since the afternoon he had driven Victoria to the Hammonds' he had had daily debates with an imaginary man in his own likeness who, to the detriment of his reading of law, sat across his table and argued with him. The imaginary man was unprincipled, and had no dignity, but he had such influence over Austen Vane that he had induced him to drive twice within sight of Fairview gate, when Austen Vane had turned round again. The imaginary man was for going to call on her and letting subsequent events take care of themselves; Austen Vane had an uncomfortable quality of reducing a matter first of all to its simplest terms. He knew that Mr. Flint's views were as fixed, ineradicable, and unchangeable as an epitaph cut in a granite monument; he felt (as Mr. Flint had) that their first conversation had been but a forerunner of

a strife to come between them; and add to this the facts
that Mr. Flint was very rich and Austen Vane poor, that
Victoria's friends were not his friends, and that he had
grave doubts that the interest she had evinced in him
sprang from any other incentive than a desire to have
communication with various types of humanity, his hesitation as to entering Mr. Flint's house was natural enough.

It was of a piece with Mr. Crewe's good fortune of
getting what he wanted that the day of the garden-party
was the best that September could do in that country,
which is to say that it was very beautiful. A pregnant
stillness enwrapped the hills, a haze shot with gold dust,
like the filmiest of veils, softened the distant purple and
the blue-black shadows under the pines. Austen awoke
from his dream in this enchanted borderland to find himself in a long line of wagons filled with people in their
Sunday clothes, — the men in black, and the young women
in white, with gay streamers, — wending their way
through the rear-entrance drive of Wedderburn, where one
of Mr. Crewe's sprucest employees was taking up the
invitation cards like tickets, — a precaution to prevent the
rowdy element from Ripton coming and eating up the
refreshments. Austen obediently tied Pepper in a field,
as he was directed, and made his way by a path through
the woods towards the house, where the Ripton Band could
be heard playing the second air in the programme, "Don't
you wish you'd Waited?"

For a really able account of that memorable entertainment see the *Ripton Record* of that week, for we cannot hope
to vie with Mr. Pardriff when his heart is really in his
work. How describe the noble figure of Mr. Crewe as it
burst upon Austen when he rounded the corner of the
house? Clad in a rough-and-ready manner, with a Gladstone collar to indicate the newly acquired statesmanship,
and fairly radiating geniality, Mr. Crewe stood at the foot
of the steps while the guests made the circuit of the driveway; and they carefully avoided, in obedience to a warning sign, the grass circle in the centre. As man and wife
confronted him, Mr. Crewe greeted them in hospitable

but stentorian tones that rose above the strains of " Don't
you wish you'd Waited?" It was Mr. Ball who introduced his townspeople to the great man who was to
represent them.

" How are you?" said Mr. Crewe, with his eyes on the
geraniums. " Mr. and Mrs. Perley Wright, eh? Make
yourselves at home. Everything's free — you'll find the
refreshments on the back porch — just have an eye to the
signs posted round, that's all." And Mr. and Mrs. Perley Wright, overwhelmed by such a welcome, would pass
on into a back eddy of neighbours, where they would
stick, staring at a sign requesting them please not to pick
the flowers.

" Can't somebody stir 'em up?" Mr. Crewe shouted in
an interval when the band had stopped to gather strength
for a new effort. " Can't somebody move 'em round to see
the cows and what's in the house and the automobile and
the horses? Move around the driveway, please. It's so
hot here you can't breathe. Some of you wanted to see
what was in the house. Now's your chance."

This graceful appeal had some temporary effect, but
the congestion soon returned, when a man of the hour
appeared, a man whose genius scattered the groups and
who did more to make the party a success than any single
individual, — Mr. Hamilton Tooting, in a glorious white
silk necktie with purple flowers.

" I'll handle 'em, Mr. Crewe," he said; " a little brains'll
start 'em goin'. Come along here, Mr. Wright, and I'll
show you the best cows this side of the Hudson River —
all pedigreed prize winners. Hello, Aust, you take hold
and get the wimmen-folks interested in the cabinets.
You know where they are."

" There's a person with some sense," remarked Mrs.
Pomfret, who had been at a little distance among a group
of summer-resident ladies and watching the affair with
shining eyes. " I'll help. Come, Edith; come, Victoria—
where's Victoria? — and dear Mrs. Chillingham. We
American women are so deplorably lacking in this kind
of experience. Alice, take some of the women into the

garden. I'm going to interest that dear, benevolent man who looks so helpless, and doing his best to have a good time."

The dear, benevolent man chanced to be Mr. Job Braden, who was standing somewhat apart with his hands in his pockets. He did not move as Mrs. Pomfret approached him, holding her glasses to her eyes.

"How are you?" exclaimed that lady, extending a white-gloved hand with a cordiality that astonished her friends. "It is so pleasant to see you here, Mr. — Mr. —"

"How be you?" said Mr. Braden, taking her fingers in the gingerly manner he would have handled one of Mr. Crewe's priceless curios. The giraffe Mr. Barnum had once brought to Ripton was not half as interesting as this immaculate and mysterious production of foreign dressmakers and French maids, but he refrained from betraying it. His eye rested on the lorgnette.

"Near-sighted, be you?" he inquired, — a remark so unexpected that for the moment Mrs. Pomfret was deprived of speech.

"I manage to see better with — with these," she gasped, "when we get old — you know."

"You hain't old," said Mr. Braden, gallantly. "If you be," he added, his eye travelling up and down the Parisian curves, "I wouldn't have suspected it — not a mite."

"I'm afraid you are given to flattery, Mr. — Mr. —" she replied hurriedly. "Whom have I the pleasure of speaking to?"

"Job Braden's my name," he answered, "but you have the advantage of me."

"How?" demanded the thoroughly bewildered Mrs. Pomfret.

"I hain't heard your name," he said.

"Oh, I'm Mrs. Pomfret — a very old friend of Mr. Crewe's. Whenever he has — his friends with him, like this, I come over and help him. It is so difficult for a bachelor to entertain, Mr. Braden."

"Well," said Mr. Braden, bending alarmingly near her ear, "there's one way out of it."

" What's that ? " said Mrs. Pomfret.

" Git married," declared Mr. Braden.

" How very clever you are, Mr. Braden! I wish poor dear Mr. Crewe would get married — a wife could take so many burdens off his shoulders. You don't know Mr. Crewe very well, do you ? "

" Callate to — so so," said Mr. Braden.

Mrs. Pomfret was at sea again.

" I mean, do you see him often ? "

" Seen him once," said Mr. Braden. " G-guess that's enough."

" You're a shrewd judge of human nature, Mr. Braden," she replied, tapping him on the shoulder with the lorgnette, " but you can have no idea how good he is — how unceasingly he works for others. He is not a man who gives much expression to his feelings, as no doubt you have discovered, but if you knew him as I do, you would realize how much affection he has for his country neighbours — and how much he has their welfare at heart."

" Loves 'em — does he — loves 'em ? "

" He is like an English gentleman in his sense of responsibility," said Mrs. Pomfret; " over there, you know, it is a part of a country gentleman's duty to improve the condition of his —his neighbours. And then Mr. Crewe is so fond of his townspeople that he couldn't resist doing *this* for them," and she indicated with a sweep of her eyeglasses the beatitude with which they were surrounded.

" Wahn't no occasion to," said Mr. Braden.

" What !" cried Mrs. Pomfret, who had been walking on ice for some time.

" This hain't England — is it ? Hain't England ? "

" No," she admitted, " but — "

" Hain't England," said Mr. Braden, and leaned forward until he was within a very few inches of her pearl ear-ring. " He'll be chose all right — d-don't fret — he'll be chose."

" My dear Mr. Braden, I've no doubt of it — Mr. Crewe's so popular," she cried, removing her ear-ring abruptly from the danger zone. " Do make yourself at home," she added, and retired from Mr. Braden's company a trifle

I

disconcerted, — a new experience for Mrs. Pomfret.   She wondered whether all country people were like Mr. Braden, but decided, after another experiment or two, that he was an original.   More than once during the afternoon she caught sight of him, beaming upon the festivities around him.   But she did not renew the conversation.

To Austen Vane, wandering about the grounds, Mr. Crewe's party presented a sociological problem of no small interest.   Mr. Crewe himself interested him, and he found himself speculating how far a man would go who charged the fastnesses of the politicians with a determination not to be denied and a bank account to be reckoned with. Austen talked to many of the Leith farmers whom he had known from boyhood, thanks to his custom of roaming the hills; they were for the most part honest men whose occupation in life was the first thought, and they were content to leave politics to Mr. Braden — that being his profession. To the most intelligent of these Mr. Crewe's garden-party was merely the wanton whim of a millionaire.   It was an open secret to them that Job Braden for reasons of his own had chosen Mr. Crewe to represent them, and they were mildly amused at the efforts of Mrs. Pomfret and her assistants to secure votes which were as certain as the sun's rising on the morrow.

It was some time before Austen came upon the object of his search — though scarce admitting to himself that it had an object.   In greeting him, after inquiring about his railroad case, Mr. Crewe had indicated with a wave of his hand the general direction of the refreshments ; but it was not until Austen had tried in all other quarters that he made his way towards the porch where the lemonade and cake and sandwiches were.   It was, after all, the most popular place, though to his mind the refreshments had little to do with its popularity.   From the outskirts of the crowd he perceived Victoria presiding over the punch-bowl that held the lemonade.   He liked to think of her as Victoria ; the name had no familiarity for him, but seemed rather to enhance the unattainable quality of her.

Surrounding Victoria were several clean-looking, freckled,

"Do tell me how old he is, and how many more you have."

and tanned young men of undergraduate age wearing straw hats with coloured ribbons, who showed every eagerness to obey and even anticipate the orders she did not hesitate to give them. Her eye seemed continually on the alert for those of Mr. Crewe's guests who were too bashful to come forward, and discerning them she would send one of her lieutenants forward with supplies. Sometimes she would go herself to the older people ; and once, perceiving a tired woman holding a baby (so many brought babies, being unable to leave them), Victoria impulsively left her post and seized the woman by the arm.

"Do come and sit down," she cried; "there's a chair beside me. And oh, what a nice baby ! Won't you let me hold him ? "

"Why, yes, ma'am," said the woman, looking up at Victoria with grateful, patient eyes, and then with awe at what seemed to her the priceless embroidery on Victoria's waist, " won't he spoil your dress ? "

"Bless him, no," said Victoria, poking her finger into a dimple — for he was smiling at her. "What if he does ? " and forthwith she seized him in her arms and bore him to the porch, amidst the laughter of those who beheld her, and sat him down on her knee in front of the lemonade bowl, the tired mother beside her. "Will a little lemonade hurt him ? Just a very, very little, you know ? "

"Why, no, ma'am," said the mother.

"And just a teeny bit of cake," begged Victoria, daintily breaking off a piece, while the baby gurgled and snatched for it. "Do tell me how old he is, and how many more you have."

"He's eleven months on the twenty-seventh," said the mother, "and I've got four more." She sighed, her eyes wandering back to the embroidery. "What between them and the housework and the butter makin', it hain't easy. Be you married ? "

"No," said Victoria, laughing and blushing a little.

"You'll make a good wife for somebody," said the woman. "I hope you'll get a good man."

"I hope so, too," said Victoria, blushing still deeper

amidst the laughter, " but there doesn't seem to be much chance of it, and good men are very scarce."

" I guess you're right," said the mother, soberly. " Not but what my man's good enough, but he don't seem to get along, somehow. The farm's wore out, and the mortgage comes around so regular."

" Where do you live ? " asked Victoria, suddenly growing serious.

" Fitch's place. 'Tain't very far from the Four Corners, on the Avalon road."

" And you are Mrs. Fitch ? "

" Callate to be," said the mother. " If it ain't askin' too much, I'd like to know your name."

" I'm Victoria Flint. I live not very far from the Four Corners—that is, about eight miles. May I come over and see you sometime ? "

Although Victoria said this very simply, the mother's eyes widened until one might almost have said they expressed a kind of terror.

" Land sakes alive, be you Mr. Flint's daughter ? I might have knowed it from the lace — that dress must have cost a fortune. But I didn't think to find you so common."

Victoria did not smile. She had heard the word " common " so used before, and knew that it was meant for a compliment, and she turned to the woman with a very expressive light in her eyes.

" I will come to see you — this very week," she said. And just then her glance, seemingly drawn in a certain direction, met that of a tall young man which had been fixed upon her during the whole of this scene. She coloured again, abruptly handed the baby back to his mother, and rose.

" I'm neglecting all these people," she said, " but do sit there and rest yourself and — have some more lemonade."

She bowed to Austen, and smiled a little as she filled the glasses, but she did not beckon him. She gave no further sign of her knowledge of his presence until he stood beside her — and then she looked up at him.

"I have been looking for you, Miss Flint," he said.

"I suppose a man would never think of trying the obvious places first," she replied. "Hastings, don't you see that poor old woman over there? She looks so thirsty — give her this."

The boy addressed, with a glance at Austen, did as he was bid, and she sent off a second on another errand.

"Let me help," said Austen, seizing the cake; and being seized at the same time, by an unusual and inexplicable tremor of shyness, thrust it at the baby.

"Oh, he can't have any more; do you want to kill him?" cried Victoria, seizing the plate, and adding mischievously, "I don't believe you're of very much use — after all!"

"Then it's time I learned," said Austen. "Here's Mr. Jenney. I'm sure he'll have a piece."

"Well," said Mr. Jenney, the same Mr. Jenney of the apple orchard, but holding out a horny hand with unmistakable warmth, "how be *you*, Austen?" Looking about him, Mr. Jenney put his hand to his mouth, and added, "Didn't expect to see you trailin' on to this here kite." He took a piece of cake between his thumb and forefinger and glanced bashfully at Victoria.

"Have some lemonade, Mr. Jenney? Do," she urged.

"Well, I don't care if I do," he said, "— just a little mite." He did not attempt to stop her as she filled the glass to the brim, but continued to regard her with a mixture of curiosity and admiration. "Seen you nursin' the baby and makin' folks at home. Guess you have the knack of it better'n some I could mention."

This was such a palpable stroke at their host that Victoria laughed, and made haste to turn the subject from herself.

"Mr. Vane seems to be an old friend of yours," she said.

"Why," said Mr. Jenney, laying his hand on Austen's shoulder, "I callate he is. Austen's broke in more'n one of my colts afore he went West and shot that feller. He's as good a judge of horse-flesh as any man in this part of the State. Hear Tom Gaylord and the boys wanted him to be State senator."

"Why didn't you accept, Mr. Vane?"

"Because I don't think the boys could have elected me," answered Austen, laughing.

"He's as popular a man as there is in the county," declared Mr. Jenney. "He was a mite wild as a boy, but sence he's sobered down and won that case against the railrud, he could get any office he'd a mind to. He's always adoin' little things for folks, Austen is."

"Did — did that case against the railroad make him so popular?" asked Victoria, glancing at Austen's broad back — for he had made his escape with the cake.

"I guess it helped considerable," Mr. Jenney admitted.

"Why?" asked Victoria.

"Well, it was a fearless thing to do—plumb against his own interests with old Hilary Vane. Austen's a bright lawyer, and I have heard it said he was in line for his father's place as counsel."

"Do — do people dislike the railroad?"

Mr. Jenney rubbed his beard thoughtfully. He began to wonder who this young woman was, and a racial caution seized him.

"Well," he said, "folks has an idea the railrud runs this State to suit themselves. I guess they hain't far wrong. I've be'n to the Legislature and seen some signs of it. Why, Hilary Vane himself has charge of the most considerable part of the politics. Who be you?" Mr. Jenney demanded suddenly.

"I'm Victoria Flint," said Victoria.

"Godfrey!" exclaimed Mr. Jenney, "you don't say so! I might have known it — seen you on the rud more than once. But I don't know all you rich folks apart. Wouldn't have spoke so frank if I'd knowed who you was."

"I'm glad you did, Mr. Jenney," she answered. "I — I wanted to know what people think."

"Well, it's almighty complicated," said Mr. Jenney, shaking his head. "I don't know by rights what to think. As long as I've said what I have, I'll say this: that the politicians is all for the railrud, and I hain't got a

mite of use for the politicians. I'll vote for a feller like
Austen Vane every time, if he'll run, and I know other
folks that will."

After Mr. Jenney had left her, Victoria stood motionless, gazing off into the haze, until she was startled by the
voice of Hastings Weare beside her.

" Say, Victoria, who is that man ? " he asked.

" What man ? "

Hastings nodded towards Austen, who, with a cake
basket in his hand, stood chatting with a group of country
people on the edge of the porch.

" Oh, that man! " said Victoria. " His name's Austen
Vane, and he's a lawyer in Ripton."

" All I can say is," replied Hastings, with a light in his
face, " he's one I'd like to tie to. I'll bet he could whip
any four men you could pick out."

Considering that Hastings had himself proposed — although in a very mild form — more than once to Victoria, this was generous.

" I daresay he could," she agreed absently.

" It isn't only the way he's built," persisted Hastings,
" he looks as if he were going to be somebody some day.
Introduce me to him, will you ? "

" Certainly," said Victoria. " Mr. Vane," she called, " I
want to introduce — an admirer, Mr. Hastings Weare."

" I just wanted to know you," said Hastings, redden-
ing, " and Victoria — I mean Miss Flint — said she'd introduce me."

" I'm much obliged to her," said Austen, smiling.

" Are you in politics ? " asked Hastings.

" I'm afraid not," answered Austen, with a glance at
Victoria.

" You're not helping Humphrey Crewe, are you ? "

" No," said Austen, and added with an illuminating
smile, " Mr. Crewe doesn't need any help."

" I'm glad you're not," exclaimed the downright Hastings, with palpable relief in his voice that an idol had not
been shattered. " I think Humphrey's a fakir, and all
this sort of thing tommyrot. He wouldn't get *my* vote

by giving me lemonade and cake and letting me look at his cows. If you ever run for office, I'd like to cast it for you. My father is only a summer resident, but since he has gone out of business he stays here till Christmas, and I'll be twenty-one in a year."

Austen had ceased to smile; he was looking into the boy's eyes with that serious expression which men and women found irresistible.

"Thank you, Mr. Weare," he said simply.

Hastings was suddenly overcome with the shyness of youth. He held out his hand, and said, "I'm awfully glad to have met you," and fled.

Victoria, who had looked on with a curious mixture of feelings, turned to Austen.

"That was a real tribute," she said. "Is this the way you affect everybody whom you meet?"

They were standing almost alone. The sun was nearing the western hills beyond the river, and people had for some time been wending their way towards the field where the horses were tied. He did not answer her question, but asked one instead.

"Will you let me drive you home?"

"Do you think you deserve to, after the shameful manner in which you have behaved?"

"I'm quite sure that I don't deserve to," he answered, still looking down at her.

"If you did deserve to, being a woman, I probably shouldn't let you," said Victoria, flashing a look upwards; "as it is, you may."

His face lighted, but she halted in the grass, with her hands behind her, and stared at him with a puzzled expression.

"I'm sure you're a dangerous man," she declared. "First you take in poor little Hastings, and now you're trying to take me in."

"Then I wish I were still more dangerous," he laughed, "for apparently I haven't succeeded."

"I want to talk to you seriously," said Victoria; "that is the only reason I'm permitting you to drive me home."

"I am devoutly thankful for the reason then," he said, — "my horse is tied in the field."

"And aren't you going to say good-by to your host and hostess ? "

"Hostess ? " he repeated, puzzled.

"Hostesses," she corrected herself, " Mrs. Pomfret and Alice. I thought you had eyes in your head," she added, with a fleeting glance at them.

"Is Crewe engaged to Miss Pomfret ? " he asked.

"Are all men simpletons ? " said Victoria. " He doesn't know it yet, but he is."

"I think I'd know it, if I were," said Austen, with an emphasis that made her laugh.

"Sometimes fish don't know they're in a net until — until the morning after," said Victoria. "That has a horribly dissipated sound — hasn't it ? I know to a moral certainty that Mr. Crewe will eventually lead Miss Pomfret away from the altar. At present," she could not refrain from adding, "he thinks he's in love with some one else."

"Who ? "

"It doesn't matter," she replied. "Humphrey's perfectly happy, because he believes most women are in love with him, and he's making up his mind in that magnificent, thorough way of his whether she is worthy to be endowed with his heart and hand, his cows, and all his stocks and bonds. He doesn't know he's going to marry Alice. It almost makes one a Calvinist, doesn't it. He's predestined, but perfectly happy."

"Who is he in love with?" demanded Austen, ungrammatically.

"I'm going to say good-by to him. I'll meet you in the field, if you don't care to come. It's only manners, after all, although the lemonade's all gone and I haven't had a drop."

"I'll go along too," he said.

"Aren't you afraid of Mrs. Pomfret ? "

"Not a bit ! "

"I am," said Victoria, "but I think you'd better come just the same."

Around the corner of the house they found them, — Mr. Crewe urging the departing guests to remain, and not to be bashful in the future about calling.

"We don't always have lemonade and cake," he was saying, " but you can be sure of a welcome, just the same. Good-by, Vane, glad you came. Did they show you through the stables? Did you see the mate to the horse I lost? Beauty, isn't he? Stir 'em up and get the money. I guess we won't see much of each other politically. You're anti-railroad. I don't believe that tack'll work — we can't get along without corporations, you know. You ought to talk to Flint. I'll give you a letter of introduction to him. I don't know what I'd have done without that man Tooting in your father's office. He's a wasted genius in Ripton. What? Good-by, you'll find your wagon, I guess. Well, Victoria, where have you been keeping yourself? I've been so busy I haven't had time to look for you. You're going to stay to dinner, and Hastings, and all the people who have helped."

"No, I'm not," answered Victoria, with a glance at Austen, before whom this announcement was so delicately made, " I'm going home."

"But when am I to see you?" cried Mr. Crewe, as near genuine alarm as he ever got. "You never let me see you. I was going to drive you home in the motor by moonlight."

"We all know that you're the most original person, Victoria," said Mrs. Pomfret, "full of whims and strange fancies," she added, with the only brief look at Austen she had deigned to bestow on him. "It never pays to count on you for twenty-four hours. I suppose you're off on another wild expedition."

"I think I've earned the right to it," said Victoria; "I've poured lemonade for Humphrey's constituents the whole afternoon. And besides, I never said I'd stay for dinner. I'm going home. Father's leaving for California in the morning."

"He'd better stay at home and look after her," Mrs. Pomfret remarked, when Victoria was out of hearing.

" Since Mrs. Harry Haynes ran off, one can never tell what a woman will do. It wouldn't surprise me a bit if Victoria eloped with a handsome nobody like that. Of course he's after her money, but he wouldn't get it, not if I know Augustus Flint."

" Is he handsome ? " said Mr. Crewe, as though the idea were a new one. " Great Scott, I don't believe she gives him a thought. She's only going as far as the field with him. She insisted on leaving her horse there instead of putting him in the stable."

" Catch Alice going as far as the field with him," said Mrs. Pomfret, " but I've done my duty. It's none of my affair."

In the meantime Austen and Victoria had walked on some distance in silence.

" I have an idea with whom Mr. Crewe is in love," he said at length.

" So have I," replied Victoria, promptly. " Humphrey's in love with himself. All he desires in a wife — if he desires one — is an inanimate and accommodating looking-glass, in whom he may see what he conceives to be his own image daily. James, you may take the mare home. I'm going to drive with Mr. Vane."

She stroked Pepper's nose while Austen undid the hitch-rope from around his neck.

" You and I are getting to be friends, aren't we, Pepper ? " she asked, as the horse, with quivering nostrils, thrust his head into her hand. Then she sprang lightly into the buggy by Austen's side. The manner of these acts and the generous courage with which she defied opinion appealed to him so strongly that his heart was beating faster than Pepper's hoof-beats on the turf of the pasture.

" You are very good to come with me," he said gravely, when they had reached the road; " perhaps I ought not to have asked you."

" Why ? " she asked, with one of her direct looks.

" It was undoubtedly selfish," he said, and added, more lightly, " I don't wish to put you into Mrs. Pomfret's bad graces."

Victoria laughed.

"She thought it her duty to tell father the time you drove me to the Hammonds'. She said I asked you to do it."

"What did he say?" Austen inquired, looking straight ahead of him.

"He didn't say much," she answered. "Father never does. I think he knows that I am to be trusted."

"Even with me?" he asked quizzically, but with a deeper significance.

"I don't think he realizes how dangerous you are," she replied, avoiding the issue. "The last time I saw you, you were actually trying to throw a fat man out of your window. What a violent life you lead, Mr. Vane. I hope you haven't shot any more people."

"I saw you," he said.

"Is that the way you spend your time in office hours, — throwing people out of the windows?"

"It was only Tom Gaylord."

"He's the man Mr. Jenney said wanted you to be a senator, isn't he?" she asked.

"You have a good memory," he answered her. "Yes. That's the reason I tried to throw him out of the window."

"Why didn't you be a senator?" she asked abruptly. "I always think of you in public life. Why waste your opportunities?"

"I'm not at all sure that was an opportunity. It was only some of Tom's nonsense. I should have had all the politicians in the district against me."

"But you aren't the kind of man who would care about the politicians, surely. If Humphrey Crewe can get elected by the people, I should think you might."

"I can't afford to give garden-parties and buy lemonade," said Austen, and they both laughed. He did not think it worth while mentioning Mr. Braden.

"Sometimes I think you haven't a particle of ambition," she said. "I like men with ambition."

"I shall try to cultivate it," said Austen.

" You seem to be popular enough."

" Most worthless people are popular, because they don't tread on anybody's toes."

" Worthless people don't take up poor people's suits, and win them," she said. " I saw Zeb Meader the other day, and he said you could be President of the United States."

" Zeb meant that I was eligible — having been born in this country," said Austen. " But where did you see him?"

" I — I went to see him."

" All the way to Mercer?"

" It isn't so far in an automobile," she replied, as though in excuse, and added, still more lamely, " Zeb and I became great friends, you know, in the hospital."

He did not answer, but wondered the more at the simplicity and kindness in one brought up as she had been which prompted her to take the trouble to see the humblest of her friends : nay, to take the trouble to have humble friends.

The road wound along a ridge, and at intervals was spread before them the full glory of the September sunset, — the mountains of the west in blue-black silhouette against the saffron sky, the myriad dappled clouds, the crimson fading from the still reaches of the river, and the wine-colour from the eastern hills. Both were silent under the spell, but a yearning arose within him when he glanced at the sunset glow on her face : would sunsets hereafter bring sadness?

His thoughts ran riot as the light faded in the west. Hers were not revealed. And the silence between them seemed gradually to grow into a pact, to become a subtler and more intimate element than speech. A faint tang of autumn smoke was in the air, a white mist crept along the running waters, a silver moon like a new-stamped coin rode triumphant in the sky, impatient to proclaim her glory; and the shadows under the ghost-like sentinel trees in the pastures grew blacker. At last Victoria looked at him.

" You are the only man I know who doesn't insist on talking," she said. " There are times when — "

"When there is nothing to say," he suggested.

She laughed softly. He tried to remember the sound of it afterwards, when he rehearsed this phase of the conversation, but couldn't.

"It's because you like the hills, isn't it?" she asked. "You seem such an out-of-door person, and Mr. Jenney said you were always wandering about the country-side."

"Mr. Jenney also made other reflections about my youth," said Austen.

She laughed again, acquiescing in his humour, secretly thankful not to find him sentimental.

"Mr. Jenney said something else that — that I wanted to ask you about," she went on, breathing more deeply. "It was about the railroad."

"I am afraid you have not come to an authority," he replied.

"You said the politicians would be against you if you tried to become a State senator. Do you believe that the politicians are owned by the railroad?"

"Has Jenney been putting such things into your head?"

"Not only Mr. Jenney, but — I have heard other people say that. And Humphrey Crewe said that you hadn't a chance politically, because you had opposed the railroad and had gone against your own interests."

Austen was amazed at this new exhibition of courage on her part, though he was sorely pressed.

"Humphrey Crewe isn't much of an authority, either," he said briefly.

"Then you won't tell me?" said Victoria. "Oh, Mr. Vane," she cried, with sudden vehemence, "if such things are going on here, I'm sure my father doesn't know about them. This is only one State, and the railroad runs through so many. He can't know everything, and I have heard him say that he wasn't responsible for what the politicians did in his name. If they are bad, why don't you go to him and tell him so? I'm sure he'd listen to you."

"I'm sure he'd think me a presumptuous idiot," said Austen. "Politicians are not idealists anywhere — the very word has become a term of reproach. Undoubtedly your father desires to set things right as much as any one else — probably more than any one."

"Oh, I know he does," exclaimed Victoria.

"If politics are not all that they should be," he went on, somewhat grimly, with an unpleasant feeling of hypocrisy, "we must remember that they are nobody's fault in particular, and can't be set right in an instant by any one man, no matter how powerful."

She turned her face to him gratefully, but he did not meet her look. They were on the driveway of Fairview.

"I suppose you think me very silly for asking such questions," she said.

"No," he answered gravely, "but politics are so intricate a subject that they are often not understood by those who are in the midst of them. I admire — I think it is very fine in you to want to know."

"You are not one of the men who would not wish a woman to know, are you?"

"No," he said, "no, I'm not."

The note of pain in his voice surprised and troubled her. They were almost in sight of the house.

"I asked you to come to Fairview," she said, assuming a lightness of tone, "and you never appeared. I thought it was horrid of you to forget, after we'd been such friends."

"I didn't forget," replied Austen.

"Then you didn't want to come."

He looked into her eyes, and she dropped them.

"You will have to be the best judge of that," he said.

"But what am I to think?" she persisted.

"Think the best of me you can," he answered, as they drew up on the gravel before the open door of Fairview house. A man was standing in the moonlight on the porch.

"Is that you, Victoria?"

"Yes, father."

"I was getting worried," said Mr. Flint, coming down on the driveway.

"I'm all right," she said, leaping out of the buggy, "Mr. Vane brought me home."

"How are you, Hilary?" said Mr. Flint.

"I'm Austen Vane, Mr. Flint," said Austen.

"How are you?" said Mr. Flint, as curtly as the barest politeness allowed. "What was the matter with your own horse, Victoria?"

"Nothing," she replied, after an instant's pause. Austen wondered many times whether her lips had trembled. "Mr. Vane asked me to drive with him, and I came. Won't — won't you come in, Mr. Vane?"

"No, thanks," said Austen, "I'm afraid I have to go back to Ripton."

"Good-by, and thank you," she said, and gave him her hand. As he pressed it, he thought he felt the slightest pressure in return, — and then she fled up the steps. As he drove away, he turned once to look at the great house, with its shades closely drawn, as it stood amidst its setting of shrubbery silent under the moon.

An hour later he sat in Hanover Street before the supper Euphrasia had saved for him. But though he tried nobly, his heart was not in the relation, for her benefit, of Mr. Crewe's garden-party.

CHAPTER IX

MR. CREWE ASSAULTS THE CAPITAL

THOSE portions of the biographies of great men which deal with the small beginnings of careers are always eagerly devoured, and for this reason the humble entry of Mr. Crewe into politics may be of interest. Great revolutions have had their origins in back cellars; great builders of railroads have begun life with packs on their shoulders, trudging over the wilderness which they were to traverse in after years in private cars. The history of Napoleon Bonaparte has not a Sunday-school moral, but we can trace therein the results of industry after the future emperor got started. Industry, and the motto *nil desperandum* lived up to, and the watchword "thorough," and a touch of unsuspected genius, and *l'audace, toujours l'audace*, and a man may go far in life.

Mr. Humphrey Crewe possessed, as may have been surmised, a dash of all these gifts. For a summary of his character one would not have used the phrase (as a contemporary of his remarked) of "a shrinking violet." The phrase, after all, would have fitted very few great men; genius is sure of itself, and seeks its peers.

The State capital is an old and beautiful and somewhat conservative town. Life there has its joys and sorrows and passions, its ambitions and heartburnings, to be sure; a most absorbing novel could be written about it, and the author need not go beyond the city limits or approach the state-house or the Pelican Hotel. The casual visitor in that capital leaves it with a sense of peace, the echo of church bells in his ear, and (if in winter) the impression of dazzling snow. Comedies do not necessarily require a wide stage, nor tragedies an amphitheatre for their enactment.

No casual visitor, for instance, would have suspected from the faces or remarks of the inhabitants whom he chanced to meet that there was excitement in the capital over the prospective arrival of Mr. Humphrey Crewe for the legislative session that winter. Legislative sessions, be it known, no longer took place in the summer, — a great relief to Mr. Crewe and to farmers in general, who wished to be at home in haying time.

The capital abounded in comfortable homes and boasted not a few dwellings of larger pretensions. Chief among these was the Duncan house — still so called, although Mr. Duncan, who built it, had been dead these fifteen years, and his daughter and heiress, Janet, had married an Italian Marquis and lived in a Roman palace, rehabilitated by the Duncan money. Mr. Duncan, it may be recalled by some readers of "Coniston," had been a notable man in his day, who had married the heiress of the State, and was president of the Central Railroad, now absorbed in the United Northeastern. The house was a great square of brick, with a wide cornice, surrounded by a shaded lawn; solidly built, in the fashion of the days when rich people stayed at home, with a conservatory and a library that had once been Mr. Duncan's pride. The Marchesa cared very little about the library, or about the house, for that matter; a great aunt and uncle, spinster and bachelor, were living in it that winter, and they vacated for Mr. Crewe. He travelled to the capital on the legislative pass the Northeastern Railroads had so kindly given him, and brought down his horses and his secretary and servants from Leith a few days before the first of January, when the session was to open, and laid out his bills for the betterment of the State on that library table where Mr. Duncan had lovingly thumbed his folios. Mr. Crewe, with characteristic promptitude, set his secretary to work to make a list of the persons of influence in the town, preparatory to a series of dinner-parties; he dropped into the office of Mr. Ridout, the counsel of the Northeastern and of the Winona Corporation in the capital, to pay his respects as a man of affairs, and incidentally to leave copies of his bills for the improvement of the State.   Mr. Ridout was politely interested, and promised to read the bills, and agreed that they ought to pass.

Mr. Crewe also examined the Pelican Hotel, so soon to be a hive, and stood between the snowbanks in the capital park contemplating the statue of the great statesman there, and repeating to himself the quotation inscribed beneath.   " The People's Government, made for the People, made by the People, and answerable to the People." And he wondered, idly, — for the day was not cold, — how he would look upon a pedestal with the Gladstone collar and the rough woollen coat that would lend themselves so readily to reproduction in marble.   Stranger things had happened, and grateful States had been known to reward benefactors.

At length comes the gala night of nights, — the last of the old year, — and the assembling of the five hundred legislators and of the army that is wont to attend them. The afternoon trains, steaming hot, are crowded to the doors, the station a scene of animation, and Main Street, dazzling in snow, is alive with a stream of men, with eddies here and there at the curbs and in the entries. What hand-shaking, and looking over of new faces, and walking round and round !   What sightseeing by the country members and their wives who have come to attend the inauguration of the new governor, the Honourable Asa P. Gray !   There he is, with the whiskers and the tall hat and the comfortable face, which wears already a look of gubernatorial dignity and power.   He stands for a moment in the lobby of the Pelican Hotel, — thronged now to suffocation, — to shake hands genially with new friends, who are led up by old friends with two fingers on the elbow.   The old friends crack jokes and whisper in the ear of the governor-to-be, who presently goes upstairs, accompanied by the Honourable Hilary Vane, to the bridal suite, which is reserved for him, and which has fire-proof carpet on the floor.   The Honourable Hilary has a room next door, connecting with the new governor's by folding doors, but this fact is not generally known to country

members. Only old timers, like Bijah Bixby and Job
Braden, know that the Honourable Hilary's room cor-
responds to one which in the old Pelican was called
the Throne Room, Number Seven, where Jethro Bass sat
in the old days and watched unceasingly the groups in
the street from the window.

But Jethro Bass has been dead these twenty years, and
his lieutenants shorn of power. An empire has arisen out
of the ashes of the ancient kingdoms. Bijah and Job are
old, all-powerful still in Clovelly and Leith — influential
still in their own estimations; still kicking up their heels
behind, still stuttering and whispering into ears, still
" going along by when they are talking sly." But there
are no guerrillas now, no condottieri who can be hired:
the empire has a paid and standing army, as an empire
should. The North Country chiefs, so powerful in the
clan warfare of bygone days, are generals now, — chiefs
of staff. The captain-general, with a minute piece of
Honey Dew under his tongue, sits in Number Seven. A
new Number Seven, — with electric lights and a bathroom
and a brass bed. *Tempora mutantur.* There is an empire and a feudal system, did one but know it. The clans
are part of the empire, and each chief is responsible for
his clan — did one but know it. One doesn't know it.

The Honourable Brush Bascom, Duke of Putnam, member of the House, has arrived unostentatiously — as is his
custom — and is seated in his own headquarters, number
ten (with a bathroom). Number nine belongs from year
to year to Mr. Manning, division superintendent of that
part of the Northeastern which was the old Central, — a
thin gentleman with side-whiskers. He loves life in the
capital so much that he takes his vacations there in the
winter, — during the sessions of the Legislature, — presumably because it is gay. There are other rooms, higher up,
of important men, to be sure, but to enter which it is not
so much of an honour. The Honourable Bill Fleming,
postmaster of Brampton in Truro (Ephraim Prescott
being long since dead and Brampton a large place now),
has his vacation during the session in room thirty-six (no

bathroom); and the Honourable Elisha Jane, Earl of Haines County in the North Country, and United States consul somewhere, is home on his annual vacation in room fifty-nine (no bath). Senator Whitredge has a room, and Senator Green, and Congressmen Eldridge and Fairplay — (no baths, and only temporary).

The five hundred who during the next three months are to register the laws find quarters as best they can. Not all of them are as luxurious as Mr. Crewe in the Duncan house, or the Honourable Brush Bascom in number ten of the Pelican, the rent of either of which would swallow the legislative salary in no time. The Honourable Nat Billings, senator from the Putnam County district, is comfortably installed, to be sure. By gradual and unexplained degrees, the constitution of the State has been changed until there are only twenty senators. Noble five hundred! Steadfast twenty!

A careful perusal of the biographies of great men of the dynamic type leads one to the conclusion that much of their success is due to an assiduous improvement of every opportunity, — and Mr. Humphrey Crewe certainly possessed this quality, also. He is in the Pelican Hotel this evening, meeting the men that count. Mr. Job Braden, who had come down with the idea that he might be of use in introducing the new member from Leith to the notables, was met by this remark: —

"You can't introduce me to any of 'em — they all know who I am. Just point any of 'em out you think I ought to know, and I'll go up and talk to 'em. What? Come up to my house after a while and smoke a cigar. The Duncan house, you know — the big one with the conservatory."

Mr. Crewe was right — they all knew him. The Leith millionaire, the summer resident, was a new factor in politics, and the rumours of the size of his fortune had reached a high-water mark in the Pelican Hotel that evening. Pushing through the crowd in the corridor outside the bridal suite waiting to shake hands with the new governor, Mr. Crewe gained an entrance in no time, and did not hesitate to interrupt the somewhat protracted felicitations of an Irish member of the Newcastle delegation.

"How are you, Governor?" he said, with the bonhomie of a man of the world. "I'm Humphrey Crewe, from Leith. You got a letter from me, didn't you, congratulating you upon your election? We didn't do badly for you up there. What?"

"How do you do, Mr. Crewe?" said Mr. Gray, with dignified hospitality, while their fingers slid over each other's; "I'm glad to welcome you here. I've noticed the interest you've taken in the State, and the number of — ahem — very useful societies to which you belong."

"Good," said Mr. Crewe, "I do what I can. I just dropped in to shake your hand, and to say that I hope we'll pull together."

The governor lifted his eyebrows a little.

"Why, I hope so, I'm sure, Mr. Crewe," said he.

"I've looked over the policy of the State for the last twenty years in regard to public improvements and the introduction of modern methods as concerns husbandry, and I find it deplorable. You and I, Governor, live in a progressive age, and we can't afford not to see something done. What? It is my desire to do what I can to help make your administration a notable advance upon those of your predecessors."

"Why — I greatly appreciate it, Mr. Crewe," said Mr. Gray.

"I'm sure you do. I've looked over your record, and I find you've had experience in State affairs, and that you are a successful and conservative business man. That is the type we want — eh? Business men. You've read over the bills I sent you by registered mail?"

"Ahem," said Mr. Gray, "I've been a good deal occupied since election day, Mr. Crewe."

"Read 'em," said Mr. Crewe, "and I'll call in on you at the state-house day after to-morrow at five o'clock promptly. We'll discuss 'em, Governor, and if, by the light of your legislative experience, you have any suggestions to make, I shall be glad to hear 'em. Before

putting the bills in their final shape I've taken the trouble
to go over them with my friend, Mr. Flint — our mutual
friend, let us say."

"I've had the pleasure of meeting Mr. Flint," said
Mr. Gray.   "I — ahem — can't say that I know him intimately."

Mr. Crewe looked at Mr. Gray in a manner which plainly
indicated that he was not an infant.

"My relations with Mr. Flint and the Northeastern
have been very pleasant," said Mr. Crewe.   "I may say
that I am somewhat of a practical railroad and business
man myself."

"We need such men," said Mr. Gray.   "Why, how do
you do, Cary?   How are the boys up in Wheeler?"

"Well, good-by, Governor.   See you day after to-morrow
at five precisely," said Mr. Crewe.

The next official call of Mr. Crewe was on the Speaker-
to-be, Mr. Doby of Hale (for such matters are cut and
dried), but any amount of pounding on Mr. Doby's door
(number seventy-five) brought no response.   Other rural
members besides Mr. Crewe came and pounded on that
door, and went away again; but Mr. Job Braden suddenly
appeared from another part of the corridor, smiling be-
nignly, and apparently not resenting the refusal of his
previous offers of help.

"W-want the Speaker?" he inquired.

Mr. Crewe acknowledged that he did.

"Ed only sleeps there," said Mr. Braden.   "Guess
you'll find him in the Railroad Room."

"Railroad Room?"

"Hilary Vane's, Number Seven."   Mr. Braden took hold
of the lapel of his fellow-townsman's coat.   "Callated you
didn't know it all," he said; "that's the reason I come
down — so's to help you some."

Mr. Crewe, although he was not wont to take a second
place, followed Mr. Braden down the stairs to the door
next to the governor's, where he pushed ahead of his
guide, through the group about the doorway, — none of
whom, however, were attempting to enter.   They stared

in some surprise at Mr. Crewe as he flung open the door without knocking, and slammed it behind him in Mr. Braden's face. But the bewilderment caused by this act of those without was as nothing to the astonishment of those within — had Mr. Crewe but known it. An oil painting of the prominent men gathered about the marble-topped table in the centre of the room, with an outline key beneath it, would have been an appropriate work of art to hang in the state-house, as emblematic of the statesmanship of the past twenty years. The Honourable Hilary Vane sat at one end in a padded chair; Mr. Manning, the division superintendent, startled out of a meditation, was upright on the end of the bed; Mr. Ridout, the Northeastern's capital lawyer, was figuring at the other end of the table; the Honourable Brush Bascom was bending over a wide, sad-faced gentleman of some two hundred and fifty pounds who sat at the centre in his shirt-sleeves, poring over numerous sheets in front of him which were covered with names of the five hundred. This gentleman was the Honourable Edward Doby of Hale, who, with the kind assistance of the other gentlemen above-named, was in this secluded spot making up a list of his committees, undisturbed by eager country members. At Mr. Crewe's entrance Mr. Bascom, with great presence of mind, laid down his hat over the principal list, while Mr. Ridout, taking the hint, put the Revised Statutes on the other. There was a short silence; and the Speaker-to-be, whose pencil had been knocked out of his hand, recovered himself sufficiently to relight an extremely frayed cigar.

Not that Mr. Crewe was in the least abashed. He chose this opportunity to make a survey of the situation, nodded to Mr. Ridout, and walked up to the padded arm-chair.

"How are you, Mr. Vane?" he said. "I thought I'd drop in to shake hands with you, especially as I have business with the Speaker, and heard he was here. But I'm glad to have met you for many reasons. I want you to be one of the vice-presidents of the State Economic League

"I THOUGHT I'D DROP IN TO SHAKE HANDS WITH YOU."

— it won't cost you anything.   Ridout has agreed to let his name go on."

The Honourable Hilary, not being an emotional man, merely grunted as he started to rise to his feet.   What he was about to say was interrupted by a timid knock, and there followed another brief period of silence.

" It ain't anybody," said Mr. Bascom, and crossing the room, turned the key in the lock.   The timid knock was repeated.

" I suppose you're constantly interrupted here by unimportant people," Mr. Crewe remarked.

" Well," said Mr. Vane, slowly, boring into Mr. Crewe with his eye, " that statement isn't far out of the way."

" I don't believe you've ever met me, Mr. Vane.   I'm Humphrey Crewe.   We have a good friend in common in Mr. Flint."

The Honourable Hilary's hand passed over Mr. Crewe's lightly.

" Glad to meet you, Mr. Crewe," he said, and a faint twinkle appeared in his eye.   " Job has told everybody you were coming down.   Glad to welcome a man of your — ahem — stamp into politics."

" I'm a plain business man," answered Mr. Crewe, modestly; " and although I have considerable occupation, I believe that one in my position has duties to perform. I've certain bills — "

" Yes, yes," agreed the Honourable Hilary; " do you know Mr. Brush Bascom and Mr. Manning?   Allow me to introduce you, — and General Doby."

" How are you, General?" said Mr. Crewe to the Speaker-to-be, " I'm always glad to shake the hand of a veteran. Indeed, I have thought that a society — "

" I earned my title," said General Doby, somewhat sheepishly, " fighting on Governor Brown's staff.   There were twenty of us, and we were resistless, weren't we, Brush?"

" Twenty on a staff!" exclaimed Mr. Crewe.

" Oh, we furnished our own uniforms and paid our own way — except those of us who had passes," declared the

General, as though the memory of his military career did not give him unalloyed pleasure. " What's the use of State sovereignty if you can't have a glittering army to follow the governor round ? "

Mr. Crewe had never considered this question, and he was not the man to waste time in speculation.

" Doubtless you got a letter from me, General Doby," he said. " We did what we could up our way to put you in the Speaker's chair."

General Doby creased a little in the middle, to signify that he was bowing.

" I trust it will be in my power to reciprocate, Mr. Crewe," he replied.

" We want to treat Mr. Crewe right," Mr. Bascom put in.

" You have probably made a note of my requests," Mr. Crewe continued. " I should like to be on the Judiciary Committee, for one thing. Although I am not a lawyer, I know something of the principles of law, and I understand that this and the Appropriations Committee are the most important. I may say with truth that I should be a useful member of that, as I am accustomed to sitting on financial boards. As my bills are of some considerable importance and deal with practical progressive measures, I have no hesitation in asking for the chairmanship of Public Improvements, — and of course a membership in the Agricultural is essential, as I have bills for them. Gentlemen," he added to the room at large, " I have typewritten manifolds of those bills which I shall be happy to leave here — at headquarters." And suiting the action to the word, he put down a packet on the table.

The Honourable Brush Bascom, accompanied by Mr. Ridout, walked to the window and stood staring at the glitter of the electric light on the snow. The Honourable Hilary gazed steadily at the table, while General Doby blew his nose with painful violence.

" I'll do what I can for you, certainly, Mr. Crewe," he said. " But — what is to become of the other four hundred and ninety-nine ? The ways of a Speaker are hard, Mr. Crewe, and I have to do justice to all."

"Well," answered Mr. Crewe, "of course I don't want to be unreasonable, and I realize the pressure that's put upon you. But when you consider the importance of the work I came down here to do — "

"I do consider it," said the Speaker, politely. "It's a little early to talk about the make-up of committees. I hope to be able to get at them by Sunday. You may be sure I'll do my best for you."

"We'd better make a note of it," said Mr. Crewe; "give me some paper," and he was reaching around behind General Doby for one of the precious sheets under Mr. Bascom's hat, when the general, with great presence of mind, sat on it. We have it, from a malicious and untrustworthy source, that the Northeastern Railroads paid for a new one.

"Here, here," cried the Speaker, "make the memorandum here."

At this critical juncture a fortunate diversion occurred. A rap — three times — of no uncertain quality was heard at the door, and Mr. Brush Bascom hastened to open it. A voice cried out : —

"Is Manning here? The boys are hollering for those passes," and a wiry, sallow gentleman burst in, none other than the Honourable Elisha Jane, who was taking his consular vacation. When his eyes fell upon Mr. Crewe he halted abruptly, looked a little foolish, and gave a questioning glance at the Honourable Hilary.

"Mountain passes, Lish? Sit down. Did I ever tell you that story about the slide in Ricket's Gulch?" asked the Honourable Brush Bascom. "But first let me make you acquainted with Mr. Humphrey Crewe of Leith. Mr. Crewe has come down here with the finest lot of bills you ever saw, and we're all going to take hold and put 'em through. Here, Lish, I'll give you a set."

"Read 'em, Mr. Jane," urged Mr. Crewe. "I don't claim much for 'em, but perhaps they will help to set a few little matters right — I hope so."

Mr. Jane opened the bills with deliberation, and cast his eyes over the headings.

"I'll read 'em this very night, Mr. Crewe," he said solemnly; "this meeting you is a particular pleasure, and I have heard in many quarters of these measures."

"Well," admitted Mr. Crewe, "they may help some. I have a few other matters to attend to this evening, so I must say good-night, gentlemen. Don't let me interfere with those 'mountain passes,' Mr. Manning."

With this parting remark, which proved him to be not merely an idealist in politics, but a practical man, Mr. Crewe took his leave. And he was too much occupied with his own thoughts to pay any attention to the click of the key as it turned in the lock, or to hear United States Senator Whitredge rap (three times) on the door after he had turned the corner, or to know that presently the sliding doors into the governor's bridal suite were to open a trifle, large enough for the admission of the body of the Honourable Asa P. Gray.

Number Seven still keeps up its reputation as the seat of benevolence, and great public benefactors still meet there to discuss the welfare of their fellow-men : the hallowed council chamber now of an empire, seat of the Governor-general of the State, the Honourable Hilary Vane, and his advisers. For years a benighted people, with a fond belief in their participation of Republican institutions, had elected the noble five hundred of the House and the stanch twenty of the Senate. Noble five hundreds (biggest Legislature in the world) have come and gone ; debated, applauded, fought and on occasions denounced, kicked over the traces, and even wept — to no avail. Behold that political institution of man, representative government ! There it is on the stage, curtain up, a sublime spectacle for all men to see, and thrill over speeches about the Rights of Man, and the Forefathers in the Revolution ; about Constituents who do not constitute. The High Heavens allow it and smile, and it is well for the atoms that they think themselves free American representatives, that they do not feel the string of predestination around their ankles. The senatorial twenty, from their high carved seats, see the strings and smile, too ; yes, and see their own strings, and smile. Wisdom does not wish for flight. " The people " having changed the constitution, the blackbirds are reduced from four and forty to a score. This is cheaper — for the people.

Democracy on the front of the stage before an applauding audience ; performers absorbed in their parts, forgetting that the landlord has to be paid in money yet to be earned. Behind the stage, the real play, the absorbing interest, the high stakes — occasional discreet laughter through the peep-hole when an actor makes an impassioned appeal to the gods. Democracy in front, the Feudal System, the Dukes and Earls behind — but in plain clothes ; Democracy in stars and spangles and trappings and insignia. Or, a better figure, the Fates weaving the web in that mystic chamber, Number Seven, pausing now and again to smile as a new thread is put in. Proclamations, constitutions, and creeds crumble before conditions; the Law of Dividends is the high law, and the Forum an open vent through which the white steam may rise heavenward and be resolved again into water.

Mr. Crewe took his seat in the popular assemblage next day, although most of the five hundred gave up theirs to the ladies who had come to hear his Excellency deliver his inaugural. The Honourable Asa made a splendid figure, all agreed, and read his speech in a firm and manly voice. A large part of it was about the people; some of it about the sacred government they had inherited from their fore-fathers ; still another concerned the high character and achievements of the inhabitants within the State lines; the name of Abraham Lincoln was mentioned, and, with even greater reverence and fervour, the Republican party which had ennobled and enriched the people — and incidentally elected the governor. There was a noble financial policy, a curtailment of expense. The forests should be protected, roads should be built, and, above all, corporations should be held to a strict accounting.

Needless to say, the speech gave great satisfaction to all, and many old friends left the hall exclaiming that they didn't believe Asa had it in him. As a matter of fact (known only to the initiated), Asa didn't have it in him until last night, before he squeezed through the crack in the folding doors from room number six to room Number Seven. The inspiration came to him then, when he was ennobled by the Governor-general, who represents the Empire. Perpetual Governor-general, who quickens into life puppet governors of his own choosing! Asa has agreed, for the honour of the title of governor of his State, to act the part, open the fairs, lend his magnificent voice to those phrases which it rounds so well. It is fortunate, when we smoke a fine cigar from Havana, that we cannot look into the factory. The sight would disturb us. It was well for the applauding, deep-breathing audience in the state-house that first of January that they did not have a glimpse in room Number Seven the night before, under the sheets that contained the list of the Speaker's committees; it was well that they could not go back to Ripton into the offices on the square, earlier in December, where Mr. Hamilton Tooting was writing the noble part of that inaugural from memoranda given him by the Honourable Hilary Vane. Yes, the versatile Mr. Tooting, and none other, doomed forever to hide the light of his genius under a bushel! The financial part was written by the Governor-general himself — the Honourable Hilary Vane. And when it was all finished and revised, it was put into a long envelope which bore this printed address: *Augustus P. Flint, Pres't United Northeastern Railroads, New York.* And came back with certain annotations on the margin, which were duly incorporated into it. This is the private history (which must never be told) of the document which on January first became, as far as fame and posterity is concerned, the Honourable Asa P. Gray's — forever and forever.

Mr. Crewe liked the inaugural, and was one of the first to tell Mr. Gray so, and to express his pleasure and appreciation of the fact that his request (mailed in November) had been complied with, that the substance of his bills had been recommended in the governor's programme.

He did not pause to reflect on the maxim, that platforms are made to get in by and inaugurals to get started by.

Although annual efforts have been made by various public-spirited citizens to build a new state-house, economy — with assistance from room Number Seven — has triumphed. It is the same state-house from the gallery of which poor William Wetherell witnessed the drama of the Woodchuck Session, although there are more members now, for the population of the State has increased to five hundred thousand. It is well for General Doby, with his two hundred and fifty pounds, that he is in the Speaker's chair; five hundred seats are a good many for that hall, and painful in a long session. The Honourable Brush Bascom can stretch his legs, because he is fortunate enough to have a front seat. Upon inquiry, it turns out that Mr. Bascom has had a front seat for the last twenty years — he has been uniformly lucky in drawing. The Honourable Jacob Botcher (ten years' service) is equally fortunate; the Honourable Jake is a man of large presence, and a voice that sounds as if it came, oracularly, from the caverns of the earth. He is easily heard by the members on the back seats, while Mr. Bascom is not. Mr. Ridout, the capital lawyer, is in the House this year, and singularly enough has a front seat likewise. It was Mr. Crewe's misfortune to draw number 415, in the extreme corner of the room, and next the steam radiator. But he was not of the metal to accept tamely such a ticketing from the hat of destiny (via the Clerk of the House). He complained, as any man of spirit would, and Mr. Utter, the polite clerk, is profoundly sorry, — and says it may be managed. Curiously enough, the Honourable Brush Bascom and the Honourable Jacob Botcher join Mr. Crewe in his complaint, and reiterate that it is an outrage that a man of such ability and deserving prominence should be among the submerged four hundred and seventy. It is managed in a mysterious manner we don't pretend to fathom, and behold Mr. Crewe in the front of the Forum, in the seats of the mighty, where he can easily be pointed out from

the gallery at the head of the five hundred, between
those shining leaders and parliamentarians, the Honourables Brush Bascom and Jake Botcher.

For Mr. Crewe has not come to the Legislature, like the
country members in the rear, to acquire a smattering of
parliamentary procedure by the day the Speaker is presented with a gold watch, at the end of the session.   Not
he!   Not the practical business man, the member of
boards, the chairman and president of societies.   He has
studied the Rules of the House and parliamentary law,
you may be sure.   Genius does not come unprepared, and
is rarely caught napping.   After the Legislature adjourned that week the following telegram was sent over
the wires:—

Augustus P. Flint, New York.
  *Kindly use your influence with Doby to secure my com-
mittee appointments.   Important as per my conversation
with you.*
                                        Humphrey Crewe.

Nor was Mr. Crewe idle from Saturday to Monday night,
when the committees were to be announced.   He sent to
the *State Tribune* office for fifty copies of that valuable
paper, which contained a two-column-and-a-half article
on Mr. Crewe as a legislator and financier and citizen,
with a summary of his bills and an argument as to how
the State would benefit by their adoption; an accurate list
of Mr. Crewe's societies was inserted, and an account
of his life's history, and of those ancestors of his who
had been born or lived within the State.   Indeed, the
accuracy of this article as a whole did great credit to
the editor of the *State Tribune*, who must have spent a
tremendous amount of painstaking research upon it; and
the article was so good that Mr. Crewe regretted (undoubtedly for the editor's sake) that a request could not be
appended to it such as is used upon marriage and funeral
notices: "New York, Boston, and Philadelphia papers
please copy."

Mr. Crewe thought it his duty to remedy as much as

possible the unfortunate limited circulation of the article, and he spent as much as a whole day making out a list of friends and acquaintances whom he thought worthy to receive a copy of the *Tribune*, — marked personal. Victoria Flint got one, and read it to her father at the breakfast table. (Mr. Flint did not open his.) Austen Vane wondered why any man in his obscure and helpless position should have been honoured, but honoured he was. He sent his to Victoria, too, and was surprised to find that she knew his handwriting and wrote him a letter to thank him for it: a letter which provoked on his part much laughter, and elements of other sensations which, according to Charles Reade, should form the ingredients of a good novel. But of this matter later.

Mrs. Pomfret and Alice each got one, and each wrote Mr. Crewe appropriate congratulations. (Alice's answer supervised.) Mrs. Chillingham got one; the Honourable Hilary Vane got one — marked in red ink, lest he should have skipped it in his daily perusal of the paper. Mr. Brush Bascom got one likewise. But the list of Mr. Crewe's acquaintances is too long and too broad to dwell upon further in these pages.

The Monday-night session came at last, that sensational hour when the Speaker makes those decisions to which he is supposed to have given birth over Sunday in the seclusion of his country home at Hale. Monday-night sessions are, as a rule, confined in attendance to the Honourable Brush Bascom and Mr. Ridout and a few other conscientious members who do not believe in cheating the State, but to-night all is bustle and confusion, and at least four hundred members are pushing down the aisles and squeezing past each other into the narrow seats, and reading the *State Tribune* or the ringing words of the governor's inaugural which they find in the racks on the back of the seats before them. Speaker Doby, who has been apparently deep in conference with the most important members (among them Mr. Crewe, to whom he has whispered that a violent snow-storm is raging in Hale), raps for order; and after a few preliminaries hands

L

to Mr. Utter, the clerk, amidst a breathless silence, the paper on which the parliamentary career of so many ambitious statesmen depends.

It is not a pleasure to record the perfidy of man, nor the lack of judgment which prevents him, in his circumscribed lights, from recognizing undoubted geniuses when he sees them. Perhaps it was jealousy on General Doby's part, and a selfish desire to occupy the centre of the stage himself, but at any rate we will pass hastily over the disagreeable portions of this narrative. Mr. Crewe settled himself with his feet extended, and with a complacency which he had rightly earned by leaving no stone unturned, to listen. He sat up a little when the Appropriations Committee, headed by the Honourable Jake Botcher, did not contain his name — but it might have been an oversight of Mr. Utter's; when the Judiciary (Mr. Ridout's committee) was read it began to look like malice; committee after committee was revealed, and the name of Humphrey Crewe might not have been contained in the five hundred except as the twelfth member of forestry, until it appeared at the top of National Affairs. Here was a broad enough field, certainly,— the Trusts, the Tariff, the Gold Standard, the Foreign Possessions, — and Mr. Crewe's mind began to soar in spite of himself. Public Improvements was reached, and he straightened. Mr. Beck, a railroad lawyer from Belfast, led it. Mr. Crewe arose, as any man of spirit would, and walked with dignity up the aisle and out of the house. This deliberate attempt to crush genius would inevitably react on itself. The Honourable Hilary Vane and Mr. Flint should be informed of it at once.

CHAPTER X

A MAN with a sense of humour once went to the capital as a member of the five hundred from his town, and he never went back again. One reason for this was that he died the following year, — literally, the doctors said, from laughing too much. I know that this statement will be received incredulously, and disputed by those who claim that laughter is a good thing; the honourable gentleman died from too much of a good thing. He was overpowered by having too much to laugh at, and the undiscerning thought him a fool, and the Empire had no need of a court jester. But many of his sayings have lived, nevertheless. He wrote a poem, said to be a plagiarism, which contains the quotation at the beginning of this chapter: "For bills may come, and bills may go, but I go on forever." The first person singular is supposed to relate to the United Northeastern Railroads. It was a poor joke at best.

It is needless to say that the gentleman referred to had a back seat among the submerged four hundred and seventy, — and that he kept it. No discerning and powerful well-wishers came forward and said to him, " Friend, go up higher." He sat, doubled up, in number 460, and the gods gave him compensation in laughter; he disturbed the Solons around him, who were interested in what was going on in front, and trying to do their duty to their constituents by learning parliamentary procedure before the Speaker got his gold watch and shed tears over it.

The gentleman who laughed and died is forgotten, as he deserves to be, and it never occurred to anybody that he might have been a philosopher, after all. There is something irresistibly funny about predestination; about men who are striving and learning and soberly voting upon measures with which they have as little to do as guinea-pigs. There were certain wise and cynical atheists who did not attend the sessions at all except when they received mysterious hints to do so. These were chiefly from Newcastle. And there were others who played poker in the state-house cellar waiting for the Word to come to them, when they went up and voted (prudently counting their chips before they did so), and descended again. The man with a sense of humour laughed at these, too, and at the twenty blackbirds in the Senate, — but not so heartily. He laughed at their gravity, for no gravity can equal that of gentlemen who play with stacked cards.

The risible gentleman laughed at the proposed legislation, about which he made the song, and he likened it to a stream that rises hopefully in the mountains, and takes its way singing at the prospect of reaching the ocean, but presently flows into a hole in the ground to fill the forgotten caverns of the earth, and is lost to the knowledge and sight of man. The caverns he labelled respectively *Appropriations, Railroad, Judiciary*, and their guardians were unmistakably the Honourables Messrs. Bascom, Botcher, and Ridout. The greatest cavern of all he called *The Senate*.

If you listen, you can hear the music of the stream of bills as it is rising hopefully and flowing now : "*Mr. Crewe of Leith gives notice that on to-morrow or some subsequent day he will introduce a bill entitled ' An act for the Improvement of the State Highways.' Mr. Crewe of Leith gives notice, etc. ' An act for the Improvement of the Practice of Agriculture.' 'An act relating to the State Indebtedness.' ' An act to increase the State Forest Area.' 'An act to incorporate the State Economic League.' 'An act to incorporate the State Children's Charities Association.' 'An act in relation to Abandoned Farms.'*" These were some of the most important, and they were duly introduced on the morrow, and gravely referred by the Speaker to various committees. As might be expected, a man whose watchword is "thorough" immediately got a list of those committees, and lost no time in hunting up the chairmen and the various available members thereof.

As a man of spirit, also, Mr. Crewe wrote to Mr. Flint, protesting as to the manner in which he had been treated concerning committees. In the course of a week he received a kind but necessarily brief letter from the Northeastern's president to remind him that he persisted in a fallacy ; as a neighbour, Mr. Flint would help him to the extent of his power, but the Northeastern Railroads could not interfere in legislative or political matters. Mr. Crewe was naturally pained by the lack of confidence of his friend; it seems useless to reiterate that he was far from being a fool, and no man could be in the capital a day during the session without being told of the existence of Number Seven, no matter how little the informant might know of what might be going on there. Mr. Crewe had been fortunate enough to see the inside of that mysterious room, and, being a sufficiently clever man to realize the importance and necessity of government by corporations, had been shocked at nothing he had seen or heard. However, had he had a glimpse of the Speaker's lists under the hopelessly crushed hat of Mr. Bascom, perhaps he might have been shocked, after all.

It was about this time that a touching friendship began which ought, in justice, to be briefly chronicled. It was impossible for the Honourable Brush Bascom and the Honourable Jacob Botcher to have Mr. Crewe sitting between them and not conceive a strong affection for him. The Honourable Brush, though not given to expressing his feelings, betrayed some surprise at the volumes Mr. Crewe had contributed to the stream of bills ; and Mr. Botcher, in a Delphic whisper, invited Mr. Crewe to visit him in room forty-eight of the Pelican that evening. To tell the truth, Mr. Crewe returned the feeling of his companions warmly, and he had even entertained the idea of asking them both to dine with him that evening.

Number forty-eight (the Honourable Jake's) was a free-and-easy democratic resort. No three knocks and a password before you turn the key here. Almost before your knuckles hit the panel you heard Mr. Botcher's hearty voice shouting "Come in," in spite of the closed transom. The Honourable Jake, being a teetotaller, had no bathroom, and none but his intimate friends ever looked in the third from the top bureau drawer.

The proprietor of the Pelican, who in common with the rest of humanity had fallen a victim to the rough and honest charms and hearty good fellowship of the Honourable Jake, always placed a large padded arm-chair in number forty-eight before the sessions, knowing that the Honourable Jake's constituency would be uniformly kind to him. There Mr. Botcher was wont to sit (when he was not depressing one of the tiles in the rotunda), surrounded by his friends and their tobacco smoke, discussing in his frank and manly fashion the public questions of the day.

Mr. Crewe thought it a little strange that, whenever he entered a room in the Pelican, a silence should succeed the buzz of talk which he had heard through the closed transom; but he very naturally attributed this to the constraint which ordinary men would be likely to feel in his presence. In the mouth of one presumptuous member the word "railroad" was cut in two by an agate glance from the Honourable Brush, and Mr. Crewe noted with some surprise that the Democratic leader of the House, Mr. Painter, was seated on Mr. Botcher's mattress, with an expression that was in singular contrast to the look of bold defiance which he had swept over the House that afternoon in announcing his opposition policy. The vulgar political suggestion might have crept into a more trivial mind than Mr. Crewe's that Mr. Painter was being "put to bed," the bed being very similar to that of Procrustes. Mr. Botcher extracted himself from the nooks and crannies of his arm-chair.

"How are you, Crewe?" he said hospitably; "we're all friends here — eh, Painter? We don't carry our quarrels outside the swinging doors. You know Mr. Crewe — by sight, of course. Do you know these other gentlemen, Crewe? I didn't expect you so early."

The "other gentlemen" said that they were happy to make the acquaintance of their fellow-member from Leith, and seemingly with one consent began to edge towards the door.

"Don't go, boys," Mr. Bascom protested. "Let me finish that story."

Some of "the boys" seemed to regard this statement as humorous, — more humorous, indeed, than the story itself. And when it was finished they took their departure, a trifle awkwardly, led by Mr. Painter.

"They're a little mite bashful," said Mr. Botcher, apologetically.

"How many more of those bills have you got?" demanded Mr. Bascom, from the steam radiator, with characteristic directness.

"I put 'em all in this morning," said Mr. Crewe, "but I have thought since of two or three other conditions which might be benefited by legislation."

"Well," said Mr. Bascom, kindly, "if you have any more I was going to suggest that you distribute 'em round among the boys. That's the way I do, and most folks don't guess they're your bills. See?"

"What harm is there in that?" demanded Mr. Crewe. "I'm not ashamed of 'em."

"Brush was only lookin' at it from the point of view of gettin' 'em through," honest Mr. Botcher put in, in stentorian tones. "It doesn't do for a new member to be thought a hog about legislation."

Now the Honourable Jacob only meant this in the kindest manner, as we know, and to give inexperience a hint from well-intentioned experience. On the other hand, Mr. Crewe had a dignity and a position to uphold. He was a personality. People who went too far with him were apt to be rebuked by a certain glassy quality in his eye, and this now caused the Honourable Jake to draw back perceptibly.

"I see no reason why a public-spirited man should be open to such an imputation," said Mr. Crewe.

"Certainly not, certainly not," said Mr. Botcher, in

stentorian tones of apology, "I was only trying to give
you a little friendly advice, but I may have put it too
strong. Brush and I — I may as well be plain about it,
Mr. Crewe — have taken a liking to you. Couldn't help
it, sir, sitting next to you as we do. We take an interest
in your career, and we don't want you to make any mistakes. Ain't that about it, Brush?"

"That's about it," said Mr. Bascom.

Mr. Crewe was too big a man not to perceive and
appreciate the sterling philanthropy which lay beneath
the exteriors of his new friends, who scorned to flatter
him.

"I understand the spirit in which your advice is given,
gentlemen," he replied magnanimously, "and I appreciate
it. We are all working for the same things, and we all believe that they must be brought about in the same practical
way. For instance, we know as practical men that the
railroad pays a large tax in this State, and that property
must take a hand — a very considerable hand — in legislation. You gentlemen, as important factors in the Republican organization, are loyal to — er — that property, and
perhaps for wholly desirable reasons cannot bring forward
too many bills under your own names. Whereas I — "

At this point in Mr. Crewe's remarks the Honourable
Jacob Botcher was seized by an appalling coughing fit
which threatened to break his arm-chair, probably owing
to the fact that he had swallowed something which he
had in his mouth the wrong way. Mr. Bascom, assisted
by Mr. Crewe, pounded him relentlessly on the back.

"I read that article in the *Tribune* about you with
great interest," said Mr. Bascom, when Mr. Botcher's
coughing had subsided. "I had no idea you were so —
ahem — well equipped for a political career. But what
we wanted to speak to you about was this," he continued,
as Mr. Crewe showed signs of breaking in, "those committee appointments you desired."

"Yes," said Mr. Crewe, with some pardonable heat,
"the Speaker doesn't seem to know which side his bread's
buttered on."

"What I was going to say," proceeded Mr. Bascom, "was that General Doby is a pretty good fellow. Personally, I happen to know that the general feels very badly that he couldn't give you what you wanted. He took a shine to you that night you saw him."

"Yes," Mr. Botcher agreed, for he had quite recovered, "the general felt bad — feels bad, I should say. He perceived that you were a man of ability, sir — "

"And that was just the reason," said the Honourable Brush, "that he couldn't make you more useful just now."

"There's a good deal of jealousy, my dear sir, against young members of ability," said Mr. Botcher, in his most oracular and impressive tones. " The competition amongst those — er — who have served the party is very keen for the positions you desired. I personally happen to know that the general had you on the Judiciary and Appropriations, and that some of your — er — well-wishers persuaded him to take you off for your own good."

"It wouldn't do for the party leaders to make you too prominent all at once," said Mr. Bascom. " You are bound to take an active part in what passes here. The general said, 'At all events I will give Mr. Crewe one chairmanship by which he can make a name for himself suited to his talents,' and he insisted on giving you, in spite of some remonstrances from your friends, National Affairs. The general urged, rightly, that with your broad view and knowledge of national policy, it was his duty to put you in that place whatever people might say."

Mr. Crewe listened to these explanations in some surprise ; and being a rational man, had to confess that they were more or less reasonable.

"Scarcely any bills come before that committee," he objected.

"Ah," replied Mr. Bascom, "that is true. But the chairman of that committee is generally supposed to be in line for — er — national honours. It has not always happened in the past, because the men have not proved worthy. But the opportunity is always given to that chairman to make a speech upon national affairs which is listened to with the deepest interest."

" Is that so?" said Mr. Crewe. He wanted to be of service, as we know. He was a man of ideas, and the opening sentences of the speech were already occurring to him.

" Let's go upstairs and see the general now," suggested Mr. Botcher, smiling that such a happy thought should have occurred to him.

" Why, I guess we couldn't do any better," Mr. Bascom agreed.

" Well," said Mr. Crewe, " I'm willing to hear what he's got to say, anyway."

Taking advantage of this generous concession, Mr. Botcher hastily locked the door, and led the way up the stairway to number seventy-five. After a knock or two here, the door opened a crack, disclosing, instead of General Doby's cherubic countenance, a sallow face with an exceedingly pointed nose. The owner of these features, having only Mr. Botcher in his line of vision, made what was perhaps an unguarded remark.

" Hello, Jake, the general's in number nine — Manning sent for him about half an hour ago."

It was Mr. Botcher himself who almost closed the door on the gentleman's sharp nose, and took Mr. Crewe's arm confidingly.

" We'll go up to the desk and see Doby in the morning, — he's busy," said the Honourable Jake.

" What's the matter with seeing him now?" Mr. Crewe demanded. " I know Manning. He's the division superintendent, isn't he?"

Mr. Botcher and Mr. Bascom exchanged glances.

" Why, yes — " said Mr. Bascom, " yes, he is. He's a great friend of General Doby's, and their wives are great friends."

" Intimate friends, sir," said the Honourable Jake.

" Well," said Mr. Crewe, " we won't bother 'em but a moment."

It was he who led the way now, briskly, the Honourable Brush and the Honourable Jake pressing closely after him. It was Mr. Crewe who, without pausing to knock, pushed open the door of number nine, which was not quite closed; and it was Mr. Crewe who made the important discovery that the lugubrious division superintendent had a sense of humour. Mr. Manning was seated at a marble-topped table writing on a salmon-coloured card, in the act of pronouncing these words: —

"For Mr. Speaker and Mrs. Speaker and all the little Speakers, to New York and return."

Mr. Speaker Doby, standing before the marble-topped table with his hands in his pockets, heard the noise behind him and turned, and a mournful expression spread over his countenance.

"Don't mind me," said Mr. Crewe, waving a hand in the direction of the salmon-coloured tickets; "I hope you have a good time, General. When do you go?"

"Why," exclaimed the Speaker, "how are you, Mr. Crewe, how are you? It's only one of Manning's little jokes."

"That's all right, General," said Mr. Crewe, "I haven't been a director in railroads for nothing. I'm not as green as he thinks. Am I, Mr. Manning?"

"It never struck me that green was your colour, Mr. Crewe," answered the division superintendent, smiling a little as he tore the tickets into bits and put them in the waste-basket.

"Well," said Mr. Crewe, "you needn't have torn 'em up on my account. I travel on the pass which the Northeastern gives me as a legislator, and I'm thinking seriously of getting Mr. Flint to send me an annual, now that I'm in politics and have to cover the State."

"We thought you were a reformer, Mr. Crewe," the Honourable Brush Bascom remarked.

"I am a practical man," said Mr. Crewe, "a railroad man, a business man, and as such I try to see things as they are."

"Well," said General Doby, who by this time had regained his usual genial air of composure, "I'm glad you said that, Mr. Crewe. As these gentlemen will tell you, if I'd had my wish I'd have had you on every important committee in the House."

"Chairman of every important committee, General," corrected the Honourable Jacob Botcher.

"Yes, chairman of 'em," assented the general, after a glance at Mr. Crewe's countenance to see how this statement fared. "But the fact is, the boys are all jealous of you — on the quiet. I suppose you suspected something of the kind."

"I should have imagined there might be some little feeling," Mr. Crewe assented modestly.

"Exactly," cried the general, "and I had to combat that feeling when I insisted upon putting you at the head of National Affairs. It does not do for a new member, whatever his prominence in the financial world, to be pushed forward too quickly. And unless I am mighty mistaken, Mr. Crewe," he added, with his hand on the new member's shoulder, "you will make yourself felt without any boosting from me."

"I did not come here to remain idle, General," answered Mr. Crewe, considerably mollified.

"Certainly not," said the general, "and I say to some of those men, 'Keep your eye on the gentleman who is Chairman of National Affairs.'"

After a little more of this desultory and pleasant talk, during which recourse was had to the bathroom for several tall and thin glasses ranged on the shelf there, Mr. Crewe took his departure in a most equable frame of mind. And when the door was closed and locked behind him, Mr. Manning dipped his pen in the ink, once more produced from a drawer in the table the salmon-coloured tickets, and glanced again at the general with a smile.

"For Mr. Speaker and Mrs. Speaker and all the little Speakers, to New York and return."

CHAPTER XI

THE HOPPER

IT is certainly not the function of a romance to relate, with the exactness of a House journal, the proceedings of a Legislature. Somebody has likened the state-house to pioneer Kentucky, a dark and bloody ground over which the battles of selfish interests ebbed and flowed, — no place for an innocent and unselfish bystander like Mr. Crewe, who desired only to make of his State an Utopia; whose measures were for the public good — not his own. But if any politician were fatuous enough to believe that Humphrey Crewe was a man to introduce bills and calmly await their fate; a man who, like Senator Sanderson, only came down to the capital when he was notified by telegram, that politician was entirely mistaken.

No sooner had his bills been assigned to the careful and just consideration of the committees in charge of the Honourable Brush Bascom, Mr. Botcher, and others than Mr. Crewe desired of each a day for a hearing. Every member of the five hundred was provided with a copy; nay, nearly every member was personally appealed to to appear and speak for the measures. Foresters, road builders, and agriculturists (expenses paid) were sent for from other States; Mr. Ball and others came down from Leith, and gentlemen who for a generation had written letters to the newspapers turned up from other localities. In two cases the largest committee rooms proved too small for the gathering which was the result of Mr. Crewe's energy, and the legislative hall had to be lighted. The *State Tribune* gave column reports of the hearings, and little editorial pushes besides. And yet, when all was over, when it had been proved beyond a doubt that, if the State would consent to spend a little money, she would take the foremost rank among her forty odd sisters for progression, the bills were still under consideration by those hard-headed statesmen, Mr. Bascom and Mr. Botcher and their associates.

It could not be because these gentlemen did not know the arguments and see the necessity. Mr. Crewe had had them to dinner, and had spent so much time in their company presenting his case — to which they absolutely agreed — that they took to a forced seclusion. The member from Leith also wrote letters and telegrams, and sent long typewritten arguments and documents to Mr. Flint. Mr. Crewe, although far from discouraged, began to think there was something mysterious about all this seemingly unnecessary deliberation.

Mr. Crewe, though of great discernment, was only mortal, and while he was fighting his battle single-handed, how was he to know that the gods above him were taking sides and preparing for conflict? The gods do not give out their declarations of war for publication to the Associated Press; and old Tom Gaylord, who may be likened to Mars, had no intention of sending Jupiter notice until he got his cohorts into line. The strife, because it was to be internecine, was the more terrible. Hitherto the Gaylord Lumber Company, like the Winona Manufacturing Company of Newcastle (the mills of which extended for miles along the Tyne), had been a faithful ally of the Empire; and, on occasions when it was needed, had borrowed the Imperial army to obtain grants, extensions, and franchises.

The fact is that old Tom Gaylord, in the autumn previous, had quarrelled with Mr. Flint about lumber rates, which had been steadily rising. Mr. Flint had been polite, but firm; and old Tom, who, with all his tremendous properties, could ship by no other railroad than the Northeastern, had left the New York office in a black rage. A more innocent citizen than old Tom would have put his case (which was without doubt a strong one) before the Railroad Commission of the State, but old Tom knew well enough that the Railroad Commission was in reality an economy board of the Northeastern system, as much under Mr. Flint's orders as the conductors and brakemen. Old Tom, in consulting the map, conceived an unheard-of effrontery, a high treason which took away the breath of his secretary and treasurer when it was pointed out to him. The plan contemplated a line of railroad from the heart of the lumber regions down the south side of the valley of the Pingsquit to Kingston, where the lumber could take to the sea. In short, it was a pernicious revival of an obsolete state of affairs, *competition*, and if persisted in, involved nothing less than a fight to a finish with the army, the lobby of the Northeastern. Other favoured beings stood aghast when they heard of it, and hastened to old Tom with timely counsel; but he had reached a frame of mind which they knew well. He would listen to no reason, and maintained stoutly that there were other lawyers in the world as able in political sagacity and lobby tactics as Hilary Vane; the Honourable Galusha Hammer, for instance, an old and independent and wary war-horse who had more than once wrung compromises out of the Honourable Hilary. The Honourable Galusha Hammer was sent for, and was now industriously, if quietly and unobtrusively, at work. The Honourable Hilary was likewise at work, equally quietly and unobtrusively. When the powers fall out, they do not open up at once with long-distance artillery. There is always a chance of a friendly settlement. The news was worth a good deal, for instance, to Mr. Peter Pardriff (brother of Paul, of Ripton), who refrained, with praiseworthy self-control, from publishing it in the *State Tribune*, although the temptation to do so must have been great. And most of the senatorial twenty saw the trouble coming and braced their backs against it, but in silence. The capital had seen no such war as this since the days of Jethro Bass.

In the meantime Mr. Crewe, blissfully ignorant of this impending conflict, was preparing a speech on national affairs and national issues which was to startle an unsuspecting State. Mrs. Pomfret, who had received many clippings and pamphlets, had written him weekly letters

of a nature spurring to his ambition, which incidentally
contained many references to Alice's interest in his career.
And Mr. Crewe's mind, when not intent upon affairs of
State, sometimes reverted pleasantly to thoughts of Victoria
Flint; it occurred to him that the Duncan house was
large enough for entertaining, and that he might invite
Mrs. Pomfret to bring Victoria and the inevitable Alice
to hear his oration, for which Mr. Speaker Doby had set
a day.

In his desire to give other people pleasure, Mr. Crewe
took the trouble to notify a great many of his friends and
acquaintances as to the day of his speech, in case they
might wish to travel to the State capital and hear him
deliver it. Having unexpectedly received in the mail a
cheque from Austen Vane in settlement of the case of the
injured horse, Austen was likewise invited.

Austen smiled when he opened the letter, and with its
businesslike contents there seemed to be wafted from it
the perfume and suppliance of a September day in the
Vale of the Blue. From the window of his back office,
looking across the railroad tracks, he could see Sawanec,
pale in her winter garb against a pale winter sky, and
there arose in him the old restless desire for the woods
and fields which at times was almost irresistible. His
thoughts at length descending from the azure above Sawanec, his eyes fell again on Mr. Crewe's typewritten
words : " It may be of interest to you that I am to deliver, on the 15th instant, and as the Chairman of the
House Committee on National Affairs, a speech upon
national policies which is the result of much thought,
and which touches upon such material needs of our State
as can be supplied by the Federal Government."

Austen had a brief fancy, whimsical as it was, of going
to hear him. Mr. Crewe, as a type absolutely new to
him, interested him. He had followed the unusual and
somewhat surprising career of the gentleman from Leith
with some care, even to the extent of reading of Mr.
Crewe's activities in the *State Tribunes* which had been
sent him. Were such qualifications as Mr. Crewe pos-

sessed, he wondered, of a kind to sweep their possessor into high office? Were industry, persistency, and a capacity for taking advantage of a fair wind sufficient?

Since his return from Pepper County, Austen Vane had never been to the State capital during a session, although it was common for young lawyers to have cases before the Legislature. It would have been difficult to say why he did not take these cases, aside from the fact that they were not very remunerative. On occasions gentlemen from different parts of the State, and some from outside of it who had certain favours to ask at the hands of the lawmaking body, had visited his back office and closed the door after them, and in the course of the conversation had referred to the relationship of the young lawyer to Hilary Vane. At such times Austen would freely acknowledge the debt of gratitude he owed his father for being in the world — and refer them politely to Mr. Hilary Vane himself. In most cases they had followed his advice, wondering not a little at this isolated example of quixotism.

During the sessions, except for a day or two at week ends which were often occupied with conferences, the Honourable Hilary's office was deserted; or rather, as we have seen, his headquarters were removed to room Number Seven in the Pelican Hotel at the capital. Austen got many of the lay clients who came to see his father at such times; and — without giving an exaggerated idea of his income — it might be said that he was beginning to have what may be called a snug practice for a lawyer of his experience. In other words, according to Mr. Tooting, who took an intense interest in the matter, "not wearing the collar" had been more of a financial success for Austen than that gentleman had imagined. There proved to be many clients to whom the fact that young Mr. Vane did not carry a "retainer pass" actually appealed. These clients paid their bills, but they were neither large nor influential, as a rule, with the notable exception of the Gaylord Lumber Company, where the matters for trial were not large. If young Tom Gaylord had had his way,

M

Austen would have been the chief counsel for the corporation.

To tell the truth, Austen Vane had a secret aversion to going to the capital during a session, a feeling that such a visit would cause him unhappiness. In spite of his efforts, and indeed in spite of Hilary's, Austen and his father had grown steadily apart. They met in the office hallway, in the house in Hanover Street when Hilary came home to sleep, and the elder Mr. Vane was not a man to thrive on small talk. His world was the battle-field from which he directed the forces of the great corporation which he served, and the cherished vision of a son in whom he could confide his plans, upon whose aid and counsel he could lean, was gone forever. Hilary Vane had troublesome half-hours, but on the whole he had reached the conclusion that this son, like Sarah Austen, was one of those inexplicable products in which an extravagant and inscrutable nature sometimes indulged. On the rare evenings when the two were at home together, the Honourable Hilary sat under one side of the lamp with a pile of documents and newspapers, and Austen under the other with a book from the circulating library. No public questions could be broached upon which they were not as far apart as the poles, and the Honourable Hilary put literature in the same category as embroidery. Euphrasia, when she paused in her bodily activity to darn their stockings, used to glance at them covertly from time to time, and many a silent tear of which they knew nothing fell on her needle.

On the subject of his protracted weekly absences at the State capital, the Honourable Hilary was as uncommunicative as he would have been had he retired for those periods to a bar-room. He often grunted and cleared his throat and glanced at his son when their talk bordered upon these absences; and he was even conscious of an extreme irritation against himself as well as Austen because of the instinct that bade him keep silent. He told himself fiercely that he had nothing to be ashamed of, nor would he have acknowledged that it was a kind of shame that

bade him refrain even from circumstantial accounts of
what went on in room Number Seven of the Pelican. He
had an idea that Austen knew and silently condemned; and
how extremely maddening was this feeling to the Honourable Hilary may well be imagined. All his life long he
had deemed himself morally invulnerable, and now to be
judged and ethically found wanting by the son of Sarah
Austen was, at times, almost insupportable. Were the
standards of a long life to be suddenly reversed by a
prodigal son?

To get back to Austen. On St. Valentine's Day of
that year when, to tell the truth, he was seated in his
office scribbling certain descriptions of nature suggested
by the valentines in Mr. Hayman's stationery store, the
postman brought in a letter from young Tom Gaylord.
Austen laughed as he read it. "The Honourable Galusha
Hammer is well named," young Tom wrote, "but the
conviction has been gaining ground with me that a hammer is about as much use as a shovel would be at the
present time. It is not the proper instrument. But the
old man" (it was thus young Tom was wont to designate
his parent) "is pig-headed when he gets to fighting, and
won't listen to reason. If he believes he can lick the
Northeastern with a Hammer, he is durned badly mistaken,
and I told him so. I have been giving him sage advice
in little drops — after meals. I tell him there is only one
man in the State who has sense enough even to shake the
Northeastern, and that's you. He thinks this a pretty
good joke. Of course I realize where your old man is
planted, and that you might have some natural delicacy
and wish to refrain from giving him a jar. But come
down for an hour and let me talk to you, anyway. The
new statesman from Leith is cutting a wide swath. Not
a day passes but his voice is heard roaring in the Forum;
he has visited all the State institutions, dined and wined
the governor and his staff and all the ex-governors he can
lay his hands on, and he has that hard-headed and caustic journalist, Mr. Peter Pardriff, of the *State Tribune*,
hypnotized. He has some swells up at his house to hear

his speech on national affairs, among them old Flint's daughter, who is a ripper to look at, although I never got nearer to her than across the street. As you may guess, it is something of a card for Crewe to have Flint's daughter here."

Austen sat for a long time after reading this letter, idly watching the snow-clouds gathering around Sawanec. Then he tore up the paper, on which he had been scribbling, into very small bits, consulted a time-table, and at noon, in a tumult of feelings, he found himself in a back seat of the express, bound for the capital.

Arriving at the station, amidst a hurry and bustle of legislators and politicians coming and going, many of whom nodded to him, he stood for a minute in the whirling snow reflecting. Now that he was here, where was he to stay? The idea of spending the night at the Pelican was repellent to him, and he was hesitating between two more modest hostelries when he was hailed by a giant with a flowing white beard, a weather-beaten face, and a clear eye that shone with a steady and kindly light. It was James Redbrook, the member from Mercer.

"Why, how be you, Austen?" he cried, extending a welcome hand; and, when Austen had told him his dilemma: "Come right along up to my lodgings. I live at the Widow Peasley's, and there's a vacant room next to mine."

Austen accepted gratefully, and as they trudged through the storm up the hill, he inquired how legislative matters were progressing. Whereupon Mr. Redbrook unburdened himself.

"Say, I just warmed up all over when I see you, Austen. I'm so glad to run across an honest man. We ain't forgot in Mercer what you did for Zeb Meader, and how you went against your interests. And I guess it ain't done you any harm in the State. As many as thirty or forty members have spoke to me about it. And down here I've got so I just can't hold in any more."

"Is it as bad as that, Mr. Redbrook?" asked Austen, with a serious glance at the farmer's face.

"It's so bad I don't know how to begin," said the member from Mercer, and paused suddenly. "But I don't want to hurt your feelings, Austen, seeing your father is — where he is."

"Go on," said Austen, "I understand."

"Well," said Mr. Redbrook, "it just makes me tremble as an American citizen. The railrud sends them slick cusses down here that sit in the front seats who know all this here parliamentary law and the tricks of the trade, and every time any of us gets up to speak our honest minds, they have us ruled out of order or get the thing laid on the table until some Friday morning when there ain't nobody here, and send it along up to the Senate. They made that fat feller, Doby, Speaker, and he's stuffed all the important committees so that you can't get an honest measure considered. You can talk to the committees all you've a mind to, and they'll just listen and never do anything. There's five hundred in the House, and it ain't any more of a Legislature than a camp-meetin' is. What do you suppose they done last Friday morning, when there wahn't but twenty men at the session? We had an anti-pass law, and all these fellers were breakin' it. It forbid anybody riding on a pass except railroad presidents, directors, express messengers, and persons in misfortune, and they stuck in these words, '*and others to whom passes have been granted by the proper officers.*' Ain't that a disgrace to the State? And those twenty senators passed it before we got back on Tuesday. You can't get a bill through that Legislature unless you go up to the Pelican and get permission of Hilary —"

Here Mr. Redbrook stopped abruptly, and glanced contritely at his companion.

"I didn't mean to get goin' so," he said, "but sometimes I wish this American government'd never been started."

"I often feel that way myself, Mr. Redbrook," said Austen.

"I knowed you did. I guess I can tell an honest man when I see one. It's treason to say anything against this

Northeastern louder than a whisper. They want an electric railrud bad up in Greenacre, and when some of us spoke for it and tried to get the committee to report it, those cheap fellers from Newcastle started such a catcall we had to set down."

By this time they were at the Widow Peasley's, stamping the snow from off their boots.

"How general is this sentiment?" Austen asked, after he had set down his bag in the room he was to occupy.

"Why," said Mr. Redbrook, with conviction, "there's enough feel as I do to turn that House upside down — if we only had a leader. If you was only in there, Austen."

"I'm afraid I shouldn't be of much use," Austen answered. "They'd have given me a back seat, too."

The Widow Peasley's was a frame and gabled house of Revolutionary days with a little terrace in front of it and a retaining wall built up from the sidewalk. Austen, on the steps, stood gazing across at a square mansion with a wide cornice, half hidden by elms and maples and pines. It was set far back from the street, and a driveway entered the picket-fence and swept a wide semicircle to the front door and back again. Before the door was a sleigh of a pattern new to him, with a seat high above the backs of two long-bodied, deep-chested horses, their heads held with difficulty by a little footman with his arms above him. At that moment two figures in furs emerged from the house. The young woman gathered up the reins and leaped lightly to the box, the man followed; the little groom touched his fur helmet and scrambled aboard as the horses sprang forward to the music of the softest of bells. The sleigh swept around the curve, avoided by a clever turn a snow-pile at the entrance, the young woman raised her eyes from the horses, stared at Austen, and bowed. As for Austen, he grew warm as he took off his hat, and he realized that his hand was actually trembling. The sleigh flew on up the hill, but she turned once more to look behind her, and he still had his hat in his hand, the snowflakes falling on his bared head. Then he was aware that James Redbrook was gazing at him curiously.

"That's Flint's daughter, ain't it?" inquired the member from Mercer. "Didn't callate you'd know *her*."

Austen flushed. He felt exceedingly foolish, but an answer came to him.

"I met her in the hospital. She used to go there to see Zeb Meader."

"That's so," said Mr. Redbrook; "Zeb told me about it, and she used to come to Mercer to see him after he got out. She ain't much like the old man, I callate."

"I don't think she is," said Austen.

"I don't know what she's stayin' with that feller Crewe for," the farmer remarked; "of all the etarnal darn idiots — why, Brush Bascom and that Botcher and the rest of 'em are trailin' him along and usin' him for the best thing that ever came down here. He sets up to be a practical man, and don't know as much as some of us hayseeds in the back seats. Where be you goin'?"

"I was going to the Pelican."

"Well, I've got a committee meetin' of Agriculture," said Mr. Redbrook. "Could you be up here at Mis' Peasley's about eight to-night?"

"Why, yes," Austen replied, "if you want to see me."

"I do want to see you," said Mr. Redbrook, significantly, and waved a farewell.

Austen took his way slowly across the state-house park, threading among the groups between the snowbanks towards the wide façade of the Pelican Hotel. Presently he paused, and then with a sudden determination crossed the park diagonally into Main Street, walking rapidly southward and scrutinizing the buildings on either side until at length these began to grow wide apart, and he spied a florist's sign with a greenhouse behind it. He halted again, irresolutely, in front of it, flung open the door, and entered a boxlike office filled with the heated scents of flowers. A little man eyed him with an obsequious interest which he must have accorded to other young men on similar errands. Austen may be spared a repetition of the very painful conversation that ensued; suffice it to say that, after mature deliberation, violets were chosen. He had a notion—not analyzed—that she would prefer violets to roses. The information that the flowers were for the daughter of the president of the Northeastern Railroads caused a visible quickening of the little florist's regard, an attitude which aroused a corresponding disgust and depression in Austen.

"Oh, yes," said the florist, "she's up at Crewe's." He glanced at Austen apologetically. "Excuse me," he said, "I ought to know you. Have you a card?"

"No," said Austen, with emphasis.

"And what name, please?"

"No name," said the donor, now heartily repenting of his rashness, and slamming the glass door in a manner that made the panes rattle behind him.

As he stood hesitating on the curb of the crossing, he began to wish that he had not left Ripton.

"Hello, Austen," said a voice, which he recognized as the Honourable Brush Bascom's, "didn't know you ever came down here in session time."

"What are you doing down here, Brush?" Austen asked.

Mr. Bascom grinned in appreciation of this pleasantry.

"I came for my health," he said; "I prefer it to Florida."

"I've heard that it agrees with some people," said Austen.

Mr. Bascom grinned again.

"Just arrived?" he inquired.

"Just," said Austen.

"I thought you'd get here sooner or later," said Mr. Bascom. "Some folks try stayin' away, but it ain't much use. You'll find the Honourable Hilary doing business at the same old stand, next to the governor, in Number Seven up there." And Mr. Bascom pointed to the well-known window on the second floor.

"Thanks, Brush," said Austen, indifferently. "To tell the truth, I came down to hear that promising protégé of yours speak on national affairs. I understand you're pushing his bills along."

Mr. Bascom, with great deliberation, shut one of his little eyes.

"So long," he said, "come and see me when you get time."

Austen went slowly down the street and entered the smoke-clouded lobby of the Pelican. He was a man to draw attention, and he was stared at by many politicians there and spoken to by some before he reached the stairs. Mounting, he found the door with the numeral 7, and knocked. The medley of voices within ceased; there were sounds of rattling papers, and of closing of folding doors. The key turned in the lock, and State Senator Nathaniel Billings appeared in the doorway, with a look of polite inquiry on his convivial face. This expression, when he saw Austen, changed to something like consternation.

"Why, hello, hello," said the senator. "Come in, come in. The Honourable Hilary's here. When'd you come down?"

"Hello, Nat," said Austen, and went in.

The Honourable Hilary sat in his usual arm-chair; Mr. Botcher severely strained the tensile strength of the bedsprings; Mr. Hamilton Tooting stood before the still waving portières in front of the folding doors; and Mr. Manning, the division superintendent, sat pensively, with his pen in his mouth, before the marble-topped table from which everything had been removed but a Bible. Two gentlemen, whom Austen recognized as colleagues of Mr. Billings in the State Senate, stood together in a window, pointing out things of interest in the street. Austen walked up to his father and laid a hand on his shoulder.

"How are you, Judge?" he said. "I only came in to pay my respects. I hope I have not disturbed any —entertainment going on here," he added, glancing in turn at the thoughtful occupants of the room, and then at the curtains which hid the folding doors to the apartment of his Excellency.

"Why, no," answered the Honourable Hilary, his customary grunt being the only indication of surprise on his part; "didn't know you were coming down."

"I didn't know it myself until this morning," said Austen.

" Legislative case, I suppose," remarked the Honourable Jacob Botcher, in his deep voice.

" No, merely a pleasure trip, Mr. Botcher."

The Honourable Jacob rubbed his throat, the two State senators in the window giggled, and Mr. Hamilton Tooting laughed.

" I thought you took to the mountains in such cases, sir," said Mr. Botcher.

" I came for intellectual pleasure this time," said Austen. " I understand that Mr. Crewe is to deliver an epoch-making speech on the national situation to-morrow."

This was too much even for the gravity of Mr. Manning; Mr. Tooting and Mr. Billings and his two colleagues roared, though the Honourable Jacob's laugh was not so spontaneous.

" Aust," said Mr. Tooting, admiringly, " you're all right."

" Well, Judge," said Austen, patting his father's shoulder again, " I'm glad to see you so comfortably fixed. Good-by, and give my regards to the governor. I'm sorry to have missed him," he added, glancing at the portières that hid the folding doors.

" Are you stopping here?" asked the Honourable Hilary.

" No, I met Mr. Redbrook of Mercer, and he took me up to his lodgings. If I can do anything for you, a message will reach me there."

" Humph," said the Honourable Hilary, while the others exchanged significant glances.

Austen had not gone half the length of the hall when he was overtaken by Mr. Tooting.

" Say, Aust, what's up between you and Redbrook?" he asked.

" Nothing. Why?" Austen asked, stopping abruptly.

" Well, I suppose you know there's an anti-railroad feeling growing in that House, and that Redbrook has more influence with the farmers than any other man."

" I didn't know anything about Mr. Redbrook's influence," said Austen.

Mr. Tooting looked unconvinced.

" Say, Aust, if anything's in the wind, I wish you'd let me know.   I'll keep it quiet."

" I think I shall be safe in promising that, Ham," said Austen.   " When there's anything in the wind, you generally find it out first."

" There's trouble coming for the railroad," said Mr. Tooting.   " I can see that.   And I guess you saw it before I did."

"They say a ship's about to sink when the rats begin to leave it," said Austen.

Although Austen spoke smilingly, Mr. Tooting looked pained.

" There's no chance for young men in that system," he said.

" Young men write the noble parts of the governor's inaugurals," said Austen.

" Yes," said Mr. Tooting, bitterly, " but you never get to be governor and read 'em.   You've got to be a 'come on' with thirty thousand dollars to be a Northeastern governor and live next door to the Honourable Hilary in the Pelican.   Well, so long, Aust.   If anything's up, give me the tip, that's all I ask."

Reflecting on the singular character of Mr. Tooting, Austen sought the Gaylords' headquarters, and found them at the furthermost end of the building from the Railroad Room.   The door was opened by young Tom himself, whose face became wreathed in smiles when he saw who the visitor was.

" It's Austen! " he cried.   "I thought you'd come down when you got that appeal of mine."

Austen did not admit the self-sacrifice as he shook Tom's hand; but remembered, singularly enough, the closing sentences of Tom's letter — which had nothing whatever to do with the Gaylord bill.

At this moment a commotion arose within the room, and a high, tremulous, but singularly fierce and compelling voice was heard crying out : —

" Get out !   Get out, d—n you, all of you, and don't

come back until you've got some notion of what you're a-goin' to do. Get out, I say!"

These last words were pronounced with such extraordinary vigour that four gentlemen seemed to be physically impelled from the room. Three of them Austen recognized as dismissed and disgruntled soldiers from the lobby army of the Northeastern; the fourth was the Honourable Galusha Hammer, whose mode of progress might be described as "stalking," and whose lips were forming the word "intolerable." In the corner old Tom himself could be seen, a wizened figure of wrath.

"Who's that?" he demanded of his son, "another d—d fool?"

"No," replied young Tom, "it's Austen Vane."

"What's he doin' here?" old Tom demanded, with a profane qualification as to the region. But young Tom seemed to be the only being capable of serenity amongst the flames that played around him.

"I sent for him because he's got more sense than Galusha and all the rest of 'em put together," he said.

"I guess that's so," old Tom agreed unexpectedly, "but it ain't sayin' much. Bring him in — bring him in, and lock the door."

In obedience to these summons, and a pull from young Tom, Austen entered and sat down.

"You've read the Pingsquit bill?" old Tom demanded.

"Yes," said Austen.

"Just because you won a suit against the Northeastern, and nearly killed a man out West, Tom seems to think you can do anything. He wouldn't give me any peace until I let him send for you," Mr. Gaylord remarked testily. "Now you're down here, what have you got to propose?"

"I didn't come here to propose anything, Mr. Gaylord," said Austen.

"What!" cried Mr. Gaylord, with one of his customary and forceful exclamations. "What'd you come down for?"

"I've been asking myself that question ever since I came, Mr. Gaylord," said Austen, "and I haven't yet arrived at any conclusion."

Young Tom looked at his friend and laughed, and Mr. Gaylord, who at first gave every indication of being about to explode with anger, suddenly emitted a dry cackle.

"You ain't a d—n fool, anyway," he declared.

"I'm beginning to think I am," said Austen.

"Then you've got sense enough to know it," retorted old Tom. "Most of 'em haven't." And his glance, as it fell upon the younger man, was almost approving. Young Tom's was distinctly so.

"I told you Austen was the only lawyer who'd talk common sense to you," he said.

"I haven't heard much of it yet," said old Tom.

"Perhaps I ought to tell you, Mr. Gaylord," said Austen, smiling a little, "that I didn't come down in any legal capacity. That's only one of Tom's jokes."

"Then what in h—l did you bring him in here for?" demanded old Tom of his son.

"Just for a quiet little powwow," said young Tom, "to make you laugh. He's made you laugh before."

"I don't want to laugh," said old Tom, pettishly. Nevertheless, he seemed to be visibly cooling. "If you ain't in here to make money," he added to Austen, "I don't care how long you stay."

"Say, Austen," said young Tom, "do you remember the time we covered the old man with shavings at the mills in Avalon, and how he chased us with a two-by-four scantling?"

"I'd made pulp out'n you if I'd got you," remarked Mr. Gaylord, with a reminiscent chuckle that was almost pleasant. "But you were always a goldurned smart boy, Austen, and you've done well with them little suits." He gazed at Austen a moment with his small, filmy-blue eye. "I don't know but what you might take hold here and make it hot for those d—d rascals in the Northeastern, after all. You couldn't botch it worse'n Hammer has, and you might do some good. I said I'd make 'em dance, and by G—d, I'll do it, if I have to pay that feller Levering in New York, and it takes the rest of my life. Look the situation over, and come back to-morrow and tell me what you think of it."

"I can tell you what I think of it now, Mr. Gaylord," said Austen.

"What's that?" old Tom demanded sharply.

"That you'll never get the bill passed, this session or next, by lobbying."

For the moment the elder Mr. Gaylord was speechless, but young Tom Gaylord clapped his hand heartily on his friend's shoulder.

"That's the reason I wanted to get you down here, Austen," he cried; "that's what I've been telling the old man all along — perhaps he'll believe you."

"Then you won't take hold?" said Mr. Gaylord, his voice trembling on the edge of another spasm. "You refuse business?"

"I refuse that kind of business, Mr. Gaylord," Austen answered quietly, though there was a certain note in his voice that young Tom knew well, and which actually averted the imminent explosion from Mr. Gaylord, whose eyes glared and watered. "But aside from that, you must know that the Republican party leaders in this State are the heads of the lobby of the Northeastern Railroads."

"I guess I know about Number Seven as well as you do," old Tom interjected.

Austen's eye flashed.

"Now hold on, father," said young Tom, "that's no way to talk to Austen."

"Knowing Number Seven," Austen continued, "you probably realize that the political and business future of nearly every one of the twenty State senators depends upon the favour of the Northeastern Railroads."

"I know that the d——d fools won't look at money," said Mr. Gaylord; "Hammer's tried 'em."

"I told you that before you started in," young Tom remarked, "but when you get mad, you won't listen to sense. And then there's the Honourable Asa Gray, who wants to represent the Northeastern some day in the United States Senate."

"The bill ought to pass," shrieked old Tom; "it's a d—d outrage. There's no reason why I shouldn't be allowed to build a railroad if I've got the money to do it. What in blazes are we comin' to in this country if we can't git competition? If Flint stops that bill, I'll buy a newspaper and go to the people with the issue and throw his d—d monopoly into bankruptcy."

"It's all very well to talk about competition and monopolies and lobbies," said young Tom, "but how about the Gaylord Lumber Company? How about the times you used the lobby, with Flint's permission? This kind of virtuous talk is beautiful to listen to when you and Flint get into a row."

At this remark of his son's, the intermittent geyser of old Tom's wrath spouted up again with scalding steam, and in a manner utterly impossible to reproduce upon paper. Young Tom waited patiently for the exhibition to cease, which it did at length in a coughing fit of sheer exhaustion that left his father speechless, if not expressionless, pointing a lean and trembling finger in the direction of a valise on the floor.

"You'll go off in a spell of that kind some day," said young Tom, opening the valise and extracting a bottle. Uncorking it, he pressed it to his father's lips, and with his own pocket-handkerchief (old Tom not possessing such an article) wiped the perspiration from Mr. Gaylord's brow and the drops from his shabby black coat. "There's no use gettin' mad at Austen. He's dead right —you can't lobby this thing through, and you knew it before you started. If you hadn't lost your temper, you wouldn't have tried."

"We'll see, by G—d, we'll see," said the indomitable old Tom, when he got his breath. "You young men think you know a sight, but you haven't got the stuff in you we old fellers have. Where would I be if it wasn't for fightin'? You mark my words, before this session's ended I'll scare h—l out of Flint —see if I don't."

Young Tom winked at his friend.

"Let's go down to supper," he said.

The dining room of the Pelican Hotel during a midweek of a busy session was a scene of bustle and confusion not likely to be forgotten. Every seat was taken, and gentlemen waited their turn in the marble-flagged rotunda who had not the honour of being known to Mr. Giles, the head waiter. If Mr. Hamilton Tooting were present, and recognized you, he would take great pleasure in pointing out the celebrities, and especially that table over which the Honourable Hilary Vane presided, with the pretty, red-cheeked waitress hovering around it. At the Honourable Hilary's right hand was the division superintendent, and at his left, Mr. Speaker Doby — a most convenient and congenial arrangement ; farther down the board were State Senator Nat Billings, Mr. Ridout (when he did not sup at home), the Honourables Brush Bascom and Elisha Jane, and the Honourable Jacob Botcher made a proper ballast for the foot. This table was known as the Railroad Table, and it was very difficult, at any distance away from it, to hear what was said, except when the Honourable Jacob Botcher made a joke. Next in importance and situation was the Governor's Table — now occupied by the Honourable Asa Gray. Mr. Tooting's description would not have stopped here.

Sensations are common in the Pelican Hotel, but when Austen Vane walked in that evening between the Gaylords, father and son, many a hungry guest laid down his knife and fork and stared. Was the younger Vane (known to be anti-railroad) to take up the Gaylords' war against his own father? All the indications were that way, and a rumour flew from table to table — leaping space, as rumours will — that the Gaylords had sent to Ripton for Austen. There was but one table in the room the occupants of which appeared not to take any interest in the event, or even to grasp that an event had occurred. The Railroad Table was oblivious.

After supper Mr. Tooting found Austen in the rotunda, and drew him mysteriously aside.

"Say, Aust, the Honourable Hilary wants to see you to-night," he whispered.

"Did he send you with the message?" Austen demanded.

"That's right," said Mr. Tooting. "I guess you know what's up."

Austen did not answer. At the foot of the stairway was the tall form of Hilary Vane himself, and Austen crossed the rotunda.

"Do you want to see me, Judge?" he asked.

The Honourable Hilary faced about quickly.

"Yes, if you've got any spare time."

"I'll go to your room at half-past nine to-night, if that's convenient."

"All right," said the Honourable Hilary, starting up the stairs.

Austen turned, and found Mr. Hamilton Tooting at his elbow.

N

CHAPTER XII

MR. REDBROOK'S PARTY

THE storm was over, and the bare trees, when the moon shone between the hurrying clouds, cast lacelike shadows on the white velvet surface of the snow as Austen forged his way up the hill to the Widow Peasley's in keeping with his promise to Mr. Redbrook. Across the street he paused outside the picket-fence to gaze at the yellow bars of light between the slats of the windows of the Duncan house. It was hard to realize that she was there, within a stone's throw of where he was to sleep; but the strange, half-startled expression in her eyes that afternoon and the smile — which had in it a curious quality he could not analyze — were so vivid in his consciousness as to give him pain. The incident, as he stood there ankle-deep in the snow, seemed to him another inexplicable and uselessly cruel caprice of fate.

As he pictured her in the dining room behind Mr. Crewe's silver and cut glass and flowers, it was undoubtedly natural that he should wonder whether she were thinking of him in the Widow Peasley's lamp-lit cottage, and he smiled at the contrast. After all, it was the contrast between his life and hers. As an American of good antecedents and education, with a Western experience thrown in, social gulfs, although awkward, might be crossed in spite of opposition from ladies like the Rose of Sharon, — who had crossed them. Nevertheless, the life which Victoria led seemingly accentuated — to a man standing behind a picket-fence in the snow — the voids between.

A stamping of feet in the Widow Peasley's vestibule

awoke in him that sense of the ridiculous which was never far from the surface, and he made his way thither in mingled amusement and pain. What happened there is of interest, but may be briefly chronicled. Austen was surprised, on entering, to find Mrs. Peasley's parlour filled with men ; and a single glance at their faces in the lamplight assured him that they were of a type which he understood — countrymen of that rugged New England stock to which he himself belonged, whose sons for generations had made lawyers and statesmen and soldiers for the State and nation. Some were talking in low voices, and others sat silent on the chairs and sofa, not awkwardly or uncomfortably, but with a characteristic self-possession and repose. Mr. Redbrook, towering in front of the stove, came forward.

"Here you be," he said, taking Austen's hand warmly and a little ceremoniously; "I asked 'em here to meet ye."

"To meet me ! " Austen repeated.

"Wanted they should know you," said Mr. Redbrook. "They've all heard of you and what you did for Zeb."

Austen flushed. He was aware that he was undergoing a cool and critical examination by those present, and that they were men who used all their faculties in making up their minds.

"I'm very glad to meet any friends of yours, Mr. Redbrook," he said. "What I did for Meader isn't worth mentioning. It was an absolutely simple case."

" 'Twahn't so much what ye did as *how ye did* it," said Mr. Redbrook. "It's kind of rare in these days," he added, with the manner of commenting to himself on the circumstance, "to find a young lawyer with brains that won't sell 'em to the railrud. That's what appeals to me, and to some other folks I know — especially when we take into account the situation you was in and the chances you had."

Austen's silence under this compliment seemed to create an indefinable though favourable impression, and the member from Mercer permitted himself to smile.

"These men are all friends of mine, and members of

the House," he said, "and there's more would have come if they'd had a longer notice. Allow me to make you acquainted with Mr. Widgeon of Hull."

"We kind of wanted to look you over," said Mr. Widgeon, suiting the action to the word. "That's natural, ain't it?"

"Kind of size you up," added Mr. Jarley of Wye, raising his eyes. "Callate you're *sizable* enough."

"Wish you was in the House," remarked Mr. Adams of Barrett. "None of us is much on talk, but if we had you, I guess we could lay things wide open."

"If you was thar, and give it to 'em as hot as you did when you was talkin' for Zeb, them skunks in the front seats wouldn't know whether they was afoot or hoss-back," declared Mr. Williams of Devon, a town adjoining Mercer.

"I used to think railrud gov'ment wahn't so bad until I come to the House this time," remarked a stocky member from Oxford; "it's sheer waste of money for the State to pay a Legislature. They might as well run things from the New York office — you know that."

"*We* might as well wear so many Northeastern uniforms with brass buttons," a sinewy hill farmer from Lee put in. He had a lean face that did not move a muscle, but a humorous gray eye that twinkled.

In the meantime Mr. Redbrook looked on with an expression of approval which was (to Austen) distinctly pleasant, but more or less mystifying.

"I guess you ain't disappointed 'em much," he declared, when the round was ended; "most of 'em knew me well enough to understand that cattle and live stock in general, includin' humans, is about as I represent 'em to be."

"We have some confidence in your judgment, Brother Redbrook," answered Mr. Terry of Lee, "and now we've looked over the goods, it ain't set back any, I callate."

This observation, which seemed to meet with a general assent, was to Austen more mystifying than ever. He laughed.

"Gentlemen," he said, "I feel as though some expression of thanks were due you for this kind and most unexpected reception." Here a sudden seriousness came into his eyes which served, somehow, only to enhance his charm of manner, and a certain determined ring into his voice. "You have all referred to a condition of affairs," he added, "about which I have thought a great deal, and which I deplore as deeply as you do. There is no doubt that the Northeastern Railroads have seized the government of this State for three main reasons : to throttle competition; to control our railroad commission in order that we may not get the service and safety to which we are entitled, — so increasing dividends ; and to make and maintain laws which enable them to bribe with passes, to pay less taxes than they should, and to manipulate political machinery."

"That's right," said Mr. Jarley of Wye, with a decided emphasis.

"That's the kind of talk I like to hear," exclaimed Mr. Terry.

"And nobody's had the gumption to fight 'em," said Mr. Widgeon.

"It looks," said Austen, "as though it must come to a fight in the end. I do not think they will listen to reason. I mean," he added, with a flash of humour, "that they will listen to it, but not act upon it. Gentlemen, I regret to have to say, for obvious reasons, something which you all know, that my father is at the head of the Northeastern machine, which is the Republican party organization."

There was a silence.

"You went again' him, and we honour you for it, Austen," said Mr. Redbrook, at length.

"I want to say," Austen continued, "that I have tried to look at things as Mr. Vane sees them, and that I have a good deal of sympathy for his point of view. Conditions as they exist are the result of an evolution for which no one man is responsible. That does not alter the fact that the conditions are wrong. But the railroads, before they consolidated, found the political boss in power, and had to pay him for favours. The citizen was the culprit to start with, just as he is the culprit now, because he does not take sufficient interest in his government to make it honest. We mustn't blame the railroads too severely, when they grew strong enough, for substituting their own political army to avoid being blackmailed. Long immunity has re-enforced them in the belief that they have but one duty — to pay dividends. I am, afraid," he added, " that they will have to be enlightened somewhat as Pharaoh was enlightened."

" Well, that's sense, too," said Mr. Widgeon; " I guess you're the man to enlighten 'em."

" Moderate talk appeals to me," declared Mr. Jarley.

" And when that fails," said Mr. Terry, " hard, tellin' blows."

" Don't lose track of the fact that we've got our eye on you," said Mr. Emerson of Oxford, who had a blacksmith's grip, and came back to renew it after he had put on his overshoes. He was the last to linger, and when the door had closed on him Austen turned to Mr. Redbrook.

" Now what does all this mean?" he demanded.

" It means," said Mr. Redbrook, "that when the time comes, we want you to run for governor."

Austen went to the mantelpiece, and stood for a long time with his back turned, staring at a crayon portrait of Colonel Peasley, in the uniform in which he had fallen at the battle of Gettysburg. Then he swung about and seized the member from Mercer by both broad shoulders.

" James Redbrook," he said, " until to-night I thought you were about as long-headed and sensible a man as there was in the State."

" So I be," replied Mr. Redbrook, with a grin. " You ask young Tom Gaylord."

" So Tom put you up to this nonsense."

" It ain't nonsense," retorted Mr. Redbrook, stoutly, " and Tom didn't put me up to it. It's the best notion that ever came into my mind."

Austen, still clinging to Mr. Redbrook's shoulders, shook his head slowly.

" James," he said, " there are plenty of men who are
better equipped than I for the place, and in a better situation to undertake it. I — I'm much obliged to you. But
I'll help. I've got to go," he added; "the Honourable
Hilary wants to see me."

He went into the entry and put on his overshoes and
his coat, while James Redbrook regarded him with a curious mingling of pain and benevolence on his rugged face.

" I won't press you now, Austen," he said, " but think
on it. For God's sake, think on it."

Outside, Austen paused in the snow once more, his brain
awhirl with a strange exaltation the like of which he had
never felt before. Although eminently human, it was
not the fact that honest men had asked him to be their
governor which uplifted him, — but that they believed
him to be as honest as themselves. In that hour he had
tasted life as he had never yet tasted it, he had lived as he
might never live again. Not one of them, he remembered
suddenly, had uttered a sentence of the political claptrap
of which he had heard so much. They had spoken from
the soul ; not bitterly, not passionately, but their words
had rung with the determination which had made their
forefathers and his leave home, toil, and kindred to fight
and die at Bunker Hill and Gettysburg for a principle. It
had been given him to look that night into the heart of a
nation, and he was awed.

As he stood there under the winter moon, he gradually
became conscious of music, of an air that seemed the very
expression of his mood. His eyes, irresistibly drawn
towards the Duncan house, were caught by the fluttering
of lace curtains at an open window. The notes were
those of a piano, — though the instrument mattered little,
— that with which they were charged for him set the
night wind quivering. It was not simple music, although
it had in it a grand simplicity. At times it rose, vibrant
with inexpressible feeling, and fell again into gentler,
yearning cadences that wrung the soul with a longing
that was world-old and world-wide, that reached out
towards the unattainable stars — and, reaching, became

immortal. Thus was the end of it, fainting as it drifted heavenward.

Then the window was closed.

Austen walked on; whither, he knew not. After a certain time of which he had no cognizance he found himself under the glaring arc-light that hung over Main Street before the Pelican Hotel, in front of what was known as the ladies' entrance. He slipped in there, avoiding the crowded lobby with its shifting groups and its haze of smoke, — plainly to be seen behind the great plates of glass, — went upstairs, and gained room Number Seven unnoticed. Then, after the briefest moment of hesitation, he knocked. A voice responded — the Honourable Hilary's. There was but one light burning in the room, and Mr. Vane sat in his accustomed chair in the corner, alone. He was not reading, nor was he drowsing, but his head was dropped forward a little on his breast. He raised it slowly at his son's entrance, and regarded Austen fixedly, though silently.

"You wanted to see me, Judge?" said Austen.

"Come at last, have you?" said Mr. Vane.

"I didn't intend to be late," said Austen.

"Seem to have a good deal of business on hand these days," the Honourable Hilary remarked.

Austen took a step forward, and stopped. Mr. Vane was preparing a piece of Honey Dew.

"If you would like to know what the business was, Judge, I am here to tell you."

The Honourable Hilary grunted.

"I ain't good enough to be confided in, I guess," he said; "I wouldn't understand motives from principle."

Austen looked at his father for a few moments in silence. To-night he seemed at a greater distance than ever before, and more lonely than ever. When Austen had entered the room and had seen him sitting with his head bowed forward, the hostility of months of misunderstanding had fallen away from the son, and he had longed to fly to him as he had as a child after punishment. Differences in after life, alas, are not always to be bridged thus.

"Judge," he said slowly, with an attempt to control his voice, "wouldn't it have been fairer to wait awhile, before you made a remark like that? Whatever our dealings may have been, I have never lied to you. Anything you may want to know, I am here to tell you."

"So you're going to take up lobbying, are you? I had a notion you were above lobbying."

Austen was angered. But like all men of character, his face became stern under provocation, and he spoke more deliberately.

"Before we go any farther," he said, "would you mind telling me who your informant is on this point?"

"I guess I don't need an informant. My eyesight is as good as ever," said the Honourable Hilary.

"Your deductions are usually more accurate. If any one has told you that I am about to engage in lobbying, they have lied to you."

"Wouldn't engage in lobbying, would you?" the Honourable Hilary asked, with the air of making a casual inquiry.

Austen flushed, but kept his temper.

"I prefer the practice of law," he replied.

"Saw you were associatin' with saints," his father remarked.

Austen bit his lip, and then laughed outright, — the canonization of old Tom Gaylord being too much for him.

"Now, Judge," he said, "it isn't like you to draw hasty conclusions. Because I sat down to supper with the Gaylords it isn't fair to infer that they have retained me in a legislative case."

The Honourable Hilary did not respond to his son's humour, but shifted the Honey Dew to the left cheek.

"Old Tom going in for reform?"

"He may bring it about," answered Austen, instantly becoming serious again, "whether he's going in for it or not."

For the first time the Honourable Hilary raised his eyes to his son's face, and shot at him a penetrating look of characteristic shrewdness. But he followed in conversation the same rule as in examining a witness, rarely asking a direct question, except as a tactical surprise.

"Old Tom ought to have his railroad, oughtn't he?"

"So far as I can see, it would be a benefit to the people of that part of the State," said Austen.

"Building it for the people, is he?"

"His motive doesn't count. The bill should be judged on its merits, and proper measures for the safeguarding of public interests should be put into it."

"Don't think the bill will be judged on its merits, do you?"

"No, I don't," replied Austen, "and neither do you."

"Did you tell old Tom so?" asked Mr. Vane, after a pause. "Did you tell old Tom so when he sent for you to take hold?"

"He didn't send for me," answered Austen, quietly, "and I have no business dealings with him except small suits. What I did tell him was that he would never get the bill through this session or next by lobbying."

The Honourable Hilary never showed surprise. He emitted a grunt which evinced at once impatience and amusement.

"Why not?" he asked.

"Well, Judge, I'll tell you what I told him — although you both know. It's because the Northeastern owns the Republican party machine, which is the lobby, and because most of the twenty State senators are dependent upon the Northeastern for future favours."

"Did you tell Tom Gaylord that?" demanded Mr. Vane. "What did he say?"

Austen braced himself. He did not find the answer easy.

"He said he knew about Number Seven as well as I did."

The Honourable Hilary rose abruptly — perhaps in some secret agitation — Austen could not discern. His father walked as far as the door, and turned slowly and faced him, but he did not speak. His mouth was tightly closed, almost as in pain, and Austen went towards him, appealingly.

"Judge," he said, "you sent for me. You have asked

me questions which I felt obliged in honesty to answer.
God knows I don't wish to differ with you, but circumstances
seem always against us. I will talk plainly, if you will
let me. I try to look at things from your point of view.
I know that you believe that a political system should
go hand in hand with the great commercial system which
you are engaged in building. I disagree with your
beliefs, but I do not think that your pursuit of them
has not been sincere, and justified by your conscience. I
suppose that you sent for me to know whether Mr. Gaylord has employed me to lobby for his bill. He has not,
because I refused that employment. But I will tell you
that, in my opinion, if a man of any ability whatever
should get up on the floor of the House and make an
argument for the Pingsquit bill, the sentiment against
the Northeastern and its political power is so great that
the House would compel the committee to report the bill,
and pass it. You probably know this already, but I mention it for your own good if you do not, in the hope
that, through you, the Northeastern Railroads may be
induced to relax their grip upon the government of this
State."

The Honourable Hilary advanced, until only the marble-
topped table was between himself and his son. A slight
noise in the adjoining room caused him to turn his head
momentarily. Then he faced Austen again.

" Did you tell Gaylord this ? " he asked.

Austen made a gesture of distaste, and turned away.

" No," he said, " I reserved the opinion, whatever it is
worth, for your ears alone."

" I've heard that kind of calculation before," said the Honourable Hilary. " My experience is that they never come
to much. As for this nonsense about the Northeastern
Railroads running things," he added more vigorously, " I
guess when it's once in a man's head there's no getting it
out. The railroad employs the best lawyers it can find to
look after its interests. I'm one of 'em, and I'm proud of
it. If I hadn't been one of 'em, the chances are you'd never
be where you are, that you'd never have gone to college and

the law school. The Republican party realizes that the Northeastern is most vitally connected with the material interests of this State; that the prosperity of the road means the prosperity of the State. And the leaders of the party protect the road from vindictive assaults on it like Gaylord's, and from scatterbrains and agitators like your friend Redbrook."

Austen shook his head sadly as he gazed at his father. He had always recognized the futility of arguments, if argument on this point ever arose between them.

"It's no use, Judge," he said. "If material prosperity alone were to be considered, your contention would have some weight. The perpetuation of the principle of American government has to be thought of. Government by a railroad will lead in the end to anarchy. You are courting destruction as it is."

"If you came in here to quote your confounded Emerson—" the Honourable Hilary began, but Austen slipped around the table and took him by the arm and led him perforce to his chair.

"No, Judge, that isn't Emerson," he answered. "It's just common sense, only it sounds to you like drivel. I'm going now,—unless you want to hear some more about the plots I've been getting into. But I want to say this. I ask you to remember that you're my father, and that— I'm fond of you. And that, if you and I happen to be on opposite sides, it won't make any difference as far as my feelings are concerned. I'm always ready to tell you frankly what I'm doing, if you wish to know. Good-by. I suppose I'll see you in Ripton at the end of the week." And he pressed his father's shoulder.

Mr. Vane looked up at his son with a curious expression. Perhaps (as when Austen returned from the shooting of Mr. Blodgett in the West) there was a smattering of admiration and pride in that look, and something of an affection which had long ceased in its strivings for utterance. It was the unconscious tribute, too,—slight as was its exhibition,—of the man whose life has been spent in the conquest of material things to the man who has the audacity,

"I ASK YOU TO REMEMBER THAT YOU'RE MY FATHER, AND THAT — I'M
FOND OF YOU."

insensate though it seem, to fling these to the winds in his
search after ideals.

"Good-by, Austen," said Mr. Vane.

Austen got as far as the door, cast another look back
at his father, — who was sitting motionless, with head
bowed, as when he came, — and went out. So Mr. Vane
remained for a full minute after the door had closed, and
then he raised his head sharply and gave a piercing glance
at the curtains that separated Number Seven from the
governor's room.   In three strides he had reached them,
flung them open, and the folding doors behind them, —
already parted by four inches. The gas was turned low,
but under the chandelier was the figure of a young man
struggling with an overcoat. The Honourable Hilary did
not hesitate, but came forward with a swiftness that paralyzed the young man, who turned upon him a face on
which was meant to be written surprise and a just indignation, but in reality was a mixture of impudence and pallid
fright. The Honourable Hilary, towering above him, and
with that grip on his arm, was a formidable person.

"Listening, were you, Ham?" he demanded.

"No," cried Mr. Tooting, with a vehemence he meant
for force. "No, I wasn't. Listening to who?"

"Humph!" said the Honourable Hilary, still retaining
with one hand the grip on Mr. Tooting's arm, and with
the other turning up the gas until it flared in Mr. Tooting's
face. "What are you doing in the governor's room?"

"I left my overcoat in here this afternoon when you
sent me to bring up the senator."

"Ham," said Mr. Vane, "it isn't any use lying to me."

"I ain't lying to you," said Mr. Tooting, "I never did.
I often lied *for* you," he added, "and you didn't raise any
objections that I remember."

Mr. Vane let go of the arm contemptuously.

"I've done dirty work for the Northeastern for a good
many years," cried Mr. Tooting, seemingly gaining confidence now that he was free; "I've slaved for 'em, and
what have they done for me? They wouldn't even back
me for county solicitor when I wanted the job."

"Turned reformer, Ham?"

"I guess I've got as much right to turn reformer as some folks I know."

"I guess you have," agreed the Honourable Hilary, unexpectedly. He seated himself on a chair, and proceeded to regard Mr. Tooting in a manner extremely disconcerting to that gentleman. This quality of impenetrability, of never being sure when he was angry, had baffled more able opponents of Hilary Vane than Mr. Hamilton Tooting. "Good-night, Ham."

"I want to say — " Mr. Tooting began.

"Good-night, Ham," said Mr. Vane, once more.

Mr. Tooting looked at him, slowly buttoned up his overcoat, and departed.

CHAPTER XIII

THE REALM OF PEGASUS

THE eventful day of Mr. Humphrey Crewe's speech on national affairs dawned without a cloud in the sky. The snow was of a dazzling whiteness and sprinkled with diamond dust, and the air of such transcendent clearness that Austen could see — by leaning a little out of the Widow Peasley's window — the powdered top of Holdfast Mountain some thirty miles away. For once, a glance at the mountain sufficed him, and he directed his gaze through the trees at the Duncan house, engaging in a pleasant game of conjecture as to which was *her* window. In such weather the heights of Helicon seemed as attainable as the peak of Holdfast, and he had but to beckon a shining Pegasus from out a sun-shaft in the sky. Obstacles were mere specks on the snow.

He forgot to close the window, and dressed in a temperature which would have meant, for many mortals, pneumonia. The events of yesterday, painful and agitating as they had been, had fallen away in the prospect that lay before him — he would see her to-day, and speak with her. These words, like a refrain, were humming in his head as honest Mr. Redbrook talked during breakfast, while Austen's answers may have been both intelligent and humorous. Mr. Redbrook, at least, gave no sign that they were not. He was aware that Mr. Redbrook was bringing arguments to bear on the matter of the meeting of the evening before, but he fended these lightly, while in spirit he flung a gem-studded bridle over the neck of Pegasus.

And after breakfast — away from the haunts of men! Away from the bickerings, the subjection of mean spirits,

material loss and gain and material passion! By eight
o'clock (the Widow Peasley's household being an early
and orderly one) he was swinging across the long hills,
cleaving for himself a furrowed path in the untrodden
snow, breathing deep as he gazed across the blue spaces
from the crests. Bellerophon or Perseus, aided by im-
mortals, felt no greater sense of achievements to come
than he. Out here, on the wind-swept hills that rolled
onward and upward to the mountains, the world was his.

With the same speed he returned, still by untrodden
paths until he reached the country road that ended in
the city street. Some who saw him paused in their steps,
caught unconsciously by the rhythmic perfection of his
motion. Ahead of him he beheld the state-house, its dial
aflame in the light, emblematic to him of the presence
within it of a spirit which cleansed it of impurities. *She*
would be there; nay, when he looked at the dial from
a different angle, was there. As he drew nearer, there
rose out of the void her presence beside him which he had
daily tried to summon since that autumn afternoon — her
voice and her eyes, and many of the infinite expressions
of each and both. Sprites that they were, they had failed
him until to-day, when he was to see her again!

And then, somehow, he had threaded the groups beside
the battle-flags in the corridor, and mounted the stairway.
The doorkeeper of the House looked into his face, and,
with that rare knowledge of mankind which doorkeepers
possess, let him in. There were many ladies on the floor
(such being the chivalrous custom when a debate or a
speech of the importance of Mr. Crewe's was going on),
but Austen swept them with a glance of disappointment.
Was it possible, after all, that she had not come, or —
more agitating thought — had gone back to New York?

At this disturbing point in his reflections Austen became
aware that the hall was ringing with a loud and compelling voice which originated in front of the Speaker's desk.

The Honourable Humphrey Crewe was delivering his
long-heralded speech on national affairs, and was arrayed
for the occasion in a manner befitting the American states-

man, with the conventional frock coat, which he wore unbuttoned. But the Gladstone collar and a tie gave the touch of individuality to his dress which was needed to set him aside as a marked man. Austen suddenly remembered, with an irresistible smile, that one of the reasons which he had assigned for his visit to the capital was to hear this very speech, to see how Mr. Crewe would carry off what appeared to be a somewhat difficult situation. Whether or not this motive had drawn others, — for the millionaire's speech had not lacked advertisement, — it is impossible to say, but there was standing room only on the floor of the House that day.

The fact that Mr. Crewe was gratified could not be wholly concealed. The thing that fascinated Austen Vane and others who listened was the aplomb with which the speech was delivered. The member from Leith showed no trace of the nervousness naturally to be expected in a maiden effort, but spoke with the deliberation of an old campaigner, of the man of weight and influence that he was. He leaned, part of the time, with his elbow on the clerk's desk, with his feet crossed ; again, when he wished to emphasize a point, he came forward and seized with both hands the back of his chair. Sometimes he thrust his thumb in his waistcoat pocket, and turned with an appeal to Mr. Speaker Doby, who was apparently too thrilled and surprised to indulge in conversation with those on the bench beside him, and who made no attempt to quell hand-clapping and even occasional whistling; again, after the manner of experts, Mr. Crewe addressed himself forcibly to an individual in the audience, usually a sensitive and responsive person like the Honourable Jacob Botcher, who on such occasions assumed a look of infinite wisdom and nodded his head slowly. There was no doubt about it that the compelling personality of Mr. Humphrey Crewe was creating a sensation. Genius is sure of itself, and statesmen are born, not made.

Able and powerful as was Mr. Crewe's discourse, the man and not the words had fastened the wandering attention of Austen Vane. He did not perceive his friend of

o

the evening before, Mr. Widgeon, coming towards him up the side aisle, until he felt a touch on the arm.

"Take my seat. It ain't exactly a front one," whispered the member from Hull, "my wife's cousin's comin' on the noon train. Not a bad speech, is it?" he added. "Acts like a veteran. I didn't callate he had it in him."

Thus aroused, Austen made his way towards the vacant chair, and when he was seated raised his eyes to the gallery rail, and Mr. Crewe, the legislative chamber, and its audience ceased to exist. It is quite impossible — unless one is a poetical genius — to reproduce on paper that gone and sickly sensation which is, paradoxically, so exquisite. The psychological cause of it in this instance was, primarily, the sight, by Austen Vane, of his own violets on a black, tailor-made gown trimmed with wide braid, and secondarily of an oval face framed in a black hat, the subtle curves of which no living man could describe. The face was turned in his direction, and he felt an additional thrill when he realized that she must have been watching him as he came in, for she was leaning forward with a gloved hand on the railing.

He performed that act of conventionality known as a bow, and she nodded her head — black hat and all. The real salutation was a divine ray which passed between their eyes — hers and his — over the commonplace mortals between. And after that, although the patient legislative clock in the corner which had marked the space of other great events (such as the Woodchuck Session) continued to tick, undisturbed in this instance by the pole of the sergeant-at-arms, time became a lost dimension for Austen Vane. He made a few unimportant discoveries such as the fact that Mrs. Pomfret and her daughter were seated beside Victoria, listening with a rapt attention; and that Mr. Crewe had begun to read statistics; and that some people were gaping and others leaving. He could look up at the gallery without turning his head, and sometimes he caught her momentary glance, and again, with her chin in her hand, she was watching Mr. Crewe with a little smile creasing the corners of her eyes.

A horrible thought crossed Austen's mind — perhaps they were not his violets after all! Because she had smiled at him, yesterday and to-day, he had soared heavenwards on wings of his own making. Perhaps they were Mr. Crewe's violets. Had she not come to visit Mr. Crewe, to listen to his *pièce de résistance*, without knowing that he, Austen Vane, would be in the capital? The idea that her interest in Austen Vane was possibly connected with the study of mankind had a sobering effect on him; and the notion that she had another sort of interest in Mr. Crewe seemed ridiculous enough, but disturbing, and supported by facts.

Austen had reached this phase in his reflections when he was aroused by a metallic sound which arose above the resonant tones of the orator of the day. A certain vessel, to the use of which, according to Mr. Dickens, the entire male portion of the American nation was at one time addicted, — a cuspidor, in plain language, — had been started, by some unknown agency in the back seats, rolling down the centre aisle, and gathering impetus as it went, bumped the louder on each successive step until it hurled itself with a clash against the clerk's desk, at the feet of the orator himself. During its descent a titter arose which gradually swelled into a roar of laughter, and Austen's attention was once more focussed upon the member from Leith. But if any man had so misjudged the quality of Humphrey Crewe as to suppose for an instant that he could be put out of countenance by such a manœuvre, that man was mightily mistaken. Mr. Crewe paused, with his forefinger on the page, and fixed a glassy eye on the remote neighbourhood in the back seats where the disturbance had started.

"I am much obliged to the gentleman," he said coldly, "but he has sent me an article which I never use, under any conditions. I would not deprive him of its convenience."

Whereupon, it is not too much to say, Mr. Crewe was accorded an ovation, led by his stanch friend and admirer, the Honourable Jacob Botcher, although that worthy *had* been known to use the article in question.

Mr. Speaker Doby glanced at the faithful clock, and arose majestically.

" I regret to say," he announced, " that the time of the gentleman from Leith is up."

Mr. Botcher rose slowly to his feet.

" Mr. Speaker," he began, in a voice that rumbled through the crevices of the gallery, " I move you, sir, that a vote of thanks be accorded to the gentleman from Leith for his exceedingly able and instructive speech on national affairs."

" Second the motion," said the Honourable Brush Bascom, instantly.

" And leave to print in the *State Tribune!*" cried a voice from somewhere among the submerged four hundred and seventy.

" Gentlemen of the House," said Mr. Crewe, when the laughter had subsided, " I have given you a speech which is the result of much thought and preparation on my part. I have not flaunted the star-spangled banner in your faces, or indulged in oratorical fireworks. Mine have been the words of a plain business man, and I have not indulged in wild accusations or flights of imagination. Perhaps, if I had," he added, " there are some who would have been better pleased. I thank my friends for their kind attention and approbation."

Nevertheless, amidst somewhat of a pandemonium, the vote of thanks was given and the House adjourned; while Mr. Crewe's friends of whom he had spoken could be seen pressing around him and shaking him by the hand. Austen got to his feet, his eyes again sought the gallery, whence he believed he received a look of understanding from a face upon which amusement seemed plainly written. She had turned to glance down at him, despite the fact that Mrs. Pomfret was urging her to leave. Austen started for the door, and managed to reach it long before his neighbours had left the vicinity of their seats. Once in the corridor, his eye singled her out amongst those descending the gallery stairs, and he had a little thrill of pride and despair when he realized that she was the object of the scrutiny, too, of the men around him; the women were interested, likewise, in Mrs. Pomfret, whose appearance, although appropriate enough for a New York matinée, proclaimed her as hailing from that mysterious and fabulous city of wealth. This lady, with her lorgnette, was examining the faces about her in undisguised curiosity, and at the same time talking to Victoria in a voice which she took no pains to lower.

"I think it outrageous," she was saying. "If some Radical member had done that in Parliament, he would have been expelled from the House. But of course in Parliament they wouldn't have those horrid things to roll down the aisles. Poor dear Humphrey! The career of a gentleman in politics is a thankless one in this country. I wonder at his fortitude."

Victoria's eyes alone betokened her amusement.

"How do you do, Mr. Vane?" she said. "I'm so glad to see you again."

Austen said something which he felt was entirely commonplace and inadequate to express his own sentiments, while Alice gave him an uncertain bow, and Mrs. Pomfret turned her glasses upon him.

"You remember Mr. Vane," said Victoria; "you met him at Humphrey's."

"Did I?" answered Mrs. Pomfret. "How do you do? Can't something be done to punish those rowdies?"

Austen grew red.

"Mr. Vane isn't a member of the House," said Victoria.

"Oh," exclaimed Mrs. Pomfret. "Something ought to be done about it. In England such a thing wouldn't be allowed to drop for a minute. If I lived in this State, I think I should do something. Nobody in America seems to have the spirit even to make a protest."

Austen turned quietly to Victoria.

"When are you going away?" he asked.

"To-morrow morning — earlier than I like to think of. I have to be in New York by to-morrow night."

She flashed at him a look of approbation for his self-control, and then, by a swift transition which he had often remarked, her expression changed to one of amusement, although a seriousness lurked in the depths of her eyes. Mrs. Pomfret had gone on, with Alice, and they followed.

"And — am I not to see you again before you go?" he exclaimed.

He didn't stop to reason then upon the probable consequences of his act in seeking her. Nature, which is stronger than reason, was compelling him.

"That depends," said Victoria.

"Upon whom?"

"Upon you."

They were on the lower stairs by this time, and there was silence between them for a few moments as they descended, — principally because, after this exalting remark, Austen could not trust himself to speak.

"Will you go driving with me?" he asked, and was immediately thunderstruck at his boldness.

"Yes," she answered, simply.

"How soon may I come?" he demanded.

She laughed softly, but with a joyous note which was not hidden from him as they stepped out of the darkened corridor into the dazzling winter noonday.

"I will be ready at three o'clock," she said.

He looked at his watch.

"Two hours and a half!" he cried.

"If that is too early," she said mischievously, "we can go later."

"Too early!" he repeated. But the rest of his protest was cut short by Mr. Crewe.

"Hello, Victoria, what did you think of my speech?"

"The destinies of the nation are settled," said Victoria. "Do you know Mr. Vane?"

"Oh, yes, how are you?" said Mr. Crewe; "glad to see you," and he extended a furred glove. "Were you there?"

"Yes," said Austen.

"I'll send you a copy. I'd like to talk it over with you. Come on, Victoria, I've arranged for an early lunch. Come on, Mrs. Pomfret — get in, Alice."

Mrs. Pomfret, still protesting against the profane inter-ruption to Mr. Crewe's speech, bent her head to enter Mr. Crewe's booby sleigh, which had his crest on the panel. Alice was hustled in next, but Victoria avoided his ready assistance and got in herself, Mr. Crewe getting in beside her.

"Au revoir," she called out to Austen, as the door slammed. The coachman gathered his horses together, and off they went at a brisk trot. Then the little group which had been watching the performance dispersed. Halfway across the park Austen perceived some one sig-nalling violently to him, and discovered his friend, young Tom Gaylord.

"Come to dinner with me," said young Tom, "and tell me whether the speech of your friend from Leith will send him to Congress. I saw you hobnobbing with him just now. What's the matter, Austen? I haven't seen that guilty expression on your face since we were at college together."

"What's the best livery-stable in town?" Austen asked.

"By George, I wondered why you came down here. Who are you going to take out in a sleigh? There's a girl in it, is there?"

"Not yet, Tom," said Austen.

"I've often asked myself why I ever had any use for such a secretive cuss as you," declared young Mr. Gaylord. "But if you're really goin' to get interested in girls, you ought to see old Flint's daughter. I wrote you about her. Why," exclaimed Tom, "wasn't she one of those that got into Crewe's sleigh?"

"Tom," said Austen, "where did you say that livery-stable was?"

"Oh, dang the livery-stable!" answered Mr. Gaylord. "I hear there's quite a sentiment for you for governor. How about it? You know I've always said you could be United States senator and President. If you'll only say the word, Austen, we'll work up a movement around the State that'll be hard to beat."

"Tom," said Austen, laying his hand on young Mr. Gaylord's farther shoulder, "you're a pretty good fellow. Where did you say that livery-stable was?"

"I'll go sleigh-riding with you," said Mr. Gaylord. " I guess the Pingsquit bill can rest one afternoon."

"Tom, I don't know any man I'd rather take than you," said Austen.

The unsuspecting Tom was too good-natured to be offended, and shortly after dinner Austen found himself in the process of being looked over by a stout gentleman named Putter, proprietor of Putter's Livery, who claimed to be a judge of men as well as horses. Austen had been through his stalls and chosen a mare.

" Durned if you don't look like a man who can handle a hoss," said Mr. Putter. "And as long as you're a friend of Tom Gaylord's I'll let you have her. Nobody drives that mare but me. What's your name?"

" Vane."

" Ain't any relation to old Hilary, be you?"

" I'm his son," said Austen, "only he doesn't boast about it."

" Godfrey! " exclaimed Mr. Putter, with a broad grin, " I guess you kin have her. Ain't you the man that shot a feller out West? Seems to me I heerd somethin' about it."

" Which one did you hear about?" Austen asked.

" Good Lord! " said Mr. Putter, "you didn't shoot more'n one, did you?"

It was just three o'clock when Austen drove into the semicircle opposite the Widow Peasley's, rang Mr. Crewe's door-bell, and leaped into the sleigh once more, the mare's nature being such as to make it undesirable to leave her. Presently Mr. Crewe's butler appeared, and stood dubiously in the vestibule.

" Will you tell Miss Flint that Mr. Vane has called for her, and that I cannot leave the horse?"

The man retired with obvious disapproval. Then Austen heard Victoria's voice in the hallway: —

" Don't make a goose of yourself, Humphrey." Here she appeared, the colour fresh in her cheeks, her slender figure clad in a fur which even Austen knew was priceless. She sprang into the sleigh, the butler, with annoying deliberation, and with the air of saying that this was an affair of which he washed his hands, tucked in Mr. Putter's best robe about her feet, the mare leaped forward, and they were off, out of the circle and flying up the hill on the hard snow-tracks.

"Whew!" exclaimed Victoria, "what a relief! Are you staying in that dear little house?" she asked, with a glance at the Widow Peasley's.

"Yes," said Austen.

"I wish I were."

He looked at her shyly. He was not a man to do homage to material gods, but the pomp and circumstance with which she was surrounded had had a sobering effect upon him, and added to his sense of the instability and unreality of the present moment. He had an almost guilty feeling of having broken an unwritten law, of abducting a princess, and the old Duncan house had seemed to frown protestingly that such an act should have taken place under its windows. If Victoria had been — to him — an ordinary mortal in expensive furs instead of a princess, he would have snapped his fingers at the pomp and circumstance. These typified the comforts which, in a wild and forgetful moment, he might ask her to leave. Not that he believed she would leave them. He had lived long enough to know that an interest by a woman in a man — especially a man beyond the beaten track of her observation — did not necessarily mean that she might marry him if he asked her. And yet — oh, Tantalus! — here she was beside him, for one afternoon again his very own, their two souls ringing with the harmony of whirling worlds in sunlit space. He sought refuge in this thought; he strove, in oblivion, to drain the cup of the hour of its nectar, even as he had done before. Generations of Puritan Vanes (whose descendant alone had harassed poor Sarah Austen) were in his blood; and there they hung in the long gallery of Time, mutely but sternly forbidding when he raised his hand to the stem.

In silence they reached the crest where the little city ended abruptly in view of the paradise of the silent hills, — his paradise, where there were no palaces or thought of palaces. The wild wind of the morning was still. In this realm at least, a heritage from his mother, seemingly untrodden by the foot of man, the woman at his side was his. From Holdfast over the spruces to Sawanec in the blue distance he was lord, a domain the wealth of which could not be reckoned in the coin of Midas. He turned to her as they flew down the slope, and she averted her face, perchance perceiving in that look a possession from which a woman shrinks; and her remark, startlingly indicative of the accord between them, lent a no less startling reality to the enchantment.

"This is your land, isn't it?" she said.

"I sometimes feel as though it were," he answered. "I was out here this morning, when the wind was at play," and he pointed with his whip at a fantastic snow-drift, "before I saw you."

"You looked as though you had come from it," she answered. "You seemed — I suppose you will think me silly — but you seemed to bring something of this with you into that hall. I always think of you as out on the hills and mountains."

"And you," he said, "belong here, too."

She drew a deep breath.

"I wish I did. But you — you really do belong here. You seem to have absorbed all the clearness of it, and the strength and vigour. I was watching you this morning, and you were so utterly out of place in those surroundings." Victoria paused, her colour deepening.

His blood kept pace with the mare's footsteps, but he did not reply.

"What did you think of Humphrey's speech?" she asked, abruptly changing the subject.

"I thought it a surprisingly good one, — what I heard of it," he answered. "That wasn't much. I didn't think he'd do as well."

"Humphrey's clever in a great many ways," Victoria

agreed. "If he didn't have such an impenetrable conceit, he might go far, because he learns quickly, and has an industry that is simply appalling. But he hasn't quite the manner for politics, has he?"

"I think I should call his manner a drawback," said Austen, "though not by any means an insurmountable one."

Victoria laughed.

"The other qualities all need to be very great," she said. "He was furious at me for coming out this afternoon. He had it all arranged to drive over to the Forge, and had an early lunch."

"And I," said Austen, "have all the more reason to be grateful to you."

"Oh, if you knew the favour you were doing me," she cried, "bringing me out here where I can breathe. I hope you don't think I dislike Humphrey," she went on. "Of course, if I did, I shouldn't visit him. You see, I have known him for so long."

"I hadn't a notion that you disliked him," said Austen. "I am curious about his career; that's one reason I came down. He somehow inspires curiosity."

"And awe," she added. "Humphrey's career has all the fascination of a runaway locomotive. One watches it transfixed, awaiting the inevitable crash."

Their eyes met, and they both laughed.

"It's no use trying to be a humbug," said Victoria, "I can't. And I do like Humphrey, in spite of his career."

And they laughed again. The music of the bells ran faster and faster still, keeping time to a wilder music of the sunlit hills and sky; nor was it strange that her voice, when she spoke, did not break the spell, but laid upon him a deeper sense of magic.

"This brings back the fairy books," she said, "and all those wonderful and never-to-be-forgotten sensations of the truant, doesn't it? You've been a truant — haven't you?"

"Yes," he laughed, "I've been a truant, but I never quite realized the possibilities of the part — until to-day."

She was silent a moment, and turned away her head, surveying the landscape that fell away for miles beyond.

"When I was a child," she said, "I used to think that by opening a door I could step into an enchanted realm like this. Only I could never find the door. Perhaps," she added, gayly pursuing the conceit, "it was because you had the key, and I didn't know you in those days." She gave him a swift, searching look, smiling, whimsical yet startled, — so elusive that the memory of it afterwards was wont to come and go like a flash of light. "Who are you?" she asked.

His blood leaped, but he smiled in delighted understanding of her mood. Sarah Austen had brought just such a magic touch to an excursion, and even at that moment Austen found himself marvelling a little at the strange resemblance between the two.

"I am a plain person whose ancestors came from a village called Camden Street," he replied. "Camden Street is there, on a shelf of the hills, and through the arch of its elms you can look off over the forests of the lowlands until they end in the blue reaches of the ocean, — if you could see far enough."

"If you could see far enough," said Victoria, unconsciously repeating his words. "But that doesn't explain you," she exclaimed. "You are like nobody I ever met, and you have a supernatural faculty of appearing suddenly, from nowhere, and whisking me away like the lady in the fable, out of myself and the world I live in. If I become so inordinately grateful as to talk nonsense, you mustn't blame me. Try not to think of the number of times I've seen you, or when it was we first met."

"I believe," said Austen, gravely, "it was when a mammoth beast had his cave on Holdfast, and the valleys were covered with cocoanut-palms."

"And you appeared suddenly then, too, and rescued me. You have always been uniformly kind," she said, "but — a little intangible."

"A myth," he suggested, "with neither height, breadth, nor thickness."

"You have height and breadth," she answered, measuring him swiftly with her eye; "I am not sure about the thickness. Perhaps. What I mean to say is, that you seem to be a person in the world, but not of it. Your exits and entrances are too mysterious, and then you carry me out of it, — although I invite myself, which is not at all proper."

"I came down here to see you," he said, and took a firmer grip on the reins. "I exist to that extent."

"That's unworthy of you," she cried. "I don't believe you would have known I was here unless you had caught sight of me."

"I should have known it," he said.

"How?"

"Because I heard you playing. I am sure it was you playing."

"Yes, it was I," she answered simply, "but I did not know that — you heard. Where were you?"

"I suppose," he replied, "a sane witness would have testified that I was in the street — one of those partial and material truths which are so misleading."

She laughed again, joyously.

"Seriously, why did you come down here?" she insisted. "I am not so absorbed in Humphrey's career that I cannot take an interest in yours. In fact, yours interests me more, because it is more mysterious. Humphrey's," she added, laughing, "is charted from day to day, and announced in bulletins. He is more generous to his friends than — you."

"I have nothing to chart," said Austen, "except such pilgrimages as this, — and these, after all, are unchartable. Your friend, Mr. Crewe, on the other hand, is well away on his voyage after the Golden Fleece. I hope he is provided with a Lynceus."

She was silent for a long time, but he was feverishly conscious of her gaze upon him, and did not dare to turn his eyes to hers. The look in them he beheld without the aid of physical vision, and in that look was the world-old riddle of her sex typified in the image on the African desert — which Napoleon had tried to read, and failed. And while wisdom was in the look, there was in it likewise the eternal questioning of a fate quite as inscrutable, against which wisdom would avail nothing. It was that look which, for Austen, revealed in her in their infinite variety all women who had lived; those who could resist, and those who could yield, and yielding all, bestow a gift which left them still priceless; those to whom sorrow might bring sadness, and knowledge mourning, and yet could rob them of no jot of sweetness. And knowing this, he knew that to gain her now (could such a high prize be gained!) would be to lose her. If he were anything to her (realize it or not as she might), it was because he found strength to resist this greatest temptation of his life. Yield, and his guerdon was lost, and he would be Austen Vane no longer—yield, and his right to act, which would make him of value in her eyes as well as in his own, was gone forever.

Well he knew what the question in her eyes meant — or something of what it meant, so inexplicably is the soul of woman linked to events. He had pondered often on that which she had asked him when he had brought her home over the hills in the autumn twilight. He remembered her words, and the very inflection of her voice. " Then you won't tell me ? " How could he tell her ? He became aware that she was speaking now, in an even tone.

" I had an odd experience this morning, when I was waiting for Mrs. Pomfret outside the state-house," she said. "A man was standing looking up at the statue of the patriot with a strange, rapt expression on his face, — such a good face, — and he was so big and honest and uncompromising I wanted to talk to him. I didn't realize that I was staring at him so hard, because I was trying to remember where I had seen him before, — and then I remembered suddenly that it was with you."

" With me ? " Austen repeated.

" You were standing with him, in front of the little house, when I saw you yesterday. His name was Redbrook. It appears that he had seen me," Victoria replied, "when I went to Mercer to call on Zeb Meader. And he asked me if I knew you."

"Of course you denied it," said Austen.

"I couldn't, very well," laughed Victoria, "because you had confessed to the acquaintance first."

"He merely wished to have the fact corroborated. Mr. Redbrook is a man who likes to be sure of his ground."

"He told me a very interesting thing about you," she continued slowly, with her eye upon Austen's profile. "He said that a great many men wanted you to be their candidate for governor of the State, — more than you had any idea of, — and that you wouldn't consent. Mr. Redbrook grew so enthusiastic that he forgot, for the moment, my — relationship to the railroad. He is not the only person with whom I have talked who has — forgotten it, or hasn't known of it."

Austen was silent.

"Why won't you be a candidate," she asked, in a low voice, "if such men as that want you?"

"I am afraid Mr. Redbrook exaggerates," he said. "The popular demand of which he spoke is rather mythical. And I should be inclined to accuse him, too, of a friendly attempt to install me in your good graces."

"No," answered Victoria, smiling, with serious eyes, "I won't be put off that way. Mr. Redbrook isn't the kind of man that exaggerates — I've seen enough of his type to know that. And he told me about your — reception last night at the Widow Peasley's. You wouldn't have told me," she added reproachfully.

He laughed.

"It was scarcely a subject I could have ventured," he said.

"But I asked you," she objected. "Now tell me, why did you refuse to be their candidate? It wasn't because you were not likely to get elected, was it?"

He permitted himself a glance which was a tribute of admiration — a glance which she returned steadfastly.

"It isn't likely that I should have been elected," he

answered, "but you are right — that is not the reason I
refused."

"I thought not," she said, "I did not believe you were
the kind of man to refuse for that reason. And you would
have been elected."

"What makes you think so?" he asked curiously.

"I have been thinking since I saw you last — yes, and
I have been making inquiries. I have been trying to find
out things — which you will not tell me." She paused,
with a little catch of her breath, and went on again. "Do
you believe I came all the way up here just to hear Humphrey Crewe make a speech and to drive with him in a
high sleigh and listen to him talk about his career? When
serious men of the people like Mr. Redbrook and that nice
Mr. Jenney at Leith and a lot of others who do not ordinarily care for politics are thinking and indignant, I have
come to the conclusion there must be a cause for it. They
say that the railroad governs them through disreputable
politicians, — and I — I am beginning to believe it is
true. I have had some of the politicians pointed out to
me in the Legislature, and they look like it."

Austen did not smile. She was speaking quietly, but
he saw that she was breathing deeply, and he knew that
she possessed a courage which went far beyond that of
most women, and an insight into life and affairs.

"I am going to find out," she said, "whether these
things are true."

"And then?" he asked involuntarily.

"If they are true, I am going to tell my father about
them, and ask him to investigate. Nobody seems to have
the courage to go to him."

Austen did not answer. He felt the implication; he
knew that, without realizing his difficulties, and carried
on by a feeling long pent up, she had measured him un-
justly, and yet he felt no resentment, and no shock.
Perhaps he might feel that later. Now he was filled only
with a sympathy that was yet another common bond between them. Suppose she did find out? He knew that
she would not falter until she came to the end of her in-

vestigation, to the revelation of Mr. Flint's code of business ethics. Should the revolt take place, she would be satisfied with nothing less than the truth, even as he, Austen Vane, had not been satisfied. And he thought of the life-long faith that would be broken thereby.

They had made the circle of the hills, and the sparkling lights of the city lay under them like blue diamond points in the twilight of the valley. The crests behind them deepened in purple as the saffron faded in the west, and a gossamer cloud of Tyrian dye floated over Holdfast. In silence they turned for a last lingering look, and in silence went down the slope into the world again, and through the streets to the driveway of the Duncan house. It was only when they had stopped before the door that she trusted herself to speak.

"I ought not to have said what I did," she began, in a low voice; "I didn't realize — but I cannot understand you."

"You have said nothing which you need ever have cause to regret," he replied. He was too great for excuses, too great for any sorrow save what she herself might feel, as great as the silent hills from which he came.

She stood for a moment on the edge of the steps, her eyes lustrous, — yet gazing into his with a searching, troubled look that haunted him for many days. But her self-command was unshaken, her power to control speech was the equal of his. And this power of silence in her — revealed in such instants — was her greatest fascination for Austen, the thing which set her apart among women; which embodied for him the whole charm and mystery of her sex.

"Good-by," she said simply.

"Good-by," he said, and seized her hand — and drove away.

Without ringing the bell Victoria slipped into the hall, — for the latch was not caught, — and her first impulse was to run up the staircase to her room. But she heard Mrs. Pomfret's voice on the landing above and fled, as to

P

a refuge, into the dark drawing-room, where she stood for
a moment motionless, listening for the sound of his sleigh-
bells as they fainted on the winter's night. Then she
seated herself to think, if she could, though it is difficult
to think when one's heart is beating a little wildly. It
was Victoria's nature to think things out. For the first
time in her life she knew sorrow, and it made it worse
that that sorrow was indefinable. She felt an accountable
attraction for this man who had so strangely come into
her life, whose problems had suddenly become her problems. But she did not connect the attraction for Austen
Vane with her misery. She recalled him as he had left
her, big and strong and sorrowful, with a yearning look
that was undisguised, and while her faith in him came
surging back again, she could not understand.

Gradually she became aware of men's voices, and turned
with a start to perceive that the door of the library was
open, and that Humphrey Crewe and another were standing in the doorway against the light. With an effort of
memory she identified the other man as the Mr. Tooting
who had made himself so useful at Mr. Crewe's garden-
party.

"I told you I could make you governor, Mr. Crewe,"
Mr. Tooting was saying. "Say, why do you think the
Northeastern crowd — why do you think Hilary Vane
is pushing your bills down the sidings? I'll tell you,
because they know you're a man of ability, and they're
afraid of you, and they know you're a gentleman, and
can't be trusted with their deals, so they just shunted
you off at Kodunk with a jolly about sendin' you to Congress if you made a hit on a national speech. I've been
in the business a good many years, and I've seen and done
some things for the Northeastern that stick in my throat"
— (at this point Victoria sat down again and gripped the
arms of her chair). "I don't like to see a decent man
sawbucked the way they're teeterin' you, Mr. Crewe. I
know what I'm talkin' about, and I tell you that Ridout
and Jake Botcher and Brush Bascom haven't any more
notion of lettin' your bills out of committee than they

have Gaylord's. Why? Because they've got orders not to."

"You're making some serious charges, Mr. Tooting," said Mr. Crewe.

"And what's more, I can prove 'em. You know yourself that anybody who talks against the Northeastern is booted down and blacklisted. You've seen that, haven't you?"

"I have observed," said Mr. Crewe, "that things do not seem to be as they should in a free government."

"And it makes your blood boil as an American citizen, don't it? It does mine," said Mr. Tooting, with fine indignation. "I was a poor boy, and had to earn my living, but I've made up my mind I've worn the collar long enough — if I have to break rocks. And I want to repeat what I said a little while ago," he added, weaving his thumb into Mr. Crewe's buttonhole; "I know a thing or two, and I've got some brains, as they know, and I can make you governor of this State if you'll only say the word. It's a cinch."

Victoria started to rise once more, and realized that to escape she would have to cross the room directly in front of the two men. She remained sitting where she was in a fearful fascination, awaiting Humphrey Crewe's answer. There was a moment's pause.

"I believe you made the remark, Mr. Tooting," he said, "that in your opinion there is enough anti-railroad sentiment in the House to pass any bill which the railroad opposes."

"If a leader was to get up there, like you, with the arguments I could put into his hands, they would make the committee discharge that Pingsquit bill of the Gaylords', and pass it."

"On what do you base your opinion?" asked Mr. Crewe.

"Well," said Mr. Tooting, "I guess I'm a pretty shrewd observer and have had practice enough. But you know Austen Vane, don't you?"

Victoria held her breath.

"I've a slight acquaintance with him," replied Mr. Crewe; "I've helped him along in one or two minor legal matters. He seems to be a little — well, pushing, you might say."

"I want to tell you one thing about Austen," continued Mr. Tooting. "Although I don't stand much for old Hilary, I'd take Austen Vane's opinion on most things as soon as that of any man in the State. If he only had some sense about himself, he could be governor next time — there's a whole lot that wants him. I happen to know some of 'em offered it to him last night."

"Austen Vane governor!" exclaimed Mr. Crewe, with a politely deprecating laugh.

"It may sound funny," said Mr. Tooting, stoutly; "I never understood what he has about him. He's never done anything but buck old Hilary in that damage case and send back a retainer pass to old Flint, but he's got something in his make-up that gets under your belt, and a good many of these old hayseeds'll eat out of his hand, right now. Well, I don't want this to go any farther, — you're a gentleman, — but Austen came down here yesterday and had the whole thing sized up by last night. Old Hilary thought the Gaylords sent for him to lobby their bill through. They may have sent for him, all right, but he wouldn't lobby for 'em. He could have made a pile of money out of 'em. Austen doesn't seem to care about money — he's queer. He says as long as he has a horse and a few books and a couple of sandwiches a day he's all right. Hilary had him up in Number Seven tryin' to find out what he came down for, and Austen told him pretty straight — what he didn't tell the Gaylords, either. He kind of likes old Hilary, — because he's his father, I guess, — and he said there were enough men in that House to turn Hilary and his crowd upside down. That's how I know for certain. If Austen Vane said it, I'll borrow money to bet on it," declared Mr. Tooting.

"You don't think young Vane is going to get into the race?" queried Mr. Crewe.

"No," said Mr. Tooting, somewhat contemptuously. "No, I tell you he hasn't got that kind of sense. He never took any trouble to get ahead, and I guess he's sort of sensitive about old Hilary. It'd make a good deal of a scandal in the family, with Austen as an anti-railroad candidate." Mr. Tooting lowered his voice to a tone that was caressingly confidential. "I tell you, and you sleep on it, a man of your brains and money can't lose. It's a chance in a million, and when you win you've got this little State tight in your pocket, and a desk in the millionaire's club at Washington. Well, so long," said Mr. Tooting, "you think that over."

"You have, at least, put things in a new and interesting light," said Mr. Crewe. "I will try to decide what my duty is."

"Your duty's pretty plain to me," said Mr. Tooting. "If I had money, I'd know that the best way to use it is for the people, — ain't that so?"

"In the meantime," Mr. Crewe continued, "you may drop in to-morrow at three."

"You'd better make it to-morrow night, hadn't you?" said Mr. Tooting, significantly. "There ain't any back way to this house."

"As you choose," said Mr. Crewe.

They passed within a few feet of Victoria, who resisted an almost uncontrollable impulse to rise and confront them. The words given her to use were surging in her brain, and yet she withheld them — why, she knew not. Perhaps it was because, after such communion as the afternoon had brought, the repulsion she felt for Mr. Tooting aided her to sit where she was. She heard the outside door open and close, and she saw Humphrey Crewe walk past her again into his library, and that door closed, and she was left in darkness. Darkness indeed for Victoria, who throughout her life had lived in light alone; in the light she had shed, and the light which she had kindled in others. With a throb which was an exquisite pain, she understood now the compassion in Austen's eyes, and she saw so simply and so clearly why he had not told her that her face burned with the shame of her demand. The one of all others to whom she could go in this trouble was denied her, and his lips were sealed, who would have spoken honestly and without prejudice. She rose and went quietly out into the biting winter night, and stood staring through the trees at the friendly reddened windows of the little cottage across the way with a yearning that passed her understanding. Out of those windows, to Victoria, shone honesty and truth, and the peace which these alone may bring.

CHAPTER XIV

THE DESCENDANTS OF HORATIUS

So the twenty honourable members of the State Senate had been dubbed by the man who had a sense of humour and a smattering of the classics, because they had been put there to hold the bridge against the Tarquins who would invade the dominions of the Northeastern. Twenty picked men, and true they were indeed, but a better name for their body would have been the Life Guard of the Sovereign. The five hundred far below them might rage and at times revolt, but the twenty in their shining armour stood undaunted above the vulnerable ground and smiled grimly at the mob. The citadel was safe.

The real Horatius of the stirring time of which we write was that old and tried veteran, the Honourable Brush Bascom; and Spurius Lartius might be typified by the indomitable warrior, the Honourable Jacob Botcher; while the Honourable Samuel Doby of Hale, Speaker of the House, was unquestionably Herminius. How the three held the bridge that year will be told in as few and as stirring words as possible. A greater than Porsena confronted them, and well it was for them, and for the Empire, that the Body Guard of the Twenty stood behind them.

> "Lars Porsena of Clusium,
> By the Nine Gods he swore."

The morning after the *State Tribune* had printed that memorable speech on national affairs — statistics and all, with an editorial which gave every evidence of Mr. Peter Pardriff's best sparkle — Mr. Crewe appeared on the floor of the House with a new look in his eye which made discerning men turn and stare at him. It was the look of

the great when they are justly indignant, when their trust
— nobly given — has been betrayed. Washington, for
instance, must have had just such a look on the battle-
field of Trenton. The Honourable Jacob Botcher, pressing forward as fast as his bulk would permit and with the
newspaper in his hand, was met by a calm and distant
manner which discomposed that statesman, and froze his
stout index finger to the editorial which "perhaps Mr.
Crewe had not seen."

Mr. Crewe was too big for resentment, but he knew
how to meet people who didn't measure up to his standards. Yes, he had seen the editorial, and the weather
still continued fine. The Honourable Jacob was left behind scratching his head, and presently he sought a front
seat in which to think, the back ones not giving him room
enough. The brisk, cheery greeting of the Honourable
Brush Bascom fared no better, but Mr. Bascom was a
philosopher, and did not disturb the great when their
minds were revolving on national affairs and the welfare
of humanity in general. Mr. Speaker Doby and Mr.
Ridout got but abstract salutations also, and were cor-
respondingly dismayed.

That day, and for many days thereafter, Mr. Crewe
spent some time — as was entirely proper — among the
back seats, making the acquaintance of his humbler fellow-
members of the submerged four hundred and seventy. He
had too long neglected this, so he told them, but his mind
had been on high matters. During many of his mature
years he had pondered as to how the welfare of community
and State could be improved, and the result of that thought
was embodied in the bills of which they had doubtless received copies. If not, down went their names in a leather-
bound memorandum, and they got copies in the next
mails.

The delight of some of the simple rustic members at
this unbending of a great man may be imagined. To tell
the truth, they had looked with little favour upon the intimacy which had sprung up between him and those tyran-
nical potentates, Messrs. Botcher and Bascom, and many

who had the courage of their convictions expressed them
very frankly.   Messrs. Botcher and Bascom were, when all
was said, mere train despatchers of the Northeastern, who
might some day bring on a wreck the like of which the
State had never seen.   Mr. Crewe was in a receptive
mood; indeed his nature, like Nebuchadnezzar's, seemed
to have experienced some indefinable and vital change.
Was this the Mr. Crewe the humble rural members had
pictured to themselves?   Was this the Mr. Crewe who,
at the beginning of the session, had told them roundly
it was their duty to vote for his bills?

Mr. Crewe was surprised, he said, to hear so much
sentiment against the Northeastern Railroads.   Yes, he
was a friend of Mr. Flint's — they were neighbours in
the country.   But if these charges had any foundation
whatever, they ought to be looked into — they ought to
be taken up.   A sovereign people should not be governed
by a railroad.   Mr. Crewe was a business man, but first of
all he was a citizen ; as a business man he did not intend
to talk vaguely, but to investigate thoroughly.   And
then, if charges should be made, he would make them
specifically, and as a citizen contend for the right.

It is difficult to restrain one's pen in dealing with a
hero, but it is not too much to say that Mr. Crewe impressed many of the country members favourably.   How,
indeed, could he help doing so?   His language was
moderate, his poise that of a man of affairs, and there was
a look in his eye and a determination in his manner that
boded ill for the Northeastern if he should, after weighing
the facts, decide that they ought to be flagellated.   His
friendship with Mr. Flint and the suspicion that he
might be inclined to fancy Mr. Flint's daughter would
not influence him in the least; of that many of his hearers
were sure.   Not a few of them were invited to dinner at
the Duncan house, and shown the library and the conservatory.

"Walk right in," said Mr. Crewe.   "You can't hurt the
flowers unless you bump against the pots, and if you
walk straight you can't do that.   I brought the plants

down from my own hothouse in Leith. Those are French geraniums — very hard to get. They're double, you see, and don't look like the scrawny things you see in this country. Yes (with a good-natured smile), I guess they do cost something. I'll ask my secretary what I paid for that plant. Is that dinner, Waters? Come right in, gentlemen, we won't wait for ceremony."

Whereupon the delegation would file into the dining room in solemn silence behind the imperturbable Waters, with dubious glances at Mr. Waters' imperturbable understudy in green and buff and silver buttons. Honest red hands, used to milking at five o'clock in the morning, and hands not so red that measured dry goods over rural counters for insistent female customers fingered in some dismay what seemed an inexplicable array of table furniture.

"It don't make any difference which fork you take," said the good-natured owner of this palace of luxury, "only I shouldn't advise you to use one for the soup — you wouldn't get much of it — what? Yes, this house suits me very well. It was built by old man Duncan, you know, and his daughter married an Italian nobleman and lives in a castle. The State ought to buy the house for a governor's mansion. It's a disgrace that our governor should have to live in the Pelican Hotel, and especially in a room next to that of the chief counsel of the Northeastern, with only a curtain and a couple of folding doors between."

"That's right," declared an up-state member; "the governor hadn't ought to live next to Vane. But as to gettin' him a house like this — kind of royal, ain't it? Couldn't do justice to it on fifteen hundred a year, could he? Costs you a little mite more to live in it, don't it?"

"It costs me something," Mr. Crewe admitted modestly. "But then our governors are all rich men, or they couldn't afford to pay the Northeastern lobby campaign expenses. Not that I believe in a rich man for governor, gentlemen. My contention is that the State should pay its governors a sufficient salary to make them independent of the North-eastern, a salary on which they can live as befits a chief executive."

These sentiments, and others of a similar tenor, were usually received in silence by his rural guests, but Mr. Crewe, being a broad-minded man of human understanding, did not set down their lack of response to surliness or suspicion of a motive, but rather to the innate caution of the hill farmer ; and doubtless, also, to a natural awe of the unwonted splendour with which they were surrounded. In a brief time his kindly hospitality became a byword in the capital, and fabulous accounts of it were carried home at week ends to toiling wives and sons and daughters, to incredulous citizens who sat on cracker boxes and found the Sunday papers stale and unprofitable for weeks thereafter. The geraniums — the price of which Mr. Crewe had forgotten to find out — were appraised at four figures, and the conservatory became the hanging gardens of Babylon under glass ; the functionary in buff and green and silver buttons and his duties furnished the subject for long and heated arguments. And incidentally everybody who had a farm for sale wrote to Mr. Crewe. Since the motives of every philanthropist and public benefactor are inevitably challenged by cynics, there were many who asked the question, "What did Mr. Crewe want?" It is painful even to touch upon this when we know that Mr. Crewe was merely doing his duty as he saw it, when we know that he spelled the word, mentally, with a capital D.

There were many, too, who remarked that a touching friendship in the front seats (formerly plainly visible to the naked eye from the back) had been strained — at least. Mr. Crewe still sat with Mr. Botcher and Mr. Bascom, but he was not a man to pretend after the fires had cooled. The Honourable Jacob Botcher, with his eyes shut so tight that his honest face wore an expression of agony, seemed to pray every morning for the renewal of that friendship when the chaplain begged the Lord to guide the Legislature into the paths of truth ; and the Honourable Brush Bascom wore an air of resignation which was painful to see. Conversation languished, and the cosey and familiar haunts of the Pelican knew Mr. Crewe no more.

Mr. Crewe never forgot, of course, that he was a gentleman, and a certain polite intercourse existed. During the sessions, as a matter of fact, Mr. Bascom had many things to whisper to Mr. Botcher, and Mr. Botcher to Mr. Bascom, and in order to facilitate this Mr. Crewe changed seats with the Honourable Jacob. Neither was our hero a man to neglect, on account of strained relations, to insist upon his rights. His eyes were open now, and he saw men and things political as they were ; he knew that his bills for the emancipation of the State were prisoners in the maw of the dragon, and not likely to see the light of law. Not a legislative day passed that he did not demand, with a firmness and restraint which did him infinite credit, that Mr. Bascom's and Mr. Botcher's committees report those bills to the House either favourably or unfavourably. And we must do exact justice, likewise, to Messrs. Bascom and Botcher; they, too, incited perhaps thereto by Mr. Crewe's example, answered courteously that the very excellent bills in question were of such weight and importance as not to be decided on lightly, and that there were necessary State expenditures which had first to be passed upon. Mr. Speaker Doby, with all the will in the world, could do nothing : and on such occasions (Mr. Crewe could see) Mr. Doby bore a striking resemblance to the picture of the mock-turtle in " Alice in Wonderland " — a fact which had been pointed out by Miss Victoria Flint. In truth, all three of these gentlemen wore, when questioned, such a sorrowful and injured air as would have deceived a more experienced politician than the new member from Leith. The will to oblige was infinite.

There was no doubt about the fact that the session was rapidly drawing to a close; and likewise that the committees guided by the Honourables Jacob Botcher and Brush Bascom, composed of members carefully picked by that judge of mankind, Mr. Doby, were wrestling day and night (behind closed doors) with the intellectual problems presented by the bills of the member from Leith. It is not to be supposed that a man of Mr. Crewe's shrewdness would rest at the word of the chairmen. Other members were catechized, and in justice to Messrs. Bascom and Botcher it must be admitted that the assertions of these gentlemen were confirmed. It appeared that the amount of thought which was being lavished upon these measures was appalling.

By this time Mr. Crewe had made some new friends, as was inevitable when such a man unbent. Three of these friends owned, by a singular chance, weekly newspapers, and having conceived a liking as well as an admiration for him, began to say pleasant things about him in their columns—which Mr. Crewe (always thoughtful) sent to other friends of his. These new and accidental newspaper friends declared weekly that measures of paramount importance were slumbering in committees, and cited the measures. Other friends of Mr. Crewe were so inspired by affection and awe that they actually neglected their business and spent whole days in the rural districts telling people what a fine man Mr. Crewe was and circulating petitions for his bills; and incidentally the committees of Mr. Botcher and Mr. Bascom were flooded with these petitions, representing the spontaneous sentiment of an aggrieved populace.

> " Just then a scout came flying,
>   All wild with haste and fear :
> ' To arms ! to arms ! Sir Consul :
>   Lars Porsena is here.'
> On the low hills to westward
>   The Consul fixed his eye,
> And saw the swarthy storm of dust
>   Rise fast along the sky."

It will not do to push a comparison too far, and Mr. Hamilton Tooting, of course, ought not to be made to act the part of Tarquin the Proud. Like Tarquin, however, he had been deposed—one of those fatuous acts which the wisest will commit. No more could the Honourable Hilary well be likened to Pandora, for he only opened the box wide enough to allow one mischievous sprite to take wings — one mischievous sprite that was to prove a host. Talented and invaluable lieutenant that he was, Mr. Tooting had become an exile, to explain to any audience who should make it worth his while the mysterious acts by which the puppets on the stage were moved, and who moved them; who, for instance, wrote the declamation which his Excellency Asa Gray recited as his own. Mr. Tooting, as we have seen, had a remarkable business head, and combined with it — as Austen Vane remarked — the rare instinct of the Norway rat which goes down to the sea in ships — when they are safe. Burrowing continually amongst the bowels of the vessel, Mr. Tooting knew the weak timbers better than the Honourable Hilary Vane, who thought the ship as sound as the day Augustus Flint had launched her. But we have got a long way from Horatius in our imagery.

Little birds flutter around the capital, picking up what crumbs they may. One of them, occasionally fed by that humanitarian, the Honourable Jacob Botcher, whispered a secret that made the humanitarian knit his brows. He was the scout that came flying (if by a burst of imagination we can conceive the Honourable Jacob in this aërial act) — came flying to the Consul in room Number Seven with the news that Mr. Hamilton Tooting had been detected on two evenings slipping into the Duncan house. But the Consul — strong man that he was — merely laughed. The Honourable Elisha Jane did some scouting on his own account. Some people are so small as to be repelled by greatness, to be jealous of high gifts and power, and it was perhaps inevitable that a few of the humbler members whom Mr. Crewe had entertained should betray his hospitality, and misinterpret his pure motives.

It was a mere coincidence, perhaps, that after Mr. Jane's investigation the intellectual concentration which one of the committees had bestowed on two of Mr. Crewe's bills came to an end. These bills, it is true, carried no appropriation, and were, respectively, the acts to incorporate the State Economic League and the

Children's Charities Association. These suddenly appeared in the House one morning, with favourable recommendations, and, *mirabile dictu*, the end of the day saw them through the Senate and signed by his Excellency the governor. At last Mr. Crewe had stamped the mark of his genius on the statute books, and the Honourable Jacob Botcher, holding out an olive branch, took the liberty of congratulating him.

A vainer man, a lighter character than Humphrey Crewe, would have been content to have got something, and let it rest at that. Little Mr. Botcher or Mr. Speaker Doby, with his sorrowful smile, guessed the iron hand within the velvet glove of the Leith statesman; little they knew the man they were dealing with. Once aroused, he would not be pacified by bribes of cheap olive branches and laurels. When the proper time came, he would fling down the gauntlet before Rome itself, and then let Horatius and his friends beware.

The hour has struck at last — and the man is not wanting. The French Revolution found Napoleon ready, and our own Civil War General Ulysses Grant. Of that ever memorable session but three days remained, and those who had been prepared to rise in the good cause had long since despaired. The Pingsquit bill, and all other bills that spelled *liberty*, were still prisoners in the hands of grim jailers, and Thomas Gaylord, the elder, had worn several holes in the carpet of his private room in the Pelican, and could often be descried from Main Street running up and down between the windows like a caged lion, while young Tom had been spied standing, with his hands in his pockets, smiling on the world.

Young Tom had his own way of doing things, though he little dreamed of the help Heaven was to send him in this matter. There was, in the lower House, a young man by the name of Harper, a lawyer from Brighton, who was sufficiently eccentric not to carry a pass. The light of fame, as the sunset gilds a weathercock on a steeple, sometimes touches such men for an instant and makes them immortal. The name of Mr. Harper is remembered,

because it is linked with a greater one.   But Mr. Harper
was the first man over the wall.

History chooses odd moments for her entrances. It was
at the end of one of those busy afternoon sessions, with a
full house, when Messrs. Bascom, Botcher, and Ridout had
done enough of blocking and hacking and hewing to satisfy those doughty defenders of the bridge, that a slight,
unprepossessing-looking young man with spectacles arose
to make a motion.   The Honourable Jacob Botcher, with
his books and papers under his arm, was already picking
his way up the aisle, nodding genially to such of the
faithful as he saw ; Mr. Bascom was at the Speaker's
desk, and Mr. Ridout receiving a messenger from the Honourable Hilary at the door.   The Speaker, not without
some difficulty, recognized Mr. Harper amidst what seemed
the beginning of an exodus — and Mr. Harper read his
motion.

Men halted in the aisles, and nudged other men to make
them stop talking.   Mr. Harper's voice was not loud, and
it shook a trifle with excitement, but those who heard passed
on the news so swiftly to those who had not that the House
was sitting (or standing) in amazed silence by the time
the motion reached the Speaker, who had actually risen to
receive it.   Mr. Doby regarded it for a few seconds and
raised his eyes mournfully to Mr. Harper himself, as much
as to say that he would give the young man a chance to
take it back if he could — if the words had not been spoken
which would bring the offender to the block in the bloom
and enthusiasm of youth.   Misguided Mr. Harper had
committed unutterable treason to the Empire!

" The gentleman from Brighton, Mr. Harper," said the
Speaker, sadly, " offers the following resolution, and
moves its adoption : ' Resolved, that the Committee on
Incorporations be instructed to report House bill number
302, entitled *An act to incorporate the Pingsquit Railroad*,
by eleven-thirty o'clock to-morrow morning ' — the gentleman from Putnam, Mr. Bascom."

The House listened and looked on entranced, as though
they were the spectators to a tragedy.   And indeed it

seemed as though they were. Necks were craned to see Mr. Harper; he didn't look like a hero, but one never can tell about these little men. He had hurled defiance at the Northeastern Railroads, and that was enough for Mr. Redbrook and Mr. Widgeon and their friends, who prepared to rush into the fray trusting to Heaven for speech and parliamentary law. O for a leader now! Horatius is on the bridge, scarce concealing his disdain for this puny opponent, and Lartius and Herminius not taking the trouble to arm. Mr. Bascom will crush this one with the flat of his sword.

"Mr. Speaker," said that gentleman, informally, "as Chairman of the Committee on Incorporations, I rise to protest against such an unheard-of motion in this House. The very essence of orderly procedure, of effective business, depends on the confidence of the House in its committees, and in all of my years as a member I have never known of such a thing. Gentlemen of the House, your committee are giving to this bill and other measures their undivided attention, and will report them at the earliest practicable moment. I hope that this motion will be voted down."

Mr. Bascom, with a glance around to assure himself that most of the hundred members of the Newcastle delegation — vassals of the Winona Corporation and subject to the Empire — had not made use of their passes and boarded, as usual, the six o'clock train, took his seat. A buzz of excitement ran over the house, a dozen men were on their feet, including the plainly agitated Mr. Harper himself. But who is this, in the lunar cockpit before the Speaker's desk, demanding firmly to be heard — so firmly that Mr. Harper, with a glance at him, sits down again; so firmly that Mr. Speaker Doby, hypnotized by an eye, makes the blunder that will eventually cost him his own head?

"The gentleman from Leith, Mr. Crewe."

As though sensing a drama, the mutterings were hushed once more. Mr. Jacob Botcher leaned forward, and cracked his seat; but none, even those who had tasted of his hospitality, recognized that the Black Knight had en-

Q

tered the lists — the greatest deeds of this world, and the heroes of them, coming unheralded out of the plain clay. Mr. Crewe was the calmest man under the roof as he saluted the Speaker, walked up to the clerk's desk, turned his back to it, and leaned both elbows on it; and he regarded the sea of faces with the identical self-possession he had exhibited when he had made his famous address on national affairs. He did not raise his voice at the beginning, but his very presence seemed to compel silence, and curiosity was at fever heat. What was he going to say?

"Gentlemen of the House," said Mr. Crewe, "I have listened to the gentleman from Putnam with some — amusement. He has made the statement that he and his committee are giving to the Pingsquit bill and other measures — some other measures — their undivided attention. Of this I have no doubt whatever. He neglected to define the species of attention he is giving them — I should define it as the kindly care which the warden of a penitentiary bestows upon his charges."

Mr. Crewe was interrupted here. The submerged four hundred and seventy had had time to rub their eyes and get their breath, to realize that their champion had dealt Mr. Bascom a blow to cleave his helm, and a roar of mingled laughter and exultation arose in the back seats, and there was more craning to see the glittering eyes of the Honourable Brush and the expressions of his two companions-in-arms. Mr. Speaker Doby beat the stone with his gavel, while Mr. Crewe continued to lean back calmly until the noise was over.

"Gentlemen," he went on, "I will enter at the proper time into a situation — known, I believe, to most of you — that brings about a condition of affairs by which the gentleman's committee, or the gentleman himself, with his capacious pockets, does not have to account to the House for every bill assigned to him by the Speaker. I have taken the trouble to examine a little into the gentleman's past record — he has been chairman of such committees for years past, and I find no trace that bills inimical to certain great interests have ever been reported back by him. The Pingsquit bill involves the vital principle of competition. I have read it with considerable care and believe it to be, in itself, a good measure, which deserves a fair hearing. I have had no conversation whatever with those who are said to be its promoters. If the bill is to pass, it has little enough time to get to the Senate. By the gentleman from Putnam's own statement his committee have given it its share of attention, and I believe this House is entitled to know the verdict, is entitled to accept or reject a report. I hope the motion will prevail."

He sat down amidst a storm of applause which would have turned the head of a lesser man. No such personal ovation had been seen in the House for years. How the Speaker got order; how the Honourable Brush Bascom declared that Mr. Crewe would be called upon to prove his statements; how Mr. Botcher regretted that a new member of such promise should go off at half-cock; how Mr. Ridout hinted that the new member might think he had an animus; how Mr. Terry of Lee and Mr. Widgeon of Hull denounced, in plain hill language, the North-eastern Railroads and lauded the man of prominence who had the grit to oppose them, need not be gone into. Mr. Crewe at length demanded the previous question, which was carried, and the motion was carried, too, two hundred and fifty to one hundred and fifty-two. The House adjourned.

We will spare the blushes of the hero of this occasion, who was threatened with suffocation by an inundation from the back seats. In answer to the congratulations and queries, he replied modestly that nobody else seemed to have had the sand to do it, so he did it himself. He regarded it as a matter of duty, however unpleasant and unforeseen; and if, as they said, he had been a pioneer, education and a knowledge of railroads and the world had helped him. Whereupon, adding tactfully that he desired the evening to himself to prepare for the battle of the morrow (of which he foresaw he was to bear the burden), he extricated himself from his admirers and made his way unostentatiously out of a side door into his sleigh. For the man who had kindled a fire — the blaze of which was to mark an epoch — he was exceptionally calm. Not so the only visitor whom Waters had instructions to admit that evening.

"Say, you hit it just right," cried the visitor, too exultant to take off his overcoat. "I've been down through the Pelican, and there ain't been such excitement since Snow and Giddings had the fight for United States senator in the '80's. The place is all torn up, and you can't get a room there for love or money. They tell me they've been havin' conferences steady in Number Seven since the session closed, and Hilary Vane's sent for all the Federal and State office-holders to be here in the morning and lobby. Botcher and Jane and Bascom are circulatin' like hot water, tellin' everybody that because they wouldn't saddle the State with a debt with your bills you turned sour on 'em, and that you're more of a corporation and railroad man than any of 'em. They've got their machine to working a thousand to the minute, and everybody they have a slant on is going into line. One of them fellers, a conductor, told me he had to go with 'em. But our boys ain't idle, I can tell you that. I was in the back of the gallery when you spoke up, and I shook 'em off the leash right away."

Mr. Crewe leaned back from the table and thrust his hands in his pockets and smiled. He was in one of his delightful moods.

"Take off your overcoat, Tooting," he said; "you'll find one of my best political cigars over there, in the usual place."

"Well, I guessed about right, didn't I?" inquired Mr. Tooting, biting off one of the "political cigars." "I gave you a pretty straight tip, didn't I, that young Tom Gaylord was goin' to have somebody make that motion to-day? But say, it's funny he couldn't get a better one than that feller Harper. If you hadn't come along, they'd have smashed him to pulp. I'll bet the most surprised man in the State to-night, next to Brush Bascom, is young Tom

Gaylord.   It's a wonder he ain't been up here to thank you."

"Maybe he has been," replied Mr. Crewe.   "I told Waters to keep everybody out to-night because I want to know exactly what I'm going to say on the floor to-morrow.   I don't want 'em to give me trouble.   Did you bring some of those papers with you ? "

Mr. Tooting fished a bundle from his overcoat pocket. The papers in question, of which he had a great number stored away in Ripton, represented the foresight, on Mr. Tooting's part, of years.   He was a young man with a praiseworthy ambition to get on in the world, and during his apprenticeship in the office of the Honourable Hilary Vane many letters and documents had passed through his hands.   A less industrious person would have neglected the opportunity.   Mr. Tooting copied them ; and some, which would have gone into the waste-basket, he laid carefully aside, bearing in mind the adage about little scraps of paper — if there is one.   At any rate, he now had a manuscript collection which was unique in its way, which would have been worth much to a great many men, and with characteristic generosity he was placing it at the disposal of Mr. Crewe.

Mr. Crewe, in reading them, had other sensations.   He warmed with indignation as an American citizen that a man should sit in a mahogany office in New York and dictate the government of a free and sovereign State; and he found himself in the grip of a righteous wrath when he recalled what Mr. Flint had written to him.   "As a neighbour, it will give me the greatest pleasure to help you to the extent of my power, but the Northeastern Railroads cannot interfere in legislative or political matters."   The effrontery of it was appalling !   Where, he demanded of Mr. Tooting, did the common people come in ?   And this extremely pertinent question Mr. Tooting was unable to answer.

But the wheels of justice had begun to turn.

Mr. Tooting had not exaggerated the tumult and affright at the Pelican Hotel.   The private telephone in Num-

ber Seven was busy all evening, while more or less prominent gentlemen were using continually the public ones in
the boxes in the reading room downstairs. The Feudal
System was showing what it could do, and the word had
gone out to all the holders of fiefs that the vassals should
be summoned. The Duke of Putnam had sent out a general call to the office-holders in that county. Theirs not
to reason why — but obey; and some of them, late as was
the hour, were already travelling (free) towards the capital. Even the congressional delegation in Washington
had received telegrams, and sent them again to Federal
office-holders in various parts of the State. If Mr. Crewe
had chosen to listen, he could have heard the tramp of
armed men. But he was not of the metal to be dismayed
by the prospect of a great conflict. He was as cool as
Cromwell, and after Mr. Tooting had left him to take
charge once more of his own armies in the field, the gentleman from Leith went to bed and slept soundly.

The day of the battle dawned darkly, with great flakes
flying. As early as seven o'clock the later cohorts began
to arrive, and were soon as thick as bees in the Pelican,
circulating in the lobby, conferring in various rooms of
which they had the numbers with occupants in bed and
out. A wonderful organization, that Feudal System, which
could mobilize an army overnight! And each unit of it,
like the bee, working unselfishly for the good of the
whole; like the bee, flying straight for the object to be
attained. Every member of the House from Putnam
County, for instance, was seen by one of these indefatigable
captains, and if the member had a mortgage or an ambition, or a wife and family that made life a problem, or a
situation on the railroad or in some of the larger manufacturing establishments, let him beware! If he lived in lodgings in the town, he stuck his head out of the window to
perceive a cheery neighbour from the country on his doorstep. Think of a system which could do this, not for Putnam County alone, but for all the counties in the State!

The Honourable Hilary Vane, captain-general of the
Forces, had had but four hours' sleep, and his Excellency,

the Honourable Asa Gray, when he arose in the twilight
of the morning, had to step carefully to avoid the cigar butts
on the floor which — like so many empty cartridge shells —
were unpleasant reminders that a rebellion of no mean
magnitude had arisen against the power to which he owed
allegiance, and by the favour of which he was attended with
pomp and circumstance wherever he chose to go.

Long before eleven o'clock the paths to the state-house
were thronged with people. Beside the office-holders and
their friends who were in town, there were many residents of the capital city in the habit of going to hear the
livelier debates. Not that the powers of the Empire had
permitted debates on most subjects, but there could be no
harm in allowing the lower House to discuss as fiercely as
they pleased dog and sheep laws and hedgehog bounties.
But now! The oldest resident couldn't remember a
case of high treason and rebellion against the Northeastern such as this promised to be, and the sensation
took on an added flavour from the fact that the arch
rebel was a figure of picturesque interest, a millionaire
with money enough to rent the Duncan house and fill its
long-disused stable with horses, who was a capitalist himself and a friend of Mr. Flint's; of whom it was said that
he was going to marry Mr. Flint's daughter!

Long before eleven, too, the chiefs over tens and the
chiefs over hundreds had gathered their men and
marched them into the state-house; and Mr. Tooting,
who was everywhere that morning, noticed that some
of these led soldiers had pieces of paper in their hands.
The chaplain arose to pray for guidance, and the House
was crowded to its capacity, and the gallery filled with
eager and expectant faces — but the hero of the hour had
not yet arrived. When at length he did walk down the
aisle, as unconcernedly as though he were an unknown
man entering a theatre, feminine whispers of "There he is!"
could plainly be heard above the buzz, and simultaneous
applause broke out in spots, causing the Speaker to rap
sharply with his gavel. Poor Mr. Speaker Doby! He
looked more like the mock-turtle than ever! and might

have exclaimed, too, that once he had been a real turtle: only yesterday, in fact, before he had made the inconceivable blunder of recognizing Mr. Humphrey Crewe. Mr. Speaker Doby had spent a part of the night in room Number Seven listening to things about himself. Herminius the unspeakable has given the enemy a foothold in Rome.

Apparently unaware that he was the centre of interest, Mr. Crewe, carrying a neat little bag full of papers, took his seat beside the Honourable Jacob Botcher, nodding to that erstwhile friend as a man of the world should. And Mr. Botcher, not to be outdone, nodded back.

We shall skip over the painful interval that elapsed before the bill in question was reached: painful, at least, for every one but Mr. Crewe, who sat with his knees crossed and his arms folded. The hosts were facing each other, awaiting the word; the rebels prayerfully watching their gallant leader; and the loyal vassals — whose wavering ranks had been added to overnight — with their eyes on Mr. Bascom. And in justice to that veteran it must be said, despite the knock-out blow he had received, that he seemed as debonair as ever.

> "Now while the three were tightening
> The harness on their backs."

Mr. Speaker Doby read many committee reports, and at the beginning of each there was a stir of expectation that it might be the signal for battle. But at length he fumbled among his papers, cleared away the lump in his throat, and glanced significantly at Mr. Bascom.

"The Committee on Incorporations, to whom was referred House bill number 302, entitled *An act to incorporate the Pingsquit Railroad*, having considered the same, report the same with the following resolution: 'Resolved, that it is inexpedient to legislate. Brush Bascom, for the Committee.' Gentlemen, are you ready for the question? As many as are of opinion that the report of the Committee should be adopted — the gentleman from Putnam, Mr. Bascom."

Again let us do exact justice, and let us not be led by

our feelings to give a prejudiced account of this struggle. The Honourable Brush Bascom, skilled from youth in the use of weapons, opened the combat so adroitly that more than once the followers of his noble opponent winced and trembled. The bill, Mr. Bascom said, would have been reported that day, anyway — a statement received with mingled cheers and jeers. Then followed a brief and somewhat intimate history of the Gaylord Lumber Company, not at all flattering to that corporation. Mr. Bascom hinted at an animus: there was no more need for a railroad in the Pingsquit Valley than there was for a merry-go-round in the cellar of the state-house. (Loud laughter from everybody, some irreverent person crying out that a merry-go-round was better than poker tables.) When Mr. Bascom came to discuss the gentleman from Leith, and recited the names of the committees for which Mr. Crewe — in his desire to be of service to the State — had applied, there was more laughter, even amongst Mr. Crewe's friends, and Mr. Speaker Doby relaxed so far as to smile sadly. Mr. Bascom laid his watch on the clerk's desk and began to read the list of bills Mr. Crewe had introduced, and as this reading proceeded some of the light-minded showed a tendency to become slightly hysterical. Mr. Bascom said that he would like to see all those bills grow into laws, — with certain slight changes, — but that he could not conscientiously vote to saddle the people with another Civil War debt. It was well for the State, he hinted, that those committees were composed of stanch men who would do their duty in all weathers, regardless of demagogues who sought to gratify inordinate ambitions.

The hope of the revolutionists bore these strokes and others as mighty with complacency, as though they had been so many playful taps; and while the battle surged hotly around him he sat calmly listening or making occasional notes with a gold pencil. Born leader that he was, he was biding his time. Mr. Bascom's attack was met, valiantly but unskilfully, from the back seats. The Honourable Jacob Botcher arose, and filled the hall with extracts from the "Book of Arguments" — in which he had been coached overnight by the Honourable Hilary Vane.   Mr. Botcher's tone towards his erstwhile friend was regretful,— a good man gone wrong through impulse and inexperience.   " I am, sir," said Mr. Bascom to the Speaker, "sincerely sorry —sincerely sorry that an individual of such ability as the member from Leith should be led, by the representations of political adventurers and brigands and malcontents, into his present deplorable position of criticising a State which is his only by adoption, the political conditions of which were as sound and as free from corporate domination, sir, as those of any State in the broad Union." (*Loud cheers.*) This appeal to State pride by Mr. Botcher is a masterstroke, and the friends of the champion of the liberties of the people are beginning (some of them) to be a little nervous and doubtful.

Following Mr. Botcher were wild and scattering speeches from the back benches — unskilful and pitiable counterstrokes.   Where was the champion ?   Had he been tampered with overnight, and persuaded of the futility of rebellion?   Persuaded that his head would be more useful on his own neck in the councils of the nation than on exhibition to the populace from the point of a pike ?   It looks, to a calm spectator from the gallery, as though the rebel forces are growing weaker and more demoralized every moment.   Mr. Redbrook's speech, vehement and honest, helps a little; people listen to an honest and forceful man, however he may lack technical knowledge, but the majority of the replies are mere incoherent denunciations of the Northeastern Railroads.

On the other hand, the astounding discipline amongst the legions of the Empire excites the admiration and despair even of their enemies; there is no random fighting here and breaking of ranks to do useless hacking.   A grave farmer with a beard delivers a short and temperate speech (which he has by heart), mildly inquiring what the State would do without the Northeastern Railroads; and the very moderation of this query coming from a plain and hard-headed agriculturist (the boss of Grenville, if

one but knew it!) has a telling effect. And then to cap
the climax, to make the attitude of the rebels even more
ridiculous in the minds of thinking people, Mr. Ridout
is given the floor. Skilled in debate when he chooses to
enter it, his knowledge of the law only exceeded by his
knowledge of how it is to be evaded — to Lartius is
assigned the task of following up the rout. And Mr.
Crewe has ceased taking notes.

When the House leader and attorney for the Northeastern took his seat, the victory to all appearances was
won. It was a victory for conservatism and established
order against sensationalism and anarchy — Mr. Ridout
had contrived to make that clear without actually saying
so. It was as if the Ute Indians had sought to capture
Washington and conduct the government. Just as ridiculous as that! The debate seemed to be exhausted, and
the long-suffering Mr. Doby was inquiring for the fiftieth
time if the House were ready for the question, when Mr.
Crewe of Leith arose and was recognized. In three months he
had acquired such a remarkable knowledge of the game of
parliamentary tactics as to be able, patiently, to wait until
the bolt of his opponents had been shot; and a glance sufficed to revive the drooping spirits of his followers, and to
assure them that their leader knew what he was about.

"Mr. Speaker," he said, "I have listened with great
care to the masterly defence of that corporation on which
our material prosperity and civic welfare is founded
(*laughter*); I have listened to the gentleman's learned
discussion of the finances of that road, tending to prove
that it is an eleemosynary institution on a grand scale. I
do not wish to question unduly the intellects of those
members of this House who by their votes will prove that
they have been convinced by the gentleman's argument."
Here Mr. Crewe paused and drew a slip of paper from his
pocket and surveyed the back seats. "But I perceive,"
he continued, "that a great interest has been taken in this
debate — so great an interest that since yesterday numbers
of gentlemen have come in from various parts of the State
to listen to it (*laughter and astonishment*), gentlemen

who hold Federal and State offices. (*Renewed laughter and searching of the House.*) I repeat, Mr. Speaker, that I do not wish to question the intellects of my fellow-members, but I notice that many of them who are seated near the Federal and State office-holders in question have in their hands slips of paper similar to this. And I have reason to believe that these slips were written by somebody in room Number Seven of the Pelican Hotel." (*Tremendous commotion, and craning to see whether one's neighbour has a slip. The faces of the redoubtable three a study.*)

"I procured one of these slips," Mr. Crewe continued, "through a fellow-member who has no use for it — whose intelligence, in fact, is underrated by the gentlemen in Number Seven. I will read the slip.

"'Vote *yes* on the question. *Yes* means that the report of the Committee will be accepted, and that the Pingsquit bill will *not* pass. Wait for Bascom's signal, and destroy this paper.'"

There was no need, indeed, for Mr. Crewe to say any more than that — no need for the admirable discussion of railroad finance from an expert's standpoint which followed to controvert Mr. Ridout's misleading statements. The reading of the words on the slip of paper of which he had so mysteriously got possession (through Mr. Hamilton Tooting) was sufficient to bring about a disorder that — for a full minute — Mr. Speaker Doby found it impossible to quell. The gallery shook with laughter, and honourable members with slips of paper in their hands were made as conspicuous as if they had been caught wearing dunces' caps.

It was then only, with belated wisdom, that Mr. Bascom and his two noble companions gave up the fight, and let the horde across the bridge — too late, as we shall see. The populace, led by a redoubtable leader, have learned their strength. It is true that the shining senatorial twenty of the body-guard stand ready to be hacked to pieces at their posts before the Pingsquit bill shall become a law; and should unutterable treason take place here, his Excellency is prepared to be drawn and quartered

rather than sign it. It is the Senate which, in this somewhat inaccurate repetition of history, hold the citadel if
not the bridge; and in spite of the howling mob below
their windows, scornfully refuse even to discuss the
Pingsquit bill. The Honourable Hilary Vane, whose
face they study at dinner time, is not worried. Popular
wrath does not continue to boil, and many changes will
take place in the year before the Legislature meets
again.

This is the Honourable Hilary's public face. But are
there not private conferences in room Number Seven of
which we can know nothing — exceedingly uncomfortable
conferences for Horatius and his companions? Are there
not private telegrams and letters to the president of the
Northeastern in New York advising him that the Pingsquit bill has passed the House, and that a certain
Mr. Crewe is primarily responsible? And are there not
queries — which history may disclose in after years — as
to whether Mr. Crewe's abilities as a statesman have not
been seriously underrated by those who should have been
the first to perceive them? Verily, pride goeth before a
fall.

In this modern version of ours, the fathers throng about
another than Horatius after the session of that memorable
morning. Publicly and privately, Mr. Crewe is being
congratulated, and we know enough of his character to
appreciate the modesty with which the congratulations
are accepted. He is the same Humphrey Crewe that he
was before he became the corner-stone of the temple;
success is a mere outward and visible sign of intrinsic
worth in the inner man, and Mr. Crewe had never for a
moment underestimated his true value.

"There's no use wasting time in talking about it," he
told the grateful members who sought to press his hands.
"Go home and organize. I've got your name. Get your
neighbours into line, and keep me informed. I'll pay
for the postage-stamps. I'm no impractical reformer,
and if we're going to do this thing, we'll have to do it
right."

They left him, impressed by the force of this argument, with an added respect for Mr. Crewe, and a vague feeling that they were pledged to something which made not a few of them a trifle uneasy.   Mr. Redbrook was one of these.

The felicitations of his new-found friend and convert, Mr. Tooting, Mr. Crewe cut short with the terseness of a born commander.

"Never mind that," he said, "and follow 'em up and get 'em pledged if you can."

Get 'em pledged!   Pledged to what?   Mr. Tooting evidently knew, for he wasted no precious moments in asking questions.

There is no time at this place to go into the feelings of Mr. Tom Gaylord the younger when he learned that his bill had passed the House.   He, too, meeting Mr. Crewe in the square, took the opportunity to express his gratitude to the member from Leith.

" Come in on Friday afternoon, Gaylord," answered Mr. Crewe.   " I've got several things to talk to you about. Your general acquaintance around the State will be useful, and there must be men you know of in the lumber sections who can help us considerably."

" Help us ? " repeated young Tom, in some surprise.

" Certainly," replied Mr. Crewe ; " you don't think we're going to drop the fight here, do you?   We've got to put a stop in this State to political domination by a railroad, and as long as there doesn't seem to be any one else to take hold, I'm going to.   Your bill's a good bill, and we'll pass it next session."

Young Tom regarded Mr. Crewe with a frank stare.

" I'm going up to the Pingsquit Valley on Friday," he answered.

" Then you'd better come up to Leith to see me as soon as you get back," said Mr. Crewe.   " These things can't wait, and have to be dealt with practically."

Young Tom had not been the virtual head of the Gaylord Company for some years without gaining a little knowledge of politics and humanity.   The invitation to

Leith he valued, of course, but he felt that it would not do to accept it with too much ardour. He was, he said, a very busy man.

"That's the trouble with most people," declared Mr. Crewe; "they won't take the time to bother about politics, and then they complain when things don't go right. Now I'm givin' my time to it, when I've got other large interests to attend to."

On his way back to the Pelican, young Tom halted several times reflectively, as certain points in this conversation — which he seemed to have missed at the time — came back to him. His gratitude to Mr. Crewe as a public benefactor was profound, of course; but young Tom's sense of humour was peculiar, and he laughed more than once, out loud, at nothing at all. Then he became grave again, and went into the hotel and wrote a long letter, which he addressed to Mr. Austen Vane.

And now, before this chapter which contains these memorable events is closed, one more strange and significant fact is to be chronicled. On the evening of the day which saw Mr. Crewe triumphantly leading the insurgent forces to victory, that gentleman sent his private secretary to the office of the *State Tribune* to leave an order for fifty copies of the paper to be delivered in the morning. Morning came, and the fifty copies, and Mr. Crewe's personal copy in addition, were handed to him by the faithful Waters when he entered his dining room at an early hour. Life is full of disillusions. Could this be the *State Tribune* he held in his hand? The *State Tribune* of Mr. Peter Pardriff, who had stood so stanchly for Mr. Crewe and better things? Who had hitherto held the words of the Leith statesman in such golden estimate as to curtail advertising columns when it was necessary to print them for the public good?

Mr. Crewe's eye travelled from column to column, from page to page, in vain. By some incredible oversight on the part of Mr. Pardriff, the ringing words were not there, — nay, the soul-stirring events of that eventful day appeared, on closer inspection, to have been deliberately edited out! The terrible indignation of the righteous arose as Mr. Crewe read (in the legislative proceedings of the day before) that the Pingsquit bill had been discussed by certain members — of whom he was one — and passed. This was all — literally all! If Mr. Pardriff had lived in the eighteenth century, he would probably have referred as casually to the Boston massacre as a street fight — which it was.

Profoundly disgusted with human kind,— as the noblest of us will be at times,— Mr. Crewe flung down the paper, and actually forgot to send the fifty copies to his friends!

CHAPTER XV

THE DISTURBANCE OF JUNE SEVENTH

AFTER Mr. Speaker Doby had got his gold watch from
an admiring and apparently reunited House, and had
wept over it, the Legislature adjourned. This was about
the first of April, that sloppiest and windiest of months
in a northern climate, and Mr. Crewe had intended, as
usual, to make a little trip southward to a club of which
he was a member. A sense of duty, instead, took him to
Leith, where he sat through the days in his study, dictating letters, poring over a great map of the State which
he had hung on the wall, and scanning long printed lists.
If we could stand behind him, we should see that these
are what are known as check-lists, or rosters of the voters in
various towns.

Mr. Crewe also has an unusual number of visitors for
this muddy weather, when the snow-water is making
brooks of the roads. Interested observers — if there
were any — might have remarked that his friendship with
Mr. Hamilton Tooting had increased, that gentleman
coming up from Ripton at least twice a week, and aiding
Mr. Crewe to multiply his acquaintances by bringing
numerous strangers to see him. Mr. Tooting, as we
know, had abandoned the law office of the Honourable
Hilary Vane and was now engaged in travelling over the
State, apparently in search of health. These were signs,
surely, which the wise might have read with profit: in
the offices, for instance, of the Honourable Hilary Vane
in Ripton Square, where seismic disturbances were registered; but the movement of the needle (to the Honourable Hilary's eye) was almost imperceptible. What
observer, however experienced, would have believed that
such delicate tracings could herald a volcanic eruption?

Throughout the month of April the needle kept up its persistent registering, and the Honourable Hilary continued to smile. The Honourable Jacob Botcher, who had made a trip to Ripton and had cited that very decided earthquake shock of the Pingsquit bill, had been ridiculed for his pains, and had gone away again comforted by communion with a strong man. The Honourable Jacob had felt little shocks in his fief: Mr. Tooting had visited it, sitting with his feet on the tables of hotel waiting-rooms, holding private intercourse with gentlemen who had been disappointed in office. Mr. Tooting had likewise been a sojourner in the domain of the Duke of Putnam. But the Honourable Brush was not troubled, and had presented Mr. Tooting with a cigar.

In spite of the strange omission of the *State Tribune* to print his speech and to give his victory in the matter of the Pingsquit bill proper recognition, Mr. Crewe was too big a man to stop his subscription to the paper. Conscious that he had done his duty in that matter, neither praise nor blame could affect him; and although he had not been mentioned since, he read it assiduously every afternoon upon its arrival at Leith, feeling confident that Mr. Peter Pardriff (who had always in private conversation proclaimed himself emphatically for reform) would not eventually refuse — to a prophet — public recognition. One afternoon towards the end of that month of April, when the sun had made the last snow-drift into a pool, Mr. Crewe settled himself on his south porch and opened the *State Tribune*, and his heart gave a bound as his eye fell upon the following heading to the leading editorial: —

A WORTHY PUBLIC SERVANT FOR GOVERNOR

Had his reward come at last? Had Mr. Peter Pardriff seen the error of his way? Mr. Crewe leisurely folded back the sheet, and called to his secretary, who was never far distant.

"Look here," he said, " I guess Pardriff's recovered his senses. Look here!"

The tired secretary, ready with his pencil and notebook to order fifty copies, responded, staring over his employer's shoulder. It has been said of men in battle that they have been shot and have run forward some hundred feet without knowing what has happened to them. And so Mr. Crewe got five or six lines into that editorial before he realized in full the baseness of Mr. Pardriff's treachery.

"These are times" (so ran Mr. Pardriff's composition) "when the sure and steadying hand of a strong man is needed at the helm of State. A man of conservative, business habits of mind; a man who weighs the value of traditions equally with the just demands of a new era; a man with a knowledge of public affairs derived from long experience;" (! ! !) "a man who has never sought office, but has held it by the will of the people, and who himself is a proof that the conduct of State institutions in the past has been just and equitable. One who has served with distinction upon such boards as the Railroad Commission, the Board of Equalization, etc., etc." (! ! !) "A stanch Republican, one who puts party before —" here the newspaper began to shake a little, and Mr. Crewe could not for the moment see whether the next word were *place* or *principle*. He skipped a few lines. The *Tribune*, it appeared, had a scintillating idea, which surely must have occurred to others in the State. "Why not the Honourable Adam B. Hunt of Edmundton for the next governor?"

The Honourable Adam B. Hunt of Edmundton!

It is a pleasure to record, at this crisis, that Mr. Crewe fixed upon his secretary as steady an eye as though Mr. Pardriff's bullet had missed its mark.

"Get me," he said coolly, "the 'State Encyclopædia of Prominent Men.'" (Just printed. Fogarty and Co., Newcastle, publishers.)

The secretary fetched it, open at the handsome and lifelike steel-engraving of the Honourable Adam, with his broad forehead and kindly, twinkling eyes, and the tuft of beard on his chin; with his ample statesman's coat in natural creases, and his white shirt-front and little black tie. Mr. Crewe gazed at this work of art long and earnestly. The Honourable Adam B. Hunt did not in the least have the appearance of a bolt from the blue. And then Mr. Crewe read his biography.

Two things he shrewdly noted about that biography; it was placed, out of alphabetical order, fourth in the book, and it was longer than any other with one exception — that of Mr. Ridout, the capital lawyer. Mr. Ridout's place was second in this invaluable volume, he being preceded only by a harmless patriarch. These facts were laid before Mr. Tooting, who was directed by telephone to come to Leith as soon as he should arrive in Ripton from his latest excursion. It was nine o'clock at night when that long-suffering and mud-bespattered individual put in an appearance at the door of his friend's study.

"Because I didn't get on to it," answered Mr. Tooting, in response to a reproach for not having registered a warning — for he was Mr. Crewe's seismograph. "I knew old Adam was on the Railroads' governor's bench, but I hadn't any notion he'd been moved up to the top of the batting-list. I told you right. Ridout was going to be their next governor if you hadn't singed him with the Pingsquit bill. This was done pretty slick, wasn't it? Hilary got back from New York day before yesterday, and Pardriff has the editorial to-day. Say, I always told you Pardriff wasn't a reformer, didn't I?"

Mr. Crewe looked pained.

"I prefer to believe the best of people until I know the worst," he said. "I did not think Mr. Pardriff capable of ingratitude."

What Mr. Crewe meant by this remark is enigmatical.

"He ain't," replied Mr. Tooting, "he's grateful for that red ticket he carries around with him when he travels, and he's grateful to the Honourable Adam B. Hunt for favours to come. Peter Pardriff's a grateful cuss, all right, all right."

Mr. Crewe tapped his fingers on the desk thoughtfully.

"The need of a reform campaign is more apparent than ever," he remarked.

Mr. Tooting put his tongue in his cheek; and, seeing a dreamy expression on his friend's face, accidentally helped himself to a cigar out of the wrong box.

"It's up to a man with a sense of duty and money to make it," Mr. Tooting agreed, taking a long pull at the Havana.

"As for the money," replied Mr. Crewe, "the good citizens of the State should be willing to contribute largely. I have had a list of men of means prepared, who will receive notices at the proper time."

Mr. Hamilton Tooting spread out his feet, and appeared to be studying them carefully.

"It's funny you should have mentioned cash," he said, after a moment's silence, "and it's tough on you to have to be the public-spirited man to put it up at the start. I've got a little memorandum here," he added, fumbling apologetically in his pocket; "it certainly costs something to move the boys around and keep 'em indignant."

Mr. Tooting put the paper on the edge of the desk, and Mr. Crewe, without looking, reached out his hand for it, the pained expression returning to his face.

"Tooting," he said, "you've got a very flippant way of speaking of serious things. It strikes me that these expenses are out of all proportion to the simplicity of the task involved. It strikes me — ahem — that you might find, in some quarters at least, a freer response to a movement founded on principle."

"That's right," declared Mr. Tooting, "I've thought so myself. I've got mad, and told 'em so to their faces. But you've said yourself, Mr. Crewe, that we've got to deal with this thing practically."

"Certainly," Mr. Crewe interrupted. He loved the word.

"And we've got to get workers, haven't we? And it costs money to move 'em round, don't it? We haven't got a bushel basket of passes. Look here," and he pushed another paper at Mr. Crewe, "here's ten new ones who've made up their minds that you're the finest man in the State. That makes twenty."

Mr. Crewe took that paper deprecatingly, but neverthe-less began a fire of cross-questions on Mr. Tooting as to the personality, habits, and occupations of the discerning ten in question, making certain little marks of his own against each name. Thus it will be seen that Mr. Crewe knew perfectly what he was about — although no one else did except Mr. Tooting, who merely looked mysterious when questioned on the streets of Ripton or Newcastle or Kingston. It was generally supposed, however, that the gentleman from Leith was going to run for the State Senate, and was attempting to get a following in other counties, in order to push through his measures next time. Hence the tiny fluctuations of Hilary Vane's seismograph — an instrument, as will be shown, utterly out-of-date. Not so the motto *toujours l'audace*. Geniuses continue (at long intervals) to be born, and to live up to that motto.

That seismograph of the Honourable Hilary's persisted in tracing only a slightly ragged line throughout the beautiful month of May, in which favourable season the campaign of the Honourable Adam B. Hunt took root and flourished — apparently from the seed planted by the *State Tribune*. The ground, as usual, had been carefully prepared, and trained gardeners raked, and watered, and weeded the patch. It had been decreed and countersigned that the Honourable Adam B. Hunt was the flower that was to grow this year.

There must be something vitally wrong with an in-strument which failed to register the great earthquake shock of June the seventh !

Now that we have come to the point where this shock is to be recorded on these pages, we begin to doubt whether our own pen will be able adequately to register it, and whether the sheet is long enough and broad enough upon which to portray the relative importance of the dis-turbance created. The trouble is, that there is nothing to measure it by. What other event in the history of the State produced the vexation of spirit, the anger, the tears, the profanity ; the derision, the laughter of fools, the con-tempt ; the hope, the glee, the prayers, the awe, the dumb amazement at the superb courage of this act? No, for a just comparison we shall have to reach back to history and fable: David and Goliath; Theseus and the Minotaur; or, better still, Cadmus and the Dragon! It was Cadmus (if we remember rightly) who wasted no time whatever, but actually jumped down the dragon's throat and cut him up from the inside! And it was Cadmus, likewise, who afterwards sowed the dragon's teeth.

That wondrous clear and fresh summer morning of June the seventh will not be forgotten for many years. The trees were in their early leaf in Ripton Square, and the dark pine patches on Sawanec looked (from Austen's little office) like cloud shadows against the shimmer of the tender green. He sat at his table, which was covered with open law-books and papers, but his eyes were on the distant mountain, and every scent-laden breeze wafted in at his open window seemed the bearer of a tremulous, wistful, yet imperious message — " Come! " Throughout the changing seasons Sawanec called to him in words of love: sometimes her face was hidden by cloud and fog — and yet he heard her voice! Sometimes her perfume — as to-day — made him dream; sometimes, when the western heavens were flooded with the golden light of the infinite, she veiled herself in magic purple, when to gaze at her was an exquisite agony, and she became as one forbidden to man. Though his soul cried out to her across the spaces, she was not for him. She was not for him!

With a sigh he turned to his law-books again, and sat for a while staring steadfastly at a section of the Act of Consolidation of the Northeastern Railroads which he had stumbled on that morning. The section, if he read its meaning aright, was fraught with the gravest consequences for the Northeastern Railroads; if he read its meaning aright, the Northeastern Railroads had been violating it persistently for many years and were liable for unknown sums in damages. The discovery of it had dazed him, and the consequences resulting from a successful suit under the section would be so great that he had searched diligently, though in vain, for some modification of it since its enactment. Why had not some one discovered it before? This query appeared to be unanswerable, until the simple — though none the less remarkable — solution came to him, that perhaps no definite occasion had hitherto arisen for seeking it. Undoubtedly the Railroads' attorneys must know of its existence — his own father, Hilary Vane, having been instrumental in drawing up the Act. And a long period had elapsed under which the Northeastern Railroads had been a law unto themselves.

The discovery was of grave import to Austen. A month before, chiefly through the efforts of his friend, Tom, who was gradually taking his father's place in the Gaylord Lumber Company, Austen had been appointed junior counsel for that corporation. The Honourable Galusha Hammer still remained the senior counsel, but was now confined in his house at Newcastle by an illness which made the probability of his return to active life extremely doubtful; and Tom had repeatedly declared that in the event of his non-recovery Austen should have Mr. Hammer's place. As counsel for the Gaylord Lumber Company, it was clearly his duty to call the attention of young Mr. Gaylord to the section; and in case Mr. Hammer did not resume his law practice, it would fall upon Austen himself to bring the suit. His opponent in this matter would be his own father!

The consequences of this culminating conflict between them, the coming of which he had long dreaded — although he had not foreseen its specific cause — weighed heavily upon Austen. It was Tom Gaylord himself who abruptly aroused him from his revery by bursting in at the door.

"Have you heard what's up?" he cried, flinging down a newspaper before Austen's eyes. "Have you seen the *Guardian?*"

"What's the matter now, Tom?"

"Matter!" exclaimed Tom; "read that. Your friend and client, the Honourable Humphrey Crewe, is out for governor."

"Humphrey Crewe for governor!"

" On an anti-railroad platform. I might have known
something of the kind was up when he began to associate
with Tooting, and from the way he spoke to me in March.
But who'd have thought he'd have the cheek to come out
for governor ? Did you ever hear of such tommyrot ? "

Austen looked grave.

" I'm not sure it's such tommyrot," he said.

" Not tommyrot? "Tom ejaculated. "Everybody's laughing. When I passed the Honourable Hilary's door just
now, Brush Bascom and some of the old liners were there,
reciting parts of the proclamation, and the boys down in
the Ripton House are having the time of their lives."

Austen took the *Guardian*, and there, sure enough,
filling a leading column, and in a little coarser type than
the rest of the page, he read : —

DOWN WITH RAILROAD RULE!

*The Honourable Humphrey Crewe of Leith, at the request
of twenty prominent citizens, consents to become a candidate
for the Republican Nomination for Governor.*

*Ringing letter of acceptance, in which he denounces the
political power of the Northeastern Railroads, and declares
that the State is governed from a gilded suite of offices in
New York.*

" The following letter, evincing as it does a public
opinion thoroughly aroused in all parts of the State
against the present disgraceful political conditions, speaks
for itself. The standing and character of its signers give
it a status which Republican voters cannot ignore."

The letter followed. It prayed Mr. Crewe, in the name
of decency and good government, to carry the standard of
honest men to victory. Too long had a proud and sovereign State writhed under the heel of an all-devouring
corporation! Too long had the Northeastern Railroads
elected, for their own selfish ends, governors and legislatures and controlled railroad commissions! The spirit

of 1776 was abroad in the land. It was eminently fitting that the Honourable Humphrey Crewe of Leith, who had dared to fling down the gauntlet in the face of an arrogant power, should be the leader of the plain people, to recover the rights which had been wrested from them. Had he not given the highest proof that he had the people's interests at heart? He was clearly a man who "did things."

At this point Austen looked up and smiled.

"Tom," he asked, "has it struck you that this is written in the same inimitable style as a part of the message of the Honourable Asa Gray?"

Tom slapped his knee.

"That's exactly what I said!" he cried. "Tooting wrote it. I'll swear to it."

"And the twenty prominent citizens — do you know any of 'em, Tom?"

"Well," said Tom, in delighted appreciation, "I've heard of three of 'em, and that's more than any man I've met can boast of. Ed Dubois cuts my hair when I go to Kingston. He certainly is a prominent citizen in the fourth ward. Jim Kendall runs the weekly newspaper in Grantley — I understood it was for sale. Bill Clements is prominent enough up at Groveton. He wanted a trolley franchise some years ago, you remember."

"And didn't get it."

Mr. Crewe's answer was characteristically terse and businesslike. The overwhelming compliment of a request from such gentlemen must be treated in the nature of a command — and yet he had hesitated for several weeks, during which period he had cast about for another more worthy of the honour. Then followed a somewhat technical and (to the lay mind) obscure recapitulation of the iniquities the Northeastern was committing, which proved beyond peradventure that Mr. Crewe knew what he was talking about; such phrases as "rolling stock," "milking the road" — an imposing array of facts and figures. Mr. Crewe made it plain that he was a man who "did things." And if it were the will of Heaven that he became governor, certain material benefits would as inevitably ensue as the day follows the night. The list of the material benefits, for which there was a crying need, bore a strong resemblance to a summary of the worthy measures upon which Mr. Crewe had spent so much time and labour in the last Legislature.

Austen laid down the paper, leaned back in his chair, and thrust his hands in his pockets, and with a little vertical pucker in his forehead, regarded his friend.

" What do you think of that?" Tom demanded. " Now, what *do* you think of it? "

" I think," said Austen, " that he'll scare the life out of the Northeastern before he gets through with them."

" What! " exclaimed Tom, incredulously. He had always been willing to accept Austen's judgment on men and affairs, but this was pretty stiff. " What makes you think so ? "

" Well, people don't know Mr. Crewe, for one thing. And they are beginning to have a glimmer of light upon the Railroad."

" Do you mean to say he has a chance for the nomination ? "

" I don't know. It depends upon how much the voters find out about him before the convention."

Tom sat down rather heavily.

" You could have been governor," he complained reproachfully, " by raising your hand. You've got more ability than any man in the State, and you sit here gazin' at that mountain and lettin' a darned fool millionaire walk in ahead of you."

Austen rose and crossed over to Mr. Gaylord's chair, and, his hands still in his pockets, looked down thoughtfully into that gentleman's square and rugged face.

" Tom," he said, " there's no use discussing this delusion of yours, which seems to be the only flaw in an otherwise sane character. We must try to keep it from the world."

Tom laughed in spite of himself.

" I'm hanged if I understand you," he declared, " but I

never did. You think Crewe and Tooting may carry off the governorship, and you don't seem to care."

"I do care," said Austen, briefly. He went to the window and stood for a moment with his back to his friend, staring across at Sawanec. Tom had learned by long experience to respect these moods, although they were to him inexplicable. At length Austen turned.

"Tom," he said, "can you come in to-morrow about this time? If you can't, I'll go to your office if you will let me know when you'll be in. There's a matter of business I want to talk to you about."

Tom pulled out his watch.

"I've got to catch a train for Mercer," he replied, "but I will come in in the morning and see you."

A quarter of an hour later Austen went down the narrow wooden flight of stairs into the street, and as he emerged from the entry almost bumped into the figure of a young man that was hurrying by. He reached out and grasped the young man by the collar, pulling him up so short as almost to choke him.

"Hully gee!" cried the young man whose progress had been so rudely arrested. "Great snakes!" (A cough.) "What're you tryin' to do? Oh," (apologetically) "it's you, Aust. Let me go. This day ain't long enough for me. Let me go."

Austen kept his grip and regarded Mr. Tooting thoughtfully.

"I want to speak to you, Ham," he said; "better come upstairs."

"Say, Aust, on the dead, I haven't time. Pardriff's waitin' for some copy now."

"Just for a minute, Ham," said Austen; "I won't keep you long."

"Leggo my collar, then, if you don't want to choke me. Say, I don't believe you know how strong you are."

"I didn't know you wore a collar any more, Ham," said Austen.

Mr. Tooting grinned in appreciation of this joke.

"You must think you've got one of your Wild West necktie parties on," he gasped. "I'll come. But if you love me, don't let the boys in Hilary's office see me."

"They use the other entry," answered Austen, indicating that Mr. Tooting should go up first — which he did. When they reached the office Austen shut the door, and stood with his back against it, regarding Mr. Tooting thoughtfully.

At first Mr. Tooting returned the look with interest: *swagger* — *aggression* would be too emphatic, and *defiance* would not do. His was the air, perhaps, of Talleyrand when he said, " There seems to be an inexplicable something in me that brings bad luck to governments that neglect me : " the air of a man who has made a brilliant *coup d'état.* All day he had worn that air — since five o'clock in the morning, when he had sprung from his pallet. The world might now behold the stuff that was in Hamilton Tooting. Power flowed out of his right hand from an inexhaustible reservoir which he had had the sagacity to tap, and men leaped into action at his touch. He, the once neglected, had the destiny of a State in his keeping.

Gradually, however, it became for some strange reason difficult to maintain that aggressive stare upon Austen Vane, who shook his head slowly.

"Ham, why did you do it?" he asked.

"Why?" cried Mr. Tooting, fiercely biting back a treasonable smile. "Why not? Ain't he the best man in the State to make a winner? Hasn't he got the money, and the brains, and the get-up-and-git? Why, it's a sure thing. I've been around the State, and I know the sentiment. We've got 'em licked, right now. What have you got against it? You're on our side, Aust."

"Ham," said Austen, "are you sure you have the names and addresses of those twenty prominent citizens right, so that any voter may go out and find 'em?"

"What are you kidding about, Aust?" retorted Mr. Tooting, biting back the smile again. "Say, you never get down to business with me. You don't blame Crewe for comin' out, do you?"

"I don't see how Mr. Crewe could have resisted such an overwhelming demand," said Austen. "He couldn't shirk such a duty. He says so himself, doesn't he?"

"Oh, go on!" exclaimed Mr. Tooting, who was not able to repress a grin.

"The letter of the twenty must have been a great surprise to Mr. Crewe. He says he was astonished. Did the whole delegation go up to Leith, or only a committee?"

Mr. Tooting's grin had by this time spread all over his face — a flood beyond his control.

"Well, there's no use puttin' it on with you, Aust. That was done pretty slick, that twenty-prominent-citizen business, if I do say it myself. But you don't know that feller Crewe — he's a full-size cyclone when he gets started, and nothin' but a range of mountains could stop him."

"It must be fairly exciting to — ride him, Ham."

"Say, but it just is. Kind of breathless, though. He ain't very well known around the State, and he was bound to run — and I just couldn't let him come out without any clothes on."

"I quite appreciate your delicacy, Ham."

Mr. Tooting's face took on once more a sheepish look, which changed almost immediately to one of disquietude.

"Say, I'll come back again some day and kid with you. I've got to go, Aust — that's straight. This is my busy day."

"Wouldn't you gain some time if you left by the window?" Austen asked.

At this suggestion Mr. Tooting's expressive countenance showed genuine alarm.

"Say, you ain't going to put up any Wild West tricks on me, are you? I heard you nearly flung Tom Gaylord out of the one in the other room."

"If this were a less civilized place, Ham, I'd initiate you into what is known as the bullet dance. As it is, I have a great mind to speed you on your way by assisting you downstairs."

Mr. Hamilton Tooting became ashy pale.

" I haven't done anything to you, Aust. Say — you didn't — ? " He did not finish.

Terrified by something in Austen's eye, which may or may not have been there at the time of the Blodgett incident, Mr. Tooting fled without completing his inquiry. And, his imagination being great, he reproduced for himself such a vivid sensation of a bullet-hole in his spine that he missed his footing near the bottom, and measured his length in the entry. Such are the humiliating experiences which sometimes befall the Talleyrands — but rarely creep into their biographies.

Austen, from the top of the stairway, saw this catastrophe, but did not smile. He turned on his heel, and made his way slowly around the corner of the passage into the other part of the building, and paused at the open doorway of the Honourable Hilary's outer office. By the street windows sat the Honourable Brush Bascom, sphinx-like, absorbing wisdom and clouds of cigar smoke which emanated from the Honourable Nat Billings.

" Howdy, Austen? " said Brush, genially, " lookin' for the Honourable Hilary? Flint got up from New York this morning, and sent for him a couple of hours ago. He'll be back at two."

" Have you read the pronunciamento? " inquired Mr. Billings. " Say, Austen, knowin' your sentiments, I wonder you weren't one of the twenty prominent citizens."

" All you anti-railroad fellers ought to get together," Mr. Bascom suggested; " you've got us terrified since your friend from Leith turned the light of publicity on us this morning. I hear Ham Tooting's been in and made you an offer."

News travels fast in Ripton.

" Austen kicked him downstairs," said Jimmy Towle, the office boy, who had made a breathless entrance during the conversation, and felt it to be the psychological moment to give vent to the news with which he was bursting.

" Is that straight? " Mr. Billings demanded. He wished

he had done it himself. "Is that straight?" he repeated, but Austen had gone.

"Of course it's straight," said Jimmy Towle, vigorously. A shrewd observer of human nature, he had little respect for Senator Billings. "Ned Johnson saw him pick himself up at the foot of Austen's stairway."

The Honourable Brush's agate eyes caught the light, and he addressed Mr. Billings in a voice which, by dint of long training, only carried a few feet.

"There's the man the Northeastern's got to look out for," he said. "The Humphrey Crewes don't count. But if Austen Vane ever gets started, there'll be trouble. Old man Flint's got some such idea as that, too. I overheard him givin' it to old Hilary once, up at Fairview, and Hilary said he couldn't control him. I guess nobody else can control him. I wish I'd seen him kick Ham downstairs."

"I'd like to kick *him* downstairs," said Mr. Billings, savagely biting off another cigar.

"I guess you hadn't better try it, Nat," said Mr. Bascom.

Meanwhile Austen had returned to his own office, and shut the door. His luncheon hour came and went, and still he sat by the open window gazing out across the teeming plain, and up the green valley whence the Blue came singing from the highlands. In spirit he followed the water to Leith, and beyond, where it swung in a wide circle and hurried between wondrous hills like those in the backgrounds of the old Italians: hills of close-cropped pastures, dotted with shapely sentinel oaks and maples which cast sharp, rounded shadows on the slopes at noonday; with thin fantastic elms on the gentle sky-lines, and forests massed here and there — silent, impenetrable: hills from a story-book of a land of mystery. The river coursed between them on its rocky bed, flinging its myriad gems to the sun. This was the Vale of the Blue, and she had touched it with meaning for him, and gone.

He drew from his coat a worn pocket-book, and from the pocket-book a letter. It was dated in New York in February, and though he knew it by heart he found a strange solace in the pain which it gave him to reread it. He stared at the monogram on the paper, which seemed so emblematic of her; for he had often reflected that her things — even such minute insignia as this — belonged to her. She impressed them not only with her taste, but with her character. The entwined letters, V. F., of the design were not, he thought, of a meaningless, frivolous daintiness, but stood for something. Then he read the note again. It was only a note.

"MY DEAR MR. VANE : I have come back to find my mother ill, and I am taking her to France. We are sailing, unexpectedly, to-morrow, there being a difficulty about a passage later. I cannot refrain from sending you a line before I go to tell you that I did you an injustice. You will no doubt think it strange that I should write to you, but I shall be troubled until it is off my mind. I am ashamed to have been so stupid. I think I know now why you would not consent to be a candidate, and I respect you for it.

"Sincerely your friend,
"VICTORIA FLINT."

What did she know? What had she found out? Had she seen her father and talked to him? That was scarcely possible, since her mother had been ill and she had left at once. Austen had asked himself these questions many times, and was no nearer the solution. He had heard nothing of her since, and he told himself that perhaps it was better, after all, that she was still away. To know that she was at Fairview, and not to be able to see her, were torture indeed.

The note was formal enough, and at times he pretended to be glad that it was. How could it be otherwise? And why should he interpret her interest in him in other terms than those in which it was written? She had a warm heart — that he knew; and he felt for her sake that he had no right to wish for more than the note expressed. After several unsuccessful attempts, he had answered it in a line, "I thank you, and I understand."

s

CHAPTER XVI

THE "BOOK OF ARGUMENTS" IS OPENED

THE Honourable Hilary Vane returned that day from Fairview in no very equable frame of mind. It is not for us to be present at the Councils on the Palatine when the "Book of Arguments" is opened, and those fitting the occasion are chosen and sent out to the faithful who own printing-presses and free passes. The Honourable Hilary Vane bore away from the residence of his emperor a great many memoranda in an envelope, and he must have sighed as he drove through the leafy roads for Mr. Hamilton Tooting, with his fertile mind and active body. A year ago, and Mr. Tooting would have seized these memoranda of majesty, and covered their margins with new suggestions: Mr. Tooting, on occasions, had even made additions to the "Book of Arguments" itself — additions which had been used in New York and other States with telling effect against Mr. Crewes there. Mr. Tooting knew by heart the time of going to press of every country newspaper which had passes (in exchange for advertising!). It was two o'clock when the Honourable Hilary reached his office, and by three all the edicts would have gone forth, and the grape-shot and canister would have been on their way to demolish the arrogance of this petty Lord of Leith.

"Tooting's a dangerous man, Vane. You oughtn't to have let him go," Mr. Flint had said. "I don't care a snap of my finger for the other fellow."

How Mr. Tooting's ears would have burned, and how his blood would have sung with pride to have heard himself called dangerous by the president of the Northeastern!

He who, during all the valuable years of his services, had never had a sign that that potentate was cognizant of his humble existence.

The Honourable Brush Bascom, as we know, was a clever man; and although it had never been given him to improve on the "Book of Arguments," he had ideas of his own. On reading Mr. Crewe's defiance that morning, he had, with characteristic promptitude and a desire to be useful, taken the first train out of Putnam for Ripton, to range himself by the side of the Honourable Hilary in the hour of need. The Feudal System anticipates, and Mr. Bascom did not wait for a telegram.

On the arrival of the chief counsel from Fairview other captains had put in an appearance, but Mr. Bascom alone was summoned, by a nod, into the private office. What passed between them seems too sacred to write about. The Honourable Hilary would take one of the slips from the packet and give it to Mr. Bascom.

"If that were recommended, editorially, to the *Hull Mercury*, it might serve to clear away certain misconceptions in that section."

"Certain," Mr. Bascom would reply.

"It has been thought wise," the Honourable Hilary continued, "to send an annual to the *Groveton News*. Roberts, his name is. Suppose you recommend to Mr. Roberts that an editorial on this subject would be timely."

Slip number two. Mr. Bascom marks it *Roberts*. Subject: "What would the State do without the Railroad?"

"And Grenville, being a Prohibition centre, you might get this worked up for the *Advertiser* there."

Mr. Bascom's agate eyes are full of light as he takes slip number three. Subject: "Mr. Humphrey Crewe has the best-stocked wine cellar in the State, and champagne every night for dinner." Slip number four, taken direct from the second chapter of the "Book of Arguments": "Mr. Crewe is a reformer because he has been disappointed in his inordinate ambitions," etc. Slip number five: "Mr. Crewe is a summer resident, with a house in New York," etc., etc.

Slip number six, "Book of Arguments," paragraph 1, chapter 1: "Humphrey Crewe, Defamer of our State." Assigned, among others, to the *Ripton Record*.

"Paul Pardriff went up to Leith to-day," said Mr. Bascom.

"Go to see him," replied the Honourable Hilary. "I've been thinking for some time that the advertising in the *Ripton Record* deserves an additional annual."

Mr. Bascom, having been despatched on this business, and having voluntarily assumed control of the Empire Bureau of Publication, the chief counsel transacted other necessary legal business with State Senator Billings and other gentlemen who were waiting. At three o'clock word was sent in that Mr. Austen Vane was outside, and wished to speak with his father as soon as the latter was at leisure. Whereupon the Honourable Hilary shooed out the minor clients, leaned back in his chair, and commanded that his son be admitted.

"Judge," said Austen, as he closed the door behind him, "I don't want to bother you."

The Honourable Hilary regarded his son for a moment fixedly out of his little eyes.

"Humph!" he said.

Austen looked down at his father. The Honourable Hilary's expression was not one which would have aroused, in the ordinary man who beheld him, a feeling of sympathy or compassion: it was the impenetrable look with which he had faced his opponents for many years. But Austen felt compassion.

"Perhaps I'd better come in another time — when you are less busy," he suggested.

"Who said I was busy?" inquired the Honourable Hilary.

Austen smiled a little sadly. One would have thought, by that smile, that the son was the older and wiser of the two.

"I didn't mean to cast any reflection on your habitual industry, Judge," he said.

"Humph!" exclaimed Mr. Vane. "I've got more to

do than sit in the window and read poetry, if that's what you mean."

"You never learned how to enjoy life, did you, Judge?" he said. "I don't believe you ever really had a good time. Own up."

"I've had sterner things to think about. I've had to earn my living — and give you a good time."

"I appreciate it," said Austen.

"Humph! Sometimes I think you don't show it a great deal," the Honourable Hilary answered.

"I show it as far as I can, Judge," said his son. "I can't help the way I was made."

"I try to take account of that," said the Honourable Hilary.

Austen laughed.

"I'll drop in to-morrow morning," he said.

But the Honourable Hilary pointed to a chair on the other side of the desk.

"Sit down. To-day's as good as to-morrow," he remarked, with sententious significance, characteristically throwing the burden of explanation on the visitor.

Austen found the opening unexpectedly difficult. He felt that this was a crisis in their relations, and that it had come at an unfortunate hour.

"Judge," he said, trying to control the feeling that threatened to creep into his voice, "we have jogged along for some years pretty peaceably, and I hope you won't misunderstand what I'm going to say."

The Honourable Hilary grunted.

"It was at your request that I went into the law. I have learned to like that profession. I have stuck to it as well as my wandering, Bohemian nature will permit, and while I do not expect you necessarily to feel any pride in such progress as I have made, I have hoped — that you might feel an interest."

The Honourable Hilary grunted again.

"I suppose I am by nature a free-lance," Austen continued. "You were good enough to acknowledge the force of my argument when I told you it would be best for me to strike out for myself. And I suppose it was inevitable, such being the case, and you the chief counsel for the Northeastern Railroads, that I should at some time or another be called upon to bring suits against your client. It would have been better, perhaps, if I had not started to practise in this State. I did so from what I believe was a desire common to both of us to — to live together."

The Honourable Hilary reached for his Honey Dew, but he did not speak.

"To live together," Austen repeated. "I want to say that, if I had gone away, I believe I should always have regretted the fact." He paused, and took from his pocket a slip of paper. "I made up my mind from the start that I would always be frank with you. In spite of my desire to amass riches, there are some suits against the Northeastern which I have — somewhat quixotically — refused. Here is a section of the act which permitted the consolidation of the Northeastern Railroads. You are no doubt aware of its existence."

The Honourable Hilary took the slip of paper in his hand and stared at it. "*The rates for fares and freights existing at the time of the passage of this act shall not be increased on the roads leased or united under it.*" What his sensations were when he read it no man might have read in his face, but his hand trembled a little, and a long silence ensued before he gave it back to his son with the simple comment : —

"Well?"

"I do not wish to be understood to ask your legal opinion, although you probably know that lumber rates have been steadily raised, and if a suit under that section were successful the Gaylord Lumber Company could recover a very large sum of money from the Northeastern Railroads," said Austen. "Having discovered the section, I believe it to be my duty to call it to the attention of the Gaylords. What I wish to know is, whether my taking the case would cause you any personal inconvenience or distress? If so, I will refuse it."

"No," answered the Honourable Hilary, "it won't.

Bring suit. Much use it'll be. Do you expect they can recover under that section?"

"I think it is worth trying," said Austen.

"Why didn't somebody try it before?" asked the Honourable Hilary.

"See here, Judge, I wish you'd let me out of an argument about it. Suit is going to be brought, whether I bring it or another man. If you would prefer for any reason that I shouldn't bring it—I won't. I'd much rather resign as counsel for the Gaylords—and I am prepared to do so."

"Bring suit," answered the Honourable Hilary, quickly, "bring suit by all means. And now's your time. This seems to be a popular season for attacking the property which is the foundation of the State's prosperity." ("Book of Arguments," chapter 3.)

In spite of himself, Austen smiled again. Long habit had accustomed Hilary Vane to put business considerations before family ties; and this habit had been the secret of his particular success. And now, rather than admit by the least sign the importance of his son's discovery of the statute (which he had had in mind for many years, and to which he had more than once, by the way, called Mr. Flint's attention), the Honourable Hilary deliberately belittled the matter as part and parcel of the political tactics against the Northeastern.

Scars caused by differences of opinion are soon healed; words count for nothing, and it is the soul that attracts or repels. Mr. Vane was not analytical, he had been through a harassing day, and he was unaware that it was not Austen's opposition, but Austen's smile, which set the torch to his anger. Once, shortly after his marriage, when he had come home in wrath after a protracted quarrel with Mr. Tredway over the orthodoxy of the new minister, in the middle of his indignant recital of Mr. Tredway's unwarranted attitude, Sarah Austen had smiled. The smile had had in it, to be sure, nothing of conscious superiority, but it had been utterly inexplicable to Hilary Vane. He had known for the first time what it was to feel murder in the heart, and if he had not rushed out of the room, he was sure he would have strangled her. After all, the Hilary Vanes of this world cannot reasonably be expected to perceive the humour in their endeavours.

Now the son's smile seemed the reincarnation of the mother's. That smile was in itself a refutation of motive on Austen's part which no words could have made more emphatic; it had in it (unconsciously, too) compassion for and understanding of the Honourable Hilary's mood and limitations. Out of the corner of his mental vision — without grasping it — the Honourable Hilary perceived this vaguely. It was the smile in which a parent privately indulges when a child kicks his toy locomotive because its mechanism is broken. It was the smile of one who, unforgetful of the scheme of the firmament and the spinning planets, will not be moved to anger by him who sees but the four sides of a pit.

Hilary Vane grew red around the eyes — a danger signal of the old days.

"Take the suit," he said. "If you don't, I'll make it known all over the State that you started it. I'll tell Mr. Flint to-morrow. Take it, do you hear me? You ask me if I have any pride in you. I answer, yes. I'd like to see what you can do. I've done what I could for you, and now I wash my hands of you. Go, ruin yourself if you want to. You've always been headed that way, and there's no use trying to stop you. You don't seem to have any notion of decency or order, or any idea of the principle on which this government was based. Attack property — destroy it. So much the better for you and your kind. Join the Humphrey Crewes — you belong with 'em. Give those of us who stand for order and decency as much trouble as you can. Brand us as rascals trying to enrich ourselves with politics, and proclaim yourselves saints nobly striving to get back the rights of the people. If you don't bring that suit, I tell you I'll give you the credit for it — and I mean what I say."

Austen got to his feet. His own expression, curiously enough, had not changed to one of anger. His face had set, but his eyes held the look that seemed still to express compassion, and what he felt was a sorrow that went to the depths of his nature. What he had so long feared — what he knew they had both feared — had come at last.

"Good-by, Judge," he said.

Hilary Vane stared at him dumbly. His anger had not cooled, his eyes still flamed, but he suddenly found himself bereft of speech. Austen put his hand on his father's shoulder, and looked down silently into his face. But Hilary was stiff as in a rigour, expressionless save for the defiant red in his eye.

"I don't think you meant all that, Judge, and I don't intend to hold it against you."

Still Hilary stared, his lips in the tight line which was the emblem of his character, his body rigid. He saw his son turn and walk to the door, and turn again with his handle on the knob, and Hilary did not move. The door closed, and still he sat there, motionless, expressionless.

Austen was hailed by those in the outer office, but he walked through them as though the place were empty. Rumours sprang up behind him of which he was unconscious; the long-expected quarrel had come; Austen had joined the motley ranks of the rebels under Mr. Crewe. Only the office boy, Jimmy Towle, interrupted the jokes that were flying by repeating, with dogged vehemence, "I tell you it ain't so. Austen kicked Ham downstairs. Ned Johnson saw him." Nor was it on account of this particular deed that Austen was a hero in Jimmy's eyes.

Austen, finding himself in the square, looked at his watch. It was four o'clock. He made his way under the maples to the house in Hanover Street, halted for a moment contemplatively before the familiar classic pillars of its porch, took a key from his pocket, and (unprecedented action!) entered by the front door. Climbing to the attic, he found two valises — one of which he had brought back from Pepper County — and took them to his own room. They held, with a little crowding, most of his possessions, including a photograph of Sarah Austen, which he left on the bureau to the last. Once or twice he paused in his packing to gaze at the face, striving to fathom the fleeting quality of her glance which the photograph had so strangely caught. In that glance nature had stamped her enigma—for Sarah Austen was a child of nature. Hers was the gentle look of wild things —but it was more; it was the understanding of the unwritten law of creation, the law by which the flowers grow, and wither; the law by which the animal springs upon its prey, and, unerring, seeks its mate; the law of the song of the waters, and the song of the morning stars; the law that permits evil and pain and dumb, incomprehensible suffering; the law that floods at sunset the mountain lands with colour and the soul with light; and the law that rends the branches in the blue storm. Of what avail was anger against it, or the puny rage of man? Hilary Vane, not recognizing it, had spent his force upon it, like a hawk against a mountain wall, but Austen looked at his mother's face and understood. In it was not the wisdom of creeds and cities, but the unworldly wisdom which comprehends and condones.

His packing finished, with one last glance at the room Austen went downstairs with his valises and laid them on the doorstep. Then he went to the stable and harnessed Pepper, putting into the buggy his stable blanket and halter and currycomb, and, driving around to the front of the house, hitched the horse at the stone post, and packed the valises in the back of the buggy. After that he walked slowly to the back of the house and looked in at the kitchen window. Euphrasia, her thin arms bare to the elbow, was bending over a wash-tub. He spoke her name, and as she lifted her head a light came into her face which seemed to make her young again. She dried her hands hastily on her apron as she drew towards him. He sprang through the window, and patted her on the back — his usual salutation. And as she raised her eyes to his (those ordinarily sharp eyes of Euphrasia's), they shone with an admiration she had accorded to no other human being since he had come into the world. Terms of endearment she had, characteristically, never used, but she threw her soul into the sounding of his name.

"Off to the hills, Austen? I saw you a-harnessing of Pepper."

"Phrasie," he said, still patting her, "I'm going to the country for a while."

"To the country?" she repeated.

"To stay on a farm for a sort of vacation."

Her face brightened.

"Goin' to take a real vacation, be you?"

He laughed.

"Oh, I don't have to work very hard, Phrasie. You know I get out a good deal. I just thought — I just thought I'd like to sleep in the country — for a while."

"Well," answered Euphrasia, "I guess if you've took the notion, you've got to go. It was that way with your mother before you. I've seen her leave the house on a bright Sabbath half an hour before meetin' to be gone the whole day, and Hilary and all the ministers in town couldn't stop her."

"I'll drop in once in a while to see you, Phrasie. I'll be at Jabe Jenney's."

"Jabe's is not more than three or four miles from Flint's place," Euphrasia remarked.

"I've thought of that," said Austen.

"You'd thought of it!"

Austen coloured.

"The distance is nothing," he said quickly, "with Pepper."

"And you'll come and see me?" asked Euphrasia.

"If you'll do something for me," he said.

"I always do what you want, Austen. You know I'm not able to refuse you."

He laid his hands on her shoulders.

"You'll promise?" he asked.

"I'll promise," said Euphrasia, solemnly.

He was silent for a moment, looking down at her.

"I want you to promise to stay here and take care of the Judge."

Fright crept into her eyes, but his own were smiling, reassuring.

"Take care of him!" she cried, the very mention of Hilary raising the pitch of her voice. "I guess I'll have to. Haven't I took care of him nigh on forty years, and small thanks and recompense I get for it except when you're here. I've wore out my life takin' care of him" (more gently). "What do you mean by makin' me promise such a thing, Austen?"

"Well," said Austen, slowly, "the Judge is worried now. Things are not going as smoothly with him as — as usual."

"Money?" demanded Euphrasia. "He ain't lost money, has he?"

A light began to dance in Austen's eyes in spite of the weight within him.

"Now, Phrasie," he said, lifting her chin a little, "you know you don't care any more about money than I do."

"Lord help me," she exclaimed, "Lord help me if I didn't! And as long as you don't care for it, and no sense can be knocked into your head about it, I hope you'll marry somebody that does know the value of it. If Hilary was to lose what he has now, before it comes rightly to you, he'd ought to be put in jail."

Austen laughed, and shook his head.

"Phrasie, the Lord did you a grave injustice when he didn't make you a man, but I suppose he'll give you a recompense hereafter. No, I believe I am safe in saying that the Judge's securities are still — secure. Not that I really know — or care" (shakes of the head from Euphrasia). "Poor old Judge! Worse things than finance are troubling him now."

"Not a woman!" cried Euphrasia, horror-stricken at the very thought. "He hasn't took it into his head after all these years —"

"No," said Austen, laughing, "no, no. It's not quite as bad as that, but it's pretty bad."

"In Heaven's name, what is it?" she demanded.

"Reformers," said Austen.

"Reformers?" she repeated. "What might they be?"

"Well," answered Austen, "you might call them a new kind of caterpillar — only they feed on corporations instead of trees."

Euphrasia shook her head vigorously.

"Go 'long," she exclaimed. "When you talk like that I never can follow you, Austen. If Hilary has any worries, I guess he brought 'em on himself. I never knew him to fail."

"Ambitious and designing persons are making trouble for his railroad."

"Well, I never took much stock in that railroad," said Euphrasia, with emphasis. "I never was on it but an engine gave out, and the cars was jammed, and it wasn't less than an hour late. And then they're eternally smashin' folks or runnin' 'em down. You served 'em right when you made 'em pay that Meader man six thousand dollars, and I told Hilary so." She paused, and stared at Austen fixedly as a thought came into her head. "You ain't leavin' him because of this trouble, are you, Austen?"

"Phrasie," he said, "I — I don't want to quarrel with him now. I think it would be easy to quarrel with him."

"You mean him quarrel with you," returned Euphrasia. "I'd like to see him! If he did, it wouldn't take me long to pack up and leave."

"That's just it. I don't want that to happen. And I've had a longing to go out and pay a little visit to Jabe up in the hills, and drive his colts for him. You see," he said, "I've got a kind of affection for the Judge."

Euphrasia looked at him, and her lips trembled.

"He don't deserve it," she declared, "but I suppose he's your father."

"He can't get out of that," said Austen.

"I'd like to see him try it," said Euphrasia. "Come in soon, Austen," she whispered, "come in soon."

She stood on the lawn and watched him as he drove away, and he waved good-by to her over the hood of the buggy. When he was out of sight she lifted her head, gave her eyes a vigorous brush with her checked apron, and went back to her washing.

It was not until Euphrasia had supper on the table that Hilary Vane came home, and she glanced at him sharply as he took his usual seat. It is a curious fact that it is possible for two persons to live together for more than a third of a century, and at the end of that time understand each other little better than at the beginning. The sole bond between Euphrasia and Hilary was that of Sarah Austen and her son. Euphrasia never knew when Hilary was tired, or when he was cold, or hungry, or cross, although she provided for all these emergencies. Her service to him was unflagging, but he had never been under the slightest delusion that it was not an inheritance from his wife. There must have been some affection between Mr. Vane and his housekeeper, hidden away in the strong boxes of both, but up to the present this was only a theory — not quite as probable as that about the inhabitants of Mars.

He ate his supper to-night with his usual appetite, which had always been sparing ; and he would have eaten the same amount if the Northeastern Railroads had been going into the hands of a receiver the next day. Often he did not exchange a word with Euphrasia between home-coming and bed-going, and this was apparently to be one of these occasions. After supper he went, as usual, to sit on the steps of his porch, and to cut his piece of Honey Dew, which never varied a milligram. Nine o'clock struck, and Euphrasia, who had shut up the back of the house, was on her way to bed with her lamp in her hand, when she came face to face with him in the narrow passageway.

" Where's Austen? " he asked.

Euphrasia halted. The lamp shook, but she raised it to the level of his eyes.

" Don't you know ? " she demanded.

" No," he said, with unparalleled humility.

She put down the lamp on the little table that stood beside her.

"He didn't tell you he was a-goin'?"

"No," said Hilary.

"Then how did you know he wasn't just buggy-ridin'?" she said.

Hilary Vane was mute.

"You've be'n to his room!" she exclaimed. "You've seen his things are gone!"

He confessed it by his silence. Then, with amazing swiftness and vigour for one of her age, Euphrasia seized him by the arms and shook him.

"What have you done to him?" she cried; "what have you done to him? You sent him off. You've never understood him — you've never behaved like a father to him. You ain't worthy to have him." She flung herself away and stood facing Hilary at a little distance. "What a fool I was! What a fool! I might have known it, — and I promised him."

"Promised him?" Hilary repeated. The shaking, the vehemence and anger, of Euphrasia seemed to have had no effect whatever on the main trend of his thoughts.

"Where has he gone?"

"You can find out for yourself," she retorted bitterly. "I wish on your account it was to China. He came here this afternoon, as gentle as ever, and packed up his things, and said he was goin' away because you was worried. Worried!" she exclaimed scornfully. "*His* worry and *his* trouble don't count — but yours. And he made me promise to stay with you. If it wasn't for him," she cried, picking up the lamp, "I'd leave you this very night."

She swept past him, and up the narrow stairway to her bedroom.

CHAPTER XVII

BUSY DAYS AT WEDDERBURN

THERE is no blast so powerful, so withering, as the blast of ridicule. Only the strongest men can withstand it, — only reformers who are such in deed, and not alone in name, can snap their fingers at it, and liken it to the crackling of thorns under a pot. Confucius and Martin Luther must have been ridiculed, Mr. Crewe reflected, and although he did not have time to assure himself on these historical points, the thought stayed him. Sixty odd weekly newspapers, filled with arguments from the Book, attacked him all at once; and if by chance he should have missed the best part of this flattering personal attention, the editorials which contained the most spice were copied at the end of the week into the columns of his erstwhile friend, the *State Tribune*, now the organ of that mysterious personality, the Honourable Adam B. Hunt. *Et tu, Brute!*

Moreover, Mr. Peter Pardriff had something of his own to say. Some gentlemen of prominence (not among the twenty signers of the new Declaration of Independence) had been interviewed by the *Tribune* reporter on the subject of Mr. Crewe's candidacy. Here are some of the answers, duly tabulated.

"*Negligible.*" — Congressman Fairplay.

"*One less vote for the Honourable Adam B. Hunt.*" — The Honourable Jacob Botcher.

"*A monumental farce.*" — Ex-Governor Broadbent.

"*Who is Mr. Crewe?*" — Senator Whitredge. (Ah ha! Senator, this want shall be supplied, at least.)

"*I have been very busy. I do not know what candidates are in the field.*" — Mr. Augustus P. Flint, president of the Northeastern Railroads. (The unkindest cut of all!)

"*I have heard that a Mr. Crewe is a candidate, but I do not know much about him. They tell me he is a summer resident at Leith.*" — The Honourable Hilary Vane.

"*A millionaire's freak — not to be taken seriously.*" — State Senator Nathaniel Billings.

The *State Tribune* itself seemed to be especially interested in the past careers of the twenty signers. Who composed this dauntless band, whose members had arisen with remarkable unanimity and martyr's zeal in such widely scattered parts of the State? Had each been simultaneously inspired with the same high thought, and — more amazing still — with the idea of the same peerless leader? The *Tribune* modestly ventured the theory that Mr. Crewe had appeared to each of the twenty in a dream, with a flaming sword pointing to the steam of the dragon's breath. Or, perhaps, a star had led each of the twenty to Leith. (This likening of Mr. H——n T——g to a star caused much merriment among that gentleman's former friends and acquaintances.) The *Tribune* could not account for this phenomenon by any natural laws, and was forced to believe that the thing was a miracle — in which case it behooved the Northeastern Railroads to read the handwriting on the wall. Unless — unless the twenty did not exist! Unless the whole thing were a joke! The *Tribune* remembered a time when a signed statement, purporting to come from a certain Mrs. Amanda P. Pillow, of 22 Blair Street, Newcastle, had appeared, to the effect that three bottles of Rand's Peach Nectar had cured her of dropsy. On investigation there was no 22 Blair Street, and Mrs. Amanda P. Pillow was as yet unborn. The one sure thing about the statement was that Rand's Peach Nectar could be had, in large or small quantities, as desired. And the *Tribune* was prepared to state, on its own authority, that a Mr. Humphrey Crewe did exist, and might reluctantly consent to take the nomination for the governorship. In industry and zeal he was said to resemble the celebrated and lamented Mr. Rand, of the Peach Nectar.

Ingratitude merely injures those who are capable of

T

it, although it sometimes produces sadness in great souls. What were Mr. Crewe's feelings when he read this drivel? When he perused the extracts from the "Book of Arguments" which appeared (with astonishing unanimity, too!) in sixty odd weekly newspapers of the State — an assortment of arguments for each county.

"Brush Bascom's doin' that work now," said Mr. Tooting, contemptuously, "and he's doin' it with a shovel. Look here! He's got the same squib in three towns within a dozen miles of each other, the one beginning 'Political conditions in this State are as clean as those of any State in the Union, and the United Northeastern Railroads is a corporation which is, fortunately, above calumny. A summer resident who, to satisfy his lust for office, is willing to defame—'"

"Yes," interrupted Mr. Crewe, "never mind reading any more of that rot."

"It's botched," said Mr. Tooting, whose artistic soul was jarred. "I'd have put that in Avalon County, and Weare, and Marshall. I know men that take all three of those papers in Putnam."

No need of balloonists to see what the enemy is about, when we have a Mr. Tooting.

"They're stung!" he cried, as he ran rapidly through the bundle of papers — Mr. Crewe having subscribed, with characteristic generosity, to the entire press of the State. "Flint gave 'em out all this stuff about the railroad bein' a sacred institution. You've got 'em on the run right now, Mr. Crewe. You'll notice that, Democrats and Republicans, they've dropped everybody else, that they've all been sicked on to you. They're scared."

"I came to that conclusion some time ago," replied Mr. Crewe, who was sorting over his letters.

"And look there!" exclaimed Mr. Tooting, tearing out a paragraph, "there's the best campaign material we've had yet. Say, I'll bet Flint takes that doddering idiot's pass away for writing that."

Mr. Crewe took the extract, and read: —

"A summer resident of Leith, who is said to be a millionaire many times over, and who had a somewhat farcical career as a legislator last winter, has announced himself as a candidate for the Republican nomination on a platform attacking the Northeastern Railroads. Mr. Humphrey Crewe declares that the Northeastern Railroads govern us. What if they do? *Every sober-minded citizen will agree that they give us a pretty good government.* More power to them."

Mr. Crewe permitted himself to smile.

"They *are* playing into our hands, sure enough. What?"

This is an example of the spirit in which the ridicule and abuse was met.

It was Senator Whitredge — only last autumn so pleased to meet Mr. Crewe at Mr. Flint's — who asked the hypocritical question, " Who is Humphrey Crewe?" A biography (in pamphlet form, illustrated, — send your name and address) is being prepared by the invaluable Mr. Tooting, who only sleeps six hours these days. We shall see it presently, when it emerges from that busy hive at Wedderburn.

Wedderburn was a hive, sure enough. Not having a balloon ourselves, it is difficult to see all that is going on there; but there can be no mistake (except by the Honourable Hilary's seismograph) that it has become the centre of extraordinary activity. The outside world has paused to draw breath at the spectacle, and members of the metropolitan press are filling the rooms of the Ripton House and adding to the prosperity of its livery-stable. Mr. Crewe is a difficult man to see these days — there are so many visitors at Wedderburn, and the representatives of the metropolitan press hitch their horses and stroll around the grounds, or sit on the porch and converse with gentlemen from various counties of the State who (as the *Tribune* would put it) have been led by a star to Leith.

On the occasion of one of these gatherings, when Mr. Crewe had been inaccessible for four hours, Mrs. Pomfret drove up in a victoria with her daughter Alice.

" I'm sure I don't know when we're going to see poor dear Humphrey again," said Mrs. Pomfret, examining the

group on the porch through her gold-mounted lenses;
"these awful people are always here when I come. I
wonder if they sleep here, in the hammocks and lounging
chairs! Alice, we must be very polite to them — so much
depends on it."

"I'm always polite, mother," answered Alice, "except
when you tell me not to be. The trouble is I never know
myself."

The victoria stopped in front of the door, and the irreproachable Waters advanced across the porch.

"Waters," said Mrs. Pomfret, "I suppose Mr. Crewe
is too busy to come out."

"I'm afraid so, madam," replied Waters; "there's a line
of gentlemen waitin' here" (he eyed them with no uncertain
disapproval), "and I've positive orders not to disturb him,
madam."

"I quite understand, at a time like this," said Mrs.
Pomfret, and added, for the benefit of her audience, "when
Mr. Crewe has been public-spirited and unselfish enough
to undertake such a gigantic task. Tell him Miss Pomfret and I call from time to time because we are *so* interested, and that the whole of Leith wishes him success."

"I'll tell him, madam," said Waters.

But Mrs. Pomfret did not give the signal for her coachman to drive on. She looked, instead, at the patient
gathering.

"Good morning, gentlemen," she said.

"Mother!" whispered Alice, "what are you going to
do?"

The gentlemen rose.

"I'm Mrs. Pomfret," she said, as though that simple
announcement were quite sufficient, — as it was, for the
metropolitan press. Not a man of them who had not seen
Mrs. Pomfret's important movements on both sides of the
water chronicled. "I take the liberty of speaking to you,
as we all seem to be united in a common cause. How is
the campaign looking?"

Some of the gentlemen shifted their cigars from one
hand to the other, and grinned sheepishly.

"You know that a woman can often get a vote when a man can't."

"I am *so* interested," continued Mrs. Pomfret; "it is so unusual in America for a gentleman to be willing to undertake such a thing, to subject himself to low criticism, and to have his pure motives questioned. Mr. Crewe has rare courage — I have always said so. And we are all going to put our shoulder to the wheel, and help him all we can."

There was one clever man there who was quick to see his opportunity, and seize it for his newspaper.

"And are you going to help Mr. Crewe in his campaign, Mrs. Pomfret?"

"Most assuredly," answered Mrs. Pomfret. "Women in this country could do so much if they only would. You know," she added, in her most winning manner, "you know that a woman can often get a vote when a man can't."

"And you, and — other ladies will go around to the public meetings?"

"Why not, my friend, if Mr. Crewe has no objection? and I can conceive of none."

"You would have an organization of society ladies to help Mr. Crewe?"

"That's rather a crude way of putting it," answered Mrs. Pomfret, with her glasses raised judicially. "Women in what you call 'society' are, I am glad to say, taking an increasing interest in politics. They are beginning to realize that it is a duty."

"Thank you," said the reporter; "and now would you mind if I took a photograph of you in your carriage?"

"Oh, mother," protested Alice, "you won't let him do that!"

"Be quiet, Alice. Lady Aylestone and the duchess are photographed in every conceivable pose for political purposes. Wymans, just drive around to the other side of the circle."

The article appeared next day, and gave, as may be imagined, a tremendous impetus to Mr. Crewe's cause. "*A new era in American politics!*" "*Society to take a hand in the gubernatorial campaign of Millionaire Humphrey Crewe!*" "*Noted social leader, Mrs. Patterson Pom-*

fret, declares it a duty, and says that English women have the right idea." And a photograph of Mrs. Patterson Pomfret herself, in her victoria, occupied a generous portion of the front page.

"What's all this rubbish about Mrs. Pomfret?" was Mr. Crewe's grateful comment when he saw it. "I spent two valuable hours with that reporter givin' him material and statistics, and I can't find that he's used a word of it."

"Never you mind about that," Mr. Tooting replied. "The more advertising you get, the better, and this shows that the right people are behind you. Mrs. Pomfret's a smart woman, all right. She knows her job. And here's more advertising," he continued, shoving another sheet across the desk, "a fine likeness of you in caricature labelled, 'Ajax defying the Lightning.' Who's Ajax? There was an Italian, a street contractor, with that name — or something like it — in Newcastle a couple of years ago — in the eighth ward."

In these days, when false rumours fly apace to the injury of innocent men, it is well to get at the truth, if possible. It is not true that Mr. Paul Pardriff, of the *Ripton Record*, has been to Wedderburn. Mr. Pardriff was getting into a buggy to go — somewhere — when he chanced to meet the Honourable Brush Bascom, and the buggy was sent back to the livery-stable. Mr. Tooting had been to see Mr. Pardriff before the world-quaking announcement of June 7th, and had found Mr. Pardriff a reformer who did not believe that the railroad should run the State. But the editor of the *Ripton Record* was a man after Emerson's own heart: "a foolish consistency is the hobgoblin of little minds" — and Mr. Pardriff did not go to Wedderburn. He went off on an excursion up the State instead, for he had been working too hard; and he returned, as many men do from their travels, a conservative. He listened coldly to Mr. Tooting's impassioned pleas for cleaner politics, until Mr. Tooting revealed the fact that his pockets were full of copy. It seems that a biography was to be printed — a biography which would, undoubtedly, be in great demand; the biography of a public benefactor, illustrated with original photographs and views in the country. Mr. Tooting and Mr. Pardriff both being men of the world, some exceeding plain talk ensued between them, and when two such minds unite, a way out is sure to be found. One can be both a conservative and a radical — if one is clever. There were other columns in Mr. Pardriff's paper besides editorial columns; editorial columns, Mr. Pardriff said, were sacred to his convictions. Certain thumb-worn schedules were referred to. Paul Pardriff, Ripton, agreed to be the publisher of the biography.

The next edition of the *Record* was an example of what Mr. Emerson meant. Three columns contained extracts of absorbing interest from the forthcoming biography and, on another page, an editorial. " The Honourable Humphrey Crewe, of Leith, is an estimable gentleman and a good citizen, whose public endeavours have been of great benefit to the community. A citizen of Avalon County, the *Record* regrets that it cannot support his candidacy for the Republican gubernatorial nomination. We are not among those who seek to impugn motives, and while giving Mr. Crewe every credit that his charges against the Northeastern Railroads are made in good faith, we beg to differ from him. That corporation is an institution which has stood the test of time, and enriches every year the State treasury by a large sum in taxes. Its management is in safe, conservative hands. No one will deny Mr. Crewe's zeal for the State's welfare, but it must be borne in mind that he is a newcomer in politics, and that conditions, seen from the surface, are sometimes deceptive. We predict for Mr. Crewe a long and useful career, but we do not think that at this time, and on this platform, he will obtain the governorship."

" Moral courage is what the age needs," had been Mr. Crewe's true and sententious remark when he read this editorial. But, bearing in mind a biblical adage, he did not blame Mr. Tooting for his diplomacy. " Send in the next man."

Mr. Tooting opened the study door and glanced over the public-spirited citizens awaiting, on the porch, the pleasure of their leader.

"Come along, Caldwell," said Mr. Tooting. "He wants your report from Kingston. Get a hustle on!"

Mr. Caldwell made his report, received many brief and businesslike suggestions, and retired, impressed. Whereupon Mr. Crewe commanded Mr. Tooting to order his automobile — an occasional and rapid spin over the country roads being the only diversion the candidate permitted himself. Wishing to be alone with his thoughts, he did not take Mr. Tooting with him on these excursions.

"And by the way," said Mr. Crewe, as he seized the steering wheel a few moments later, "just drop a line to Austen Vane, will you, and tell him I want to see him up here within a day or two. Make an appointment. It has occurred to me that he might be very useful."

Mr. Tooting stood on the driveway watching the cloud of dust settle on the road below. Then he indulged in a long and peculiarly significant whistle through his teeth, rolled his eyes heavenward, and went into the house. He remembered Austen's remark about riding a cyclone.

Mr. Crewe took the Tunbridge road. On his excursion of the day before he had met Mrs. Pomfret, who had held up her hand, and he had protestingly brought the car to a stop.

"Your horses don't frighten," he had said.

"No, but I wanted to speak to you, Humphrey," Mrs. Pomfret had replied; "you are becoming so important that nobody ever has a glimpse of you. I wanted to tell you what an interest we take in this splendid thing you are doing."

"Well," said Mr. Crewe, "it was a plain duty, and nobody else seemed willing to undertake it."

Mrs. Pomfret's eyes had flashed.

"Men of that type are scarce," she answered. "But you'll win. You're the kind of man that wins."

"Oh, yes, I'll win," said Mr. Crewe.

"You're so magnificently sure of yourself," cried Mrs.

Pomfret. "Alice is taking *such* an interest. Every day she asks, 'When is Humphrey going to make his first speech?' You'll let us know in time, won't you?"

"Did you put all that nonsense in the New York *Flare?*" asked Mr. Crewe.

"Oh, Humphrey, I hope you liked it," cried Mrs. Pomfret. "Don't make the mistake of despising what women can do. They elected the Honourable Billy Aylestone — he said so himself. I'm getting all the women interested."

"Who've you been calling on now?" he inquired.

Mrs. Pomfret hesitated.

"I've been up at Fairview to see about Mrs. Flint. She isn't much better."

"Is Victoria home?" Mr. Crewe demanded, with undisguised interest.

"Poor dear girl!" said Mrs. Pomfret, "of course I wouldn't have mentioned the subject to her, but she wanted to know all about it. It naturally makes an awkward situation between you and her, doesn't it?"

"Oh, Victoria's level-headed enough," Mr. Crewe had answered; "I guess she knows something about old Flint and his methods by this time. At any rate, it won't make any difference with me," he added magnanimously, and threw in his clutch. He had encircled Fairview in his drive that day, and was, curiously enough, headed in that direction now. Slow to make up his mind in some things, as every eligible man must be, he was now coming rapidly to the notion that he might eventually decide upon Victoria as the most fitting mate for one in his position. Still, there was no hurry. As for going to Fairview House, that might be awkward, besides being open to misconstruction by his constituents. Mr. Crewe reflected, as he rushed up the hills, that he had missed Victoria since she had been abroad — and a man so continually occupied as he did not have time to miss many people. Mr. Crewe made up his mind he would encircle Fairview every day until he ran across her.

The goddess of fortune sometimes blesses the persistent

even before they begin to persist — perhaps from sheer weariness at the remembrance of previous importuning. Victoria, on a brand-new and somewhat sensitive five-year-old, was coming out of the stone archway when Mr. Crewe (without any signal this time!) threw on his brakes. An exhibition of horsemanship followed, on Victoria's part, which Mr. Crewe beheld with admiration. The five-year-old swung about like a weathercock in a gust of wind, assuming an upright position, like the unicorn in the British coat of arms. Victoria cut him, and he came down on all fours and danced into the wire fence that encircled the Fairview domain, whereupon he got another stinging reminder that there was some one on his back.

"Bravo!" cried Mr. Crewe, leaning on the steering wheel and watching the performance with delight. Never, he thought, had Victoria been more appealing; strangely enough, he had not remembered that she was quite so handsome, or that her colour was so vivid; or that her body was so straight and long and supple. He liked the way in which she gave it to that horse, and he made up his mind that she would grace any position, however high. Presently the horse made a leap into the road in front of the motor and stood trembling, ready to bolt.

"For Heaven's sake, Humphrey," she cried, "shut off your power! Don't sit there like an idiot — do you think I'm doing this for pleasure?"

Mr. Crewe good-naturedly turned off his switch, and the motor, with a dying sigh, was silent. He even liked the notion of being commanded to do a thing; there was a relish about it that was new. The other women of his acquaintance addressed him more deferentially.

"Get hold of the bridle," he said to the chauffeur. "You've got no business to have an animal like that," was his remark to Victoria.

"Don't touch him!" she said to the man, who was approaching with a true machinist's fear of a high-spirited horse. "*You've* got no business to have a motor like that, if you can't handle it any better than you do."

"You managed him all right. I'll say that for you," said Mr. Crewe.

"No thanks to you," she replied. Now that the horse was comparatively quiet, she sat and regarded Mr. Crewe with an amusement which was gradually getting the better of her anger. A few moments since, and she wished with great intensity that she had been using the whip on his shoulders instead. Now that she had time to gather up the threads of the situation, the irresistibly comic aspect of it grew upon her, and little creases came into the corners of her eyes — which Mr. Crewe admired. She recalled — with indignation, to be sure — the conversation she had overheard in the dining room of the Duncan house, but her indignation was particularly directed, on that occasion, towards Mr. Tooting. Here was Humphrey Crewe, sitting talking to her in the road — Humphrey Crewe, whose candidacy for the governorship impugned her father's management of the Northeastern Railroads — and she was unable to take the matter seriously! There must be something wrong with her, she thought.

"So you're home again," Mr. Crewe observed, his eyes still bearing witness to the indubitable fact. "I shouldn't have known it — I've been so busy."

"Is the Legislature still in session?" Victoria soberly inquired.

"You are a little behind the times — ain't you?" said Mr. Crewe, in surprise. "How long have you been home? Hasn't anybody told you what's going on?"

"I only came up ten days ago," she answered, "and I'm afraid I've been something of a recluse. What is going on?"

"Well," he declared, "I should have thought *you'd* heard it, anyway. I'll send you up a few newspapers when I get back. I'm a candidate for the governorship."

Victoria bit her lip, and leaned over to brush a fly from the neck of her horse.

"You are getting on rapidly, Humphrey," she said. "Do you think you've got — any chance?"

"Any chance!" he repeated, with some pardonable force. "I'm sure to be nominated. There's an overwhelming sentiment among the voters of this State for decent politics. It didn't take me long to find that out. The only wonder is that somebody hasn't seen it before."

"Perhaps," she answered, giving him a steady look, "perhaps somebody has."

One of Mr. Crewe's greatest elements of strength was his imperviousness to this kind of a remark.

"If anybody's seen it," he replied, "they haven't the courage of their convictions." Such were the workings of Mr. Crewe's mind that he had already forgotten that first talk with Mr. Hamilton Tooting. "Not that I want to take too much credit on myself," he added, with becoming modesty, "I have had some experience in the world, and it was natural that I should get a fresh view. Are you coming down to Leith in a few days?"

"I may," said Victoria.

"Telephone me," said Mr. Crewe, "and if I can get off, I will. I'd like to talk to you. You have more sense than most women I know."

"You overwhelm me, Humphrey. Compliments sound strangely on your lips."

"When I say a thing, I mean it," Mr. Crewe declared. "I don't pay compliments. I'd make it a point to take a little time off to talk to you. You see, so many men are interested in this thing from various parts of the State, and we are so busy organizing, that it absorbs most of my day."

"I couldn't think of encroaching," Victoria protested.

"That's all right — you can be a great help. I've got confidence in your judgment. By the way," he asked suddenly, "you haven't seen your friend Austen Vane since you got back, have you?"

"Why do you call him my friend?" said Victoria. Mr. Crew perceived that the exercise had heightened her colour, and the transition appealed to his sense of beauty.

"Perhaps I put it a little strongly," he replied. "You

seemed to take an interest in him, for some reason. I suppose it's because you like new types."

"I like Mr. Vane very much, — and for himself," she said quietly. "But I haven't seen him since I came back. Nor do I think I am likely to see him. What made you ask about him?"

"Well, he seems to be a man of some local standing, and he ought to be in this campaign. If you happen to see him, you might mention the subject to him. I've sent for him to come up and see me."

"Mr. Vane doesn't seem to me to be a person one can send for like that," Victoria remarked judicially. "As to advising him as to what course he should take politically — that would even be straining my friendship for you, Humphrey. On reflection," she added, smiling, "there may appear to you reasons why I should not care to meddle with — politics, just now."

"I can't see it," said Mr. Crewe; "you've got a mind of your own, and you've never been afraid to use it, so far as I know. If you *should* see that Vane man, just give him a notion of what I'm trying to do."

"What are you trying to do?" inquired Victoria, sweetly.

"I'm trying to clean up this State politically," said Mr. Crewe, "and I'm going to do it. When you come down to Leith, I'll tell you about it, and I'll send you the newspapers to-day. Don't be in a hurry," he cried, addressing over his shoulder two farmers in a wagon who had driven up a few moments before, and who were apparently anxious to pass. "Wind her up, Adolphe."

The chauffeur, standing by the crank, started the engine instantly, and the gears screamed as Mr. Crewe threw in his low speed. The five-year-old whirled, and bolted down the road at a pace which would have seemed to challenge a racing car; and the girl in the saddle, bending to the motion of the horse, was seen to raise her hand in warning.

"Better stay whar you be," shouted one of the farmers; "don't go to follerin' her. The hoss is runnin' away."

Mr. Crewe steered his car into the Fairview entrance, and backed into the road again, facing the other way. He had decided to go home.

"That lady can take care of herself," he said, and started off towards Leith, wondering how it was that Mr. Flint had not confided his recent political troubles to his daughter.

"That hoss is ugly, sure enough," said the farmer who had spoken before.

Victoria flew on, down the narrow road. After twenty strides she did not attempt to disguise from herself the fact that the five-year-old was in a frenzy of fear, and running away. Victoria had been run away with before, and having some knowledge of the animal she rode, she did not waste her strength by pulling on the curb, but sought rather to quiet him with her voice, — which had no effect whatever. He was beyond appeal, his head was down, and his ears trembling backwards and straining for a sound of the terror that pursued him. The road ran through the forest, and Victoria reflected that the grade, on the whole, was downward to the East Tunbridge station, where the road crossed the track and took to the hills beyond. Once among them, she would be safe — he might run as far as he pleased. But could she pass the station? She held a firm rein, and tried to keep her mind clear.

Suddenly, at a slight bend of the road, the corner of the little red building came in sight, some hundreds of yards ahead ; and, on the side where it stood, in the clearing, was a white mass which Victoria recognized as a pile of lumber. She saw several men on the top of the pile, standing motionless; she heard one of them shout; the horse swerved, and she felt herself flung violently to the left.

Her first thought, after striking, was one of self-congratulation that her safety stirrup and habit had behaved properly. Before she could rise, a man was leaning over her — and in the instant she had the impression that he was a friend. Other people had had this impression of him on first acquaintance — his size, his genial, brick-red face, and his honest blue eyes all doubtless contributing.

"Are you hurt, Miss Flint?" he asked.

"Not in the least," she replied, springing to her feet to prove the contrary. "What's become of my horse?"

"Two of the men have gone after him," he said, staring at her with undisguised but honest admiration. Whereupon he became suddenly embarrassed, and pulled out a handkerchief the size of a table-napkin. "Let me dust you off."

"Thank you," said Victoria, laughing, and beginning the process herself. Her new acquaintance plied the handkerchief, his face a brighter brick-red than ever.

"Thank God, there wasn't a freight on the siding," he remarked, so fervently that Victoria stole a glance at him. The dusting process continued.

"There," she exclaimed, at last, adjusting her stock and shaking her skirt, "I'm ever so much obliged. It was very foolish in me to tumble off, wasn't it?"

"It was the only thing you could have done," he declared. "I had a good view of it, and he flung you like a bean out of a shooter. That's a powerful horse. I guess you're the kind that likes to take risks."

Victoria laughed at his expressive phrase, and crossed the road, and sat down on the edge of the lumber pile, in the shade.

"There seems to be nothing to do but wait," she said, "and to thank you again. Will you tell me your name?"

"I'm Tom Gaylord," he replied.

Her colour, always so near the surface, rose a little as she regarded him. So this was Austen Vane's particular friend, whom he had tried to put out of his window. A Herculean task, Victoria thought, from Tom's appearance. Tom sat down within a few feet of her.

"I've seen you a good many times, Miss Flint," he remarked, applying the handkerchief to his face.

"And I've seen you — once, Mr. Gaylord," some mischievous impulse prompted her to answer. Perhaps the impulse was more deep-seated, after all.

"Where?" demanded Tom, promptly.

"You were engaged," said Victoria, "in a struggle in a window on Ripton Square. It looked, for a time," she continued, "as if you were going to be dropped on the roof of the porch."

Tom gazed at her in confusion and surprise.

"You seem to be fond, too, of dangerous exercise," she observed.

"Do you mean to say you remembered me from that?" he exclaimed. "Oh, you know Austen Vane, don't you?"

"Does Mr. Vane acknowledge the acquaintance?" Victoria inquired.

"It's funny, but you remind me of Austen," said Tom, grinning; "you seem to have the same queer way of saying things that he has." Here he was conscious of another fit of embarrassment. "I hope you don't mind what I say, Miss Flint."

"Not at all," said Victoria. She turned, and looked across the track.

"I suppose they are having a lot of trouble in catching my horse," she remarked.

"They'll get him," Tom assured her, "one of those men is my manager. He always gets what he starts out for. What were we talking about? Oh, Austen Vane. You see, I've known him ever since I was a shaver, and I think the world of him. If he asked me to go to South America and get him a zebra to-morrow, I believe I'd do it."

"That is real devotion," said Victoria. The more she saw of young Tom, the better she liked him, although his conversation was apt to be slightly embarrassing.

"We've been through a lot of rows together," Tom continued, warming to his subject, "in school and college. You see, Austen's the kind of man who doesn't care what anybody thinks, if he takes it into his head to do a thing. It was a great piece of luck for me that he shot that fellow out West, or he wouldn't be here now. You heard about that, didn't you?"

"Yes," said Victoria, "I believe I did."

"And yet," said Tom, "although I'm as good a friend as he has, I never quite got under his skin. There's some things I wouldn't talk to him about. I've learned that. I never told him, for instance, that I saw him out in a sleigh with you at the capital."

"Oh," said Victoria; and she added, "Is he ashamed of it?"

"It's not that," replied Tom, hastily, "but I guess if he'd wanted me to know about it, he'd have told me."

Victoria had begun to realize that, in the few minutes which had elapsed since she had found herself on the roadside, gazing up into young Tom's eyes, she had somehow become quite intimate with him.

"I fancy he would have told you all there was to tell about it — if the matter had occurred to him again," she said, with the air of finally dismissing a subject already too prolonged. But Tom knew nothing of the shades and conventions of the art of conversation.

"He's never told me he knew you at all!" he exclaimed, staring at Victoria. Apparently some of the aspects of this now significant omission on Austen's part were beginning to dawn on Tom.

"It wasn't worth mentioning," said Victoria, briefly, seeking for a pretext to change the subject.

"I don't believe that," said Tom, "you can't expect me to sit here and look at you and believe that. How long has he known you?"

"I saw him once or twice last summer, at Leith," said Victoria, now wavering between laughter and exasperation. She had got herself into a quandary indeed when she had to parry the appalling frankness of such inquiries.

"The more you see of him, the more you'll admire him, I'll prophesy," said Tom. "If he'd been content to travel along the easy road, as most fellows are, he would have been counsel for the Northeastern. Instead of that — " here Tom halted abruptly, and turned scarlet. "I forgot," he said, "I'm always putting my foot in it, with ladies."

He was so painfully confused that Victoria felt herself suffering with him, and longed to comfort him.

u

"Please go on, Mr. Gaylord," she said; "I am very much interested in my neighbours here, and I know that a great many of them think that the railroad meddles in politics. I've tried to find out what they think, but it is so difficult for a woman to understand. If matters are wrong, I'm sure my father will right them when he knows the situation. He has so much to attend to." She paused. Tom was still mopping his forehead. "You may say anything you like to me, and I shall not take offence."

Tom's admiration of her was heightened by this attitude.

"Austen wouldn't join Mr. Crewe in his little game, anyway," he said. "When Ham Tooting, Crewe's manager, came to him he kicked him downstairs."

Victoria burst out laughing.

"I constantly hear of these ferocious deeds which Mr. Vane commits," she said, "and yet he seems exceptionally good-natured and mild-mannered."

"That's straight — he kicked him downstairs. Served Tooting right, too."

"There does seem to have been an element of justice in it," Victoria remarked.

"You haven't seen Austen since he left his father?" Mr. Gaylord inquired.

"Left him! Where — has he gone?"

"Gone up to live with Jabe Jenney. If Austen cared anything about money, he never would have broken with the old man, who has some little put away."

"Why did he leave his father?" asked Victoria, not taking the trouble now to conceal her interest.

"Well," said Tom, "you know they never did get along. It hasn't been Austen's fault — he's tried. After he came back from the West he stayed here to please old Hilary, when he might have gone to New York and made a fortune at the law, with his brains. But after Austen saw the kind of law the old man practised he wouldn't stand for it, and got an office of his own."

Victoria's eyes grew serious.

"What kind of law does Hilary Vane practise?" she asked.

Tom hesitated and began to mop his forehead again.

"Please don't mind me," Victoria pleaded.

"Well, all right," said Tom, "I'll tell *you* the truth, or die for it. But I don't want to make you — unhappy."

"You will do me a kindness, Mr. Gaylord," she said, "by telling me what you believe to be true."

There was a note in her voice which young Tom did not understand. Afterwards, when he reflected about the matter, he wondered if she were unhappy.

"I don't want to blame Hilary too much," he answered. "I know Austen don't. Hilary's grown up with that way of doing things, and in the old days there was no other way. Hilary is the chief counsel for the Northeastern, and he runs the Republican organization in this State for their benefit. But Austen made up his mind that there was no reason why *he* should grow up that way. He says that a lawyer should keep to his profession, and not become a lobbyist in the interest of his clients. He lived with the old man until the other day, because he has a real soft spot for him. Austen put up with a good deal. And then Hilary turned loose on him and said a lot of things he couldn't stand. Austen didn't answer, but went up and packed his bags and made Hilary's housekeeper promise to stay with him, or she'd have left, too. They say Hilary's sorry, now. He's fond of Austen, but he can't get along with him."

"Do you know what they quarrelled about?" asked Victoria, in a low voice.

"This spring," said Tom, "the Gaylord Lumber Company made Austen junior counsel. He ran across a law the other day that nobody else seems to have had sense enough to discover, by which we can sue the railroad for excessive freight rates. It means a lot of money. He went right in to Hilary and showed him the section, told him that suit was going to be brought, and offered to resign. Hilary flew off the track and said if he didn't bring suit he'd publish it all over the State that Austen started it. Galusha Hammer, our senior counsel, is sick, and I don't think he'll ever get well. That makes Austen senior counsel. But he persuaded old Tom, my father, not to bring this suit until after the political campaign, until Mr. Crewe gets through with his fireworks. Hilary doesn't know that."

"I see," said Victoria.

Down the hill, on the far side of the track, she perceived the two men approaching with a horse; then she remembered the fact that she had been thrown, and that it was her horse. She rose to her feet.

"I'm ever so much obliged to you, Mr. Gaylord," she said; "you have done me a great favour by — telling me these things. And thanks for letting them catch the horse. I'm afraid I've put you to a lot of bother."

"Not at all," said Tom, "not at all." He was studying her face. Its expression troubled and moved him strangely, for he was not an analytical person. "I didn't mean to tell you those things when I began," he apologized, "but you wanted to hear them."

"I wanted to hear them," repeated Victoria. She held out her hand to him.

"You're not going to ride home!" he exclaimed. "I'll take you up in my buggy — it's in the station shed."

She smiled, turned and questioned and thanked the men, examined the girths and bridle, and stroked the five-year-old on the neck. He was wet from mane to fetlocks.

"I don't think he'll care to run much farther," she said. "If you'll pull him over to the lumber pile, Mr. Gaylord, I'll mount him."

They performed her bidding in silence, each paying her a tribute in his thoughts. As for the five-year-old, he was quiet enough by this time. When she was in the saddle she held out her hand once more to Tom.

"I hope we shall meet soon again," she said, and smiling back at him, started on her way towards Fairview.

Tom stood for a moment looking after her, while the two men indulged in surprised comments.

"Andrews," said young Mr. Gaylord, "just fetch my buggy and follow her until she gets into the gate."

CHAPTER XVIII

A SPIRIT IN THE WOODS

EMPIRES crack before they crumble, and the first cracks seem easily mended — even as they have been mended before. A revolt in Gaul or Britain or Thrace is little to be minded, and a prophet in Judea less. And yet into him who sits in the seat of power a premonition of something impending gradually creeps — a premonition which he will not acknowledge, will not define. Yesterday, by the pointing of a finger, he created a province; to-day he dares not, but consoles himself by saying he does not wish to point. No antagonist worthy of his steel has openly defied him, worthy of recognition by the opposition of a legion. But the sense of security has been subtly and indefinably shaken.

By the strange telepathy which defies language, to the Honourable Hilary Vane, Governor of the Province, some such unacknowledged forebodings have likewise been communicated. A week after his conversation with Austen, on the return of his emperor from a trip to New York, the Honourable Hilary was summoned again to the foot of the throne, and his thoughts as he climbed the ridges towards Fairview were not in harmony with the carols of the birds in the depths of the forest and the joy of the bright June weather. Loneliness he had felt before, and to its ills he had applied the antidote of labour. The burden that sat upon his spirit to-day was not mere loneliness; to the truth of this his soul attested, but Hilary Vane had never listened to the promptings of his soul. He would have been shocked if you had told him this. Did he not confess, with his eyes shut, his sins every Sunday? Did he not publicly acknowledge his soul?

Austen Vane had once remarked that, if some keen American lawyer would really put his mind to the evasion of the Ten Commandments, the High Heavens themselves might be cheated. This saying would have shocked the Honourable Hilary inexpressibly. He had never been employed by a syndicate to draw up papers to avoid these mandates; he revered them, as he revered the Law, which he spelled with a capital. He spelled the word *Soul* with a capital likewise, and certainly no higher recognition could be desired than this!

Never in the Honourable Hilary's long, laborious, and preëminently model existence had he realized that happiness is harmony. It would not be true to assert that, on this wonderful June day, a glimmering of this truth dawned upon him. Such a statement would be open to the charge of exaggeration, and his frame of mind was pessimistic. But he had got so far as to ask himself the question, — *Cui bono?* and repeated it several times on his drive, until a verse of Scripture came, unbidden, to his lips. "*For what hath man of all his labour, and of the vexation of his heart, wherein he hath laboured under the sun?*" and "*there is one event unto all.*" Austen's saying, that he had never learned how to enjoy life, he remembered, too. What had Austen meant by that?

Hitherto Hilary Vane had never failed of self-justification in any event which had befallen him; and while this consciousness of the rectitude of his own attitude had not made him happier, there had been a certain grim pleasure in it. To the fact that he had ruined, by sheer over-righteousness, the last years of the sunny life of Sarah Austen he had been oblivious — until to-day. The strange, retrospective mood which had come over him this afternoon led his thoughts into strange paths, and he found himself wondering if, after all, it had not been in his power to make her happier. Her dryad-like face, with its sweet, elusive smile, seemed to peer at him now wistfully out of the forest, and suddenly a new and startling thought rose up within him — after six and thirty years. Perhaps she had belonged in the forest! Perhaps, be-

cause he had sought to cage her, she had pined and died!
The thought gave Hilary unwonted pain, and he strove
to put it away from him ; but memories such as these,
once aroused, are not easily set at rest, and he bent his
head as he recalled (with a new and significant pathos)
those hopeless and pitiful flights into the wilds she
loved.

Now Austen had gone. Was there a Law behind these
actions of mother and son which he had persisted in de-
nouncing as vagaries? Austen was a man : a man, Hilary
could not but see, who had the respect of his fellows,
whose judgment and talents were becoming recognized.
Was it possible that he, Hilary Vane, could have been
one of those referred to by the Preacher? During the
week which had passed since Austen's departure the
house in Hanover Street had been haunted for Hilary.
The going of his son had not left a mere void, — that
would have been pain enough. Ghosts were there, ghosts
which he could but dimly feel and see, and more than
once, in the long evenings, he had taken to the streets to
avoid them.

In that week Hilary's fear of meeting his son in the
street or in the passages of the building had been equalled
by a yearning to see him. Every morning, at the hour
Austen was wont to drive Pepper to the Ripton House
stables across the square, Hilary had contrived to be
standing near his windows — a little back, and out of
sight. And — stranger still! — he had turned from these
glimpses to the reports of the Honourable Brush Bascom
and his associates with a distaste he had never felt before.

With some such thoughts as these Hilary Vane turned
into the last straight stretch of the avenue that led to
Fairview House, with its red and white awnings gleaming
in the morning sun. On the lawn, against a white and
purple mass of lilacs and the darker background of pines,
a straight and infinitely graceful figure in white caught
his eye and held it. He recognized Victoria. She wore
a simple summer gown, the soft outline of its flounces
mingling subtly with the white clusters behind her. She

turned her head at the sound of the wheels and looked at him; the distance was not too great for a bow, but Hilary did not bow. Something in her face deterred him from this act, — something which he himself did not understand or define. He sought to pronounce the incident negligible. What was the girl, or her look, to him? And yet (he found himself strangely thinking) he had read in her eyes a trace of the riddle which had been relentlessly pursuing him ; there was an odd relation in her look to that of Sarah Austen. During the long years he had been coming to Fairview, even before the new house was built, when Victoria was in pinafores, he had never understood her. When she was a child, he had vaguely recognized in her a spirit antagonistic to his own, and her sayings had had a disconcerting ring. And now this simple glance of hers had troubled him — only more definitely.

It was a new experience for the Honourable Hilary to go into a business meeting with his faculties astray. Absently he rang the stable bell, surrendered his horse, and followed a footman to the retired part of the house occupied by the railroad president. Entering the oak-bound sanctum, he crossed it and took a seat by the window, merely nodding to Mr. Flint, who was dictating a letter. Mr. Flint took his time about the letter, but when it was finished he dismissed the stenographer with an impatient and powerful wave of the hand — as though brushing the man bodily out of the room. Remaining motionless until the door had closed, Mr. Flint turned abruptly and fixed his eyes on the contemplative figure of his chief counsel.

" Well? " he said.

" Well, Flint," answered the Honourable Hilary.

" Well," said Mr. Flint, "that bridge over Maple River has got loosened up so by the freshet that we have to keep freight cars on it to hold it down, and somebody is trying to make trouble by writing a public letter to the Railroad Commission, and calling attention to the head-on collision at Barker's Station."

"Well," replied the Honourable Hilary, again, "that won't have any influence on the Railroad Commission."

"No," said Mr. Flint, "but it all goes to increase this confounded public sentiment that's in the air, like small-pox. Another jackass pretends to have kept a table of the through trains on the Sumsic division, and says they've averaged forty-five minutes late at Edmundton. He says the through express made the run faster thirty years ago."

"I guess that's so," said the Honourable Hilary, "I was counsel for that road then. I read that letter. He says there isn't an engine on the division that could pull his hat off, up grade."

Neither of the two gentlemen appeared to deem this statement humorous.

"What these incendiaries don't understand," said Mr. Flint, "is that we have to pay dividends."

"It's because they don't get 'em," replied Mr. Vane, sententiously.

"The track slid into the water at Glendale," continued Mr. Flint. "I suppose they'll tell us we ought to rock ballast that line. You'll see the Railroad Commission, and give 'em a sketch of a report."

"I had a talk with Young yesterday," said Mr. Vane, his eyes on the stretch of lawn and forest framed by the window. For the sake of the ignorant, it may be well to add that the Honourable Orrin Young was the chairman of the Commission.

"And now," said Mr. Flint, "not that this Crewe business amounts to *that*" (here the railroad president snapped his fingers with the intensity of a small pistol shot), "but what's *he* been doing?"

"Political advertising," said the Honourable Hilary.

"Plenty of it, I guess," Mr. Flint remarked acidly. "That's one thing Tooting can't teach him. He's a natural-born genius at it."

"Tooting can help — even at that," answered Mr. Vane, ironically. "They've got a sketch of so-called North-eastern methods in forty weekly newspapers this week, with a picture of that public benefactor and martyr, Humphrey Crewe. Here's a sample of it."

Mr. Flint waved the sample away.

"You've made a list of the newspapers that printed it?" Mr. Flint demanded. Had he lived in another age he might have added, "Have the malefactors burned alive in my garden."

"Brush has seen some of 'em," said Mr. Vane, no doubt referring to the editors, "and I had some of 'em come to Ripton. They've got a lot to say about the freedom of the press, and their right to take political advertising. Crewe's matter is in the form of a despatch, and most of 'em pointed out at the top of the editorial columns that their papers are not responsible for despatches in the news columns. Six of 'em are out and out for Crewe, and those fellows are honest enough."

"Take away their passes and advertising," said Mr. Flint. ("Off with their heads!" said the Queen of Hearts.)

"I wouldn't do that if I were you, Flint; they might make capital out of it. I think you'll find that five of 'em have sent their passes back, anyway."

"Freeman will give you some new ideas" (from the "Book of Arguments," although Mr. Flint did not say so) "which have occurred to me might be distributed for editorial purposes next week. And, by the way, what have you done about that brilliant Mr. Coombes of the *Johnstown Ray*, who says 'the Northeastern Railroads give us a pretty good government'?"

The Honourable Hilary shook his head.

"Too much zeal," he observed. "I guess he won't do it again."

For a while after that they talked of strictly legal matters, which the chief counsel produced in order out of his bag. But when these were finally disposed of, Mr. Flint led the conversation back to the Honourable Humphrey Crewe, who stood harmless — to be sure — like a bull on the track which it might be unwise to run over.

"He doesn't amount to a soap bubble in a gale," Mr.

Flint declared contemptuously. "Sometimes I think we made a great mistake to notice him."

"We haven't noticed him," said Mr. Vane; "the newspapers have."

Mr. Flint brushed this distinction aside.

"That," he said irritably, "and letting Tooting go — "

The Honourable Hilary's eyes began to grow red. In former days Mr. Flint had not often questioned his judgment.

"There's one thing more I wanted to mention to you," said the chief counsel. "In past years I have frequently drawn your attention to that section of the act of consolidation which declares that rates and fares existing at the time of its passage shall not be increased."

"Well," said Mr. Flint, impatiently, "well, what of it?"

"Only this," replied the Honourable Hilary, "you disregarded my advice, and the rates on many things are higher than they were."

"Upon my word, Vane," said Mr. Flint, "I wish you'd chosen some other day to croak. What do you want me to do? Put all the rates back because this upstart politician Crewe is making a noise? Who's going to dig up that section?"

"Somebody has dug it up," said Mr. Vane.

This was the last straw.

"Speak out, man!" he cried. "What are you leading up to?"

"Just this," answered the Honourable Hilary; "that the Gaylord Lumber Company are going to bring suit under that section."

Mr. Flint rose, thrust his hands in his pockets, and paced the room twice.

"Have they got a case?" he demanded.

"It looks a little that way to me," said Mr. Vane. "I'm not prepared to give a definite opinion as yet."

Mr. Flint measured the room twice again.

"Did that old fool Hammer stumble on to this?"

"Hammer's sick," said Mr. Vane; "they say he's got Bright's disease. My son discovered that section."

There was a certain ring of pride in the Honourable Hilary's voice, and a lifting of the head as he pronounced the words "my son," which did not escape Mr. Flint. The railroad president walked slowly to the arm of the chair in which his chief counsel was seated, and stood looking down at him. But the Honourable Hilary appeared unconscious of what was impending.

"Your son!" exclaimed Mr. Flint. "So your son, the son of the man who has been my legal adviser and confidant and friend for thirty years, is going to join the Crewes and Tootings in their assaults on established decency and order! He's out for cheap political preferment, too, is he? By thunder! I thought that he had some such thing in his mind when he came in here and threw his pass in my face and took that Meader suit. I don't mind telling you that he's the man I've been afraid of all along. He's got a head on him — I saw that at the start. I trusted to you to control him, and this is how you do it."

It was characteristic of the Honourable Hilary, when confronting an angry man, to grow cooler as the other's temper increased.

"I don't want to control him," he said.

"I guess you couldn't," retorted Mr. Flint.

"That's a better way of putting it," replied the Honourable Hilary, "I couldn't."

The chief counsel for the Northeastern Railroads got up and went to the window, where he stood for some time with his back turned to the president. Then Hilary Vane faced about.

"Mr. Flint," he began, in his peculiar deep and resonant voice, "you've said some things to-day that I won't forget. I want to tell you, first of all, that I admire my son."

"I thought so," Mr. Flint interrupted.

"And more than that," the Honourable Hilary continued, "I prophesy that the time will come when you'll admire him. Austen Vane never did an underhanded thing in his life — or committed a mean action. He's be'n wild, but he's always told me the truth. I've done him injustice a good many times, but I won't stand up and listen to another man do him injustice." Here he paused, and picked up his bag. " I'm going down to Ripton to write out my resignation as counsel for your roads, and as soon as you can find another man to act, I shall consider it accepted."

It is difficult to put down on paper the sensations of the president of the Northeastern Railroads as he listened to these words from a man with whom he had been in business relations for over a quarter of a century : a man upon whose judgment he had always relied implicitly, who had been a strong fortress in time of trouble. Such sentences had an incendiary, blasphemous ring on Hilary Vane's lips — at first. It was as if the sky had fallen, and the Northeastern had been wiped out of existence.

Mr. Flint's feelings were, in a sense, akin to those of a traveller by sea who wakens out of a sound sleep in his cabin, with peculiar and unpleasant sensations, which he gradually discovers are due to cold water, and he realizes that the boat on which he is travelling is sinking.

The Honourable Hilary, with his bag, was halfway to the door, when Mr. Flint crossed the room in three strides and seized him by the arm.

" Hold on, Vane," he said, speaking with some difficulty ; " I'm — I'm a little upset this morning, and my temper got the best of me. You and I have been good friends for too many years for us to part this way. Sit down a minute, for God's sake, and let's cool off. I didn't intend to say what I did. I apologize."

Mr. Flint dropped his counsel's arm, and pulled out a handkerchief, and mopped his face. " Sit down, Hilary," he said.

The Honourable Hilary's tight lips trembled. Only three or four times in their long friendship had the president made use of his first name.

" You wouldn't leave me in the lurch now, Hilary," Mr.

Flint continued, " when all this nonsense is in the air? Think of the effect such an announcement would have! Everybody knows and respects you, and we can't do without your advice and counsel. But I won't put it on that ground. I'd never forgive myself, as long as I lived, if I lost one of my oldest and most valued personal friends in this way."

The Honourable Hilary looked at Mr. Flint, and sat down. He began to cut a piece of Honey Dew, but his hand shook. It was difficult, as we know, for him to give expression to his feelings.

" All right," he said.

Half an hour later Victoria, from under the awning of the little balcony in front of her mother's sitting room, saw her father come out bareheaded into the sun and escort the Honourable Hilary Vane to his buggy. This was an unwonted proceeding.

Victoria loved to sit in that balcony, a book lying neglected in her lap, listening to the summer sounds : the tinkle of distant cattle bells, the bass note of a hurrying bee, the strangely compelling song of the hermit-thrush, which made her breathe quickly ; the summer wind, stirring wantonly, was prodigal with perfumes gathered from the pines and the sweet June clover in the fields and the banks of flowers; in the distance, across the gentle foreground of the hills, Sawanec beckoned — did Victoria but raise her eyes! — to a land of enchantment.

The appearance of her father and Hilary had broken her revery, and a new thought, like a pain, had clutched her. The buggy rolled slowly down the drive, and Mr. Flint, staring after it a moment, went in the house. After a few minutes he emerged again, an old felt hat on his head which he was wont to wear in the country and a stick in his hand. Without raising his eyes, he started slowly across the lawn; and to Victoria, leaning forward intently over the balcony rail, there seemed an unwonted lack of purpose in his movements. Usually he struck out briskly in the direction of the pastures where his prize Guernseys were feeding, stopping on the way to pick up the manager of his farm. There are signs, unknown to men, which women read, and Victoria felt her heart beating, as she turned and entered the sitting room through the French window. A trained nurse was softly closing the door of the bedroom on the right.

"Mrs. Flint is asleep," she said.

"I am going out for a little while, Miss Oliver," Victoria answered, and the nurse returned a gentle smile of understanding.

Victoria, descending the stairs, hastily pinned on a hat which she kept in the coat closet, and hurried across the lawn in the direction Mr. Flint had taken. Reaching the pine grove, thinned by a famous landscape architect, she paused involuntarily to wonder again at the ultramarine of Sawanec through the upright columns of the trunks under the high canopy of boughs. The grove was on a plateau, which was cut on the side nearest the mountain by the line of a gray stone wall, under which the land fell away sharply. Mr. Flint was seated on a bench, his hands clasped across his stick, and as she came softly over the carpet of the needles he did not hear her until she stood beside him.

"You didn't tell me that you were going for a walk," she said reproachfully.

He started, and dropped his stick. She stooped quickly, picked it up for him, and settled herself at his side.

"I — I didn't expect to go, Victoria," he answered.

"You see," she said, "it's useless to try to slip away. I saw you from the balcony."

"How's your mother feeling?" he asked.

"She's asleep. She seems better to me since she's come back to Fairview."

Mr. Flint stared at the mountain with unseeing eyes.

"Father," said Victoria, "don't you think you ought to stay up here at least a week, and rest? I think so."

"No," he said, "no. There's a directors' meeting of a trust company to-morrow which I have to attend. I'm not tired."

Victoria shook her head, smiling at him with serious eyes.

"I don't believe you know when you are tired," she declared. "I can't see the good of all these directors' meetings. Why don't you retire, and live the rest of your life in peace? You've got — money enough, and even if you haven't," she added, with the little quiver of earnestness that sometimes came into her voice, "we could sell this big house and go back to the farmhouse to live. We used to be so happy there."

He turned abruptly, and fixed upon her a steadfast, searching stare that held, nevertheless, a strange tenderness in it.

"You don't care for all this, do you, Victoria?" he demanded, waving his stick to indicate the domain of Fairview.

She laughed gently, and raised her eyes to the green roof of the needles.

"If we could only keep the pine grove!" she sighed. "Do you remember what good times we had in the farmhouse, when you and I used to go off for whole days together?"

"Yes," said Mr. Flint, "yes."

"We don't do that any more," said Victoria. "It's only a little drive and a walk, now and then. And they seem to be growing — scarcer."

Mr. Flint moved uneasily, and made an attempt to clear his voice.

"I know it," he said, and further speech seemingly failed him. Victoria had the greater courage of the two.

"Why don't we?" she asked.

"I've often thought of it," he replied, still seeking his words with difficulty. "I find myself with more to do every year, Victoria, instead of less."

"Then why don't you give it up?"

"Why?" he asked, "why? Sometimes I wish with my whole soul I could give it up. I've always said that you had more sense than most women, but even you could not understand."

"I could understand," said Victoria.

He threw at her another glance, — a ring in her words

proclaimed their truth in spite of his determined doubt. In her eyes — had he but known it! — was a wisdom that exceeded his.

"You don't realize what you're saying," he exclaimed; "I can't leave the helm."

"Isn't it," she said, "rather the power that is so hard to relinquish?"

The feelings of Augustus Flint when he heard this question were of a complex nature. It was the second time that day he had been shocked, — the first being when Hilary Vane had unexpectedly defended his son. The word Victoria had used, *power*, had touched him on the quick. What had she meant by it? Had she been his wife and not his daughter, he would have flown into a rage. Augustus Flint was not a man given to the psychological amusement of self-examination; he had never analyzed his motives. He had had little to do with women, except Victoria. The Rose of Sharon knew him as the fountainhead from which authority and money flowed, but Victoria, since her childhood, had been his refuge from care, and in the haven of her companionship he had lost himself for brief moments of his life. She was the one being he really loved, with whom he consulted on such affairs of importance as he felt to be within her scope and province, — the cattle, the men on the place outside of the household, the wisdom of buying the Baker farm; bequests to charities, paintings, the library; and recently he had left to her judgment the European baths and the kind of treatment which her mother had required. Victoria had consulted with the physicians in Paris, and had made these decisions herself. From a child she had never shown a disposition to evade responsibility.

To his intimate business friends, Mr. Flint was in the habit of speaking of her as his right-hand man, but she was circumscribed by her sex, — or rather by Mr. Flint's idea of her sex, — and it never occurred to him that she could enter into the larger problems of his life. For this reason he had never asked himself whether such a state

x

of affairs would be desirable.   In reality it was her sympathy he craved, and such an interpretation of himself as
he chose to present to her.

So her question was a shock.   He suddenly beheld his
daughter transformed, a new personality who had been
thinking, and thinking along paths which he had never
cared to travel.

"The power!" he repeated.   "What do you mean by
that, Victoria?"

She sat for a moment on the end of the bench, gazing at
him with a questioning, searching look which he found
disconcerting.   What had happened to his daughter?
He little guessed the tumult in her breast.   She herself
could not fully understand the strange turn the conversation had taken towards the gateway of the vital things.

"It is natural for men to love power, isn't it?"

"I suppose so," said Mr. Flint, uneasily.   "I don't
know what you're driving at, Victoria."

"You control the lives and fortunes of a great many
people."

"That's just it," answered Mr. Flint, with a dash at
this opening; "my responsibilities are tremendous.   I
can't relinquish them."

"There is no — younger man to take your place?   Not
that I mean you are old, father," she continued, "but you
have worked very hard all your life, and deserve a holi-
day the rest of it."

"I don't know of any younger man," said Mr. Flint.
"I don't mean to say I'm the only person in the world
who can safeguard the stockholders' interests in the Northeastern.   But I know the road and its problems.   I don't
understand this from you, Victoria.   It doesn't sound like
you.   And as for letting go the helm now," he added, with
a short laugh tinged with bitterness, "I'd be posted all
over the country as a coward."

"Why?" asked Victoria, in the same quiet way.

"Why?   Because a lot of discontented and disappointed
people who have made failures of their lives are trying to
give me as much trouble as they can."

"Are you sure they are all disappointed and discontented, father?" she said.

"What!" exclaimed Mr. Flint, "you ask me that question? You, my own daughter, about people who are trying to make me out a rascal!"

"I don't think they are trying to make you out a rascal — at least most of them are not," said Victoria. "I don't think the — what you might call the personal aspect enters in with the honest ones."

Mr. Flint was inexpressibly amazed. He drew a long breath.

"Who are the honest ones?" he cried. "Do you mean to say that you, my own daughter, are defending these charlatans?"

"Listen, father," said Victoria. "I didn't mean to worry you, I didn't mean to bring up that subject to-day. Come — let's go for a walk and see the new barn."

But Mr. Flint remained firmly planted on the bench.

"Then you did intend to bring up the subject — some day?" he asked.

"Yes," said Victoria. She sat down again. "I have often wanted to hear — your side of it."

"Whose side have you heard?" demanded Mr. Flint.

A crimson flush crept into her cheek, but her father was too disturbed to notice it.

"You know," she said gently, "I go about the country a good deal, and I hear people talking, — farmers, and labourers, and people in the country stores who don't know that I'm your daughter."

"What do they say?" asked Mr. Flint, leaning forward eagerly and aggressively.

Victoria hesitated, turning over the matter in her mind.

"You understand, I am merely repeating what they say —"

"Yes, yes," he interrupted, "I want to know how far this thing has gone among them."

"Well," continued Victoria, looking at him bravely, "as nearly as I can remember their argument it is this:

that the Northeastern Railroads control the politics of the State for their own benefit. That you appoint the **govern-ors** and those that go to the Legislature, and that — Hilary Vane gets them elected. They say that he manages a political machine — that's the right word, isn't it? — for you. And that no laws can be passed of which you do not approve. And they say that the politicians whom Hilary Vane commands, and the men whom they put into office are all beholden to the railroad, and are of a sort which good citizens cannot support. They say that the railroad has destroyed the people's government."

Mr. Flint, for the moment forgetting or ignoring the charges, glanced at her in astonishment. The arraign-ment betrayed an amount of thought on the subject which he had not suspected.

"Upon my word, Victoria," he said, "you ought to take the stump for Humphrey Crewe."

She reached out with a womanly gesture, and laid her hand upon his.

"I am only telling you — what I hear," she said. "Won't you explain to me the way you look at it? These people don't all seem to be dishonest men or char-latans. Some of them, I know, are honest." And her colour rose again.

"Then they are dupes and fools," Mr. Flint declared vehemently. "I don't know how to explain it to you — the subject is too vast, too far-reaching. One must have had some business experience to grasp it. I don't mean to say you're not intelligent, but I'm at a loss where to begin with you. Looked at from their limited point of view, it would seem as if they had a case. I don't mean your friend, Humphrey Crewe — it's anything to get office with him. Why, he came up here and begged me — "

"I wasn't thinking of Humphrey Crewe," said Victoria.

Mr. Flint gave an ejaculation of distaste.

"He's no more of a reformer than I am. And now we've got that wild son of Hilary Vane's — the son of one of my oldest friends and associates — making trouble. He's bitten with this thing, too, and he's got some brains

in his head. Why," exclaimed Mr. Flint, stopping
abruptly and facing his daughter, "you know him! He's
the one who drove you home that evening from Crewe's
party."

"I remember," Victoria faltered, drawing her hand
away.

"I wasn't very civil to him that night, but I've always
been on the lookout for him. I sent him a pass once, and
he came up here and gave me as insolent a talking to as I
ever had in my life."

How well Victoria recalled that first visit, and how she
had wondered about the cause of it! So her father and
Austen Vane had quarrelled from the first.

"I'm sure he didn't mean to be insolent," she said, in a
low voice. "He isn't at all that sort."

"I don't know what sort he is, except that he isn't my
sort," Mr. Flint retorted, intent upon the subject which
had kindled his anger earlier in the day. "I don't pretend to understand him. He could probably have been
counsel for the road if he had behaved decently. Instead,
he starts in with suits against us. He's hit upon something now."

The president of the Northeastern dug savagely into
the ground with his stick, and suddenly perceived that
his daughter had her face turned away from his, towards
the mountain.

"Well, I won't bore you with that."

She turned with a look in her eyes that bewildered
him.

"You're not — boring me," she said.

"I didn't intend to go into all that," he explained
more calmly, "but the last few days have been trying.
We've got to expect the wind to blow from all directions."

Victoria smiled at him faintly.

"I have told you," she said, "that what you need
is a trip abroad. Perhaps some day you will remember
it."

"Maybe I'll go in the autumn," he answered, smiling

back at her. "These little flurries don't amount to anything more than mosquito-bites — only mosquitoes are irritating. You and I understand each other, Victoria, — and now listen. I'll give you the broad view of this subject, the view I've got to take, and I've lived in the world and seen more of it than some folks who think they know it all. I am virtually the trustee for thousands of stockholders, many of whom are widows and orphans. These people are innocent; they rely on my ability, and my honesty, for their incomes. Few men who have not had experience in railroad management know one-tenth of the difficulties and obstructions encountered by a railroad president who strives to do his duty by the road. My business is to run the Northeastern as economically as is consistent with good service and safety, and to give the stockholders the best return for their money. I am the steward — and so long as I am the steward," he exclaimed, "I'm going to do what I think is right, taking into consideration all the difficulties that confront me."

He got up and took a turn or two on the pine-needles. Victoria regarded him in silence. He appeared to her at that moment the embodiment of the power he represented. Force seemed to emanate from him, and she understood more clearly than ever how, from a poor boy on an obscure farm in Truro, he had risen to his present height.

"I don't say the service is what it should be," he went on, "but give me time — give me time. With all this prosperity in the country we can't handle the freight. We haven't got cars enough, tracks enough, engines enough. I won't go into that with you. But I do expect you to understand this: that politicians are politicians; they have always been corrupt as long as I have known them, and in my opinion they always will be. The Northeastern is the largest property holder in the State, pays the biggest tax, and has the most at stake. The politicians could ruin us in a single session of the Legislature — and what's more, they *would* do it. We'd have to be paying blackmail all the time to prevent measures that would compel us to go out of business. This is a fact, and not a theory. What little influence I exert politically I have to maintain in order to protect the property of my stockholders from annihilation. It isn't to be supposed," he concluded, " that I'm going to see the State turned over to a man like Humphrey Crewe. I wish to Heaven that this and every other State had a George Washington for governor and a majority of Robert Morrises in the Legislature. If they exist, in these days, the people won't elect 'em — that's all. The kind of man the people will elect, if you let 'em alone, is a man who brings in a bill and comes to you privately and wants you to buy him off."

" Oh, father," Victoria cried, " I can't believe that of the people I see about here! They seem so kind and honest and high-principled."

Mr. Flint gave a short laugh.

" They're dupes, I tell you. They're at the mercy of any political schemer who thinks it worth his while to fool 'em. Take Leith, for instance. There's a man over there who has controlled every office in that town for twenty-five years or more. He buys and sells votes and credentials like cattle. His name is Job Braden."

" Why," said Victoria, " I saw him at Humphrey Crewe's garden-party."

" I guess you did," said Mr. Flint, "and I guess Humphrey Crewe saw him before he went."

Victoria was silent, the recollection of the talk between Mr. Tooting and Mr. Crewe running through her mind, and Mr. Tooting's saying that he had done " dirty things " for the Northeastern. She felt that this was something she could not tell her father, nor could she answer his argument with what Tom Gaylord had said. She could not, indeed, answer Mr. Flint's argument at all; the subject, as he had declared, being too vast for her. And moreover, as she well knew, Mr. Flint was a man whom other men could not easily answer; he bore them down, even as he had borne her down. Involuntarily her mind turned to Austen, and she wondered what he had said; she wondered how he would have answered her father — whether he could have answered him. And she knew not what to

think. Could it be right, in a position of power and responsibility, to acknowledge evil and deal with it as evil?
That was, in effect, the gist of Mr. Flint's contention.
She did not know. She had never (strangely enough, she
thought) sought before to analyze the ethical side of her
father's character. One aspect of him she had shared with
her mother, that he was a tower of defence and strength,
and that his name alone had often been sufficient to get
difficult things done.

Was he right in this? And were his opponents char-
latans, or dupes, or idealists who could never be effective? Mr. Crewe wanted an office; Tom Gaylord had a
suit against the road, and Austen Vane was going to
bring that suit! What did she really know of Austen
Vane? But her soul cried out treason at this, and she
found herself repeating, with intensity, "I believe in
him! I believe in him!" She would have given worlds
to have been able to stand up before her father and tell
him that Austen would not bring the suit at this time —
that Austen had not allowed his name to be mentioned
for office in this connection, and had spurned Mr. Crewe's
advances. But she had not seen Austen since February.

What was his side of it? He had never told her, and
she respected his motives — yet, what was his side?
Fresh from the inevitably deep impressions which her
father's personality had stamped upon her, she wondered if Austen could cope with the argument before
which she had been so helpless.

The fact that she made of each of these two men the
embodiment of a different and opposed idea did not occur
to Victoria until that afternoon. Unconsciously, each
had impersonated the combatants in a struggle which
was going on in her own breast. Her father himself,
instinctively, had chosen Austen Vane for his antagonist
without knowing that she had an interest in him. Would
Mr. Flint ever know? Or would the time come when
she would be forced to take a side? The blood mounted
to her temples as she put the question from her.

CHAPTER XIX

MR. JABE JENNEY ENTERTAINS

Mr. Flint had dropped the subject with his last remark, nor had Victoria attempted to pursue it. Bewildered and not a little depressed (a new experience for
her), she had tried to hide her feelings. He, too, was
harassed and tired, and she had drawn him away from
the bench and through the pine woods to the pastures to
look at his cattle and the model barn he was building for
them. At half-past three, in her runabout, she had driven
him to the East Tunbridge station, where he had taken
the train for New York. He had waved her a good-by
from the platform, and smiled : and for a long time, as she
drove through the silent roads, his words and his manner
remained as vivid as though he were still by her side.
He was a man who had fought and conquered, and who
fought on for the sheer love of it.

It was a blue day in the hill country. At noon the
clouds had crowned Sawanec — a sure sign of rain; the
rain had come and gone, a June downpour, and the over-
cast sky lent (Victoria fancied) to the country-side a new
atmosphere. The hills did not look the same. It was
the kind of a day when certain finished country places
are at their best — or rather seem best to express their
meaning; a day for an event; a day set strangely apart
with an indefinable distinction. Victoria recalled such
days in her youth when weddings or garden-parties had
brought canopies into service, or news had arrived to upset
the routine of the household. Raindrops silvered the
pines, and the light winds shook them down on the
road in a musical shower.

Victoria was troubled, as she drove, over a question which had recurred to her many times since her talk that morning: had she been hypocritical in not telling her father that she had seen more of Austen Vane than she had implied by her silence? For many years Victoria had chosen her own companions; when the custom had begun, her mother had made a protest which Mr. Flint had answered with a laugh; he thought Victoria's judgment better than his wife's. Ever since that time the Rose of Sharon had taken the attitude of having washed her hands of responsibility for a course which must inevitably lead to ruin. She discussed some of Victoria's acquaintances with Mrs. Pomfret and other intimates; and Mrs. Pomfret had lost no time in telling Mrs. Flint about her daughter's sleigh-ride at the State capital with a young man from Ripton who seemed to be seeing entirely too much of Victoria. Mrs. Pomfret had marked certain danger signs, and as a conscientious woman was obliged to speak of them. Mrs. Pomfret did not wish to see Victoria make a *mésalliance*.

" My dear Fanny," Mrs. Flint had cried, lifting herself from the lace pillows, " what do you expect me to do — especially when I have nervous prostration? I've tried to do my duty by Victoria — goodness knows — to bring her up among the sons and daughters of the people who are my friends. They tell me that she has temperament — whatever that may be. I'm sure I never found out, except that the best thing to do with people who have it is to let them alone and pray for them. When we go abroad I like the Ritz and Claridge's and that new hotel in Rome. I see my friends there. Victoria, if you please, likes the little hotels in the narrow streets where you see *nobody*, and where you are *most* uncomfortable." (Miss Oliver, it's time for those seven drops.) "As I was saying, Victoria's enigmatical — hopeless, although a French *comtesse* who wouldn't look at anybody at the baths this spring became wild about her, and a certain type of elderly English peer always wants to marry her. (I suppose I *do* look pale to-day.) Victoria loves art, and really knows something about it. She adores to potter around those queer places abroad where you see strange English and Germans and Americans with red books in their hands. What am *I* to do about this young man of whom you speak — whatever his name is? I suppose Victoria will marry him — it would be just like her. But what can I do, Fanny? I can't manage her, and it's no use going to her father. He would only laugh. Augustus actually told me once there was no such thing as social position in this country!"

"American men of affairs," Mrs. Pomfret judicially replied, "are too busy to consider position. They make it, my dear, as a by-product." Mrs. Pomfret smiled, and mentally noted this aptly technical witticism for use again.

"I suppose they do," assented the Rose of Sharon, "and their daughters sometimes squander it, just as their sons squander their money."

"I'm not at all sure that Victoria is going to squander it," was Mrs. Pomfret's comforting remark. "She is too much of a personage, and she has great wealth behind her. I wish Alice were more like her, in some ways. Alice is so helpless, she has to be prodded and prompted continually. I can't leave her for a moment. And when she is married, I'm going into a sanatorium for six months."

"I hear," said Mrs. Flint, "that Humphrey Crewe is quite *épris*."

"Poor dear Humphrey!" exclaimed Mrs. Pomfret, "he can think of nothing else but politics."

But we are not to take up again, as yet, the deeds of the crafty Ulysses. In order to relate an important conversation between Mrs. Pomfret and the Rose of Sharon, we have gone back a week in this history, and have left Victoria — absorbed in her thoughts — driving over a wood road of many puddles that led to the Four Corners, near Avalon. The road climbed the song-laden valley of a brook, redolent now with scents of which the rain had robbed the fern, but at length Victoria reached an upland where the young corn was springing from the black furrows that followed the contours of the hillsides, where the big-eyed cattle lay under the heavy maples and oaks or gazed at her across the fences.

Victoria drew up in front of an unpainted farm-house straggling beside the road, a farm-house which began with the dignity of fluted pilasters and ended in a tumble-down open shed filled with a rusty sleigh and a hundred nondescript articles — some of which seemed to be moving. Intently studying this phenomenon from her runabout, she finally discovered that the moving objects were children; one of whom, a little girl, came out and stared at her.

"How do you do, Mary?" said Victoria. "Isn't your name Mary?"

The child nodded.

"I remember you," she said; "you're the rich lady mother met at the party, that got father a job."

Victoria smiled. And such was the potency of the smile that the child joined in it.

"Where's brother?" asked Victoria. "He must be quite grown up since we gave him lemonade."

Mary pointed to the woodshed.

"O dear!" exclaimed Victoria, leaping out of the runabout and hitching her horse, "aren't you afraid some of those sharp iron things will fall on him?" She herself rescued brother from what seemed untimely and certain death, and set him down in safety in the middle of the grass plot. He looked up at her with the air of one whose dignity has been irretrievably injured, and she laughed as she reached down and pulled his nose. Then his face, too, became wreathed in smiles.

"Mary, how old are you?"

"Seven, ma'am."

"And I'm five," Mary's sister chimed in.

"I want you to promise me," said Victoria, "that you won't let brother play in that shed. And the very next time I come I'll bring you both the nicest thing I can think of."

Mary began to dance.

"We'll promise, we'll promise!" she cried for both, and

at this juncture Mrs. Fitch, who had run from the wash-tub to get into her Sunday waist, came out of the door.

"So you hain't forgot me!" she exclaimed. "I was almost afeard you'd forgot me."

"I've been away," said Victoria, gently taking the woman's hand and sitting down on the doorstep.

"Don't set there," said Mrs. Fitch; "come into the parlour. You'll dirty your dress — Mary!" This last in admonition.

"Let her stay where she is," said Victoria, putting her arm around the child. "The dress washes, and it's so nice outside."

"You rich folks certainly do have strange notions," declared Mrs. Fitch, fingering the flounce on Victoria's skirt, which formed the subject of conversation for the next few minutes.

"How are you getting on?" Victoria asked at length.

A look of pain came into the woman's eyes.

"You've be'n so good to us, and done so much gettin' Eben a job on your father's place, that I don't feel as if I ought to lie to you. He done it again — on Saturday night. First time in three months. The manager up at Fairview don't know it. Eben was all right Monday."

"I'm sorry," said Victoria, simply. "Was it bad?"

"It might have be'n. Young Mr. Vane is stayin' up at Jabe Jenney's — you know, the first house as you turn off the hill road. Mr. Vane heard some way what you'd done for us, and he saw Eben in Ripton Saturday night, and made him get into his buggy and come home. I guess he had a time with Eben. Mr. Vane, he came around here on Sunday, and gave him as stiff a talkin' to as he ever got, I guess. He told Eben he'd ought to be ashamed of himself goin' back on folks who was tryin' to help him pay his mortgage. And I'll say this for Eben, he was downright ashamed. He told Mr. Vane he could lick him if he caught him drunk again, and Mr. Vane said he would. My, what a pretty colour you've got to-day!"

Victoria rose. "I'm going to send you down some washing," she said.

Mrs. Fitch insisted upon untying the horse, while Victoria renewed her promises to the children.

There were two ways of going back to Fairview, — a long and a short way, — and the long way led by Jabe Jenney's farm. Victoria came to the fork in the road, paused, — and took the long way. Several times after this, she pulled her horse down to a walk, and was apparently on the point of turning around again : a disinterested observer in a farm wagon, whom she passed, thought that she had missed her road. " The first house after you turn off the hill road," Mrs. Fitch had said. She could still, of course, keep on the hill road, but that would take her to Weymouth, and she would never get home.

It is useless to go into the reasons for this act of Victoria's. She did not know them herself. The nearer Victoria got to Mr. Jenney's, the more she wished herself back at the forks. Suppose Mrs. Fitch told him of her visit ! Perhaps she could pass the Jenneys' unnoticed. The chances of this, indeed, seemed highly favourable, and it was characteristic of her sex that she began to pray fervently to this end. Then she turned off the hill road, feeling as though she had but to look back to see the smoke of the burning bridges.

Victoria remembered the farm now; for Mr. Jabe Jenney, being a person of importance in the town of Leith, had a house commensurate with his estate. The house was not large, but its dignity was akin to Mr. Jenney's position : it was painted a spotless white, and not a shingle or a nail was out of place. Before it stood the great trees planted by Mr. Jenney's ancestors, which Victoria and other people had often paused on their drives to admire, and on the hillside was a little, old-fashioned flower garden ; lilacs clustered about the small-paned windows, and a bitter-sweet clung to the roof and pillars of the porch. These details of the place (which she had never before known as Mr. Jenney's) flashed into Victoria's mind before she caught sight of the great trees themselves looming against the sombre blue-black of the sky : the wind, rising fitfully, stirred the leaves with a sound like

falling waters, and a great drop fell upon her cheek.
Victoria raised her eyes in alarm, and across the open
spaces, toward the hills which piled higher and higher
yet against the sky, was a white veil of rain. She touched
with her whip the shoulder of her horse, recalling a farm
a quarter of a mile beyond — she must not be caught
here!

More drops followed, and the great trees seemed to
reach out to her a protecting shelter. She spoke to the
horse. Beyond the farm-house, on the other side of the
road, was a group of gray, slate-shingled barns, and here
two figures confronted her. One was that of the comfortable, middle-aged Mr. Jenney himself, standing on the
threshold of the barn, and laughing heartily, and crying:
"Hang on to him! That's right — get him by the
nose!"

The person thus addressed had led a young horse to
water at the spring which bubbled out of a sugar-kettle
hard by; and the horse, quivering, had barely touched
his nostrils to the water when he reared backward, jerk-
ing the halter-rope taut. Then followed, with bewildering
rapidity, a series of manœuvres on the part of the horse to
get away, and on the part of the person to prevent this, and
inasmuch as the struggle took place in the middle of the
road, Victoria had to stop. By the time the person had
got the horse by the nose, — shutting off his wind, — the
rain was coming down in earnest.

"Drive right in," cried Mr. Jenney, hospitably; "you'll
get wet. Look out, Austen, there's a lady comin'. Why,
it's Miss Flint!"

Victoria knew that her face must be on fire. She felt
Austen Vane's quick glance upon her, but she did not
dare look to the right or left as she drove into the barn.
There seemed no excuse for any other course.

"How be you?" said Mr. Jenney; "kind of lucky you
happened along here, wahn't it? You'd have been soaked
before you got to Harris's. How be you? I ain't seen
you since that highfalutin party up to Crewe's."

"It's very kind of you to let me come in, Mr. Jenney.

But I have a rain-coat and a boot, and — I really ought to be going on."

Here Victoria produced the rain-coat from under the seat. The garment was a dark blue, and Mr. Jenney felt of its gossamer weight with a good-natured contempt.

" That wouldn't be any more good than so much cheese-cloth," he declared, nodding in the direction of the white sheet of the storm. " Would it, Austen! "

She turned her head slowly and met Austen's eyes. Fortunate that the barn was darkened, that he might not see how deep the colour mantling in her temples! His head was bare, and she had never really marked before the superb setting of it on his shoulders, for he wore a gray flannel shirt open at the neck, revealing a bronzed throat. His sinewy arms — weather-burned, too — were bare above the elbows.

Explanations of her presence sprang to her lips, but she put them from her as subterfuges unworthy of him. She would not attempt to deceive him in the least. She *had* wished to see him again — nor did she analyze her motives. Once more beside him, the feeling of confidence, of belief in him, rose within her and swept all else away — burned in a swift consuming flame the doubts of absence. He took her hand, but she withdrew it quickly.

" This is a fortunate accident," he said, — " fortunate, at least, for me."

" Perhaps Mr. Jenney will not agree with you," she retorted.

But Mr. Jenney was hitching the horse and throwing a blanket over him. Suddenly, before they realized it, the farmer had vanished into the storm, and this unexplained desertion of their host gave rise to an awkward silence between them, which each for a while strove vainly to break. In the great moments of life, trivialities become dwarfed and ludicrous, and the burden of such occasions is on the woman.

" So you've taken to farming," she said, — " isn't it about haying time? "

He laughed.

"We begin next week. And you — you've come back in season for it. I hope that your mother is better."

"Yes," replied Victoria, simply, "the baths helped her. But I'm glad to get back, — I like my own country so much better, — and especially this part of it," she added. "I can bear to be away from New York in the winter, but not from Fairview in the summer."

At this instant Mr. Jenney appeared at the barn door bearing a huge green umbrella.

"Come over to the house — Mis' Jenney is expectin' you," he said.

Victoria hesitated. To refuse would be ungracious; moreover, she could risk no misinterpretation of her acts, and she accepted. Mrs. Jenney met her on the doorstep, and conducted her into that sanctum reserved for occasions, the parlour, with its Bible, its flat, old-fashioned piano, its samplers, its crayon portrait of Mr. and Mrs. Jenney after their honeymoon; with its aroma that suggested Sundays and best manners. Mrs. Jenney, with incredible rapidity (for her figure was not what it had been at the time of the crayon portrait), had got into a black dress, over which she wore a spotless apron. She sat in the parlour with her guest until Mr. Jenney reappeared with shining face and damp hair.

"You'll excuse me, my dear," said Mrs. Jenney, "but the supper's on the stove, and I have to run out now and then."

Mr. Jenney was entertaining. He had the shrewd, humorous outlook upon life characteristic of the best type of New England farmer, and Victoria got along with him famously. His comments upon his neighbours were kindly but incisive, except when the question of spirituous liquors occurred to him. Austen Vane he thought the world of, and dwelt upon this subject a little longer than Victoria, under the circumstances, would have wished.

"He comes out here just like it was home," said Mr. Jenney, "and helps with the hosses and cows the same as

Y

if he wasn't gettin' to be one of the greatest lawyers in the State."

"O dear, Mr. Jenney," said Victoria, glancing out of the window, "I'll really have to go home. I'm sure it won't stop raining for hours. But I shall be perfectly dry in my rain-coat, — no matter how much you may despise it."

"You're not a-going to do anything of the kind," cried Mrs. Jenney from the doorway. "Supper's all ready, and you're going to walk right in."

"Oh, I really have to go," Victoria exclaimed.

"Now I know it ain't as grand as you'd get at home," said Mr. Jenney. "It ain't what *we'd* give you, Miss Victoria, — that's only simple home fare, — it's what *you'd* give us. It's the honour of having you," he added, — and Victoria thought that no courtier could have worded an invitation better. She would not be missed at Fairview. Her mother was inaccessible at this hour, and the servants would think of her as dining at Leith. The picture of the great, lonely house, of the ceremonious dinner which awaited her single presence, gave her an irresistible longing to sit down with these simple, kindly souls. Austen was the only obstacle. He, too, had changed his clothes, and now appeared, smiling at her behind Mrs. Jenney. The look of prospective disappointment in the good woman's face decided Victoria.

"I'll stay, with pleasure," she said.

Mr. Jenney pronounced grace. Victoria sat across the table from Austen, and several times the consciousness of his grave look upon her as she talked heightened the colour in her cheek. He said but little during the meal. Victoria heard how well Mrs. Jenney's oldest son was doing in Springfield, and how the unmarried daughter was teaching, now, in the West. Asked about Europe, — that land of perpetual mystery to the native American, — the girl spoke so simply and vividly of some of the wonders she had seen that she held the older people entranced long after the meal was finished. But at length she observed, with a start, the gathering darkness. In the momentary happiness of this experience, she had been forgetful.

"I will drive home with you, if you'll allow me," said Austen.

"Oh, no, I really don't need an escort, Mr. Vane. I'm so used to driving about at night, I never think of it," she answered.

"Of course he'll drive home with you, dear," said Mrs. Jenney. "And, Jabe, you'll hitch up and go and fetch Austen back."

"Certain," Mr. Jenney agreed.

The rain had ceased, and the indistinct outline of the trees and fences betrayed the fact that the clouds were already thinning under the moon. Austen had lighted the side lamps of the runabout, revealing the shining pools on the road as they drove along — for the first few minutes in silence.

"It was very good of you to stay," he said ; "you do not know how much pleasure you have given them."

Her feminine appreciation responded to the tact of this remark : it was so distinctly what he should have said! How delicate, she thought, must be his understanding of her, that he should have spoken so!

"I was glad to stay," she answered, in a low voice. "I — enjoyed it, too."

"They have very little in their lives," he said, and added, with a characteristic touch, "I do not mean to say that your coming would not be an event in any household."

She laughed with him, softly, at this sally.

"Not to speak of the visit you are making them," she replied.

"Oh, I'm one of the family," he said ; "I come and go. Jabe's is my country house, when I can't stand the city any longer."

She saw that he did not intend to tell her why he had left Ripton on this occasion. There fell another silence. They were like prisoners, and each strove to explore the bounds of their captivity : each sought a lawful ground

of communication. Victoria suddenly remembered — with
an access of indignation — her father's words, "I do not
know what sort he is, but he is not my sort." A while
ago, and she had blamed herself vehemently for coming
to Jabe Jenney's, and now the act had suddenly become
sanctified in her sight. She did not analyze her feeling
for Austen, but she was consumed with a fierce desire
that justice should be done him. "He was honourable —
honourable!" she found herself repeating under her
breath. No man or woman could look into his face,
take his hand, sit by his side, without feeling that he
was as dependable as the stars in their courses. And
her father should know this, must be made to know it.
This man was to be distinguished from opportunists and
self-seekers, from fanatics who strike at random. His
chief possession was a priceless one — a conscience.

As for Austen, it sufficed him for the moment that he
had been lifted, by another seeming caprice of fortune,
to a seat of torture, the agony whereof was exquisite.
An hour, and only the ceaseless pricking memory of it
would abide. The barriers had risen higher since he had
seen her last, but still he might look into her face and
know the radiance of her presence. Could he only trust
himself to guard his tongue! But the heart on such
occasions will cheat language of its meaning.

"What have you been doing since I saw you last?" she
asked. "It seems that you still continue to lead a life of
violence."

"Sometimes I wish I did," he answered, with a laugh;
"the humdrum existence of getting practice enough to
keep a horse is not the most exciting in the world. To
what particular deed of violence do you refer?"

"The last achievement, which is in every one's mouth,
that of — assisting Mr. Tooting down-stairs."

"I have been defamed," Austen laughed; "he fell
down, I believe. But as I have a somewhat evil reputation, and as he came out of my entry, people draw
their own conclusions. I can't imagine who told you that
story."

"Never mind," she answered. "You see, I have certain sources of information about you."

He tingled over this, and puzzled over it so long that she laughed.

"Does that surprise you?" she asked. "I fail to see why I should be expected to lose all interest in my friends — even if they appear to have lost interest in me."

"Oh, don't say that!" he cried so sharply that she wished her words unsaid. "You can't mean it! You don't know!"

She trembled at the vigorous passion he put into the words.

"No, I don't mean it," she said gently.

The wind had made a rent in the sheet of the clouds, and through it burst the moon in her full glory, flooding field and pasture, and the black stretches of pine forest at their feet. Below them the land fell away, and fell again to the distant broadening valley, to where a mist of white vapour hid the course of the Blue. And beyond, the hills rose again, tier upon tier, to the shadowy outline of Sawanec herself against the hurrying clouds and the light-washed sky. Victoria, gazing at the scene, drew a deep breath, and turned and looked at him in the quick way which he remembered so well.

"Sometimes," she said, "it is so beautiful that it *hurts* to look at it. You love it — do you ever feel that way?"

"Yes," he said, but his answer was more than the monosyllable. "I can see that mountain from my window, and it seriously interferes with my work. I really ought to move into another building."

There was a little catch in her laugh.

"And I watch it," she continued, "I watch it from the pine grove by the hour. Sometimes it smiles, and sometimes it is sad, and sometimes it is far, far away, so remote and mysterious that I wonder if it is ever to come back and smile again."

"Have you ever seen the sunrise from its peak?" said Austen.

"No. Oh, how I should love to see it!" she exclaimed.

"Yes, you would like to see it," he answered simply. He would like to take her there, to climb, with her hand in his, the well-known paths in the darkness, to reach the summit in the rosy-fingered dawn : to see her stand on the granite at his side in the full glory of the red light, and to show her a world which she was henceforth to share with him.

Some such image, some such vision of his figure on the rock, may have been in her mind as she turned her face again toward the mountain.

"You are cold," he said, reaching for the mackintosh in the back of the trap.

"No," she said. But she stopped the horse and acquiesced by slipping her arms into the coat, and he felt upon his hand the caress of a stray wisp of hair at her neck. Under a spell of thought and feeling, seemingly laid by the magic of the night, neither spoke for a space. And then Victoria summoned her forces, and turned to him again. Her tone bespoke the subtle intimacy that always sprang up between them, despite bars and conventions.

"I was sure you would understand why I wrote you from New York," she said, "although I hesitated a long time before doing so. It was very stupid of me not to realize the scruples which made you refuse to be a candidate for the governorship, and I wanted to — to apologize."

"It wasn't necessary," said Austen, "but — I valued the note." The words seemed so absurdly inadequate to express his appreciation of the treasure which he carried with him, at that moment, in his pocket. "But, really," he added, smiling at her in the moonlight, "I must protest against your belief that I could have been an effective candidate! I have roamed about the State, and I have made some very good friends here and there among the hill farmers, like Mr. Jenney. Mr. Redbrook is one of these. But it would have been absurd of me even to think of a candidacy founded on personal friendships. I assure you," he added, smiling, "there was no self-denial in my refusal."

She gave him an appraising glance which he found at once enchanting and disconcerting.

"You are one of those people, I think, who do not know their own value. If I were a man, and such men as Mr. Redbrook and Mr. Jenney knew me and believed sufficiently in me and in my integrity of purpose to ask me to be their candidate" (here she hesitated an instant), "and I believed that the cause were a good one, I should not have felt justified in refusing. That is what I meant. I have always thought of you as a man of force and a man of action. But I did not see — the obstacle in your way." She hesitated once more, and added, with a courage which did not fail of its direct appeal, "I did not realize that you would be publicly opposing your father. And I did not realize that you would not care to criticise — mine."

On the last word she faltered and glanced at his profile. Had she gone too far?

"I felt that you would understand," he answered. He could not trust himself to speak further. How much did she know? And how much was she capable of grasping?

His reticence served only to fortify her trust — to elevate it. It was impossible for her not to feel something of that which was in him and crying for utterance. She was a woman. And if this one action had been but the holding of her coat, she would have known. A man who could keep silent under these conditions must indeed be a rock of might and honour; and she felt sure now, with a surging of joy, that the light she had seen shining from it was the beacon of truth. A question trembled on her lips — the question for which she had long been gathering strength. Whatever the outcome of this communion, she felt that there must be absolute truth between them.

"I want to ask you something, Mr. Vane — I have been wanting to for a long time."

She saw the muscles of his jaw tighten, — a manner he had when earnest or determined, — and she wondered in agitation whether he divined what she was going to say. He turned his face slowly to hers, and his eyes were troubled.

"Yes," he said.

"You have always spared my feelings," she went on. "Now — now I am asking for the truth — as you see it. Do the Northeastern Railroads wrongfully govern this State for their own ends?"

Austen, too, as he thought over it afterwards, in the night, was surprised at her concise phrasing, suggestive, as it was, of much reflection. But at the moment, although he had been prepared for and had braced himself against something of this nature, he was nevertheless overcome by the absolute and fearless directness of her speech.

"That is a question," he answered, "which you will have to ask your father."

"I have asked him," she said, in a low voice; "I want to know what — you believe."

"You have asked him!" he repeated, in astonishment.

"Yes. You mustn't think that, in asking you, I am unfair to him in any way — or that I doubt his sincerity. We have been" (her voice caught a little) "the closest friends ever since I was a child." She paused. . "But I want to know what you believe."

The fact that she emphasized the last pronoun sent another thrill through him. Did it, then, make any difference to her what he believed? Did she mean to differentiate him from out of the multitude? He had to steady himself before he answered: —

"I have sometimes thought that my own view might not be broad enough."

She turned to him again.

"Why are you evading?" she asked. "I am sure it is not because you have not settled convictions. And I have asked you — a favour."

"You have done me an honour," he answered, and faced her suddenly. "You must see," he cried, with a power and passion in his voice that startled and thrilled her in turn, "you must see that it's because I wish to be fair that I hesitate. I would tell you — anything. I do not agree with my own father, — we have been — apart

— for years because of this. And I do not agree with Mr. Flint. I am sure that they both are wrong. But I cannot help seeing their point of view. These practices are the result of an evolution, of an evolution of their time. They were forced to cope with conditions in the way they did, or go to the wall. They make the mistake of believing that the practices are still necessary to-day."

"Oh!" she exclaimed, a great hope rising within her at these words. "Oh, and you believe they are not!" His explanation seemed so simple, so inspiring. And above and beyond that, he was sure. Conviction rang in every word. Had he not, she remembered, staked his career by disagreeing with his father? Yes, and he had been slow to condemn; he had seen their side. It was they who condemned him. He must have justice — he should have it!

"I believe such practices are not necessary now," he said firmly. "A new generation has come — a generation more jealous of its political rights, and not so willing to be rid of them by farming them out. A change has taken place even in the older men, like Mr. Jenney and Mr. Redbrook, who simply did not think about these questions ten years ago. Men of this type, who could be leaders, are ready to assume their responsibilities, are ready to deal fairly with railroads and citizens alike. This is a matter of belief. I believe it — Mr. Flint and my father do not. They see the politicians, and I see the people. I belong to one generation, and they to another. With the convictions they have, added to the fact that they are in a position of heavy responsibility toward the owners of their property, they cannot be blamed for hesitating to try any experiments."

"And the practices are — bad?" Victoria asked.

"They are entirely subversive of the principles of American government, to say the least," replied Austen, grimly. He was thinking of the pass which Mr. Flint had sent him, and of the kind of men Mr. Flint employed to make the practices effective.

They descended into the darkness of a deep valley, scored out between the hills by one of the rushing tributaries of the Blue. The moon fell down behind the opposite ridge, and the road ran through a deep forest. He no longer saw the shades of meaning in her face, but in the blackness of Erebus he could have sensed her presence at his side. Speech, though of this strange kind of which neither felt the strangeness, had come and gone between them, and now silence spoke as eloquently. Twice or thrice their eyes met through the gloom, and there was light. At length she spoke with the impulsiveness in her voice that he found so appealing.

"You must see my father — you must talk to him. He doesn't know how fair you are!"

To Austen the inference was obvious that Mr. Flint had conceived for him a special animosity, which he must have mentioned to Victoria, and this inference opened the way to a wide speculation in which he was at once elated and depressed. Why had he been so singled out? And had Victoria defended him? Once before he remembered that she had told him he must see Mr. Flint. They had gained the ridge now, and the moon had risen again for them, striking black shadows from the maples on the granite-cropped pastures. A little farther on was a road which might have been called the rear entrance to Fairview.

What was he to say?

"I am afraid Mr. Flint has other things to do than to see me," he answered. "If he wished to see me, he would say so."

"Would you go to see him, if he were to ask you?" said Victoria.

"Yes," he replied, "but that is not likely to happen. Indeed, you are giving my opinion entirely too much importance in your father's eyes," he added, with an attempt to carry it off lightly; "there is no more reason why he should care to discuss the subject with me than with any other citizen of the State of my age who thinks as I do."

"Oh, yes, there is," said Victoria; "he regards you as a person whose opinion has some weight. I am sure of that. He thinks of you as a person of convictions — and he has heard things about you. You talked to him once," she went on, astonished at her own boldness, "and made him angry. Why don't you talk to him again?" she cried, seeing that Austen was silent. "I am sure that what you said about the change of public opinion in the State would appeal to him. And oh, don't quarrel with him! You have a faculty of differing with people without quarrelling with them. My father has so many cares, and he tries so hard to do right as he sees it. You must remember that he was a poor farmer's son, and that he began to work at fourteen in Brampton, running errands for a country printer. He never had any advantages except those he made for himself, and he had to fight his way in a hard school against men who were not always honourable. It is no wonder that he sometimes takes — a material view of things. But he is reasonable and willing to listen to what other men have to say, if he is not antagonized."

"I understand," said Austen, who thought Mr. Flint blest in his advocate. Indeed, Victoria's simple reference to her father's origin had touched him deeply. "I understand, but I cannot go to him. There is every reason why I cannot," he added, and she knew that he was speaking with difficulty, as under great emotion.

"But if he should send for you?" she asked. She felt his look fixed upon her with a strange intensity, and her heart leaped as she dropped her eyes.

"If Mr. Flint should send for me," he answered slowly, "I would come — and gladly. But it must be of his own free will."

Victoria repeated the words over to herself, "It must be of his own free will," waiting until she should be alone to seek their full interpretation. She turned, and looked across the lawn at Fairview House shining in the light. In another minute they had drawn up before the open door.

"Won't you come in — and wait for Mr. Jenney?" she asked.

He gazed down into her face, searchingly, and took her hand.

"Good night," he said; "Mr. Jenney is not far behind. I think — I think I should like the walk."

CHAPTER XX

MR. CREWE : AN APPRECIATION [1]

IT is given to some rare mortals with whom fame precedes grey hairs or baldness to read, while still on the rising tide of their efforts, that portion of their lives which has already been inscribed on the scroll of history — or something like it.   Mr. Crewe in kilts at five; and (prophetic picture!) with a train of cars which — so the family tradition runs — was afterwards demolished; Mr. Crewe at fourteen, in delicate health; this picture was taken abroad, with a long-suffering tutor who could speak feelingly, if he would, of embryo geniuses.   Even at this early period Humphrey Crewe's thirst for knowledge was insatiable: he cared little, the biography tells us, for galleries and churches and ruins, but his comments upon foreign methods of doing business were astonishingly precocious. He recommended to amazed clerks in provincial banks the use of cheques, ridiculed to speechless station-masters the side-entrance railway carriage with its want of room, and the size of the goods trucks.   He is said to have been the first to suggest that soda-water fountains might be run at a large profit in London.

In college, in addition to keeping up his classical courses, he found time to make an exhaustive study of the railroads of the United States, embodying these ideas in a pamphlet published shortly after graduation.   This pamphlet is now, unfortunately, very rare, but the anonymous biographer managed to get one and quote from it. If Mr. Crewe's suggestions had been carried out, seventy-five per cent of the railroad accidents might have been

[1] Paul Pardriff, Ripton.   Sent post free, on application, to voters and others.

332

eliminated. *Thorough* was his watchword even then. And even at that period he foresaw, with the prophecy of genius, the days of single-track congestion.

His efforts to improve Leith and the State in general, to ameliorate the condition of his neighbours, were fittingly and delicately dwelt upon. A desire to take upon himself the burden of citizenship led — as we know — to further self-denial. He felt called upon to go to the Legislature — and this is what he saw: —

(Mr. Crewe is quoted here at length in an admirable, concise, and hair-raising statement given in an interview to his biographer. But we have been with him, and know what he saw. It is, for lack of space, reluctantly omitted.)

And now we are to take up Mr. Crewe's career where the biography left off; to relate, in a chapter if possible, one of the most remarkable campaigns in the history of this country. A certain reformer of whose acquaintance the honest chronicler boasts (a reformer who got elected!) found, on his first visit to the headquarters he had hired — two citizens under the influence of liquor and a little girl with a skip rope. Such are the beginnings that try men's souls.

The window of every independent shopkeeper in Ripton contained a large-sized picture of the Leith statesman, his determined chin slightly thrust down into the Gladstone collar. Underneath were the words, "*I will put an end to graft and railroad rule. I am a Candidate of the People. Opening rally of the People's Campaign at the Opera House, at 8 P.M., July 10th. The Hon. Humphrey Crewe, of Leith, will tell the citizens of Ripton how their State is governed.*"

"Father," said Victoria, as she read this announcement (three columns wide, in the *Ripton Record*) as they sat at breakfast together, "do you mind my going? I can get Hastings Weare to take me."

"Not at all," said Mr. Flint, who had returned from New York in a better frame of mind. "I should like a trustworthy account of that meeting. Only," he added,

"I should advise you to go early, Victoria, in order to get a seat."

"You don't object to my listening to criticism of you?"

"Not by Humphrey Crewe," laughed Mr. Flint.

Early suppers instead of dinners were the rule at Leith on the evening of the historic day, and the candidate himself, in his red Leviathan, was not inconsiderably annoyed, on the way to Ripton, by innumerable carryalls and traps filled with brightly gowned recruits of that organization of Mrs. Pomfret's which Beatrice Chillingham had nicknamed "The Ladies' Auxiliary." In vain Mr. Crewe tooted his horn: the sound of it was drowned by the gay talk and laughter in the carryalls, and shrieks ensued when the Leviathan cut by with only six inches to spare, and the candidate turned and addressed the drivers in language more forceful than polite, and told the ladies they acted as if they were going to a Punch-and-Judy show.

"Poor dear Humphrey!" said Mrs. Pomfret, "is so much in earnest. I wouldn't give a snap for a man without a temper."

"Poor dear Humphrey!" said Beatrice Chillingham, in an undertone to her neighbour, "is exceedingly rude and ungrateful. That's what I think."

The occupants of one vehicle heard the horn, and sought the top of a grassy mound to let the Leviathan go by. And the Leviathan, with characteristic contrariness, stopped.

"Hello," said Mr. Crewe, with a pull at his cap. "I intended to be on the lookout for you."

"That is very thoughtful, Humphrey, considering how many things you have to be on the lookout for this evening," Victoria replied.

"That's all right," was Mr. Crewe's gracious reply. "I knew you'd be sufficiently broad-minded to come, and I hope you won't take offence at certain remarks I think it my duty to make."

"Don't let my presence affect you," she answered, smiling; "I have come prepared for anything."

"I'll tell Tooting to give you a good seat," he called back, as he started onward.

Hastings Weare looked up at her, with laughter-brimming eyes.

"Victoria, you're a wonder!" he remarked. "Say, do you remember that tall fellow we met at Humphrey's party, Austen Vane?"

"Yes."

"I saw him on the street in Ripton the other day, and he came right up and spoke to me. He hadn't forgotten my name. Now, he'd be my notion of a candidate. He makes you feel as if your presence in the world meant something to him."

"I think he does feel that way," replied Victoria.

"I don't blame him if he feels that way about you," said Hastings, who made love openly.

"Hastings," she answered, "when you get a little older, you will learn to confine yourself to your own opinions."

"When I do," he retorted audaciously, "they never make you blush like that."

"It's probably because you have never learned to be original," she replied. But Hastings had been set to thinking.

Mrs. Pomfret, with her foresight and her talent for management, had given the Ladies' Auxiliary notice that they were not to go farther forward than the twelfth row. She herself, with some especially favoured ones, occupied a box, which was the nearest thing to being on the stage. One unforeseen result of Mrs. Pomfret's arrangement was that the first eleven rows were vacant, with the exception of one old man and five or six schoolboys. Such is the courage of humanity in general! On the arrival of the candidate, instead of a surging crowd lining the sidewalk, he found only a fringe of the curious, whose usual post of observation was the railroad station, standing silently on the curb. Within, Mr. Tooting's duties as an usher had not been onerous. He met Mr. Crewe in the vestibule, and drew him into the private office.

"The railroad's fixed 'em," said the manager, indignantly, but *sotto voce;* "I've found that out. Hilary Vane had the word passed around town that if they came, somethin' would fall on 'em. The Tredways and all the people who own factories served notice on their men that if they paid any attention to this meeting they'd lose their job. But say, the people are watchin' you, just the same."

"How many people are in there?" Mr. Crewe demanded.

"Twenty-seven, when I came out," said Mr. Tooting, with commendable accuracy. "But it wants fifteen minutes to eight."

"And who," asked Mr. Crewe, "is to introduce me?"

An expression of indignation spread over Mr. Tooting's face.

"There ain't a man in Ripton's got sand enough!" he exclaimed. "Sol Gridley was a-goin' to, but he went to New York on the noon train. I guess it's a pleasure trip," Mr. Tooting hinted darkly.

"Why," said Mr. Crewe, "he's the fellow — "

"Exactly," Mr. Tooting replied, "and he did get a lot of 'em, travelling about. But Sol has got to work on the quiet, you understand. He feels he can't come out right away."

"And how about Amos Ricketts? Where's he?"

"Amos," said Mr. Tooting, regretfully, "was taken very sudden about five o'clock. One of his spells come on, and he sent me word to the Ripton House. He had his speech all made up, and it was a good one, too. He was going to tell folks pretty straight how the railroad beat him for mayor."

Mr. Crewe made a gesture of disgust.

"I'll introduce myself," he said. "They all know me, anyhow."

"Say," said Mr. Tooting, laying a hand on his candidate's arm. "You couldn't do any better. I've been for that all along."

"Hold on," said Mr. Crewe, listening, "a lot of people are coming in now."

What Mr. Crewe had heard, however, was the arrival of the Ladies' Auxiliary, five and thirty strong, from Leith. But stay! Who are these coming? More ladies — ladies in groups of two and three and five! ladies of Ripton whose husbands, for some unexplained reason, have stayed at home; and Mr. Tooting, as he watched them with mingled feelings, became a woman's suffragist on the spot. He dived into the private office once more, where he found Mr. Crewe seated with his legs crossed, calmly reading a last winter's playbill. (Note for a more complete biography.)

"Well, Tooting," he said, "I thought they'd begin to come."

"They're mostly women," Mr. Tooting informed him.

"Women!"

"Hold on!" said Mr. Tooting, who had the true showman's instinct. "Can't you see that folks are curious? They're afraid to come 'emselves, and they're sendin' their wives and daughters. If you get the women tonight, they'll go home and club the men into line."

Eight strokes boomed out from the tower of the neighbouring town hall, and an expectant flutter spread over the audience, — a flutter which disseminated faint odours of sachet and other mysterious substances in which feminine apparel are said to be laid away. The stage was empty, save for a table which held a pitcher of water and a glass.

"It's a pretty good imitation of a matinée," Hastings Weare remarked. "I wonder whom the front seats are reserved for. Say, Victoria, there's your friend Mr. Vane in the corner. He's looking over here."

"He has a perfect right to look where he chooses," said Victoria. She wondered whether he would come over and sit next to her if she turned around, and decided instantly that he wouldn't. Presently, when she thought Hastings was off his guard, she did turn, to meet, as she expected, Austen's glance fixed upon her. Their greeting was the signal of two people with a mutual understanding. He did not rise, and although she acknowledged to herself a

z

feeling of disappointment, she gave him credit for a nice comprehension of the situation. Beside him was his friend Tom Gaylord, who presented to her a very puzzled face. And then, if there had been a band, it would have been time to play "See, the Conquering Hero Comes!"

Why wasn't there a band? No such mistake, Mr. Tooting vowed, should be made at the next rally.

It was Mrs. Pomfret who led the applause from her box as the candidate walked modestly up the side aisle and presently appeared, alone, on the stage. The flutter of excitement was renewed, and this time it might almost be called a flutter of apprehension. But we who have heard Mr. Crewe speak are in no alarm for our candidate. He takes a glass of iced water; he arranges, with the utmost *sang-froid*, his notes on the desk and adjusts the reading-light. Then he steps forward and surveys the scattered groups.

"Ladies — " a titter ran through the audience, — a titter which started somewhere in the near neighbourhood of Mr. Hastings Weare — and rose instantly to several hysterical peals of feminine laughter. Mrs. Pomfret, outraged, sweeps the frivolous offenders with her lorgnette; Mr. Crewe, with his arm resting on the reading-desk, merely raises the palm of his hand to a perpendicular reproof, " — and gentlemen." At this point the audience is thoroughly cowed. " Ladies and gentlemen and fellow-citizens. I thank you for the honour you have done me in coming here to listen to the opening speech of my campaign to-night. It is a campaign for decency and good government, and I know that the common people of the State — of whom I have the honour to be one — demand these things. I cannot say as much for the so-called prominent citizens," said Mr. Crewe, glancing about him; " not one of your prominent citizens in Ripton would venture to offend the powers that be by consenting to introduce me to-night, or dared come into this theatre and take seats within thirty feet of this platform." Here Mr. Crewe let his eyes rest significantly on the eleven empty rows, while his hearers squirmed in terrified silence at this audacity. Even the Ripton women knew that this was high treason beneath the walls of the citadel, and many of them glanced furtively at the strangely composed daughter of Augustus P. Flint.

" I will show you that I can stand on my own feet," Mr. Crewe continued. " I will introduce myself. I am Humphrey Crewe of Leith, and I claim to have added something to the welfare and prosperity of this State, and I intend to add more before I have finished."

At this point, as might have been expected, spontaneous applause broke forth, originating in the right-hand stage box. Here was a daring defiance indeed, a courage of such a high order that it completely carried away the ladies and drew reluctant plaudits from the male element. "Give it to 'em, Humphrey ! " said one of those who happened to be sitting next to Miss Flint, and who received a very severe pinch in the arm in consequence.

" I thank the gentleman," answered Mr. Crewe, " and I propose to— (*Handclapping and sachet.*) I propose to show that you spend something like two hundred thousand dollars a year to elect legislators and send 'em to the capital, when the real government of your State is in a room in the Pelican Hotel known as the Railroad Room, and the real governor is a citizen of your town, the Honourable Hilary Vane, who sits there and acts for his master, Mr. Augustus P. Flint of New York. And I propose to prove to you that, before the Honourable Adam B. Hunt appeared as that which has come to be known as the 'regular' candidate, Mr. Flint sent for him to go to New York and exacted certain promises from him. Not that it was necessary, but the Northeastern Railroads never take any chances. (*Laughter.*) The Honourable Adam B. Hunt is what they call a 'safe' man, meaning by that a man who will do what Mr. Flint wants him to do. While I am not 'safe' because I have dared to defy them in your name, and will do what the people want me to do. (*Clapping and cheers from a gentleman in the darkness, afterwards identified as Mr. Tooting.*) Now, my friends, are you going to continue to allow a citizen of New York to nominate your governors, and do you intend, tamely, to give the Honourable Adam B. Hunt your votes?"

"They ain't got any votes," said a voice — not that of Mr. Hastings Weare, for it came from the depths of the gallery.

"'The hand that rocks the cradle sways the world,'" answered Mr. Crewe, and there was no doubt about the sincerity of the applause this time.

"The campaign of the Honourable Humphrey Crewe of Leith," said the *State Tribune* next day, "was inaugurated at the Opera House in Ripton last night before an enthusiastic audience consisting of Mr. Austen Vane, Mr. Thomas Gaylord, Jr., Mr. Hamilton Tooting, two reporters, and seventy-four ladies, who cheered the speaker to the echo. About half of these ladies were summer residents of Leith in charge of the well-known social leader, Mrs. Patterson Pomfret, — an organized league which, it is understood, will follow the candidate about the State in the English fashion, kissing the babies and teaching the mothers hygienic cooking and how to *ondulé* the hair."

After speaking for an hour and a half, the Honourable Humphrey Crewe declared that he would be glad to meet any of the audience who wished to shake his hand, and it was Mrs. Pomfret who reached him first.

"Don't be discouraged, Humphrey, — you are magnificent," she whispered.

"Discouraged!" echoed Mr. Crewe. "You can't kill an idea, and we'll see who's right and who's wrong before I get through with 'em."

"What a noble spirit!" Mrs. Pomfret exclaimed aside to Mrs. Chillingham. Then she added, in a louder tone, "Ladies, if you will kindly tell me your names, I shall be happy to introduce you to the candidate. Well, Victoria, I didn't expect to see *you* here."

"Why not?" said Victoria. "Humphrey, accept my congratulations."

"Did you like it?" asked Mr. Crewe. "I thought it was a pretty good speech myself. There's nothing like telling the truth, you know. And, by the way, I hope to see you in a day or two, before I start for Kingston. Telephone me when you come down to Leith."

The congratulations bestowed on the candidate by the daughter of the president of the Northeastern Railroads quite took the breath out of the spectators who witnessed the incident, and gave rise to the wildest conjectures. And the admiration of Mr. Hastings Weare was unbounded.

"You've got the most magnificent nerve I ever saw, Victoria," he exclaimed, as they made their way towards the door.

"You forget Humphrey," she replied.

Hastings looked at her and chuckled. In fact, he chuckled all the way home. In the vestibule they met Mr. Austen Vane and Mr. Thomas Gaylord, the latter coming forward with a certain palpable embarrassment. All through the evening Tom had been trying to account for her presence at the meeting, until Austen had begged him to keep his speculations to himself. "She can't be engaged to *him!*" Mr. Gaylord had exclaimed more than once, under his breath. "Why not?" Austen had answered; "there's a good deal about him to admire." "Because she's got more sense," said Tom doggedly. Hence he was at a loss for words when she greeted him.

"Well, Mr. Gaylord," she said, "you see no bones were broken, after all. But I appreciated your precaution in sending the buggy behind me, although it wasn't necessary."

"I felt somewhat responsible," replied Tom, and words failed him. "Here's Austen Vane," he added, indicating by a nod of the head the obvious presence of that gentleman. "You'll excuse me. There's a man here I want to see."

"What's the matter with Mr. Gaylord?" Victoria asked. "He seems so — queer."

They were standing apart, alone, Hastings Weare having gone to the stables for the runabout.

"Mr. Gaylord imagines he doesn't get along with the opposite sex," Austen replied, with just a shade of constraint.

"Nonsense!" exclaimed Victoria; "we got along perfectly the other day when he rescued me from the bushes. What's the matter with him?"

Austen laughed, and their eyes met.

"I think he is rather surprised to see you here," he said.

"And you?" returned Victoria. "Aren't you equally — out of place?"

He did not care to go into an explanation of Tom's suspicion in regard to Mr. Crewe.

"My curiosity was too much for me," he replied, smiling.

"So was mine," she replied, and suddenly demanded: "What did you think of Humphrey's speech?"

Their eyes met. And despite the attempted seriousness of her tone they joined in an irresistible and spontaneous laughter. They were again on that plane of mutual understanding and intimacy for which neither could account.

"I have no criticism to make of Mr. Crewe as an orator, at least," he said.

Then she grew serious again, and regarded him steadfastly.

"And — what he said?" she asked.

Austen wondered again at the courage she had displayed. All he had been able to think of in the theatre, while listening to Mr. Crewe's words of denunciation of the Northeastern Railroads, had been of the effect they might have on Victoria's feelings, and from time to time he had glanced anxiously at her profile. And now, looking into her face, questioning, trustful — he could not even attempt to evade. He was silent.

"I shouldn't have asked you that," she said. "One reason I came was because — because I wanted to hear the worst. You were too considerate to tell me — all."

He looked mutely into her eyes, and a great desire arose in him to be able to carry her away from it all. Many times within the past year, when the troubles and complications of his life had weighed upon him, his thoughts had turned to that Western country, limited only by the bright horizons where the sun rose and set. If he could only take her there, or into his own hills, where no man might follow them! It was a primeval longing, and, being a woman and the object of it, she saw its essential meaning in his face. For a brief moment they stood as completely alone as on the crest of Sawanec.

"Good night," she said, in a low voice.

He did not trust himself to speak at once, but went down the steps with her to the curb, where Hastings Weare was waiting in the runabout.

"I was just telling Miss Flint," said that young gentleman, "that you would have been my candidate."

Austen's face relaxed.

"Thank you, Mr. Weare," he said simply; and to Victoria, "Good night."

At the corner, when she turned, she saw him still standing on the edge of the sidewalk, his tall figure thrown into bold relief by the light which flooded from the entrance.

The account of the Ripton meeting, substantially as it appeared in the *State Tribune*, was by a singular coincidence copied at once into sixty-odd weekly newspapers, and must have caused endless merriment throughout the State. Congressman Fairplay's prophecy of "negligible" was an exaggeration, and one gentleman who had rashly predicted that Mr. Crewe would get twenty delegates out of a thousand hid himself for shame. On the whole, the "monumental farce" forecast seemed best to fit the situation. A conference was held at Leith between the candidate, Mr. Tooting, and the Honourable Timothy Watling of Newcastle, who was preparing the nominating speech, although the convention was more than two months distant. Mr. Watling was skilled in rounded periods of oratory and in other things political, and both he and Mr. Tooting reiterated their opinion that there was no particle of doubt about Mr. Crewe's nomination.

"But we'll have to fight fire with fire," Mr. Tooting declared. It was probably an accident that he happened to kick, at this instant, Mr. Watling under cover of the table. Mr. Watling was an old and valued friend.

" Gentlemen," said Mr. Crewe, " I haven't the slightest doubt of my nomination, either. I do not hesitate to say, however, that the expenses of this campaign, at this early stage, seem to me out of all proportion. Let me see what you have there."

The Honourable Timothy Watling had produced a typewritten list containing some eighty towns and wards, each followed by a name and the number of the delegates therefrom — and figures.

" They'd all be enthusiastic Crewe men — if they could be seen by the right party," declared Mr. Tooting.

Mr. Crewe ran his eye over the list.

" Whom would you suggest to see 'em ? " he asked coldly.

" There's only one party I know of that has much influence over 'em," Mr. Tooting replied, with a genial but deferential indication of his friend.

At this point Mr. Crewe's secretary left the room on an errand, and the three statesmen went into executive session. In politics, as in charity, it is a good rule not to let one's right hand know what the left hand doeth. Half an hour later the three emerged into the sunlight, Mr. Tooting and Mr. Watling smoking large cigars.

" You've got a great lay-out here, Mr. Crewe," Mr. Watling remarked. " It must have stood you in a little money, eh? Yes, I'll get mileage books, and you'll hear from me every day or two."

And now we are come to the infinitely difficult task of relating in a whirlwind manner the story of a whirlwind campaign — a campaign that was to make the oldest resident sit up and take notice. In the space of four short weeks a miracle had begun to show itself. First, there was the Kingston meeting, with the candidate, his thumb in his watch-pocket, seated in an open carriage beside Mr. Hamilton Tooting, — a carriage draped with a sheet on which was painted " Down with Railroad Ring Rule ! " The carriage was preceded by the Kingston Brass Band, producing throbbing martial melodies, and followed (we are not going to believe the *State Tribune* any longer) by a jostling and cheering crowd. The band halts before the G. A. R. Hall; the candidate alights, with a bow of acknowledgment, and goes to the private office until the musicians are seated in front of the platform, when he enters to renewed cheering and the tune of "See, the Conquering Hero Comes!"

An honest historian must admit that there were two accounts of this meeting. Both agree that Mr. Crewe introduced himself, and poured a withering sarcasm on the heads of Kingston's prominent citizens. One account, which the ill-natured declared to be in Mr. Tooting's style, and which appeared (in slightly larger type than that of the other columns) in the Kingston and local papers, stated that the hall was crowded to suffocation, and that the candidate was "accorded an ovation which lasted for fully five minutes."

Mr. Crewe's speech was printed — in this slightly larger type. Woe to the Honourable Adam B. Hunt, who had gone to New York to see whether he could be governor! Why didn't he come out on the platform? Because he couldn't. "Safe" candidates couldn't talk. His subservient and fawning reports on accidents while chairman of the Railroad Commission were ruthlessly quoted (amid cheers and laughter). What kind of railroad service was Kingston getting compared to what it should have? Compared, indeed, to what it had twenty years ago? An informal reception was held afterwards.

More meetings followed, at the rate of four a week, in county after county. At the end of fifteen days a selectman (whose name will go down in history) voluntarily mounted the platform and introduced the Honourable Humphrey Crewe to the audience; not, to be sure, as the saviour of the State; and from that day onward Mr. Crewe did not lack for a sponsor. On the other hand, the sponsors became more pronounced, and at Harwich (a free-thinking district) a whole board of selectmen and five prominent citizens sat gravely beside the candidate in the town hall.

CHAPTER XXI

ST. GILES OF THE BLAMELESS LIFE

The burden of the valley of vision : woe to the Honourable Adam B. Hunt! Where is he all this time? On the porch of his home in Edmundton, smoking cigars, little heeding the rising of the waters; receiving visits from the Honourables Brush Bascom, Nat Billings, and Jacob Botcher, and signing cheques to the order of these gentlemen for necessary expenses. Be it known that the Honourable Adam was a man of substance in this world's goods. To quote from Mr. Crewe's speech at Hull : "The Northeastern Railroads confer — they do not pay, except in passes. Of late years their books may be searched in vain for evidence of the use of political funds. The man upon whom they choose to confer your governorship is always able to pay the pipers." (Purposely put in the plural.)

Have the pipers warned the Honourable Adam of the rising tide against him? Have they asked him to gird up his loins and hire halls and smite the upstart hip and thigh? They have warned him, yes, that the expenses may be a little greater than ordinary. But it is not for him to talk, or to bestir himself in any unseemly manner, for the prize which he was to have was in the nature of a gift. In vain did Mr. Crewe cry out to him four times a week for his political beliefs, for a statement of what he would do if he were elected governor. The Honourable Adam's dignified answer was that he had always been a good Republican, and would die one. Following a time-honoured custom, he refused to say anything, but it was rumoured that he believed in the gold standard.

346

It is August, and there is rejoicing in Leith. There is no doubt now that the campaign of the people progresses; no need any more for the true accounts of the meetings, in large print, although these are still continued. The reform rallies resemble matinées no longer, and two real reporters accompany Mr. Crewe on his tours. Nay, the campaign of education has already borne fruit, which the candidate did not hesitate to mention in his talks: Edmundton has more trains, Kingston has more trains, and more cars. No need now to stand up for twenty miles on a hot day; and more cars are building, and more engines; likewise some rates have been lowered. And editors who declare that the Northeastern gives the State a pretty good government have, like the guinea pigs, long been suppressed.

In these days were many councils at Fairview and in the offices of the Honourable Hilary Vane at Ripton; councils behind closed doors, from which the councillors emerged with smiling faces that men might not know the misgivings in their hearts; councils, nevertheless, out of which leaked rumours of dissension and recrimination — conditions hitherto unheard of. One post ran to meet another, and one messenger ran to meet another; and it was even reported — though on doubtful authority — after the rally in his town the Honourable Jacob Botcher had made the remark that, under certain conditions, he might become a reformer.

None of these upsetting rumours, however, were allowed by Mr. Bascom and other gentlemen close to the Honourable Adam B. Hunt to reach that candidate, who continued to smoke in tranquillity on the porch of his home until the fifteenth day of August. At eight o'clock that morning the postman brought him a letter marked personal, the handwriting on which he recognized as belonging to the Honourable Hilary Vane. For some reason, as he read, the sensations of the Honourable Adam were disquieting; the contents of the letter, to say the least, were peculiar. "To-morrow, at noon precisely, I shall be driving along the Broad Brook road by the abandoned mill three miles towards Edmundton from Hull. I hope you will find it convenient to be there."

These were the strange words the Honourable Hilary had written, and the Honourable Adam knew that it was an order. At that very instant Mr. Hunt had been reading in the *Guardian* the account of an overflow meeting in Newcastle by his opponent, in which Mr. Crewe had made some particularly choice remarks about him, and had been cheered to the echo. The Honourable Adam put the paper down, and walked up the street to talk to Mr. Burrows, the postmaster whom, with the aid of Congressman Fairplay, he had had appointed at Edmundton. The two racked their brains for three hours; and Postmaster Burrows, who was the fortunate possessor of a pass, offered to go down to Ripton in the interest of his liege lord and see what was up. The Honourable Adam, however, decided that he could wait for twenty-four hours.

The morning of the sixteenth dawned clear, as beautiful a summer's day for a drive as any man could wish. But the spirit of the Honourable Adam did not respond to the weather, and he had certain vague forebodings as his horse jogged toward Hull, although these did not take such a definite shape as to make him feel a premonitory pull of his coat-tails. The ruined mill beside the rushing stream was a picturesque spot, and the figure of the Honourable Hilary Vane, seated on the old millstone, in the green and gold shadows of a beech, gave an interesting touch of life to the landscape. The Honourable Adam drew up and eyed his friend and associate of many years before addressing him.

"How are you, Hilary?"

"Hitch your horse," said Mr. Vane.

The Honourable Adam was some time in picking out a convenient tree. Then he lighted a cigar, and approached Mr. Vane, and at length let himself down, cautiously, on the millstone. Sitting on his porch had not improved Mr. Hunt's figure.

"This is kind of mysterious, ain't it, Hilary?" he remarked, with a tug at his goatee.

"How much have you spent?"

"I don't know but what it is," admitted Mr. Vane, who did not look as though the coming episode were to give him unqualified joy.

"Fine weather," remarked the Honourable Adam, with a brave attempt at geniality.

"The paper predicts rain to-morrow," said the Honourable Hilary.

"You don't smoke, do you?" asked the Honourable Adam.

"No," said the Honourable Hilary.

A silence, except for the music of the brook over the broken dam.

"Pretty place," said the Honourable Adam; "I kissed my wife here once — before I was married."

This remark, although of interest, the Honourable Hilary evidently thought did not require an answer.

"Adam," said Mr. Vane, presently, "how much money have you spent so far?"

"Well," said Mr. Hunt, "it has been sort of costly, but Brush and the boys tell me the times are uncommon, and I guess they are. If that crazy cuss Crewe hadn't broken loose, it would have been different. Not that I'm uneasy about him, but all this talk of his and newspaper advertising had to be counteracted some. Why, he has a couple of columns a week right here in the Edmundton *Courier*. The papers are bleedin' him to death, certain."

"How much have you spent?" asked the Honourable Hilary.

The Honourable Adam screwed up his face and pulled his goatee thoughtfully.

"What are you trying to get at, Hilary," he inquired, "sending for me to meet you out here in the woods in this curious way? If you wanted to see me, why didn't you get me to go down to Ripton, or come up and sit on my porch? You've been there before."

"Times," said the Honourable Hilary, repeating, perhaps unconsciously, Mr. Hunt's words, "are uncommon. This man Crewe's making more headway than you think.

The people don't know him, and he's struck a popular note. It's the fashion to be down on railroads these days."

"I've taken that into account," replied Mr. Hunt. "It's unlucky, and it comes high. I don't think he's got a show for the nomination, but my dander's up, and I'll beat him if I have to mortgage my house."

The Honourable Hilary grunted, and ruminated.

"How much did you say you'd spent, Adam?"

"If you think I'm not free enough, I'll loosen up a little more," said the Honourable Adam.

"How free have you been?" said the Honourable Hilary.

For some reason the question, put in this form, was productive of results.

"I can't say to a dollar, but I've got all the amounts down in a book. I guess somewhere in the neighbourhood of nine thousand would cover it."

Mr. Vane grunted again.

"Would you take a cheque, Adam?" he inquired.

"What for?" cried the Honourable Adam.

"For the amount you've spent," said the Honourable Hilary, sententiously.

The Honourable Adam began to breathe with apparent difficulty, and his face grew purple. But Mr. Vane did not appear to notice these alarming symptoms. Then the candidate turned about, as on a pivot, seized Mr. Vane by the knee, and looked into his face.

"Did you come up here with orders for me to get out?" he demanded, with some pardonable violence. "By thunder, I didn't think that of my old friend, Hilary Vane. You ought to have known me better, and Flint ought to have known me better. There ain't a mite of use of our staying here another second, and you can go right back and tell Flint what I said. Flint knows I've been waiting to be governor for eight years, and each year it's been just a year ahead. You ask him what he said to me when he sent for me to go to New York. I thought he was a man of his word, and he promised me that I should be governor this year."

The Honourable Hilary gave no indication of being moved by this righteous outburst.

"You can be governor next year, when this reform nonsense has blown over," he said. "You can't be this year, even if you stay in the race."

"Why not?" the Honourable Adam asked pugnaciously.

"Your record won't stand it — not just now," said Mr. Vane, slowly.

"My record is just as good as yours, or any man's," said the Honourable Adam.

"I never run for office," answered Mr. Vane.

"Haven't I spent the days of my active life in the service of that road — and is this my reward? Haven't I done what Flint wanted always?"

"That's just the trouble," said the Honourable Hilary; "too many folks know it. If we're going to win this time, we've got to have a man who's never had any Northeastern connections."

"Who have you picked?" demanded the Honourable Adam, with alarming calmness.

"We haven't picked anybody yet," said Mr. Vane, "but the man who goes in will give you a cheque for what you've spent, and you can be governor next time."

"Well, if this isn't the d—dest, coldest·blooded proposition ever made, I want to know!" cried the Honourable Adam. "Will Flint put up a bond of one hundred thousand dollars that I'll be nominated and elected next year? This is the clearest case of going back on an old friend I ever saw. If this is the way you fellows get scared because a sham reformer gets up and hollers against the road, then I want to serve notice on you that I'm not made of that kind of stuff. When I go into a fight, I go in to stay, and you can't pull me out by the coat-tails in favour of a saint who's never done a lick of work for the road. You tell Flint that."

"All right, Adam," said Hilary.

Some note in Hilary's voice, as he made this brief answer, suddenly sobered the Honourable Adam, and

sent a cold chill down his spine. He had had many
dealings with Mr. Vane, and he had always been as
putty in the chief counsel's hands. This simple acquiescence did more to convince the Honourable Adam that
his chances of nomination were in real danger than a long
and forceful summary of the situation could have accomplished. But like many weak men, the Honourable Adam
had a stubborn streak, and a fatuous idea that opposition
and indignation were signs of strength.

" I've made sacrifices for the road before, and effaced
myself. But by thunder, this is too much ! "

Corporations, like republics, are proverbially ungrateful. The Honourable Hilary might have voiced this sentiment, but refrained.

" Mr. Flint's a good friend of yours, Adam. He
wanted me to say that he'd always taken care of you,
and always would, so far as in his power. If you can't
be landed this time, it's common sense for you to get out,
and wait — isn't it ? We'll see that you get a cheque to
cover what you've put out."

The humour in this financial sacrifice of Mr. Flint's
(which the unknown new candidate was to make with a
cheque) struck neither the Honourable Adam nor the
Honourable Hilary. The transaction, if effected, would
resemble that of the shrine to the Virgin built by a
grateful Marquis of Mantua — which a Jew paid for.

The Honourable Adam got to his feet.

" You can tell Flint," he said, " that if he will sign a
bond of one hundred thousand dollars to elect me next
time, I'll get out. That's my last word."

" All right, Adam," replied Mr. Vane, rising also.

Mr. Hunt stared at the Honourable Hilary thoughtfully ;
and although the gubernatorial candidate was not an ob-
servant man, he was suddenly struck by the fact that the
chief counsel was growing old.

" I won't hold this against you, Hilary," he said.

" Politics," said the Honourable Hilary, " are business
matters."

" I'll show Flint that it would have been good business

to stick to me," said the Honourable Adam. " When he gets panicky, and spends all his money on new equipment and service, it's time for me to drop him. You can tell him so from me."

" Hadn't you better write him?" said the Honourable Hilary.

The rumour of the entry of Mr. Giles Henderson of Kingston into the gubernatorial contest preceded, by ten days or so, the actual event. It is difficult for the historian to unravel the precise circumstances which led to this candidacy. Conservative citizens throughout the State, it was understood, had become greatly concerned over the trend political affairs were taking; the radical doctrines of one candidate — propounded for very obvious reasons — they turned from in disgust; on the other hand, it was evident that an underlying feeling existed in certain sections that any candidate who was said to have had more or less connection with the Northeastern Railroads was undesirable at the present time. This was not to be taken as a reflection on the Northeastern, which had been the chief source of the State's prosperity, but merely as an acknowledgment that a public opinion undoubtedly existed, and ought to be taken into consideration by the men who controlled the Republican party.

This was the gist of leading articles which appeared simultaneously in several newspapers, apparently before the happy thought of bringing forward Mr. Giles Henderson had occurred to anybody. He was mentioned first, and most properly, by the editor of the *Kingston Pilot;* and the article, with comments upon it, ran like wildfire through the press of the State, — appearing even in those sheets which maintained editorially that they were for the Honourable Adam B. Hunt first and last and all the time. Whereupon Mr. Giles Henderson began to receive visits from the solid men — not politicians — of the various cities and counties. For instance, Mr. Silas Tredway of Ripton made such a pilgrimage and, as a citizen who had voted in 1860 for Abraham Lincoln

2 A

(showing Mr. Tredway himself to have been a radical once), appealed to Mr. Henderson to save the State.

At first Mr. Henderson would give no ear to these appeals, but shook his head pessimistically. He was not a politician — so much the better, we don't want a politician; he was a plain business man — exactly what is needed; a conservative, level-headed business man wholly lacking in those sensational qualities which are a stench in the nostrils of good citizens. Mr. Giles Henderson admitted that the time had come when a man of these qualities was needed — but he was not the man. Mr. Tredway was the man — so he told Mr. Tredway; Mr. Gates of Brampton was the man — so he assured Mr. Gates. Mr. Henderson had no desire to meddle in politics; his life was a happy and a full one. But was it not Mr. Henderson's duty? Cincinnatus left the plough, and Mr. Henderson should leave the ledger at the call of his countrymen.

Mr. Giles Henderson was mild-mannered and blue-eyed, with a scanty beard that was turning white; he was a deacon of the church, a member of the school board, president of the Kingston National Bank; the main business of his life had been in coal (which incidentally had had to be transported over the Northeastern Railroads); and coal rates, for some reason, were cheaper from Kingston than from many points out of the State the distances of which were nearer. Mr. Henderson had been able to sell his coal at a lower price than any other large dealer in the eastern part of the State. Mr. Henderson was the holder of a large amount of stock in the Northeastern, inherited from his father. Facts of no special significance, and not printed in the weekly newspapers. Mr. Henderson lived in a gloomy Gothic house on High Street, ate three very plain meals a day, and drank iced water. He had been a good husband and a good father, and had always voted the Republican ticket. He believed in the gold standard, a high tariff, and eternal damnation. At last his resistance was overcome, and he consented to allow his name to be used.

It was used, with a vengeance. Spontaneous praise of Mr. Giles Henderson bubbled up all over the State, and editors who were for the Honourable Adam B. Hunt suddenly developed a second choice. No man within the borders of the commonwealth had so many good qualities as the new candidate, and it must have been slightly annoying to one of that gentleman's shrinking nature to read daily, on coming down to breakfast, a list of virtues attributed to him as long as a rate schedule. How he must have longed for the record of one wicked deed to make him human!

Who will pick a flaw in the character of the Honourable Giles Henderson? Let that man now stand forth.

The news of the probable advent of Mr. Giles Henderson on the field, as well as the tidings of his actual consent to be a candidate, were not slow in reaching Leith. And — Mr. Crewe's Bureau of Information being in perfect working order — the dastardly attempt on the Honourable Adam B. Hunt's coat-tails was known there. More wonders to relate: the Honourable Adam B. Hunt had become a reformer; he had made a statement at last, in which he declared with vigour that no machine or ring was behind him; he stood on his own merits, invited the minutest inspection of his record, declared that he was an advocate of good government, and if elected would be the servant of no man and of no corporation.

Thrice-blessed State, in which there were now three reform candidates for governor!

All of these happenings went to indicate confusion in the enemy's camp, and corresponding elation in Mr. Crewe's. Woe to the reputation for political sagacity of the gentleman who had used the words "negligible" and "monumental farce"! The tide was turning, and the candidate from Leith redoubled his efforts. Had he been confounded by the advent of the Honourable Giles? Not at all. Mr. Crewe was not given to satire; his methods, as we know, were direct. Hence the real author of the following passage in his speech before an overflow meeting in the State capital remains unknown:

"My friends," Mr. Crewe had said, "I have been waiting for the time when St. Giles of the Blameless Life would be pushed forward, apparently as the only hope of our so-called 'solid citizens.' (*Prolonged laughter, and audible repetitions of Mr. Henderson's nickname, which was to stick.*) I will tell you by whose desire St. Giles became a candidate, and whose bidding he will do if he becomes governor as blindly and obediently as the Honourable Adam B. Hunt ever did. (*Shouts of "Flint!" and "The Northeastern!"*) I see you know. Who sent the solid citizens to see Mr. Henderson? (*"Flint!"*) This is a clever trick — exactly what I should have done if I'd been running their campaign — only they didn't do it early enough. They picked Mr. Giles Henderson for two reasons : because he lives in Kingston, which is anti-railroad and supported the Gaylord bill, and because he never in his life committed any positive action, good or bad — and he never will. And they made another mistake — the Honourable Adam B. Hunt wouldn't back out." (*Laughter and cheers.*)

CHAPTER XXII

IN WHICH EUPHRASIA TAKES A HAND

AUSTEN had not forgotten his promise to Euphrasia, and he had gone to Hanover Street many times since his sojourn at Mr. Jabe Jenney's. Usually these visits had taken place in the middle of the day, when Euphrasia, with gentle but determined insistence, had made him sit down before some morsel which she had prepared against his coming, and which he had not the heart to refuse. In answer to his inquiries about Hilary, she would toss her head and reply, disdainfully, that he was as comfortable as he should be. For Euphrasia had her own strict ideas of justice, and to her mind Hilary's suffering was deserved. That suffering was all the more terrible because it was silent, but Euphrasia was a stern woman. To know that he missed Austen, to feel that Hilary was being justly punished for his treatment of her idol, for his callous neglect and lack of realization of the blessings of his life — these were Euphrasia's grim compensations.

At times, even, she had experienced a strange rejoicing that she had promised Austen to remain with his father, for thus it had been given her to be the daily witness of a retribution for which she had longed during many years. Nor did she strive to hide her feelings. Their intercourse, never voluminous, had shrunk to the barest necessities for the use of speech ; but Hilary, ever since the night of his son's departure, had read in the face of his housekeeper a knowledge of his suffering, an exultation a thousand times more maddening than the little reproaches of language would have been. He avoided her more than ever, and must many times have regretted bitterly the fact that he had betrayed himself to her. As

357

for Euphrasia, she had no notion of disclosing Hilary's torture to his son. She was determined that the victory, when it came, should be Austen's, and the surrender Hilary's.

"He manages to eat his meals, and gets along as common," she would reply. "He only thinks of himself and that railroad."

But Austen read between the lines.

"Poor old Judge," he would answer; "it's because he's made that way, Phrasie. He can't help it, any more than I can help flinging law-books on the floor and running off to the country to have a good time. You know as well as I do that he hasn't had much joy out of life; that he'd like to be different, only he doesn't know how."

"I can't see that it takes much knowledge to treat a wife and son like human beings," Euphrasia retorted; "that's only common humanity. For a man that goes to meetin' twice a week, you'd have thought he'd have learned something by this time out of the New Testament. He's prayed enough in his life, goodness knows!"

Now Euphrasia's ordinarily sharp eyes were sharpened an hundred fold by affection; and of late, at odd moments during his visits, Austen had surprised them fixed on him with a penetration that troubled him.

"You don't seem to fancy the tarts as much as you used to," she would remark. "Time was when you'd eat three and four at a sittin'."

"Phrasie, one of your persistent fallacies is, that I'm still a boy."

"You ain't yourself," said Euphrasia, ignoring this pleasantry, "and you ain't been yourself for some months. I've seen it. I haven't brought you up for nothing. If *he's* troubling you, don't you worry a mite. He ain't worth it. He eats better than you do."

"I'm not worrying much about that," Austen answered, smiling. "The Judge and I will patch it up before long —I'm sure. He's worried now over these people who are making trouble for his railroad."

"I wish railroads had never been invented," cried

Euphrasia. "It seems to me they bring nothing but trouble. My mother used to get along pretty well in a stage-coach."

One evening in September, when the summer days were rapidly growing shorter and the mists rose earlier in the valley of the Blue, Austen, who had stayed late at the office preparing a case, ate his supper at the Ripton House. As he sat in the big dining room, which was almost empty, the sense of loneliness which he had experienced so often of late came over him, and he thought of Euphrasia. His father, he knew, had gone to Kingston for the night, and so he drove up Hanover Street and hitched Pepper to the stone post before the door. Euphrasia, according to an invariable custom, would be knitting in the kitchen at this hour ; and at the sight of him in the window, she dropped her work with a little, joyful cry.

"I was just thinking of you !" she said, in a low voice of tenderness which many people would not have recognized as Euphrasia's; as though her thoughts of him were the errant ones of odd moments ! "I'm so glad you come. It's lonesome here of evenings, Austen."

He entered silently and sat down beside her, in a Windsor chair which had belonged to some remote Austen of bygone days.

"You don't have as good things to eat up at Mis' Jenney's as I give you," she remarked. "Not that you appear to care much for eatables any more. Austen, are you feeling poorly ? "

"I can dig more potatoes in a day than any other man in Ripton," he declared.

"You'd ought to get married," said Euphrasia, abruptly. "I've told you that before, but you never seem to pay any attention to what I say."

"Why haven't you tried it, Phrasie ? " he retorted.

He was not prepared for what followed. Euphrasia did not answer at once, but presently her knitting dropped to her lap, and she sat staring at the old clock on the kitchen shelf.

"He never asked me," she said, simply.

Austen was silent. The answer seemed to recall, with infinite pathos, Euphrasia's long-lost youth, and he had not thought of youth as a quality which could ever have pertained to her. She must have been young once, and fresh, and full of hope for herself; she must have known, long ago, something of what he now felt, something of the joy and pain, something of the inexpressible, never ceasing yearning for the fulfilment of a desire that dwarfed all others. Euphrasia had been denied that fulfilment. And he — would he, too, be denied it ?

Out of Euphrasia's eyes, as she gazed at the mantel-shelf, shone the light of undying fires within — fires which at a touch could blaze forth after endless years, transforming the wrinkled face, softening the sterner lines of character. And suddenly there was a new bond between the two. So used are the young to the acceptance of the sacrifice of the old that they lose sight of that sacrifice. But Austen saw now, in a flash, the years of Euphrasia's self-denial, the years of memories, the years of regrets for that which might have been.

"Phrasie," he said, laying a hand on hers, which rested on the arm of the chair, "I was only joking, you know."

"I know, I know," Euphrasia answered hastily, and turned and looked into his face searchingly. Her eyes were undimmed, and the light was still in them which revealed a soul of which he had had no previous knowledge.

"I know you was, dear. I never told that to a living being except your mother. He's dead now — *he* never knew. But I told her — I couldn't help it. She had a way of drawing things out of you, and you just couldn't resist. I'll never forget that day she came in here and looked at me and took my hand — same as you have it now. She wasn't married then. I'll never forget the sound of her voice as she said, ' Euphrasia, tell me about it.' " (Here Euphrasia's own voice trembled.) "I told her, just as I'm telling you, — because I couldn't help it. Folks had to tell her things."

She turned her hand and clasped his tightly with her own thin fingers.

"And oh, Austen," she cried, "I want so that you should be happy! *She* was so unhappy, it doesn't seem right that you should be, too."

"I shall be, Phrasie," he said; "you mustn't worry about that."

For a while the only sound in the room was the ticking of the old clock with the quaint, coloured picture on its panel. And then, with a movement which, strangely, was an acute reminder of a way Victoria had, Euphrasia turned and searched his face once more.

"You're not happy," she said.

He could not put this aside —nor did he wish to. Her own confidence had been so simple, so fine, so sure of his sympathy, that he felt it would be unworthy to equivocate; the confessions of the self-reliant are sacred things. Yes, and there had been times when he had longed to unburden himself; but he had had no intimate on this plane, and — despite the great sympathy between them —that Euphrasia might understand had never occurred to him. She had read his secret.

In that instant Euphrasia, with the instinct which love lends to her sex, had gone farther; indignation seized her — and the blame fell upon the woman. Austen's words, unconsciously, were an answer to her thoughts.

"It isn't anybody's fault but my own," he said.

Euphrasia's lips were tightly closed. Long ago the idol of her youth had faded into the substance of which dreams are made — to be recalled by dreams alone; another worship had filled her heart, and Austen Vane had become — for her — the fulness and the very meaning of life itself; one to be admired of all men, to be desired of all women. Visions of Austen's courtship had at times risen in her mind, although Euphrasia would not have called it a courtship. When the time came, Austen would confer; and so sure of his judgment was Euphrasia that she was prepared to take the recipient of the priceless gift into her arms. And now! Was it possible that a woman lived who would even hesitate? Curiosity seized Euphrasia with the intensity of a passion. Who was this woman? When and where had he seen her? Ripton could not have produced her — for it was characteristic of Euphrasia that no girl of her acquaintance was worthy to be raised to such a height; Austen's wife would be an unknown of ideal appearance and attainments. Hence indignation rocked Euphrasia, and doubts swayed her. In this alone she had been an idealist, but she might have known that good men were a prey to the unworthy of the opposite sex.

She glanced at Austen's face, and he smiled at her gently, as though he divined something of her thoughts.

"If it isn't your fault that you're not happy, then the matter's easily mended," she said.

He shook his head at her, as though in reproof.

"Was yours — easily mended?" he asked.

Euphrasia was silent a moment.

"He never knew," she repeated, in a low voice.

"Well, Phrasie, it looks very much as if we were in the same boat," he said.

Euphrasia's heart gave a bound.

"Then you haven't spoke!" she cried; "I knew you hadn't. I — I was a woman — but sometimes I've thought I'd ought to have given him some sign. You're a man, Austen; thank God for it, you're a man. If a man loves a woman, he's only got to tell her so."

"It isn't as simple as that," he answered.

Euphrasia gave him a startled glance.

"She ain't married?" she exclaimed.

"No," he said, and laughed in spite of himself.

Euphrasia breathed again. For Sarah Austen had had a morality of her own, and on occasions had given expression to extreme views.

"She's not playin' with you?" was Euphrasia's next question, and her tone boded ill to any young person who would indulge in these tactics with Austen.

He shook his head again, and smiled at her vehemence.

"No, she's not playing with me — she isn't that kind.

I'd like to tell you, but I can't — I can't. It was only because you guessed that I said anything about it." He disengaged his hand, and rose, and patted her on the cheek. " I suppose I had to tell somebody," he said, " and you seemed, somehow, to be the right person, Phrasie."

Euphrasia rose abruptly and looked up intently into his face. He thought it strange afterwards, as he drove along the dark roads, that she had not answered him.

Even though the matter were on the knees of the gods, Euphrasia would have taken it thence, if she could. Nor did Austen know that she shared with him, that night, his waking hours.

The next morning Mr. Thomas Gaylord, the younger, was making his way towards the office of the Gaylord Lumber Company, conveniently situated on Willow Street, near the railroad. Young Tom was in a particularly jovial frame of mind, despite the fact that he had arrived in Ripton, on the night express, as early as five o'clock in the morning. He had been touring the State ostensibly on lumber business, but young Tom had a large and varied personal as well as commercial acquaintance, and he had the inestimable happiness of being regarded as an honest man, while his rough and genial qualities made him beloved. For these reasons and others of a more material nature, suggestions from Mr. Thomas Gaylord were apt to be well received — and Tom had been making suggestions.

Early as he was at his office — the office-boy was sprinkling the floor — young Tom had a visitor who was earlier still. Pausing in the doorway, Mr. Gaylord beheld with astonishment a prim, elderly lady in a stiff, black dress sitting upright on the edge of a capacious oak chair which seemed itself rather discomfited by what it contained, — for its hospitality had hitherto been extended to visitors of a very different sort.

" Well, upon my soul," cried young Tom, "if it isn't Euphrasia! "

" Yes, it's me," said Euphrasia; " I've be'n to market, and I had a notion to see you before I went home."

Mr. Gaylord took the office-boy lightly by the collar of his coat and lifted him, sprinkling can and all, out of the doorway and closed the door. Then he drew his revolving chair close to Euphrasia, and sat down. They were old friends, and more than once in a youth far from model Tom had experienced certain physical reproof at her hands, for which he bore no ill-will. There was anxiety on his face as he asked: —

" There hasn't been any accident, has there, Euphrasia ? "

" No," she said.

" No new row ? " inquired Tom.

" No," said Euphrasia. She was a direct person, as we know, but true descendants of the Puritans believe in the decency of preliminaries, and here was certainly an affair not to be plunged into. Euphrasia was a spinster in the strictest sense of that formidable and highly descriptive term, and she intended ultimately to discuss with Tom a subject of which she was supposed by tradition to be wholly ignorant, the mere mention of which still brought warmth to her cheeks. Such a delicate matter should surely be led up to delicately. In the meanwhile Tom was mystified.

" Well, I'm mighty glad to see you, anyhow," he said heartily. " It was good of you to call, Euphrasia. I can't offer you a cigar."

" I should think not," said Euphrasia.

Tom reddened. He still retained for her some of his youthful awe.

" I can't do the honours of hospitality as I'd wish to," he went on; " I can't give you anything like the pies you used to give me."

" You stole most of 'em," said Euphrasia.

" I guess that's so," said young Tom, laughing, " but I'll never taste pies like 'em again as long as I live. Do you know, Euphrasia, there were two reasons why those were the best pies I ever ate ? "

" What were they ? " she asked, apparently unmoved.

" First," said Tom, " because you made 'em, and second, because they were stolen."

Truly, young Tom had a way with women, had he only been aware of it.

"I never took much stock in stolen things," said Euphrasia.

"It's because you never were tempted with such pie as that," replied the audacious Mr. Gaylord.

"You're gettin' almighty stout," said Euphrasia.

As we see her this morning, could she indeed ever have had a love affair?

"I don't have to use my legs as much as I once did," said Tom. And this remark brought to an end the first phase of this conversation, — brought to an end, apparently, all conversation whatsoever. Tom racked his brain for a new topic, opened his roll-top desk, drummed on it, looked up at the ceiling and whistled softly, and then turned and faced again the imperturbable Euphrasia.

"Euphrasia," he said, "you're not exactly a politician, I believe."

"Well," said Euphrasia, "I've be'n maligned a good many times, but nobody ever went that far."

Mr. Gaylord shook with laughter.

"Then I guess there's no harm in confiding political secrets to you," he said. "I've been around the State some this week, talking to people I know, and I believe if your Austen wasn't so obstinate, we could make him governor."

"Obstinate?" ejaculated Euphrasia.

"Yes," said Tom, with a twinkle in his eye, "obstinate. He doesn't seem to want something that most men would give their souls for."

"And why should he dirty himself with politics?" she demanded. "In the years I've lived with Hilary Vane I've seen enough of politicians, goodness knows. I never want to see another."

"If Austen was governor, we'd change some of that. But mind, Euphrasia, this is a secret," said Tom, raising a warning finger. "If Austen hears about it now, the jig's up."

Euphrasia considered and thawed a little.

"They don't often have governors that young, do they?" she asked.

"No," said Tom, forcibly, "they don't. And so far as I know, they haven't had such a governor for years as Austen would make. But he won't push himself. You know, Euphrasia, I have always believed that he will be President some day."

Euphrasia received this somewhat startling prediction complacently. She had no doubt of its accuracy, but the enunciation of it raised young Tom in her estimation, and incidentally brought her nearer her topic.

"Austen ain't himself lately," she remarked.

"I knew that he didn't get along with Hilary," said Tom, sympathetically, beginning to realize now that Euphrasia had come to talk about her idol.

"It's Hilary doesn't get along with him," she retorted indignantly. "He's responsible — not Austen. Of all the narrow, pig-headed, selfish men the Lord ever created, Hilary Vane's the worst. It's Hilary drove him out of his mother's house to live with strangers. It's Austen that comes around to inquire for his father — Hilary never has a word to say about Austen." A trace of colour actually rose under Euphrasia's sallow skin, and she cast her eyes downward. "You've known him a good while, haven't you, Tom?"

"All my life," said Tom, mystified again, "all my life. And I think more of him than of anybody else in the world."

"I calculated as much," she said; "that's why I came." She hesitated. Artful Euphrasia! We will let the ingenuous Mr. Gaylord be the first to mention this delicate matter, if possible. "Goodness knows, it ain't Hilary I came to talk about. I had a notion that you'd know if — anything else was troubling Austen."

"Why," said Tom, "there can't be any business troubles outside of those Hilary's mixed up in. Austen doesn't spend any money to speak of, except what he gives away, and he's practically chief counsel for our company."

Euphrasia was silent a moment.

"I suppose there's nothing else that could bother him," she remarked. She had never held Tom Gaylord's powers of comprehension in high estimation, and the estimate had not risen during this visit. But she had undervalued him; even Tom could rise to an inspiration — when the sources of all other inspirations were eliminated.

"Why," he exclaimed, with a masculine lack of delicacy, "he may be in love!"

"That's struck you, has it?" said Euphrasia.

But Tom appeared to be thinking; he was, in truth, engaged in collecting his cumulative evidence: Austen's sleigh-ride at the capital, which he had discovered; his talk with Victoria after her fall, when she had betrayed an interest in Austen which Tom had thought entirely natural; and finally Victoria's appearance at Mr. Crewe's rally in Ripton. Young Mr. Gaylord had not had a great deal of experience in affairs of the heart, and he was himself aware that his diagnosis in such a matter would not carry much weight. He had conceived a tremendous admiration for Victoria, which had been shaken a little by the suspicion that she might be intending to marry Mr. Crewe. Tom Gaylord saw no reason why Austen Vane should not marry Mr. Flint's daughter if he chose — or any other man's daughter; partaking, in this respect, somewhat of Euphrasia's view. As for Austen himself, Tom had seen no symptoms; but then, he reflected, he would not be likely to see any. However, he perceived the object now of Euphrasia's visit, and began to take the liveliest interest in it.

"So you think Austen's in love?" he demanded.

Euphrasia sat up straighter, if anything.

"I didn't say anything of the kind," she returned.

"He wouldn't tell me, you know," said Tom; "I can only guess at it."

"And the — lady?" said Euphrasia, craftily.

"I'm up a tree there, too. All I know is that he took her sleigh-riding one afternoon at the capital, and wouldn't tell me who he was going to take. And then she fell off her horse down at East Tunbridge Station — "

" Fell off her horse ! " echoed Euphrasia, an accident comparable in her mind to falling off a roof. What manner of young woman was this who fell off horses?

" She wasn't hurt," Tom continued, " and she rode the beast home. He was a wild one, I can tell you, and she's got pluck. That's the first time I ever met her, although I had often seen her and thought she was a stunner to look at. She talked as if she took an interest in Austen."

An exact portrayal of Euphrasia's feelings at this description of the object of Austen's affections is almost impossible. A young woman who was a stunner, who rode wild horses and fell off them and rode them again, was beyond the pale not only of Euphrasia's experience but of her imagination likewise. And this hoyden had talked as though she took an interest in Austen! Euphrasia was speechless.

" The next time I saw her," said Tom, " was when she came down here to listen to Humphrey Crewe's attacks on the railroad. I thought that was a sort of a queer thing for Flint's daughter to do, but Austen didn't seem to look at it that way. He talked to her after the show was over."

At this point Euphrasia could contain herself no longer, and in her excitement she slipped off the edge of the chair and on to her feet.

" Flint's daughter ? " she cried; " Augustus P. Flint's daughter ? "

Tom looked at her in amazement.

" Didn't you know who it was ? " he stammered. But Euphrasia was not listening.

" I've seen her," she was saying; " I've seen her ridin' through Ripton in that little red wagon, drivin' herself, with a coachman perched up beside her. Flint's daughter! " Euphrasia became speechless once more, the complications opened up being too vast for intelligent comment. Euphrasia, however, grasped some of the problems which Austen had had to face. Moreover, she had learned what she had come for, and the obvious thing to do now was to go home and reflect. So, without further ceremony, she walked to the door and opened it, and turned again with her hand on the knob. "Look here, Tom Gaylord," she said, "if you tell Austen I was here, I'll never forgive you. I don't believe you've got any more sense than to do it."

And with these words she took her departure, ere the amazed Mr. Gaylord had time to show her out. Half an hour elapsed before he opened his letters.

When she arrived home in Hanover Street it was nine o'clock — an hour well on in the day for Euphrasia. Unlocking the kitchen door, she gave a glance at the stove to assure herself that it had not been misbehaving, and went into the passage on her way up-stairs to take off her gown before sitting down to reflect upon the astonishing thing she had heard. Habit had so crystallized in Euphrasia that no news, however amazing, could have shaken it. But in the passage she paused; an unwonted, or rather untimely, sound reached her ears, a sound which came from the front of the house — and at nine o'clock in the morning! Had Austen been at home, Euphrasia would have thought nothing of it. In her remembrance Hilary Vane, whether he returned from a journey or not, had never been inside the house at that hour on a week-day; and, unlike the gentleman in "La Vie de Bohéme," Euphrasia did not have to be reminded of the Sabbath.

Perhaps Austen had returned! Or perhaps it was a burglar! Euphrasia, undaunted, ran through the darkened front hall to where the graceful banister ended in a curve at the foot of the stairs, and there, on the bottom step, sat a man with his head in his hands. Euphrasia shrieked. He looked up, and she saw that it was Hilary Vane. She would have shrieked, anyway.

"What in the world's the matter with you?" she cried.

"I — I stumbled coming down the stairs," he said.

"But what are you doing at home in the middle of the morning?" she demanded.

He did not answer her. The subdued light which

2 B

crept under the porch and came in through the fan-shaped window over the door fell on his face.

"Are you sick?" said Euphrasia. In all her life she had never seen him look like that.

He shook his head, but did not attempt to rise. A Hilary Vane without vigour!

"No," he said, "no. I just came up here from the train to — get somethin' I'd left in my room."

"A likely story!" said Euphrasia. "You've never done that in thirty years. You're sick, and I'm a-going for the doctor."

She put her hand to his forehead, but he thrust it away and got to his feet, although in the effort he compressed his lips and winced.

"You stay where you are," he said; "I tell you I'm not sick, and I'm going down to the square. Let the doctors alone — I haven't got any use for 'em."

He walked to the door, opened it, and went out and slammed it in her face. By the time she had got it open again — a crack — he had reached the sidewalk, and was apparently in full possession of his powers and faculties.

CHAPTER XXIII

A FALLING-OUT IN HIGH PLACES

ALTHOUGH one of the most exciting political battles ever fought is fast coming to its climax, and a now jubilant Mr. Crewe is contesting every foot of ground in the State with the determination and pertinacity which make him a marked man; although the convention wherein his fate will be decided is now but a few days distant, and everything has been done to secure a victory which mortal man can do, let us follow Hilary Vane to Fairview. Not that Hilary has been idle. The "Book of Arguments" is exhausted, and the chiefs and the captains have been to Ripton, and received their final orders, but more than one has gone back to his fief with the vision of a changed Hilary who has puzzled them. Rumours have been in the air that the harmony between the Source of Power and the Distribution of Power is not as complete as it once was. Certainly, Hilary Vane is not the man he was — although this must not even be whispered. Senator Whitredge had told — but never mind that. In the old days an order was an order; there were no rebels then. In the old days there was no wavering and rescinding, and if the chief counsel told you, with brevity, to do a thing, you went and did it straightway, with the knowledge that it was the best thing to do. Hilary Vane had aged suddenly, and it occurred for the first time to many that, in this utilitarian world, old blood must be superseded by young blood.

Two days before the convention, immediately after taking dinner at the Ripton House with Mr. Nat Billings, Hilary Vane, in response to a summons, drove up to Fairview. One driving behind him would have observed that the Honourable Hilary's horse took his own gaits, and that the reins, most of the time, drooped listlessly on his quarters. A September stillness was in the air, a September purple clothed the distant hills, but to Hilary the glories of the day were as things non-existent. Even the groom at Fairview, who took his horse, glanced back at him with a peculiar expression as he stood for a moment on the steps with a hesitancy the man had never before remarked.

In the meantime Mr. Flint, with a pile of letters in a special basket on the edge of his desk, was awaiting his counsel; the president of the Northeastern was pacing his room, as was his wont when his activities were for a moment curbed, or when he had something on his mind; and every few moments he would glance towards his mantel at the clock which was set to railroad time. In past days he had never known Hilary Vane to be a moment late to an appointment. The door was open, and five and twenty minutes had passed the hour before he saw the lawyer in the doorway. Mr. Flint was a man of such preoccupation of mind that he was not likely to be struck by any change there might have been in his counsel's appearance.

"It's half-past three," he said.

Hilary entered, and sat down beside the window.

"You mean that I'm late," he replied.

"I've got some engineers coming here in less than an hour," said Mr. Flint.

"I'll be gone in less than an hour," said Hilary.

"Well," said Mr. Flint, "let's get down to hardtack. I've got to be frank with you, Vane, and tell you plainly that this political business is all at sixes and sevens."

"It isn't necessary to tell me that," said Hilary.

"What do you mean?"

"I mean that I know it."

"To put it mildly," the president of the Northeastern continued, "it's the worst mixed-up campaign I ever knew. Here we are with the convention only two days off, and we don't know where we stand, how many delegates we've got, or whether this upstart at Leith is going to be nominated over our heads.   Here's Adam Hunt with his back up, declaring he's a reformer, and all his section of the State behind him.   Now if that could have been handled otherwise — "

"Who told Hunt to go in?" Hilary inquired.

"Things were different then," said Mr. Flint, vigorously.   "Hunt had been promised the governorship for a long time, and when Ridout became out of the question — "

"Why did Ridout become out of the question?" asked Hilary.

Mr. Flint made a gesture of impatience.

"On account of that foolishness in the Legislature, of course."

"'That foolishness in the Legislature,' as you call it, represented a sentiment all over the State," said Hilary. "And if I'd be'n you, I wouldn't have let Hunt in this year.   But you didn't ask my opinion.   You asked me when you begged me to get Adam out, and I predicted that he wouldn't get out."

Mr. Flint took a turn up and down the room.

"I'm sorry I didn't send for him to go to New York," he said.   "Well, anyway, the campaign's been muddled, that's certain, — whoever muddled it."   And the president looked at his counsel as though he, at least, had no doubts on this point.   But Hilary appeared unaware of the implication, and made no reply.

"I can't find out what Bascom and Botcher are doing," Mr. Flint went on; "I don't get any reports — they haven't been here.   Perhaps you know.   They've had trip passes enough to move the whole population of Putnam County. Fairplay says they're gettin' delegates for Adam Hunt instead of Giles Henderson.   And Whitredge says that Jake Botcher is talking reform."

"I guess Botcher and Bascom know their business," said Mr. Vane.   If Mr. Flint had been a less concentrated man, he might have observed that the Honourable Hilary had not cut a piece of Honey Dew this afternoon.

" What is their business ? " asked Mr. Flint — a little irrelevantly for him.

" What you and I taught 'em," said Mr. Vane.

Mr. Flint considered this a moment, and decided to let it pass. He looked at the Honourable Hilary more closely, however.

" What's the matter with you, Vane ? You're not sick, are you ? "

" No."

Mr. Flint took another turn.

" Now the question is, what are we going to do? If you've got any plan, I want to hear it."

Mr. Vane was silent.

" Suppose Crewe goes into the convention with enough delegates to lock it up, so that none of the three has a majority? "

" I guess he'll do that," said Mr. Vane. He fumbled in his pocket, and drew out a typewritten list. It must be explained that the caucuses, or primaries, had been held in the various towns of the State at odd dates, and that the delegates pledged for the different candidates had been published in the newspapers from time to time — although very much in accordance with the desires of their individual newspapers. Mr. Crewe's delegates necessarily had been announced by what is known as political advertising. Mr. Flint took the Honourable Hilary's list, ran his eye over it, and whistled.

" You mean he *claims* three hundred and fifty out of the thousand."

" No," said Hilary, " he claims six hundred. He'll have three hundred and fifty."

In spite of the " Book of Arguments," Mr. Crewe was to have three hundred ! It was incredible, preposterous. Mr. Flint looked at his counsel once more, and wondered whether he could be mentally failing.

" Fairplay only gives him two hundred."

" Fairplay only gave him ten, in the beginning," said Hilary.

" You come here two days before the convention and

tell me Crewe has three hundred and fifty ! " Mr. Flint exclaimed, as though Hilary Vane were personally responsible for Mr. Crewe's delegates. A very different tone from that of other times, when conventions were mere ratifications of Imperial decrees. "Do you realize what it means if we lose control? Thousands and thousands of dollars in improvements — rolling stock, better service, new bridges, and eliminations of grade crossings. And they'll raise our tax rate to the average, which means thousands more. A new railroad commission that we can't talk to, and lower dividends — lower dividends, do you understand? That means trouble with the directors, the stockholders, and calls for explanations. And what explanations can I make which can be printed in a public report? "

"You were always pretty good at 'em, Flint," said Hilary.

This remark, as was perhaps natural, did not improve the temper of the president of the Northeastern.

"If you think I like this political business any better than you do, you're mightily mistaken," he replied. "And now I want to hear what plan you've got for the convention. Suppose there's a deadlock, as you say there will be, how are you going to handle it? Can you get a deal through between Giles Henderson and Adam Hunt? With all my other work, I've had to go into this myself. Hunt hasn't got a chance. Bascom and Botcher are egging him on and making him believe he has. When Hunt gets into the convention and begins to fall off, you've got to talk to him, Vane. And his delegates have all got to be seen at the Pelican the night before and understand that they're to swing to Henderson after two ballots. You've *got* to keep your hand on the throttle in the convention, you understand. And I don't need to impress upon you how grave are the consequences if this man Crewe gets in, with public sentiment behind him and a reactionary Lower House. You've *got* to keep your hand on the throttle."

"That's part of my business, isn't it?" Hilary asked, without turning his head.

Mr. Flint did not answer, but his eye rested again on his counsel's face.

" I'm that kind of a lawyer," Hilary continued, apparently more to himself than to his companion. " You pay me for that sort of thing more than for the work I do in the courts. Isn't that so, Flint ? "

Mr. Flint was baffled. Two qualities which were very dear to him he designated as *sane* and *safe*, and he had hitherto regarded his counsel as the sanest and safest of men. This remark made him wonder seriously whether the lawyer's mind were not giving away ; and if so, to whom was he to turn at this eleventh hour ? No man in the State knew the ins and outs of conventions as did Hilary Vane ; and, in the rare times when there had been crises, he had sat quietly in the little room off the platform as at the keyboard of an organ, and the delegates had responded to his touch. Hilary Vane had named the presidents of conventions, and the committees, and by pulling out stops could get such resolutions as he wished — or as Mr. Flint wished. But now ?

Suddenly a suspicion invaded Mr. Flint's train of thought ; he repeated Hilary's words over to himself. " I'm that kind of a lawyer," and another individuality arose before the president of the Northeastern. Instincts are curious things. On the day, some years before, when Austen Vane had brought his pass into this very room and laid it down on his desk, Mr. Flint had recognized a man with whom he would have to deal, — a stronger man than Hilary. Since then he had seen Austen's hand in various disturbing matters, and now it was as if he heard Austen speaking. "*I'm that kind of a lawyer.*" Not Hilary Vane, but Hilary Vane's son was responsible for Hilary Vane's condition — this recognition came to Mr. Flint in a flash. Austen had somehow accomplished the incredible feat of making Hilary Vane ashamed — and when such men as Hilary are ashamed, their usefulness is over. Mr. Flint had seen the thing happen with a certain kind of financiers, one day aggressive, combative, and the next broken, querulous men. Let a man cease to believe in what he is doing, and he loses force.

The president of the Northeastern used a locomotive as long as possible, but when it ceased to be able to haul a train up-grade, he sent it to the scrap-heap. Mr. Flint was far from being a bad man, but he worshipped power, and his motto was the survival of the fittest. He did not yet feel pity for Hilary — for he was angry. Only contempt, — contempt that one who had been a power should come to this. To draw a somewhat far-fetched parallel, a Captain Kidd or a Cæsar Borgia with a conscience would never have been heard of. Mr. Flint did not call it a conscience — he had a harder name for it. He had to send Hilary, thus vitiated, into the Convention to conduct the most important battle since the founding of the Empire, and Austen Vane was responsible.

Mr. Flint had to control himself. In spite of his feelings, he saw that he must do so. And yet he could not resist saying: —

"I get a good many rumours here. They tell me that there may be another candidate in the field — a dark horse."

"Who?" asked Hilary.

"There was a meeting in the room of a man named Redbrook during the Legislature to push this candidate," said Mr. Flint, eyeing his counsel significantly, "and now young Gaylord has been going quietly around the State in his interest."

Suddenly the listless figure of Hilary Vane straightened, and the old look which had commanded the respect and obedience of men returned to his eye.

"You mean my son?" he demanded.

"Yes," said Mr. Flint; "they tell me that when the time comes, your son will be a candidate on a platform opposed to our interests."

"Then," said Hilary, "they tell you a damned lie."

Hilary Vane had not sworn for a quarter of a century, and yet it is to be doubted if he ever spoke more nobly. He put his hands on the arms of his chair and lifted himself to his feet, where he stood for a moment, a tall figure

to be remembered.   Mr. Flint remembered it for many
years.   Hilary Vane's long coat was open, and seemed in
itself to express this strange and new-found vigour in its
flowing lines ; his head was thrown back, and a look on
his face which Mr. Flint had never seen there.   He drew
from an inner pocket a long envelope, and his hand
trembled, though with seeming eagerness, as he held it
out to Mr. Flint.

"Here ! " he said.

"What's this ? " asked Mr. Flint.   He evinced no
desire to take it, but Hilary pressed it on him.

" My resignation as counsel for your road."

The president of the Northeastern, bewildered by this
sudden transformation, stared at the envelope.

" What ?   Now — to-day ? " he said.

"No," answered Hilary; " read it.   You'll see it takes
effect the day after the State convention.   I'm not much
use any more — you've done your best to bring that home
to me, and you'll need a new man to do — the kind of work
I've been doing for you for twenty-five years.   But you
can't get a new man in a day, and I said I'd stay with you,
and I keep my word.   I'll go to the convention ; I'll do my
best for you, as I always have.   But I don't like it, and
after that I'm through.   After that I become a lawyer —
a lawyer, do you understand ? "

" A lawyer ? " Mr. Flint repeated.

"Yes, a lawyer.   Ever since last June, when I came
up here, I've realized what I was.   A Brush Bascom,
with a better education and more brains, but a Brush
Bascom — with the brains prostituted.   While things
were going along smoothly I didn't know — you never
attempted to talk to me this way before.   Do you remember how you took hold of me that day, and begged
me to stay ?   I do, and I stayed.   Why ?   Because I
was a friend of yours.   Association with you for twenty-
five years had got under my skin, and I thought it had
got under yours."   Hilary let his hand fall.   " To-day
you've given me a notion of what friendship is.   You've
given me a chance to estimate myself on a new basis, and

I'm much obliged to you for that. I haven't got many years left, but I'm glad to have found out what my life has been worth before I die."

He buttoned up his coat slowly, glaring at Mr. Flint the while with a courage and a defiance that were superb. And he had picked up his hat before Mr. Flint found his tongue.

"You don't mean that, Vane," he cried. "My God, think what you've said!"

Hilary pointed at the desk with a shaking finger.

"If that were a scaffold, and a rope were around my neck, I'd say it over again. And I thank God I've had a chance to say it to you." He paused, cleared his throat, and continued in a voice that all at once had become un-emotional and natural. "I've three tin boxes of the private papers you wanted. I didn't think of 'em to-day, but I'll bring 'em up to you myself on Thursday."

Mr. Flint reflected afterwards that what made him helpless must have been the sudden change in Hilary's manner to the commonplace. The president of the Northeastern stood where he was, holding the envelope in his hand, apparently without the power to move or speak. He watched the tall form of his chief counsel go through the doorway, and something told him that that exit was coincident with the end of an era.

The end of an era of fraud, of self-deception, of con-ditions that violated every sacred principle of free gov-ernment which men had shed blood to obtain.

CHAPTER XXIV

AN ADVENTURE OF VICTORIA'S

MRS. POMFRET was a proud woman, for she had at last obtained the consent of the lion to attend a lunch party. She would have liked a dinner much better, but beggars are not choosers, and she seized eagerly on the lunch. The two days before the convention Mr. Crewe was to spend at Leith; having continual conferences, of course, receiving delegations, and discussing with prominent citizens certain offices which would be in his gift when he became governor. Also, there was Mr. Watling's nominating speech to be gone over carefully, and Mr. Crewe's own speech of acceptance to be composed. He had it in his mind, and he had decided that it should have two qualities: it should be brief and forceful.

Gratitude, however, is one of the noblest qualities of man, and a statesman should not fail to reward his faithful workers and adherents. As one of the chiefest of these, Mrs. Pomfret was entitled to high consideration. Hence the candidate had consented to have a lunch given in his honour, naming the day and the hour; and Mrs. Pomfret, believing that a prospective governor should possess some of the perquisites of royalty, in a rash moment submitted for his approval a list of guests. This included two distinguished foreigners who were staying at the Leith Inn, an Englishman and an Austrian, and an elderly lady of very considerable social importance who was on a visit to Mrs. Pomfret.

Mr. Crewe had graciously sanctioned the list, but took the liberty of suggesting as an addition to it the name of Miss Victoria Flint, explaining over the telephone to Mrs. Pomfret that he had scarcely seen Victoria all summer.

and that he wanted particularly to see her.   Mrs. Pomfret declared that she had only left out Victoria because her presence might be awkward for both of them, but Mr. Crewe waved this aside as a trivial and feminine objection; so Victoria was invited, and another young man to balance the table.

Mrs. Pomfret, as may have been surmised, was a woman of taste, and her villa at Leith, though small, had added considerably to her reputation for this quality.   Patterson Pomfret had been a gentleman with red cheeks and an income, who incidentally had been satisfied with both. He had never tried to add to the income, which was large enough to pay the dues of the clubs the lists of which he thought worthy to include his name ; large enough to pay hotel bills in London and Paris and at the baths, and to fee the servants at country houses; large enough to clothe his wife and himself, and to teach Alice the three essentials of music, French, and deportment. If that man is notable who has mastered one thing well, Patterson Pomfret was a notable man: he had mastered the possibilities of his income, and never in any year had he gone beyond it by so much as a sole *à vin blanc* or a pair of red silk stockings.   When he died, he left a worthy financial successor in his wife.

Mrs. Pomfret, knowing the income, after an exhaustive search decided upon Leith as the place to build her villa. It must be credited to her foresight that, when she built, she saw the future possibilities of the place.   The proper people had started it.   And it must be credited to her genius that she added to these possibilities of Leith by bringing to it such families as she thought worthy to live in the neighbourhood — families which incidentally increased the value of the land.   Her villa had a decided French look, and was so amazingly trim and neat and generally shipshape as to be fit for only the daintiest and most discriminating feminine occupation.   The house was small, and its metamorphosis from a plain wooden farm-house had been an achievement that excited general admiration. Porches had been added, and a coat of spotless white relieved by an orange striping so original that many envied, but none dared to copy it. The striping went around the white chimneys, along the cornice, under the windows and on the railings of the porch: there were window boxes gay with geraniums and abundant awnings striped white and red, to match the flowers: a high, formal hemlock hedge hid the house from the road, through which entered a blue-stone drive that cut the close-cropped lawn and made a circle to the doorway. Under the great maples on the lawn were a tea-table, rugs, and wicker chairs, and the house itself was furnished by a variety of things of a design not to be bought in the United States of America: desks, photograph frames, writing-sets, clocks, paper-knives, flower baskets, magazine racks, cigarette boxes, and dozens of other articles for the duplicates of which one might have searched Fifth Avenue in vain.

Mr. Crewe was a little late. Important matters, he said, had detained him at the last moment, and he particularly enjoined Mrs. Pomfret's butler to listen carefully for the telephone, and twice during lunch it was announced that Mr. Crewe was wanted. At first he was preoccupied, and answered absently across the table the questions of the Englishman and the Austrian about American politics, and talked to the lady of social prominence on his right not at all; nor to Mrs. Pomfret — who excused him. Being a lady of discerning qualities, however, the hostess remarked that Mr. Crewe's eyes wandered more than once to the far end of the oval table, where Victoria sat, and even Mrs. Pomfret could not deny the attraction. Victoria wore a filmy gown of mauve that infinitely became her, and a shadowy hat which, in the semi-darkness of the dining room, was a wondrous setting for her shapely head. Twice she caught Mr. Crewe's look upon her and returned it amusedly from under her lashes, — and once he could have sworn that she winked perceptibly. What fires she kindled in his deep nature it is impossible to say.

She had kindled other fires at her side. The tall young Englishman had lost interest in American politics, had turned his back upon poor Alice Pomfret, and had forgotten the world in general. Not so the Austrian, who was on the other side of Alice, and who could not see Victoria. Mr. Crewe, by his manner and appearance, had impressed him as a person of importance, and he wanted to know more. Besides, he wished to improve his English, and Alice had been told to speak French to him. By a lucky chance, after several blind attempts, he awakened the interest of the personality.

"I hear you are what they call *reform* in America?" *This* was not the question that opened the gates.

"I don't care much for the word," answered Mr. Crewe, shortly; "I prefer the word *progressive.*"

Discourse on the word "progressive" by the Austrian — almost a monologue. But he was far from being discouraged.

"And Mrs. Pomfret tells me they play many detestable tricks on you — yes?"

"Tricks!" exclaimed Mr. Crewe, the memory of many recent ones being fresh in his mind; "I should say so. Do you know what a caucus is?"

"Caucus — caucus? It brings something to my head. Ah, I have seen a picture of it, in some English book. A very funny picture — it is in fun, yes?"

"A picture?" said Mr. Crewe. "Impossible!"

"But no," said the Austrian, earnestly, with one finger to his temples. "It is a funny picture, I know. I cannot recall. But the word *caucus* I remember. That is a droll word."

"Perhaps, Baron," said Victoria, who had been resisting an almost uncontrollable desire to laugh, "you have been reading 'Alice in Wonderland.'"

The Englishman, Beatrice Chillingham, and some others (among whom were not Mr. Crewe and Mrs. Pomfret) gave way to an extremely pardonable mirth, in which the good-natured baron joined.

"Ach!" he cried. "It is so, I have seen it in 'Alice in Wonderland.'" Here the puzzled expression returned to his face, "But they are birds, are they not?"

Men whose minds are on serious things are impatient

of levity, and Mr. Crewe looked at the baron out of cold, reproving eyes.

"No," he said, "they are not birds."

This reply was the signal for more laughter.

"A thousand pardons," exclaimed the baron. "It is I who am so ignorant. You will excuse me — yes?"

Mr. Crewe was mollified. The baron was a foreigner, he had been the object of laughter, and Mr. Crewe's chivalrous spirit resented it.

"What we call a caucus in the towns of this State," he said, "is a meeting of citizens of one party to determine who their candidates shall be. A caucus is a primary. There is a very loose primary law in this State, purposely kept loose by the politicians of the Northeastern Railroads, in order that they may play such tricks on decent men as they have been playing on me."

At this mention of the Northeastern Railroads the lady on Mr. Crewe's right, and some other guests, gave startled glances at Victoria. They observed with surprise that she seemed quite unmoved.

"I'll tell you one or two of the things those railroad lobbyists have done," said Mr. Crewe, his indignation rising with the subject, and still addressing the baron. "They are afraid to let the people into the caucuses, because they know *I'll* get the delegates. Nearly everywhere I speak to the people, I get the delegates. The railroad politicians send word to the town rings to hold 'snap caucuses' when they hear I'm coming into a town to speak, and the local politicians give out notices only a day before, and only to the voters they want in the caucus. In Hull the other day, out of a population of two thousand, twenty men elected four delegates for the railroad candidate."

"It is corruption!" cried the baron, who had no idea who Victoria was, and a very slim notion of what Mr. Crewe was talking about.

"Corruption!" said Mr. Crewe. "What can you expect when a railroad owns a State? The other day in Britain, where they elect fourteen delegates, the editor of a weekly newspaper printed false ballots with two of my men at the top and one at the bottom, and eleven railroad men in the middle. Fortunately some person with sense discovered the fraud before it was too late."

" You don't tell me ! " said the baron.

" And every State and federal office-holder has been distributing passes for the last three weeks."

"Pass?" repeated the baron. "You mean they fight with the fist — so? To distribute a pass — so," and the baron struck out at an imaginary enemy. "It is the American language. I have read it in the prize-fight. I am told to read the prize-fight and the base-ball game."

Mr. Crewe thought it obviously useless to continue this conversation.

" The railroad," said the baron, " he is the modern Machiavelli."

" I say," Mr. Rangely, the Englishman, remarked to Victoria, "this is a bit rough on you, you know."

" Oh, I'm used to it," she laughed.

" Mr. Crewe," said Mrs. Pomfret, to the table at large, " deserves tremendous credit for the fight he has made, almost single-handed. Our greatest need in this country is what you have in England, Mr. Rangely, — gentlemen in politics. Our country gentlemen, like Mr. Crewe, are now going to assume their proper duties and responsibilities." She laid her napkin on the table and glanced at Alice as she continued : " Humphrey, I shall have to appoint you, as usual, the man of the house. Will you take the gentlemen into the library ? "

Another privilege of celebrity is to throw away one's cigar, and walk out of the smoking room if one is bored. Mr. Crewe was, in a sense, the host. He indicated with a wave of his hand the cigars and cigarettes which Mrs. Pomfret had provided, and stood in a thoughtful manner before the empty fireplace, with his hands in his pockets, replying in brief sentences to the questions of Mr. Chillingham and the others. To tell the truth, Mr. Crewe was bringing to bear all of his extraordinary concentration of mind upon a problem with which he had been occupied for some years past. He was not a man, as we know, to take the important steps of life in a hurry, although, like the truly great, he was capable of making up his mind in a very brief period when it was necessary to strike. He had now, after weighing the question with the consideration which its gravity demanded, finally decided upon definite action. Whereupon he walked out of the library, leaving the other guests to comment as they would; or not comment at all, for all he cared. Like all masterful men, he went direct to the thing he wanted.

The ladies were having coffee under the maples, by the tea-table. At some little distance from the group Beatrice Chillingham was walking with Victoria, and it was evident that Victoria found Miss Chillingham's remarks amusing. These were the only two in the party who did not observe Mr. Crewe's approach. Mrs. Pomfret, when she saw the direction which he was taking, lost the thread of her conversation, and the lady who was visiting her wore a significant expression.

" Victoria," said Mr. Crewe, " let's go around to the other side of the house and look at the view."

Victoria started and turned to him from Miss Chillingham, with the fun still sparkling in her eyes. It was, perhaps, as well for Mr. Crewe that he had not overheard their conversation; but this might have applied to any man.

" Are you sure you can spare the time ? " she asked.

Mr. Crewe looked at his watch — probably from habit.

" I made it a point to leave the smoking room early," he replied.

" We're flattered — aren't we, Beatrice ? "

Miss Chillingham had a turned-up nose, and a face which was apt to be slightly freckled at this time of year ; for she contemned vanity and veils. For fear of doing her an injustice, it must be added that she was not at all bad-looking; quite the contrary ! All that can be noted in this brief space is that Beatrice Chillingham was — herself. Some people declared that she was possessed of the seven devils of her sex which Mr. Stockton wrote about.

"*I'm* flattered," she said, and walked off towards the tea-table with a glance in which Victoria read many meanings. Mr. Crewe paid no attention either to words, look, or departure.

"I want to talk to you," he said.

"You've made that very plain, at least," answered Victoria. "Why did you pretend it was the view?"

"Some conventionalities have to be observed, I suppose," he said. "Let's go around there. It *is* a good view."

"Don't you think this is a little — marked?" asked Victoria, surveying him with her hands behind her back.

"I can't help it if it is," said Mr. Crewe. "Every hour is valuable to me, and I've got to take my chances when I get 'em. For some reason, you haven't been down at Leith much this summer. Why didn't you telephone me, as I asked you?"

"Because I've suddenly grown dignified, I suppose," she said. "And then, of course, I hesitated to intrude upon such a person of importance as you have become, Humphrey."

"I've always got time to see you," he replied. "I always shall have. But I appreciate your delicacy. That sort of thing counts with a man more than most women know."

"Then I am repaid," said Victoria, "for exercising self-control."

"I find it always pays," declared Mr. Crewe, and he glanced at her with distinct approval. They were skirting the house, and presently came out upon a tiny terrace where young Ridley had made a miniature Italian garden when the Electric dividends had increased, and from which there was a vista of the shallows of the Blue. Here was a stone garden-seat which Mrs. Pomfret had brought from Italy, and over which she had quarrelled with the customs authorities. Mr. Crewe, with a wave of his hand, signified his pleasure that they should sit, and cleared his throat.

"It's just as well, perhaps," he began, "that we haven't had the chance to see each other earlier. When a man starts out upon an undertaking of the gravest importance, wherein he stakes his reputation, an undertaking for which he is ridiculed and reviled, he likes to have his judgment justified. He likes to be vindicated, especially in the eyes of — people whom he cares about. Personally, I never had any doubt that I should be the next governor, because I knew in the beginning that I had estimated public sentiment correctly. The man who succeeds in this world is the man who has sagacity enough to gauge public sentiment ahead of time, and the courage to act on his beliefs."

Victoria looked at him steadily. He was very calm, and he had one knee crossed over the other.

" And the sagacity," she added, " to choose his lieutenants in the fight."

" Exactly," said Mr. Crewe. " I have always declared, Victoria, that you had a natural aptitude for affairs."

" I have heard my father say," she continued, still maintaining her steady glance, " that Hamilton Tooting is one of the shrewdest politicians he has ever known. Isn't Mr. Tooting one of your right-hand men ? "

" He could hardly be called that," Mr. Crewe replied. " In fact, I haven't any what you might call ' right-hand men.' The large problems I have had to decide for myself. As for Tooting, he's well enough in his way ; he understands the tricks of the politicians — he's played 'em, I guess. He's uneducated ; he's merely a worker. You see," he went on, " one great reason why I've been so successful is because I've been practical. I've taken materials as I've found them."

" I see," answered Victoria, turning her head and gazing over the terrace at the sparkling reaches of the river. She remembered the close of that wintry afternoon in Mr. Crewe's house at the capital, and she was quite willing to do him exact justice, and to believe that he had forgotten it — which, indeed, was the case.

" I want to say," he continued, " that although I have known and — ahem — admired you for many years, Victoria, what has struck me most forcibly in your favour has

been your open-mindedness — especially on the great political questions this summer.   I have no idea how much
you know about them, but one would naturally have expected you, on account of your father, to be prejudiced.
Sometime, when I have more leisure, I shall go into them
fully with you.   And in the meantime I'll have my secretary send you the complete list of my speeches up to date,
and I know you will read them carefully."

" You are very kind, Humphrey," she said.

Absorbed in the presentation of his subject (which
chanced to be himself), Mr. Crewe did not observe that her
lips were parted, and that there were little creases around
her eyes.

" And sometime," said Mr. Crewe, " when all this has
blown over a little, I shall have a talk with your father.
He undoubtedly understands that there is scarcely any
question of my election.   He probably realizes, too, that he
has been in the wrong, and that railroad domination must
cease — he has already made several concessions, as you
know.   I wish you would tell him from me that when I am
governor, I shall make it a point to discuss the whole matter with him, and that he will find in me no foe of corporations.   Justice is what I stand for.   Temperamentally, I
am too conservative, I am too much of a business man, to
tamper with vested interests."

" I will tell him, Humphrey," said Victoria.

Mr. Crewe coughed, and looked at his watch once
more.

" And now, having made that clear," he said, " and
having only a quarter of an hour before I have to leave to
keep an appointment, I am going to take up another subject.   And I ask you to believe it is not done lightly, or
without due consideration, but as the result of some years
of thought."

Victoria turned to him seriously — and yet the creases
were still around her eyes.

" I can well believe it, Humphrey," she answered. " But
— have you time ? "

" Yes," he said, " I have learned the value of minutes."

"But not of hours, perhaps," she replied.

"That," said Mr. Crewe, indulgently, "is a woman's point of view. A man cannot dally through life, and your kind of woman has no use for a man who dallies. First, I will give you my idea of a woman."

"I am all attention," said Victoria.

"Well," said Mr. Crewe, putting the tops of his fingers together, "she should excel as a housewife. I haven't any use for your so-called intellectual woman. Of course, what I mean by a housewife is something a little less *bourgeoise;* she should be able to conduct an establishment with the neatness and despatch and economy of a well-run hotel. She should be able to seat a table instantly and accurately, giving to the prominent guests the prestige they deserve. Nor have I any sympathy with the notion that makes a married woman a law unto herself. She enters voluntarily into an agreement whereby she puts herself under the control of her husband: his interests, his career, his — "

"Comfort?" suggested Victoria.

"Yes, his comfort — all that comes first. And his establishment is conducted primarily, and his guests selected, in the interests of his fortunes. Of course, that goes without saying of a man in high place in public life. But he must choose for his wife a woman who is equal to all these things, — to my mind her highest achievement, — who makes the most of the position he gives her, presides at his table and entertainments, and reaches such people as, for any reason, he is unable to reach. I have taken the pains to point out these things in a general way, for obvious reasons. My greatest desire is to be fair."

"What," asked Victoria, with her eyes on the river, "what are the wages?"

Mr. Crewe laughed. Incidentally, he thought her profile very fine.

"I do not believe in flattery," he said, "but I think I should add to the qualifications personality and a sense of humour. I am quite sure I could never live with a woman who didn't have a sense of humour."

"I should think it would be a little difficult," said Victoria, "to get a woman with the qualifications you enumerate and a sense of humour thrown in."

"Infinitely difficult," declared Mr. Crewe, with more ardour than he had yet shown. "I have waited a good many years, Victoria."

"And yet," she said, "you have been happy. You have a perpetual source of enjoyment denied to some people."

"What is that?" he asked. It is natural for a man to like to hear the points of his character discussed by a discerning woman.

"Yourself," said Victoria, suddenly looking him full in the face. "You are complete, Humphrey, as it is. You are happily married already. Besides," she added, laughing a little, "the qualities you have mentioned—with the exception of the sense of humour—are not those of a wife, but of a business partner of the opposite sex. What you really want is a business partner with something like a fifth interest, and whose name shall not appear in the agreement."

Mr. Crewe laughed again. Nevertheless, he was a little puzzled over this remark.

"I am not sentimental," he began.

"You certainly are not," she said.

"You have a way," he replied, with a shade of reproof in his voice, "you have a way at times of treating serious things with a little less gravity than they deserve. I am still a young man, but I have seen a good deal of life, and I know myself pretty well. It is necessary to treat matrimony from a practical as well as a sentimental point of view. There wouldn't be half the unhappiness and divorces if people took time to do this, instead of rushing off and getting married immediately. And of course it is especially important for a man in my position to study every aspect of the problem before he takes a step."

By this time a deep and absorbing interest in a new aspect of Mr. Crewe's character had taken possession of Victoria.

"And you believe that, by taking thought, you can get the kind of a wife you want?" she asked.

"Certainly," he replied; "does that strike you as strange?"

"A little," said Victoria.   "Suppose," she added gently, "suppose that the kind of wife you'd want wouldn't want you?"

Mr. Crewe laughed again.

"That is a contingency which a strong man does not take into consideration," he answered.   "Strong men get what they want.   But upon my word, Victoria, you have a delicious way of putting things.   In your presence I quite forget the problems and perplexities which beset me.   That," he said, with delicate meaning, "that is another quality I should desire in a woman."

"It is one, fortunately, that isn't marketable," she said, "and it's the only quality you've mentioned that's worth anything."

"A woman's valuation," said Mr. Crewe.

"If it made you forget your own affairs, it would be priceless."

"Look here, Victoria," cried Mr. Crewe, uncrossing his knees, "joking's all very well, but I haven't time for it to-day.   And I'm in a serious mood.   I've told you what I want, and now that I've got to go in a few minutes, I'll come to the point.   I don't suppose a man could pay a woman a higher compliment than to say that his proposal was the result of some years of thought and study."

Here Victoria laughed outright, but grew serious again at once.

"Unless he proposed to her the day he met her.   That would be a real compliment."

"The man," said Mr. Crewe, impatiently, "would be a fool."

"Or else a person of extreme discernment," said Victoria.   "And love is lenient with fools.   By the way, Humphrey, it has just occurred to me that there's one quality which some people think necessary in a wife, which you didn't mention."

"What's that?"

"Love," said Victoria.

"Love, of course," he agreed; "I took that for granted."

"I supposed you did," said Victoria, meekly.

"Well, now, to come to the point—" he began again.

But she interrupted him by glancing at the watch on her gown, and rising.

"What's the matter?" he asked, with some annoyance.

"The fifteen minutes are up," she announced. "I cannot take the responsibility of detaining you."

"We will put in tantalizing as another attractive quality," he laughed. "I absolve you from all responsibility. Sit down."

"I believe you mentioned obedience," she answered, and sat down again at the end of the bench, resting her chin on her gloved hand, and looking at him. By this time her glances seemed to have gained a visibly disturbing effect. He moved a little nearer to her, took off his hat (which he had hitherto neglected to do), and thrust his hands abruptly into his pockets—as much as to say that he would not be responsible for their movements if they were less free.

"Hang it all, Victoria," he exclaimed, "I'm a practical man, and I try to look at this, which is one of the serious things in life, in a practical way."

"*One* of the serious things," she repeated, as though to herself.

"Yes," he said, "certainly."

"I merely asked to be sure of the weight you gave it. Go on."

"In a practical way, as I was saying. Long ago I suspected that you had most of those qualities."

"I'm overwhelmed, Humphrey," she cried, with her eyes dancing. "But—do you think I could cultivate the rest?"

"Oh, well," said Mr. Crewe, "I put it that way because no woman is perfect, and I dislike superlatives."

"I should think superlatives would be very hard to live with," she reflected. "But — dreadful thought! — suppose I should lack an essential?"

"What — for instance?"

"Love — for instance. But then you did not put it first. It was I who mentioned it, and you who took it for granted."

"*Affection* seems to be a more sensible term for it," he said. "Affection is the lasting and sensible thing. You mentioned a partnership, a word that singularly fits into my notion of marriage. I want to be honest with you, and understate my feelings on that subject."

Victoria, who had been regarding him with a curious look that puzzled him, laughed again.

"I have been hoping you haven't exaggerated them," she replied.

"They're stronger than you think," he declared. "I — I never felt this way in my life before. What I meant to say was, that I never understood running away with a woman."

"That does not surprise me," said Victoria.

"I shouldn't know where to run to," he proclaimed.

"Perhaps the woman would, if you got a clever one. At any rate, it wouldn't matter. One place is as good as another. Some go to Niagara, and some to Coney Island, and others to Venice. Personally, I should have no particular preference."

"No preference!" he exclaimed.

"I could be happy in Central Park," she declared.

"Fortunately," said Mr. Crewe, "you will never be called upon to make the trial."

Victoria was silent. Her thoughts, for the moment, had flown elsewhere, but Mr. Crewe did not appear to notice this. He fell back into the rounded hollow of the bench, and it occurred to him that he had never quite realized that profile. And what an ornament she would be to his table!

"I think, Humphrey," she said, "that we should be going back."

"One moment, and I'll have finished," he cried. "I've no doubt you are prepared for what I am going to say. I have purposely led up to it, in order that there might be no misunderstanding. In short, I have never seen another woman with personal characteristics so well suited for my life, and I want you to marry me, Victoria. I can offer you the position of the wife of a man with a public career — for which you are so well fitted."

Victoria shook her head slowly, and smiled at him.

"I couldn't fill the position," she said.

"Perhaps," he replied, smiling back at her, "perhaps I am the best judge of that."

"And you thought," she asked slowly, "that I was that kind of a woman?"

"I know it to be a practical certainty," said Mr. Crewe.

"Practical certainties," said Victoria, "are not always truths. If I should sign a contract, which I suppose, as a business man, you would want, — to live up to the letter of your specifications, — even then I could not do it. I should make life a torture for you, Humphrey. You see, I am honest with you, too — much as your offer dazzles me." And she shook her head again.

"That," exclaimed Mr. Crewe, impatiently, "is sheer nonsense. I want you, and I mean to have you."

There came a look into her eyes which Mr. Crewe did not see, because her face was turned from him.

"I could be happy," she said, "for days and weeks and years in a hut on the side of Sawanec. I could be happy in a farm-house where I had to do all the work. I am not the model housewife which your imagination depicts, Humphrey. I could live in two rooms and eat at an Italian restaurant — with the right man. And I am afraid the wrong one would wake up one day and discover that I had gone. I am sorry to disillusionize you, but I don't care a fig for balls and garden-parties and salons. It would be much more fun to run away from them to the queer places of the earth — with the right man. And I should have to possess one essential to put up with — greatness and what you call a public career."

"And what is that essential?" he asked.

"Love," said Victoria. He heard the word but faintly, for her face was still turned away from him. "You've offered me the things that are attainable by taking

thought, by perseverance, by pertinacity, by the outwit-
ting of your fellow-men, by the stacking of coins. And I
want — the unattainable, the divine gift which is bestowed,
which cannot be acquired. If it could be acquired,
Humphrey," she added, looking at him, " I am sure you
would acquire it — if you thought it worth while."

" I don't understand you," he said, — and looked it.

"No," said Victoria, " I was afraid you wouldn't. And
moreover, you never would. There is no use in my trying to make myself any clearer, and you'll have to keep
your appointment. I hesitate to contradict you, but I
am not the kind of woman you want. That is one reason
I cannot marry you. And the other is, that I do not love
you."

"You can't be in love with any one else ? " he cried.

" That does seem rather preposterous, I'll admit," she
answered. " But if I were, it wouldn't make any difference."

" You won't marry me ? " he said, getting to his feet.
There was incredulity in his voice, and a certain amount
of bewilderment. The thing was indeed incredible!

" No," said Victoria, " I won't."

And he had only to look into her face to see that it was
so. Hitherto *nil desperandum* had been a good working
motto, but something told him it was useless in this case.
He thrust on his hat and pulled out his watch.

" Well," he said, " that settles it. I must say I can't
see your point of view — but that settles it. I must say,
too, that your refusal is something of a shock after what
I had been led to expect after the past few years."

" The person you are in love with led you to expect it,
Humphrey, and that person is — yourself. You are in
love temporarily with your own ideal of me."

" And your refusal comes at an unfortunate time for
me," he continued, not heeding her words, " when I have
an affair on my hands of such magnitude, which requires
concentrated thought. But I'm not a man to cry, and
I'll make the best of it."

" If I thought it were more than a temporary dis-

appointment, I should be sorry for you," said Victoria.
" I remember that you felt something like this when Mr.
Rutter wouldn't sell you his land. The lady you really
want," she added, pointing with her parasol at the house,
" is in there, waiting for you."

Mr. Crewe did not reply to this prophecy, but followed
Victoria around the house to the group on the lawn,
where he bade his hostess a somewhat preoccupied farewell, and bowed distantly to the guests.

" He has so much on his mind," said Mrs. Pomfret.
" And oh, I quite forgot — Humphrey! " she cried, calling
after him, " Humphrey! "

" Yes," he said, turning before he reached his automobile. " What is it ? "

" Alice and I are going to the convention, you know,
and I meant to tell you that there would be ten in the
party — but I didn't have a chance." Here Mrs. Pomfret glanced at Victoria, who had been joined at once by
the tall Englishman. " Can you get tickets for ten ? "

Mr. Crewe made a memorandum.

" Yes," he said, " I'll get the tickets — but I don't see
what you want to go for."

CHAPTER XXV

MORE ADVENTURES

VICTORIA had not, of course, confided in Beatrice Chillingham what had occurred in the garden, although that lady had exhibited the liveliest interest, and had had her suspicions. After Mr. Crewe's departure Mr. Rangely, the tall young Englishman, had renewed his attentions assiduously, although during the interval in the garden he had found Miss Chillingham a person of discernment.

"She's not going to marry *that* chap, is she, Miss Chillingham?" he had asked.

"No," said Beatrice; "you have my word for it, she isn't."

As she was leaving, Mrs. Pomfret had taken Victoria's hand and drawn her aside, and looked into her face with a meaning smile.

"My dear!" she exclaimed, "he particularly asked that you be invited."

"Who?" said Victoria.

"Humphrey. He stipulated that you should be here."

"Then I'm very much obliged to him," said Victoria, "for I've enjoyed myself immensely. I like your Englishman so much."

"Do you?" said Mrs. Pomfret, searching Victoria's face, while her own brightened. "He's heir to one of the really good titles, and he has an income of his own. I couldn't put him up here, in this tiny box, because I have Mrs. Froude. We are going to take him to the convention — and if you'd care to go, Victoria — ?"

Victoria laughed.

"It isn't as serious as that," she said. "And I'm afraid I can't go to the convention — I have some things to do in the neighbourhood."

Mrs. Pomfret looked wise.

"He's a most attractive man, with the *best* prospects. It would be a splendid match for you, Victoria."

"Mrs. Pomfret," replied Victoria, wavering between amusement and a desire to be serious, "I haven't the slightest intention of making what you call a 'match.'" And there was in her words a ring of truth not to be mistaken.

Mrs. Pomfret kissed her.

"One never can tell what may happen," she said. "Think of him, Victoria. And your dear mother — perhaps you will know some day what the responsibility is of seeing a daughter well placed in life."

Victoria coloured, and withdrew her hand.

"I fear that time is a long way off, Mrs. Pomfret," she replied.

"I think so much of Victoria," Mrs. Pomfret declared a moment later to her guest; "she's like my own daughter. But at times she's so hopelessly unconventional. Why, I believe Rangely's actually going home with her."

"He asked her to drop him at the Inn," said Mrs. Froude. "He's head over heels in love already."

"It would be *such* a relief to dear Rose," sighed Mrs. Pomfret.

"I like the girl," replied Mrs. Froude, dryly. "She has individuality, and knows her own mind. Whoever she marries will have something to him."

"I devoutly hope so!" said Mrs. Pomfret.

It was quite true that Mr. Arthur Rangely had asked Victoria to drop him at the Inn. But when they reached it he made another request.

"Do you mind if I go a bit farther, Miss Flint?" he suggested. "I'd rather like the walk back."

Victoria laughed.

"Do come," she said.

He admired the country, but he looked at Victoria, and

asked an hundred exceedingly frank questions about
Leith, about Mrs. Pomfret, whom he had met at his
uncle's seat in Devonshire, and about Mr. Crewe and the
railroads in politics. Many of these Victoria parried, and
she came rapidly to the conclusion that Mr. Arthur Rangely
was a more astute person than — to a casual observer —
he would seem.

He showed no inclination to fix the limits of his walk,
and made no protest as she drove under the stone archway at the entrance of Fairview. Victoria was amused
and interested, and she decided that she liked Mr. Rangely.

"Will you come up for tea?" she asked. "I'll send
you home."

He accepted with alacrity. They had reached the
first turn when their attention was caught by the sight
of a buggy ahead of them, and facing towards them.
The horse, with the reins hanging loosely over the shafts,
had strayed to the side of the driveway and was con-
tentedly eating the shrubbery that lined it. Inside the
vehicle, hunched up in the corner of the seat, was a man
who presented an appearance of helplessness which struck
them both with a sobering effect.

"Is the fellow drunk?" said Mr. Rangely.

Victoria's answer was a little cry which startled him,
and drew his look to her. She had touched her horse
with the whip, and her eyes had widened in real alarm.

"It's Hilary Vane!" she exclaimed. "I — I wonder
what can have happened!"

She handed the reins to Mr. Rangely, and sprang out
and flew to Hilary's side.

"Mr. Vane!" she cried. "What's the matter? Are
you ill?"

She had never seen him look so. To her he had always
been as one on whom pity would be wasted, as one who
long ago had established his credit with the universe to
his own satisfaction. But now, suddenly, intense pity
welled up within her, and even in that moment she wondered if it could be because he was Austen's father. His
hands were at his sides, his head was fallen forward a

little, and his face was white. But his eyes frightened her most; instead of the old, semi-defiant expression which she remembered from childhood, they had in them a dumb suffering that went to her heart. He looked at her, tried to straighten up, and fell back again.

"N-nothing's the matter," he said, "nothing. A little spell. I'll be all right in a moment."

Victoria did not lose an instant, but climbed into the buggy at his side and gathered up the reins, and drew the fallen lap-robe over his knees.

"I'm going to take you back to Fairview," she said. "And we'll telephone for a doctor."

But she had underrated the amount of will left in him. He did not move, though indeed if he had seized the reins from her hands, he could have given her no greater effect of surprise. Life came back into the eyes at the summons, and dominance into the voice, although he breathed heavily.

"No, you're not," he said; "no, you're not. I'm going to Ripton — do you understand? I'll be all right in a minute, and I'll take the lines."

Victoria, when she got over her astonishment at this, reflected quickly. She glanced at him, and the light of his expression was already fading. There was some reason why he did not wish to go back to Fairview, and common sense told her that agitation was not good for him ; besides, they would have to telephone to Ripton for a physician, and it was quicker to drive there. Quicker to drive in her own runabout, did she dare to try to move him into it. She made up her mind.

"Please follow on behind with that trap," she called out to Rangely; "I'm going to Ripton."

He nodded understandingly, admiringly, and Victoria started Hilary's horse out of the bushes towards the entrance way. From time to time she let her eyes rest upon him anxiously.

"Are you comfortable?" she asked.

"Yes," he said, "yes. I'm all right. I'll be able to drive in a minute."

2 D

But the minutes passed, and he made no attempt to take the reins. Victoria had drawn the whalebone whip from its socket, and was urging on the horse as fast as humanity would permit ; and the while she was aware that Hilary's look was fixed upon her — in fact, never left her. Once or twice, in spite of her anxiety to get him home, Victoria blushed faintly, as she wondered what he was thinking about.

And all the while she asked herself what it was that had brought him to this condition. Victoria knew sufficient of life and had visited hospitals enough to understand that mental causes were generally responsible for such breakdowns — Hilary had had a shock. She remembered how in her childhood he had been the object of her particular animosity ; how she used to put out her tongue at him, and imitate his manner, and how he had never made the slightest attempt to conciliate her ; most people of this sort are sensitive to the instincts of children, but Hilary had not been. She remembered — how long ago it seemed now ! — the day she had given him, in deviltry, the clipping about Austen shooting Mr. Blodgett.

The Hilary Vane who sat beside her to-day was not the same man. It was unaccountable, but he was not. Nor could this changed estimate of him be attributed to her regard for Austen, for she recalled a day only a few months since — in June — when he had come up to Fairview and she was standing on the lawn, and she had looked at him without recognition; she had not, then, been able to bring herself to bow to him ; to her childhood distaste had been added the deeper resentment of Austen's wrongs. Her early instincts about Hilary had been vindicated, for he had treated his son abominably and driven Austen from his mother's home. To misunderstand and maltreat Austen Vane, of all people ! Austen, whose consideration for his father had been what it had ! Could it be that Hilary felt remorse ? Could it be that he loved Austen in some peculiar manner all his own ?

Victoria knew now — so strangely — that the man beside her was capable of love, and she had never felt that way

There was another chair against the low wainscoting, and Victoria drew it over beside Hilary and sat down in it. He did not seem to notice the action, and Euphrasia continued to stand. Standing seemed to be the natural posture of this remarkable woman, Victoria thought — a posture of vigilance, of defiance. A clock of one of the Austen grandfathers stood obscurely at the back of the hall, and the measured swing of its pendulum was all that broke the silence. *This* was Austen's home. It seemed impossible for her to realize that he could be the product of this environment — until a portrait on the opposite wall, above the stairs, came out of the gloom and caught her eye like the glow of light. At first, becoming aware of it with a start, she thought it a likeness of Austen himself. Then she saw that the hair was longer, and more wavy than his, and fell down a little over the velvet collar of a coat with a wide lapel and brass buttons, and that the original of this portrait had worn a stock. The face had not quite the strength of Austen's, she thought, but a wondrous sweetness and intellect shone from it, like an expression she had seen on his face. The chin rested on the hand, — an intellectual hand, — and the portrait brought to her mind that of a young English statesman she had seen in the National Gallery in London.

"That's Channing Austen, — he was minister to Spain."

Victoria started. It was Euphrasia who was speaking, and unmistakable pride was in her voice.

Fortunately for Victoria, who would not in the least have known what to reply, steps were heard on the porch, and Euphrasia opened the door. Mr. Rangely had returned.

"Here's the doctor, Miss Flint," he said, "and I'll wait for you outside."

Victoria rose as young Dr. Tredway came forward. They were old friends, and the doctor, it may be recalled, had been chiefly responsible for the preservation of the life of Mr. Zebulun Meader.

"I have sent for you, Doctor," she said, "against instructions and on my own responsibility. Mr. Vane is ill, although he refuses to admit it."

Dr. Tredway had a respect for Victoria and her opinions, and he knew Hilary. He opened the door a little wider, and looked critically at Mr. Vane.

"It's nothing but a spell," Hilary insisted. "I've had 'em before. I suppose it's natural that they should scare the women-folks some."

"What kind of a spell was it, Mr. Vane?" asked the doctor.

"It isn't worth talking about," said Hilary. "You might as well pick up that case of yours and go home again. I'm going down to the square in a little while."

"You see," Euphrasia put in, "he's made up his mind to kill himself."

"Perhaps," said the doctor, smiling a little, "Mr. Vane wouldn't object to Miss Flint telling me what happened."

Victoria glanced at the doctor and hesitated. Her sympathy for Hilary, her new understanding of him, urged her on — and yet never in her life had she been made to feel so distinctly an intruder. Here was the doctor, with his case; here was this extraordinary housekeeper, apparently ready to let Hilary walk to the square, if he wished, and to shut the door on their backs; and here was Hilary himself, who threatened at any moment to make his word good and depart from their midst. Only the fact that she was convinced that Hilary was in real danger made her relate, in a few brief words, what had occurred, and when she had finished Mr. Vane made no comment whatever.

Dr. Tredway turned to Hilary.

"I am going to take a mean advantage of you, Mr. Vane," he said, "and sit here awhile and talk to you. Would you object to waiting a little while, Miss Flint? I have something to say to you," he added significantly, "and this meeting will save me a trip to Fairview."

"Certainly I'll wait," she said.

"You can come along with me," said Euphrasia, "if you've a notion to."

Victoria was of two minds whether to accept this invitation. She had an intense desire to get outside, but this was counterbalanced by a sudden curiosity to see more of this strange woman who loved but one person in the world. Tom Gaylord had told Victoria that. She followed Euphrasia to the back of the hall.

"There's the parlour," said Euphrasia; "it's never be'n used since Mrs. Vane died, — but there it is."

"Oh," said Victoria, with a glance into the shadowy depths of the room, "please don't open it for me. Can't we go," she added, with an inspiration, "can't we go into — the kitchen?" She knew it was Euphrasia's place.

"Well," said Euphrasia, "I shouldn't have thought you'd care much about kitchens." And she led the way onward, through the little passage, to the room where she had spent most of her days. It was flooded with level, yellow rays of light that seemed to be searching the corners in vain for dust. Victoria paused in the doorway.

"I'm afraid you do me an injustice," she said. "I like some kitchens."

"You don't look as if you knew much about 'em," was Euphrasia's answer. With Victoria once again in the light, Euphrasia scrutinized her with appalling frankness, taking in every detail of her costume and at length raising her eyes to the girl's face. Victoria coloured. On her visits about the country-side she had met women of Euphrasia's type before, and had long ago ceased to be dismayed by their manner. But her instinct detected in Euphrasia a hostility for which she could not account.

In that simple but exquisite gown which so subtly suited her, the creation of which had aroused the artist in a celebrated Parisian dressmaker, Victoria was, indeed, a strange visitant in that kitchen. She took a seat by the window, and an involuntary exclamation of pleasure escaped her as her eyes fell upon the little, old-fashioned flower garden beneath it. The act and the exclamation for the moment disarmed Euphrasia.

"They were Sarah Austen's — Mrs. Vane's," she explained, "just as she planted them the year she died. I've always kept 'em just so."

"Mrs. Vane must have loved flowers," said Victoria.

"Loved 'em! They were everything to her — and the wild flowers, too. She used to wander off and spend whole days in the country, and come back after sunset with her arms full."

"It was nature she loved," said Victoria, in a low voice.

"That was it — nature," said Euphrasia. "She loved all nature. There wasn't a living, creeping thing that wahn't her friend. I've seen birds eat out of her hand in that window where you're settin', and she'd say to me, 'Phrasie, keep still! They'd love you, too, if they only knew you, but they're afraid you'll scrub 'em if you get hold of them, the way you used to scrub me."

Victoria smiled — but it was a smile that had tears in it. Euphrasia Cotton was standing in the shaft of sunlight at the other window, staring at the little garden.

"Yes, she used to say funny things like that, to make you laugh when you were all ready to cry. There wahn't many folks understood her. She knew every path and hilltop within miles of here, and every brook and spring, and she used to talk about that mountain just as if it was alive."

Victoria caught her breath.

"Yes," continued Euphrasia, "the mountain was alive for her. 'He's angry to-day, Phrasie. That's because you lost your temper and scolded Hilary.' It's a queer thing, but there have been hundreds of times since when he needed scoldin' bad, and I've looked at the mountain and held my tongue. It was just as if I saw *her* with that half-whimsical, half-reproachful expression in her eyes, holding up her finger at me. And there were other mornings when she'd say, 'The mountain's lonesome to-day, he wants me.' And I vow, I'd look at the mountain and it would seem lonesome. That sounds like nonsense, don't it?" Euphrasia demanded, with a sudden sharpness.

"No," said Victoria, "it seems very real to me."

The simplicity, the very ring of truth, and above all the absolute lack of self-consciousness in the girl's answer sustained the spell.

" She'd go when the mountain called her, it didn't make any difference whether it was raining — rain never appeared to do her any hurt. Nothin' *natural* ever did her any hurt. When she was a little child flittin' about like a wild creature, and she'd come in drenched to the skin, it was all I could do to catch her and change her clothes. She'd laugh at me. ' We're meant to be wet once in a while, Phrasie,' she'd say; ' that's what the rain's for, to wet us. It washes some of the wickedness out of us.' It was the unnatural things that hurt her — the unkind words and makin' her act against her nature. ' Phrasie,' she said once, ' I can't pray in the meeting-house with my eyes shut — I can't, I can't. I seem to know what they're all wishing for when they pray, — for more riches, and more comfort, and more security, and more importance. And God is such a long way off. I can't feel Him, and the pew hurts my back.' She used to read me some, out of a book of poetry, and one verse I got by heart — I guess her prayers were like that."

" Do you — remember the verse ? " asked Victoria.

Euphrasia went to a little shelf in the corner of the kitchen and produced a book, which she opened and handed to Victoria.

" There's the verse ! " she said ; " read it aloud. I guess you're better at that than I am."

And Victoria read : —

> " *Higher still and higher*
> *From the earth thou springest*
> *Like a cloud of fire;*
> *The blue deep thou wingest,*
> *And singing still dost soar, and soaring ever singest.*"

Victoria let fall the volume on her lap.

" There's another verse in that book she liked," said Euphrasia, " but it always was sad to me."

Victoria took the book, and read again: —

> " *Weary wind, who wanderest*
> *Like the world's rejected guest,*
> *Hast thou still some secret nest*
> *On the tree or billow ?* "

Euphrasia laid the volume tenderly on the shelf, and turned and faced Victoria.

" *She* was unhappy like that before she died," she exclaimed, and added, with a fling of her head towards the front of the house, " *He* killed her."

" Oh, no ! " cried Victoria, involuntarily rising to her feet. " Oh, no ! I'm sure he didn't mean to. He didn't understand her ! "

" He killed her," Euphrasia repeated. " Why didn't he understand her ? She was just as simple as a child, and just as trusting, and just as loving. He made her unhappy, and now he's driven her son out of her house, and made *him* unhappy. He's all of her I have left, and I won't see him unhappy."

Victoria summoned her courage.

" Don't you think," she asked bravely, " that Mr. Austen Vane ought to be told that his father is — in this condition ? "

" No," said Euphrasia, determinedly. " Hilary will have to send for him. This time it'll be Austen's victory."

" But hasn't he had — a victory ? " Victoria persisted earnestly. " Isn't this — victory enough ? "

" What do you mean ? " Euphrasia cried sharply.

" I mean," she answered, in a low voice, " I mean that Mr. Vane's son is responsible for his condition to-day. Oh — not consciously so. But the cause of this trouble is mental — can't you see it ? The cause of this trouble is remorse. Can't you see that it has eaten into his soul ? Do you wish a greater victory than this, or a sadder one ? Hilary Vane will not ask for his son — because he cannot. He has no more power to send that message than a man shipwrecked on an island. He can only give signals of distress — that some may heed. Would *she* have waited for such a victory as you demand ? And does Austen Vane desire it ? Don't you think that he would come to his father if he knew ? And have you any right to keep the news from him ? Have you any right to decide what their vengeance shall be ? "

Euphrasia had stood mute as she listened to these

words which she had so little expected, but her eyes flashed
and her breath came quickly. Never had she been so
spoken to ! Never had any living soul come between her
and her cherished object — the breaking of the heart of
Hilary Vane ! Nor, indeed, had that object ever been so
plainly set forth as Victoria had set it forth. And this
woman who dared to do this had herself brought unhappiness to Austen. Euphrasia had almost forgotten that,
such had been the strange harmony of their communion.

" Have *you* the right to tell Austen ? " she demanded.

" Have I ? " Victoria repeated. And then, as the full
meaning of the question came to her, the colour flooded
into her face, and she would have fled, if she could,
but Euphrasia's words came in a torrent.

" You've made him unhappy, as well as Hilary. He
loves you — but he wouldn't speak of it to you. Oh, no,
he didn't tell me who it was, but I never rested till I found
out. He never would have told me about it at all, or anybody else, but that I guessed it. I saw he was unhappy,
and I calculated it wasn't Hilary alone made him so. One
night he came in here, and I knew all at once — somehow
— there was a woman to blame, and I asked him, and he
couldn't lie to me. He said it wasn't anybody's fault but
his own — he wouldn't say any more than that, except that
he hadn't spoken to her. I always expected the time was
coming when there would be — a woman. And I never
thought the woman lived that he'd love who wouldn't love
him. I can't see how any woman could help lovin' him.

" And then I found out it was that railroad. It came
between Sarah Austen and her happiness, and now it's
come between Austen and his. Perhaps you don't love
him ! " cried Euphrasia. " Perhaps you're too rich and high
and mighty. Perhaps you're a-going to marry that fine young
man who came with you in the buggy. Since I heard who
you was, I haven't had a happy hour. Let me tell you
there's no better blood in the land than the Austen blood.
I won't mention the Vanes. If you've led him on, if you've
deceived him, I hope you may be unhappy as Sarah Austen
was — "

"Don't!" pleaded Victoria; "don't! Please don't!" and she seized Euphrasia by the arms, as though seeking by physical force to stop the intolerable flow of words. "Oh, you don't know me; you can't understand me if you say that. How can you be so cruel?"

In another moment she had gone, leaving Euphrasia standing in the middle of the floor, staring after her through the doorway.

CHAPTER XXVI

THE FOCUS OF WRATH

VICTORIA, after leaving Euphrasia, made her way around the house towards Mr. Rangely, who was waiting in the runabout, her one desire for the moment being to escape. Before she had reached the sidewalk under the trees, Dr. Tredway had interrupted her.

"Miss Flint," he called out, "I wanted to say a word to you before you went."

"Yes," she said, stopping and turning to him.

He paused a moment before speaking, as he looked into her face.

"I don't wonder this has upset you a little," he said; "a reaction always comes afterwards — even with the strongest of us."

"I am all right," she replied, unconsciously repeating Hilary's words. "How is Mr. Vane?"

"You have done a splendid thing," said the doctor, gravely. And he continued, after a moment: "It is Mr. Vane I wanted to speak to you about. He is an intimate friend, I believe, of your father's, as well as Mr. Flint's right-hand man in — in a business way in this State. Mr. Vane himself will not listen to reason. I have told him plainly that if he does not drop all business at once, the chances are ten to one that he will forfeit his life very shortly. I understand that there is a — a convention to be held at the capital the day after to-morrow, and that it is Mr. Vane's firm intention to attend it. I take the liberty of suggesting that you lay these facts before your father, as Mr. Flint probably has more influence with Hilary Vane than any other man. However," he added, seeing Victoria hesitate, "if there is any reason why you should not care to speak to Mr. Flint — "

415

"Oh, no," said Victoria; "I'll speak to him, certainly. I was going to ask you — have you thought of Mr. Austen Vane? He might be able to do something."

"Of course," said the doctor, after a moment, "it is an open secret that Austen and his father have — have, in short, never agreed. They are not now on speaking terms."

"Don't you think," asked Victoria, summoning her courage, "that Austen Vane ought to be told?"

"Yes," the doctor repeated decidedly, "I am sure of it. Everybody who knows Austen Vane as I do has the greatest admiration for him. You probably remember him in that Meader case, — he isn't a man one would be likely to forget, — and I know that this quarrel with his father isn't of Austen's seeking."

"Oughtn't he to be told — at once?" said Victoria.

"Yes," said the doctor; "time is valuable, and we can't predict what Hilary will do. At any rate, Austen ought to know — but the trouble is, he's at Jenney's farm. I met him on the way out there just before your friend the Englishman caught me. And unfortunately I have a case which I cannot neglect. But I can send word to him."

"I know where Jenney's farm is," said Victoria; "I'll drive home that way."

"Well," exclaimed Dr. Tredway, heartily, "that's good of you. Somebody who knows Hilary's situation ought to see him, and I can think of no better messenger than you."

And he helped her into the runabout.

Young Mr. Rangely being a gentleman, he refrained from asking Victoria questions on the drive out of Ripton, and expressed the greatest willingness to accompany her on this errand and to see her home afterwards. He had been deeply impressed, but he felt instinctively that after such a serious occurrence, this was not the time to continue to give hints of his admiration. He had heard in England that many American women whom he would be likely to meet socially were superficial and pleasure-loving; and Arthur Rangely came of a family which had long been cited as a vindication of a government by aristocracy, — a family which had never shirked responsibilities. It is not too much to say that he had pictured Victoria among his future tenantry; she had appealed to him first as a woman, but the incident of the afternoon had revealed her to him, as it were, under fire.

They spoke quietly of places they both had visited, of people whom they knew in common, until they came to the hills — the very threshold of Paradise on that September evening. Those hills never failed to move Victoria, and they were garnished this evening in no earthly colours, — rose-lighted on the billowy western pasture slopes and pearl in the deep clefts of the streams, and the lordly form of Sawanec shrouded in indigo against a flame of orange. And orange fainted, by the subtlest of colour changes, to azure in which swam, so confidently, a silver evening star.

In silence they drew up before Mr. Jenney's ancestral trees, and through the deepening shadows beneath these the windows of the farm-house glowed with welcoming light. At Victoria's bidding Mr. Rangely knocked to ask for Austen Vane, and Austen himself answered the summons. He held a book in his hand, and as Rangely spoke she saw Austen's look turn quickly to her, and met it through the gathering gloom between them. In an instant he was at her side, looking up questioningly into her face, and the telltale blood leaped into hers. What must he think of her for coming again? She could not speak of her errand too quickly.

"Mr. Vane, I came to leave a message."

"Yes?" he said, and glanced at the broad-shouldered, well-groomed figure of Mr. Rangely, who was standing at a discreet distance.

"Your father has had an attack of some kind, — please don't be alarmed, he seems to be recovered now, — and I thought and Dr. Tredway thought you ought to know about it. The doctor could not leave Ripton, and I offered to come and tell you."

2 E

"An attack?" he repeated.

"Yes." And she related simply how she had found
Hilary at Fairview, and how she had driven him home.
But, during the whole of her recital, she could not rid
herself of the apprehension that he was thinking her interference unwarranted, her coming an indelicate repetition
of the other visit. As he stood there listening in the
gathering dusk, she could not tell from his face what he
thought. His expression, when serious, had a determined,
combative, almost grim note in it, which came from a
habit he had of closing his jaw tightly; and his eyes were
like troubled skies through which there trembled an
occasional flash of light.

Victoria had never felt his force so strongly as now,
and never had he seemed more distant; at times — she had
thought — she had had glimpses of his soul; to-night he was
inscrutable, and never had she realized the power (which she
had known he must possess) of making himself so. And
to her? Her pride forbade her recalling at that moment
the confidences which had passed between them and
which now seemed to have been so impossible. He was
serious because he was listening to serious news — she told
herself. But it was more than this : he had shut himself
up, he was impenetrable. Shame seized her ; yes, and
anger ; and shame again at the remembrance of her talk
with Euphrasia — and anger once more. Could he think
that she would make advances to tempt his honour, and
risk his good opinion and her own?

Confidence is like a lute-string, giving forth sweet
sounds in its perfection; there are none so discordant as
when it snaps.

Victoria scarcely heard Austen's acknowledgments of
her kindness, so perfunctory did they seem, so unlike the
man she had known ; and her own protestations that she
had done nothing to merit his thanks were to her quite
as unreal. She introduced him to the Englishman.

"Mr. Rangely has been good enough to come with me,"
she said.

"I've never seen anybody act with more presence of

mind than Miss Flint," Rangely declared, as he shook
Austen's hand. "She did just the right thing, without
wasting any time whatever."

"I'm sure of it," said Austen, cordially enough. But
to Victoria's keener ear, other tones which she had heard
at other times were lacking. Nor could she, clever as
she was, see the palpable reason standing before her!

"I say," said Rangely, as they drove away, "he strikes
me as a remarkably sound chap, Miss Flint. There is
something unusual about him, something clean cut."

"I've heard other people say so," Victoria replied.
For the first time since she had known him, praise of
Austen was painful to her. What was this curious attraction that roused the interest of all who came in contact
with him? The doctor had it, Mr. Redbrook, Jabe
Jenney, — even Hamilton Tooting, she remembered.
And he attracted women as well as men — it must be
so. Certainly her own interest in him — a man beyond
the radius of her sphere — and their encounters had been
strange enough! And must she go on all her life hearing praises of him? Of one thing she was sure — who
was not? — that Austen Vane had a future. He was the
type of man which is inevitably impelled into places of
trust.

Manly men, as a rule, do not understand women. They
humour them blindly, seek to comfort them — if they
weep — with caresses, laugh with them if they have
leisure, and respect their curious and unaccountable
moods by keeping out of the way. Such a husband was
Arthur Rangely destined to make ; a man who had seen
any number of women and understood none, — as wondrous mechanisms. He had merely acquired the faculty
of appraisal, although this does not mean that he was
incapable of falling in love.

Mr. Rangely could not account for the sudden access
of gayety in Victoria's manner as they drove to Fairview
through the darkness, nor did he try. He took what the
gods sent him, and was thankful. When he reached
Fairview he was asked to dinner, as he could not possibly

get back to the Inn in time. Mr. Flint had gone to Sumner with the engineers, leaving orders to be met at the East Tunbridge station at ten ; and Mrs. Flint, still convalescent, had dined in her sitting room. Victoria sat opposite her guest in the big dining room, and Mr. Rangely pronounced the occasion decidedly jolly. He had, he proclaimed, with the exception of Mr. Vane's deplorable accident, never spent a better day in his life.

Victoria wondered at her own spirits, which were feverish, as she listened to transatlantic gossip about girls she had known who had married Mr. Rangely's friends, and stories of Westminster and South Africa, and certain experiences of Mr. Rangely's at other places than Leith on the American continent, which he had grown sufficiently confidential to relate. At times, lifting her eyes to him as he sat smoking after dinner on the other side of the library fire, she almost doubted his existence. He had come into her life at one o'clock that day — it seemed an eternity since. And a subconscious voice, heard but not heeded, told her that in the awakening from this curious dream he would be associated in her memory with tragedy, just as a tune or a book or a game of cards reminds one of painful periods of one's existence. To-morrow the episode would be a nightmare ; to-night her one desire was to prolong it.

And poor Mr. Rangely little imagined the part he was playing — as little as he deserved it. Reluctant to leave, propriety impelled him to ask for a trap at ten, and it was half past before he finally made his exit from the room with a promise to pay his respects soon — very soon.

Victoria stood before the fire listening to the sound of the wheels gradually growing fainter, and her mind refused to work. Hanover Street, Mr. Jenney's farm-house, were unrealities too. Ten minutes later — if she had marked the interval — came the sound of wheels again, this time growing louder. Then she heard a voice in the hall, her father's voice.

"Towers, who was that?"

"A young gentleman, sir, who drove home with Miss Victoria. I didn't get his name, sir."

"Has Miss Victoria retired?"

"She's in the library, sir. Here are some telegrams, Mr. Flint."

Victoria heard her father tearing open the telegrams and walking towards the library with slow steps as he read them. She did not stir from her place before the fire. She saw him enter and, with a characteristic movement which had become almost habitual of late, crush the telegrams in front of him with both hands.

"Well, Victoria?" he said.

"Well, father?"

It was characteristic of him, too, that he should momentarily drop the conversation, unravel the ball of telegrams, read one, crush them once more, — a process that seemed to give him relief. He glanced at his daughter — she had not moved. Whatever Mr. Flint's original character may have been in his long-forgotten youth on the wind-swept hill farm in Truro, his methods of attack lacked directness now; perhaps a long business and political experience were responsible for this trait.

"Your mother didn't come down to dinner, I suppose."

"No," said Victoria.

"Simpson tells me the young bull got loose and cut himself badly. He says it's the fault of the Eben Fitch you got me to hire."

"I don't believe it was Eben's fault — Simpson doesn't like him," Victoria replied.

"Simpson tells me Fitch drinks."

"Let a man get a bad name," said Victoria, "and Simpson will take care that he doesn't lose it." The unexpected necessity of defending one of her protégés aroused her. "I've made it a point to see Eben every day for the last three months, and he hasn't touched a drop. He's one of the best workers we have on the place."

"I've got too much on my mind to put up with that kind of thing," said Mr. Flint, "and I won't be worried here on the place. I *can* get capable men to tend cattle, at least. I have to put up with political rascals who rob and deceive me as soon as my back is turned, I have to put up with inefficiency and senility, but I won't have it at home."

"Fitch will be transferred to the gardener if you think best," she said.

It suddenly occurred to Victoria, in the light of a new discovery, that in the past her father's irritability had not extended to her. And this discovery, she knew, ought to have some significance, but she felt unaccountably indifferent to it. Mr. Flint walked to a window at the far end of the room and flung apart the tightly closed curtains before it.

"I never can get used to this new-fangled way of shutting everything up tight," he declared. "When I lived in Centre Street, I used to read with the curtains up every night, and nobody ever shot me." He stood looking out at the starlight for a while, and turned and faced her again.

"I haven't seen much of you this summer, Victoria," he remarked.

"I'm sorry, father. You know I always like to walk with you every day you are here." He had aroused her sufficiently to have a distinct sense that this was not the time to refer to the warning she had given him that he was working too hard. But he was evidently bent on putting this construction on her answer.

"Several times I have asked for you, and you have been away," he said.

"If you had only let me know, I should have made it a point to be at home."

"How can I tell when these idiots will give me any rest?" he asked. He crushed the telegrams again, and came down the room and stopped in front of her. "Perhaps there has been a particular reason why you have not been at home as much as usual."

"A particular reason?" she repeated, in genuine surprise.

"Read that!" he said.

believe me? I have no reason to think that you would. I am your daughter, I have been your most intimate companion, and I had the right to think that you should have formed some estimate of my character. Suppose I told you that Austen Vane has avoided me, that he would not utter a word against you or in favour of himself? Suppose I told you that I, your daughter, thought there might be two sides to the political question that is agitating you, and wished in fairness to hear the other side, — as I intended to tell you when you were less busy? Suppose I told you that Austen Vane was the soul of honour, that he saw your side and presented it as ably as you have presented it? that he had refrained in many matters which might have been of advantage to him — although I did not hear of them from him — on account of his father? Would you believe me?"

"And suppose I told you," cried Mr. Flint — so firmly fastened on him was the long habit of years of talking another down, "suppose I told you that this was the most astute and the craftiest course he could take? I've always credited him with brains. Suppose I told you that he was intriguing now, as he has been all along, to obtain the nomination for the governorship? Would you believe me?"

"No," answered Victoria, quietly.

Mr. Flint went to the lamp, unrolled the ball of telegrams, seized one and crossed the room quickly, and held it out to her. His hand shook a little.

"Read that!" he said.

She read it: "*Estimate that more than half of delegates from this section pledged to Henderson will go to Austen Vane when signal is given in convention. Am told on credible authority same is true of other sections, including many of Hunt's men and Crewe's. This is the result of quiet but persistent political work I spoke about.* BILLINGS."

She handed the telegram back to her father in silence.

"Do you believe it now?" he demanded exultantly.

"Who is the man whose name is signed to that message?" she asked.

Mr. Flint eyed her narrowly.

"What difference does that make?" he demanded.

"None," said Victoria. But a vision of Mr. Billings rose before her. He had been pointed out to her as the man who had opposed Austen in the Meader suit. "If the bishop of the diocese signed it, I would not believe that Austen Vane had anything to do with the matter."

"Ah, you defend him!" cried Mr. Flint. "I thought so — I thought so. I take off my hat to him, he is a cleverer man even than I. His own father, whom he has ruined, comes up here and defends him."

"Does Hilary Vane defend him?" Victoria asked curiously.

"Yes," said Mr. Flint, beside himself; "incredible as it may seem, he does. I have Austen Vane to thank for still another favour — he is responsible for Hilary's condition to-day. He has broken him down — he has made him an imbecile. The convention is scarcely thirty-six hours off, and Hilary is about as fit to handle it as — as Eben Fitch. Hilary, who never failed me in his life!"

Victoria did not speak for a moment, and then she reached out her hand quickly and laid it on his that still held the telegram. A lounge stood on one side of the fireplace, and she drew him gently to it, and he sat down at her side. His acquiescence to her was a second nature, and he was once more bewildered. His anger now seemed to have had no effect upon her whatever.

"I waited up to tell you about Hilary Vane, father," she said gently. "He has had a stroke, which I am afraid is serious."

"A stroke!" cried Mr. Flint. "Why didn't you tell me? How do you know?"

Victoria related how she had found Hilary coming away from Fairview, and what she had done, and the word Dr. Tredway had sent.

"Good God!" cried Mr. Flint, "he won't be able to go to the convention!" And he rose and pressed the electric button. "Towers," he said, when the butler appeared, "is Mr. Freeman still in my room? Tell him

to telephone to Ripton at once and find out how Mr.
Hilary Vane is. They'll have to send a messenger.
That accounts for it," he went on, rather to himself than
to Victoria, and he began to pace the room once more;
" he looked like a sick man when he was here. And who
have we got to put in his place? Not a soul! "

He paced awhile in silence. He appeared to have forgotten Victoria.

" Poor Hilary! " he said again, " poor Hilary! I'll go
down there the first thing in the morning."

Another silence, and then Mr. Freeman, the secretary,
entered.

" I telephoned to Dr. Tredway's, Mr. Flint. I thought
that would be quickest. Mr. Vane has left home. They
don't know where he's gone."

" Left home! It's impossible! " and he glanced at
Victoria, who had risen to her feet. " There must be
some mistake."

" No, sir. First I got the doctor, who said that Mr.
Vane was gone — at the risk of his life. And then I
talked to Mr. Austen Vane himself, who was there con-
sulting with the doctor. It appears that Mr. Hilary
Vane had left home by eight o'clock, when Mr. Austen
Vane got there."

" Hilary's gone out of his head," exclaimed Mr. Flint.
" This thing has unhinged him. Here, take these tele-
grams. No, wait a minute, I'll go out there. Call up
Billings, and see if you can get Senator Whitredge."

He started out of the room, halted, and turned his head
and hesitated.

" Father," said Victoria, " I don't think Hilary Vane is
out of his mind."

" You don't? " he said quickly. " Why? "

By some unaccountable change in the atmosphere, of
which Mr. Flint was unconscious, his normal relation to
his daughter had been suddenly reëstablished. He was
giving ear, as usual, to her judgment.

" Did Hilary Vane tell you he would go to the convention? " she asked.

" Yes." In spite of himself, he had given the word an apologetic inflection.

" Then he has gone already," she said. " I think, if you will telephone a little later to the State capital, you will find that he is in his room at the Pelican Hotel."

" By thunder, Victoria! " he ejaculated, " you may be right. It would be like him."

CHAPTER XXVII

THE ARENA AND THE DUST

Alas! that the great genius who described the battle of
Waterloo is not alive to-day and on this side of the At-
lantic, for a subject worthy of his pen is at hand, — nothing less than that convention of conventions at which the
Honourable Humphrey Crewe of Leith is one of the candidates. One of the candidates, indeed! Will it not be
known, as long as there are pensions, and a governor and
a state-house and a seal and State sovereignty and a staff,
as the *Crewe Convention?* How charge after charge was
made during the long, hot day and into the night; how the
delegates were carried out limp and speechless and starved
and wet through, and carried in to vote again, — will all
be told in time. But let us begin at the beginning, which
is the day before.

But look! it is afternoon, and the candidates are arriving at the Pelican. The Honourable Adam B. Hunt is
the first, and walks up the hill from the station escorted
by such prominent figures as the Honourables Brush Bascom and Jacob Botcher, and surrounded by enthusiastic
supporters who wear buttons with the image of their
leader — goatee and all — and the singularly prophetic
superscription, *To the Last Ditch!* Only veterans and
experts like Mr. Bascom and Mr. Botcher can recognize
the last ditch when they see it.

Another stir in the street — occasioned by the appearance
of the Honourable Giles Henderson, — of the blameless life.
Utter a syllable against him if you can! These words
should be inscribed on his buttons if he had any — but he
has none. They seem to be, unuttered, on the tongues of
the gentlemen who escort the Honourable Giles, United

States Senator Greene and the Honourable Elisha Jane, who has obtained leave of absence from his consular post to attend the convention, — and incidentally to help prepare for it.

But who and what is this? The warlike blast of a siren horn is heard, the crowd in the lobby rushes to the doors, people up-stairs fly to the windows, and the Honourable Adam B. Hunt leans out and nearly falls out, but is rescued by Division Superintendent Manning of the Northeastern Railroads, who has stepped in from Number Seven to give a little private tug of a persuasive nature to the Honourable Adam's coat-tails. A red Leviathan comes screaming down Main Street with a white trail of dust behind it, smothering the occupants of vehicles which have barely succeeded in getting out of the way, and makes a spectacular finish before the Pelican by sliding the last fifty feet on locked rear wheels.

A group in the street raises a cheer. It is the People's Champion! Dust coat, gauntlets, goggles, cannot hide him; and if they did, some one would recognize that voice, familiar now and endeared to many, and so suited to command : —

" Get that baggage off, and don't waste any time ! Jump out, Watling — that handle turns the other way. Well, Tooting, are the headquarters ready ? What was the matter that I couldn't get you on the telephone ? " (To the crowd.) " Don't push in and scratch the paint. He's going to back out in a minute, and somebody'll get hurt."

Mr. Hamilton Tooting (Colonel Hamilton Tooting that is to be — it being an open secret that he is destined for the staff) is standing hatless on the sidewalk ready to receive the great man. The crowd in the rotunda makes a lane, and Mr. Crewe, glancing neither to the right nor left, walks upstairs ; and scarce is he installed in the bridal suite, surrounded by his faithful workers for reform, than that amazing reception begins. Mr. Hamilton Tooting, looking the very soul of hospitality, stands by the doorway with an open box of cigars in his left hand, pressing them upon the visitors with his right. Reform, contrary to the preconceived opinion of many, is not made of icicles, nor answers with a stone a request for bread. As the hours run on, the visitors grow more and more numerous, and after supper the room is packed to suffocation, and a long line is waiting in the corridor, marshalled and kept in good humour by able lieutenants; while Mr. Crewe is dimly to be perceived through clouds of incense burning in his honour — and incidentally at his expense — with a welcoming smile and an appropriate word for each caller, whose waistcoat pockets, when they emerge, resemble cartridge-belts of cigars.

More cigars were hastily sent for, and more. There are to be but a thousand delegates to the convention, and at least two thousand men have already passed through the room — and those who don't smoke have friends. It is well that Mr. Crewe has stuck to his conservative habit of not squeezing hands too hard.

" Isn't that Mr. Putter, who keeps a livery-stable here? " inquired Mr. Crewe, about nine o'clock — our candidate having a piercing eye of his own.   Mr. Putter's coat, being brushed back, has revealed six cigars.

" Why, yes — yes," says Mr. Watling.

" Is he a delegate? " Mr. Crewe demanded.

" Why, I guess he must be," says Mr. Watling.

But Mr. Putter is not a delegate.

" You've stood up and made a grand fight, Mr. Crewe," says another gentleman, a little later, with a bland, smooth-shaven face and strong teeth to clinch Mr. Crewe's cigars. " I wish I was fixed so as I could vote for you."

Mr. Crewe looks at him narrowly.

" You look very much like a travelling man from New York who tried to sell me farm machinery," he answers. " Where are you from? "

" You ain't exactly what they call a tyro, are you? " says the bland-faced man; " but I guess you've missed the mark this shot.   Well, so long."

" Hold on ! " says Mr. Crewe, " Watling will talk to you."

And, as the gentleman follows Mr. Watling through the

2 F

press, a pamphlet drops from his pocket to the floor. It is marked *Catalogue of the Raines Farm Implement Company*. Mr. Watling picks it up and hands it to the gentleman, who winks again.

"Tim," he says, "where can we sit down? How much are you getting out of this? Brush and Jake Botcher are bidding high down-stairs, and the quotation on delegates has gone up ten points in ten minutes. It's mighty good of you to remember old friends, Tim, even if they're not delegates."

Meanwhile Mr. Crewe is graciously receiving others who are crowding to him.

"How are you, Mr. Giddings? How are the cows? I carry some stock that'll make you sit up — I believe I told you when I was down your way. Of course, mine cost a little money, but that's one of my hobbies. Come and see 'em some day. There's a good hotel in Ripton, and I'll have you met there and drive you back."

Thus, with a genial and kindly remark to each, he passes from one to the other, and when the members of the press come to him for his estimate of the outcome on the morrow, he treats them with the same courtly consideration.

"Estimate!" cries Mr. Crewe. "Where have your eyes been to-night, my friends? Have you seen the people coming into these headquarters? Have you seen 'em pouring into any other headquarters? All the State and federal office-holders in the country couldn't stop me now. Estimate! I'll be nominated on the first ballot."

They wrote it down.

"Thank you, Mr. Crewe," they said; "that's the kind of talk we like to hear."

"And don't forget," said Mr. Crewe, "to mention this reception in the accounts."

Mr. Tooting, who makes it a point from time to time to reconnoitre, saunters halfway down-stairs and surveys the crowded rotunda from the landing. Through the blue medium produced by the burning of many cigars (mostly Mr. Crewe's) he takes note of the burly form of Mr.

Thomas Gaylord beside that of Mr. Redbrook and other
rural figures ; he takes note of a quiet corner with a ring
of chairs surrounded by scouts and outposts, although it
requires a trained eye such as Mr. Tooting's to recognize
them as such — for they wear no uniforms. They are, in
truth, minor captains of the feudal system, and their present duties consist (as Mr. Tooting sees clearly) in pre-
venting the innocent and inquisitive from unprofitable
speech with the Honourable Jacob Botcher, who sits in
the inner angle conversing cordially with those who are
singled out for this honour. Still other scouts conduct
some of the gentlemen who have talked with Mr. Botcher
up the stairs to a mysterious room on the second floor.
Mr. Tooting discovers that the room is occupied by the
Honourable Brush Bascom ; Mr. Tooting learns with indignation that certain of these guests of Mr. Bascom's are
delegates pledged to Mr. Crewe, whereupon he rushes back
to the bridal suite to report to his chief. The cigars are
giving out again, and the rush has slackened, and he
detaches the People's Champion from the line and draws
him to the inner room.

" Brush Bascom's conducting a bourse on the second
floor and is running the price up right along," cried the
honest and indignant Mr. Tooting. "He's stringin'
Adam Hunt all right. They say he's got Adam to cough
up six thousand extra since five o'clock, but the question
is — ain't he stringin' us ? He paid six hundred for a
block of ten not quarter of an hour ago — and nine of 'em
were our delegates."

It must be remembered that these are Mr. Tooting's
words, and Mr. Crewe evidently treated them as the product of that gentleman's vivid imagination. Translated,
they meant that the Honourable Adam B. Hunt has no
chance for the nomination, but that the crafty Messrs.
Botcher and Bascom are inducing him to think that he
has — by making a supreme effort. The supreme effort
is represented by six thousand dollars.

"Are you going to lie down under that?" Mr. Tooting demanded, forgetting himself in his zeal for reform

and Mr. Crewe. But Mr. Tooting, in some alarm, perceived the eye of his chief growing virtuous and glassy.

"I guess I know when *I'm* strung, as you call it, Mr. Tooting," he replied severely. "This cigar bill alone is enough to support a large family for several months."

And with this merited reproof he turned on his heel and went back to his admirers without, leaving Mr. Tooting aghast, but still resourceful. Ten minutes later that gentleman was engaged in a private conversation with his colleague, the Honourable Timothy Watling.

"He's up on his hind legs at last," said Mr. Tooting; "it looks as if he was catching on."

Mr. Watling evidently grasped these mysterious words, for he looked grave.

"He thinks he's got the nomination cinched, don't he?"

"That's the worst of it," cried Mr. Tooting.

"I'll see what I can do," said the Honourable Tim. "He's always talking about *thorough;* let him do it thorough." And Mr. Watling winked.

"*Thorough*," repeated Mr. Tooting, delightedly.

"That's it — Colonel," said Mr. Watling. "Have you ordered your uniform yet, Ham?"

Mr. Tooting plainly appreciated this joke, for he grinned.

"I guess you won't starve if you don't get that commissionership, Tim," he retorted.

"And I guess," returned Mr. Watling, "that you won't go naked if you don't have a uniform."

Victoria's surmise was true. At ten o'clock at night, two days before the convention, a tall figure had appeared in the empty rotunda of the Pelican, startling the clerk out of a doze. He rubbed his eyes and stared, recognized Hilary Vane, and yet failed to recognize him. It was an extraordinary occasion indeed which would cause Mr. McAvoy to lose his aplomb; to neglect to seize the pen and dip it, with a flourish, into the ink, and extend its handle towards the important guest; to omit a few fitting words of welcome. It was Hilary who got the pen first, and

wrote his name in silence, and by this time Mr. McAvoy
had recovered his presence of mind sufficiently to wield
the blotter.

"We didn't expect you to-night, Mr. Vane," he said, in
a voice that sounded strange to him, "but we've kept
Number Seven, as usual. Front !"

"The old man's seen his day, I guess," Mr. McAvoy
remarked, as he studied the register with a lone reporter.
"This Crewe must have got in on 'em hard, from what
they tell me, and Adam Hunt has his dander up."

The next morning at ten o'clock, while the workmen
were still tacking down the fireproof carpets in headquarters upstairs, and before even the advance guard of
the armies had begun to arrive, the eye of the clerk was
caught by a tall young man rapidly approaching the desk.

"Is Mr. Hilary Vane here ?"

"He's in Number Seven," said Mr. McAvoy, who was
cudgelling his brains. "Give me your card, and I'll send
it up."

"I'll go up," said the caller, turning on his heel and suiting the action to the word, leaving Mr. McAvoy to make
active but futile inquiries among the few travelling men
and reporters seated about.

"Well, if you fellers don't know him, I give up,"
said the clerk, irritably, "but he looks as if he ought to
be somebody. He knows his business, anyway."

In the meantime Mr. Vane's caller had reached the first
floor; he hesitated just a moment before knocking at the
door of Number Seven, and the Honourable Hilary's voice
responded. The door opened.

Hilary was seated, as usual, beside the marble-topped
table, which was covered with newspapers and memoranda. In the room were Mr. Ridout, the capital lawyer,
and Mr. Manning, the division superintendent. There
was an instant of surprised silence on the part of the three,
but the Honourable Hilary was the only one who remained
expressionless.

"If you don't mind, gentlemen," said the visitor, "I
should like to talk to my father for a few minutes."

"Why, certainly, Austen," Mr. Ridout replied, with an attempt at heartiness. Further words seemed to fail him, and he left the room somewhat awkwardly, followed by Mr. Manning; but the Honourable Hilary appeared to take no notice of this proceeding.

"Judge," said Austen, when the door had closed behind them, "I won't keep you long. I didn't come down here to plead with you to abandon what you believe to be your duty, because I know that would be useless. I have had a talk with Dr. Tredway," he added gently, "and I realize that you are risking your life. If I could take you back to Ripton I would, but I know that I cannot. I see your point of view, and if I were in your place I should do the same thing. I only wanted to tell you this —" Austen's voice caught a little, "if — anything should happen, I shall be at Mrs. Peasley's on Maple Street, opposite the Duncan house." He laid his hand for an instant, in the old familiar way, on Hilary's shoulder, and looked down into the older man's face. It may have been that Hilary's lips trembled a little. "I — I'll see you later, Judge, when it's all over. Good luck to you."

He turned slowly, went to the door and opened it, gave one glance at the motionless figure in the chair, and went out. He did not hear the voice that called his name, for the door had shut.

Mr. Ridout and Mr. Manning were talking together in low tones at the head of the stairs. It was the lawyer who accosted Austen.

"The old gentleman don't seem to be quite himself, Austen. Don't seem well. You ought to hold him in — he can't work as hard as he used to."

"I think you'll find, Mr. Ridout," answered Austen, deliberately, "that he'll perform what's required of him with his usual efficiency."

Mr. Ridout followed Austen's figure with his eyes until he was hidden by a turn of the stairs. Then he whistled.

"I can't make that fellow out," he exclaimed. "Never could. All I know is that if Hilary Vane pulls us through this mess, in the shape he's in, it'll be a miracle.

His mind seems sound enough to-day — but he's lost his grip, I tell you. I don't wonder Flint's beside himself. Here's Adam Hunt with both feet in the trough, and no more chance of the nomination than I have, and Bascom and Botcher teasing him on, and he's got enough votes with Crewe to lock up that convention for a dark horse. And who's the dark horse?"

Mr. Manning, who was a silent man, pointed with his thumb in the direction Austen had taken.

"Hilary Vane's own son," said Mr. Ridout, voicing the gesture; "they tell me that Tom Gaylord's done some pretty slick work. Now I leave it to you, Manning, if that isn't a mess!"

At this moment the conversation was interrupted by the appearance on the stairway of the impressive form of United States Senator Whitredge, followed by a hall boy carrying the senatorial gripsack. The senator's face wore a look of concern which could not possibly be misinterpreted.

"How's Hilary?" were his first words.

Mr. Ridout and Mr. Manning glanced at each other.

"He's in Number Seven; you'd better take a look at him, Senator."

The senator drew breath, directed that his grip be put in the room where he was to repose that night, produced an amber cigar-holder from a case, and a cigar from his waistcoat pocket.

"I thought I'd better come down early," he said; "things aren't going just as they should, and that's the truth. In fact," he added, significantly tapping his pocket, "I've got a letter from Mr. Flint to Hilary which I may have to use. You understand me."

"I guessed as much," said Mr. Ridout.

"Ahem! I saw young Vane going out of the hotel just now," the senator remarked. "I am told, on pretty good authority, that under certain circumstances, which I must confess seem not unlikely at present, he may be a candidate for the nomination. The fact that he is in town tends to make the circumstance more probable."

"He's just been in to see Hilary," said Mr. Ridout.

"You don't tell me!" said the senator, pausing as he lighted his cigar; "I was under the impression that — that they were not on speaking terms."

"They've evidently got together now," said Mr. Ridout. "I wonder how old Hilary *would* feel about it. *We* couldn't do much with Austen Vane if he was governor — that's a sure thing."

The senator pondered a moment.

"It's been badly managed," he muttered; "there's no doubt of that. Hunt *must* be got out of the way. When Bascom and Botcher come, tell them I want to see them in my room, not in Number Seven."

And with this impressive command, received with nods of understanding, Senator Whitredge advanced slowly towards Number Seven, knocked, and entered. Be it known that Mr. Flint, with characteristic caution, had not confided even to the senator that the Honourable Hilary had had a stroke.

"Ah, Vane," he said, in his most affable tones, "how are you?"

The Honourable Hilary, who was looking over some papers, shot at him a glance from under his shaggy eyebrows.

"Came in here to find out — didn't you, Whitredge?" he replied.

"What?" said the senator, taken aback, and for once at a loss for words.

The Honourable Hilary rose and stood straighter than usual, and looked the senator in the eye.

"What's your diagnosis?" he asked. "Superannuated — unfit for duty — unable to cope with the situation — ready to be superseded? Is that about it?"

To say that Senator Whitredge was startled and uncomfortable would be to put his case mildly. He had never before seen Mr. Vane in this mood.

"Ha-ha!" he laughed; "the years are coming over us a little, aren't they? But I guess it isn't quite time for the youngsters to step in yet."

"No, Whitredge," said Mr. Vane, slowly, without taking his eye from the senator's, "and it won't be until this convention is over. Do you understand?"

"That's the first good news I've heard this morning," said the senator, with the uneasy feeling that, in some miraculous way, the Honourable Hilary had read the superseding orders from highest authority through his pocket.

"You may take it as good news or bad news, as you please, but it's a fact. And now I want you to tell Ridout that I wish to see him again, and to bring in Doby, who is to be chairman of the convention."

"Certainly," assented the senator, with alacrity, as he started for the door. Then he turned. "I'm glad to see you're all right, Vane," he added; "I'd heard that you were a little under the weather — a bilious attack on account of the heat — that's all I meant." He did not wait for an answer, nor would he have got one. And he found Mr. Ridout in the hall.

"Well?" said the lawyer, expectantly, and looking with some curiosity at the senator's face.

"Well," said Mr. Whitredge, with marked impatience, "he wants to see you right away."

All day long Hilary Vane held conference in Number Seven, and at six o'clock sent a request that the Honourable Adam visit him. The Honourable Adam would not come; and the fact leaked out — through the Honourable Adam.

"He's mad clean through," reported the Honourable Elisha Jane, to whose tact and diplomacy the mission had been confided. "He said he would teach Flint a lesson. He'd show him he couldn't throw away a man as useful and efficient as he'd been, like a sucked orange."

"Humph! A sucked orange. That's what he said, is it? A sucked orange," Hilary repeated.

"That's what he said," declared Mr. Jane, and remembered afterwards how Hilary had been struck by the simile.

At ten o'clock at night, at the very height of the tumult, Senator Whitredge had received an interrogatory tele-

gram from Fairview, and had called a private conference
(in which Hilary was not included) in a back room on
the second floor (where the conflicting bands of Mr.
Crewe and Mr. Hunt could not be heard), which Mr.
Manning and Mr. Jane and State Senator Billings and
Mr. Ridout attended.   Query : the Honourable Hilary
had quarrelled with Mr. Flint, that was an open secret ;
did not Mr. Vane think himself justified, from his own
point of view, in taking a singular revenge in not over-
exerting himself to pull the Honourable Adam out,
thereby leaving the field open for his son, Austen Vane,
with whom he was apparently reconciled?   Not that Mr.
Flint had hinted of such a thing !   He had, in the telegram, merely urged the senator himself to see Mr. Hunt,
and to make one more attempt to restrain the loyalty to
that candidate of Messrs. Bascom and Botcher.

The senator made the attempt, and failed signally.

It was half-past midnight by the shining face of the
clock on the tower of the state-house, and hope flamed
high in the bosom of the Honourable Adam B. Hunt —
a tribute to the bellows-like skill of Messrs. Bascom and
Botcher.   The bands in the street had blown themselves
out, the delegates were at last seeking rest, the hall boys
in the corridors were turning down the lights, and the
Honourable Adam, in a complacent and even jubilant
frame of mind, had put on his carpet slippers and taken
off his coat, when there came a knock at his door.   He
was not a little amazed and embarrassed, upon opening it,
to see the Honourable Hilary.   But these feelings gave
place almost immediately to a sense of triumph ; gone
were the days when he had to report to Number Seven.
Number Seven, in the person of Hilary (who *was* Number
Seven), had been forced to come to him !

" Well, upon my soul ! " he exclaimed heartily.
" Come in, Hilary."

He turned up the jets of the chandelier, and gazed at
his friend, and was silent.

" Have a seat, Hilary," he said, pushing up an arm-
chair.

Mr. Vane sat down. Mr. Hunt took a seat opposite, and waited for his visitor to speak. He himself seemed to find no words.

"Adam," said Mr. Vane, at length, "we've known each other for a good many years."

"That's so, Hilary. That's so," Mr. Hunt eagerly assented. What was coming?

"And whatever harm I've done in my life," Hilary continued, "I've always tried to keep my word. I told you, when we met up there by the mill this summer, that if Mr. Flint had consulted me about your candidacy, before seeing you in New York, I shouldn't have advised it — this time."

The Honourable Adam's face stiffened.

"That's what you said. But — "

"And I meant it," Mr. Vane interrupted. "I was never pledged to your candidacy, as a citizen. I've been thinking over my situation some, this summer, and I'll tell you in so many plain words what it is. I guess you know — I guess everybody knows who's thought about it. I deceived myself for a long time by believing that I earned my living as the attorney for the Northeastern Railroads. I've drawn up some pretty good papers for them, and I've won some pretty difficult suits. I'm not proud of 'em all, but let that go. Do you know what I am?"

The Honourable Adam was capable only of a startled ejaculation. Was Hilary Vane in his right senses?

"I'm merely their paid political tool," Mr. Vane continued, in the same tone. "I've sold them my brain, and my right of opinion as a citizen. I wanted to make this clear to you first of all. Not that you didn't know it, but I wished you to know that I know it. When Mr. Flint said that you were to be the Republican nominee, my business was to work to get you elected, which I did. And when it became apparent that you couldn't be nominated — "

"Hold on ! " cried the Honourable Adam.

"Please wait until I have finished. When it became

apparent that you couldn't be nominated, Mr. Flint sent
me to try to get you to withdraw, and he decreed that
the new candidate should pay your expenses up to date.
I failed in that mission."

"I don't blame you, Hilary," exclaimed Mr. Hunt.
"I told you so at the time. But I guess I'll soon be in
a position where I can make Flint walk the tracks — his
own tracks."

"Adam," said Mr. Vane, "it is because I deserve as
much of the blame as Mr. Flint that I am here."

Again Mr. Hunt was speechless. The Honourable
Hilary Vane in an apologetic mood! A surmise flashed
into the brain of the Honourable Adam, and sparkled
there. The Honourable Giles Henderson was prepared
to withdraw, and Hilary had come, by authority, to see
if he would pay the Honourable Giles' campaign expenses.
Well, he could snap his fingers at that.

"Flint has treated me like a dog," he declared.

"Mr. Flint never pretended," answered Mr. Vane, coldly,
"that the nomination and election of a governor was anything but a business transaction. His regard for you is
probably unchanged, but the interests he has at stake are
too large to admit of sentiment as a factor."

"Exactly," exclaimed Mr. Hunt. "And I hear he
hasn't treated you just right, Hilary. I understand — "

Hilary's eyes flashed for the first time.

"Never mind that, Adam," he said quietly; "I've been
treated as I deserve. I have nothing whatever to complain of from Mr. Flint. I will tell you why I came here
to-night. I haven't felt right about you since that interview, and the situation to-night is practically what it was
then. You can't be nominated."

"Can't be nominated!" gasped Mr. Hunt. And he
reached to the table for his figures. "I'll have four
hundred on the first ballot, and I've got two hundred
and fifty more pledged to me as second choice. If you've
come up here at this time of night to try to deceive me
on that, you might as well go back and wire Flint it's
no use. Why, I can name the delegates, if you'll listen."

Mr. Vane shook his head sadly. And, confident as he was, the movement sent a cold chill down the Honourable Adam's spine, for faith in Mr. Vane's judgment had become almost a second nature. He had to force himself to remember that this was not the old Hilary.

"You won't have three hundred, Adam, at any time," answered Mr. Vane. "Once you used to believe what I said, and if you won't now, you won't. But I can't go away without telling you what I came for."

"What's that?" demanded Mr. Hunt, wonderingly.

"It's this," replied Hilary, with more force than he had yet shown. "You can't get that nomination. If you'll let me know what your campaign expenses have been up to date, — all of 'em, you understand, to-night too, — I'll give you a check for them within the next two weeks."

"Who makes this offer?" demanded Mr. Hunt, with more curiosity than alarm; "Mr. Flint?"

"No," said Hilary; "Mr. Flint does not use the road's funds for such purposes."

"Henderson?"

"No," said Hilary; "I can't see what difference it makes to you."

The Honourable Adam had an eminently human side, and he laid his hand on Mr. Vane's knee.

"I think I've got a notion as to where that money would come from, Hilary," he said. "I'm much obliged to you, my friend. I wouldn't take it even if I thought you'd sized up the situation right. But — I don't agree with you this time. I know I've got the nomination. And I want to say once more, that I think you're a square man, and I don't hold anything against you."

Mr. Vane rose.

"I'm sorry, Adam," he said; "my offer holds good — after to-morrow."

"After to-morrow!"

"Yes," said the Honourable Hilary. "I don't feel right about this thing. Er — good night, Adam."

"Hold on!" cried Mr. Hunt, as a new phase of the matter struck him. "Why, if I got out — "

" What then ? " said Mr. Vane, turning around.

" Oh, I won't get out," said Mr. Hunt, " but if I did, — why, there wouldn't, according to your way of thinking, be any chance for a dark horse."

" What do you mean ? " demanded Mr. Vane.

" Now don't get mad, Hilary. I guess, and you know, that Flint hasn't treated you decently this summer after all you've done for him, and I admire the way you're standing by him. I wouldn't do it. I just wanted to say," Mr. Hunt added slowly, " that I respect you all the more for trying to get me out. If — always according to your notion of the convention — if I don't get out, and haven't any chance, they tell me on pretty good authority Austen Vane will get the nomination."

Hilary Vane walked to the door, opened it and went out, and slammed it behind him.

    *   *   *   *   *   *   *

It is morning, — a hot morning, as so many recall, — and the partisans of the three leaders are early astir, and at seven-thirty Mr. Tooting discovers something going on briskly which he terms " dealing in futures." My vote is yours as long as you are in the race, but after that I have something negotiable. The Honourable Adam Hunt strolls into the rotunda after an early breakfast, with a toothpick in his mouth, and is pointed out by the sophisticated to new arrivals as the man who spent seven thousand dollars over night, much of which is said to have stuck in the pockets of two feudal chiefs who could be named. Is it possible that there is a split in the feudal system at last? that the two feudal chiefs (who could be named) are rebels against highest authority ? A smile from the sophisticated one. This duke and baron have merely stopped to pluck a bird; it matters not whether or not the bird is an erstwhile friend — he has been outlawed by highest authority, and is fair game. The bird (with the toothpick in his mouth) creates a smile from other chiefs of the system in good standing who are not too busy to look at him. They have ceased all attempts to buttonhole him, for he is unapproachable.

The other bird, the rebel of Leith, who has never been in the feudal system at all, they have stopped laughing at. It is he who has brought the Empire to its most precarious state.

And now, while strangers from near and far throng into town, drawn by the sensational struggle which is to culminate in battle to-day, Mr. Crewe is marshalling his forces. All the delegates who can be collected, and who wear the button with the likeness and superscription of Humphrey Crewe, are drawn up beside the monument in the park, where the Ripton Band is stationed; and presently they are seen by cheering crowds marching to martial music towards the convention hall, where they collect in a body, with signs and streamers in praise of the People's Champion well to the front and centre. This is generally regarded as a piece of consummate generalship on the part of their leader. They are applauded from the galleries, — already packed, — especially from one conspicuous end where sit that company of ladies (now so famed) whose efforts have so materially aided the cause of the People's Champion. Gay streamers vie with gayer gowns, and morning papers on the morrow will have something to say about the fashionable element and the special car which brought them from Leith.

My, but it is hot!

The hall is filled now, with the thousand delegates, or their representatives who are fortunate enough to possess their credentials. Something of this matter later. General Doby, chairman of the convention, an impressive but mournful figure, could not call a roll if he wanted to. Not that he will want to! Impossible to tell, by the convenient laws of the State, whether the duly elected delegates of Hull or Mercer or Truro are here or not, since their credentials may be bought or sold or conferred. Some political giants, who have not negotiated their credentials, are recognized as they walk down the aisle: the statesmanlike figure of Senator Whitredge (a cheer); that of Senator Green (not so statesmanlike, but a cheer); Congressman Fairplay (cheers); and — Hilary Vane! His a figure that does not inspire cheers, — least of all to-day, — the man upon whose shoulders rests the political future of the Northeastern. The conservative Mr. Tredways and other Lincoln radicals of long ago who rely on his strength and judgment, are not the sort to cheer. And yet — and yet Hilary inspires some feeling when, with stooping gait, he traverses the hall, and there is a hush in many quarters as delegates and spectators watch his progress to the little room off the platform : the general's room, as the initiated know.

Ah, but few know what a hateful place it is to Hilary Vane to-day, this keyboard at which he has sat so complacently in years gone by, the envied of conventions. He sits down wearily at the basswood table, and scarcely hears the familiar sounds without, which indicate that the convention of conventions has begun. Extraordinary phenomenon at such a time, scenes of long ago and little cherished then, are stealing into his mind.

The Reverend Mr. Crane (so often chaplain of the Legislature, and known to the irreverent as the chaplain of the Northeastern) is praying now for guidance in the counsels of this great gathering of the people's representatives. God will hear Mr. Botcher better if he closes his eyes ; which he does. Now the platform is being read by State Senator Billings; closed eyes would best suit this proceeding, too. As a parallel to that platform, one can think only of the Ten Commandments. *The Republican Party (chosen children of Israel) must be kept free from the domination of corporations.* (Cheers and banner waving for a full minute.) *Some better method of choosing delegates which will more truly reflect the will of the people.* (Plank of the Honourable Jacob Botcher, whose conscience is awakening.) Never mind the rest. It is a triumph for Mr. Crewe, and is all printed in that orthodox (reform!) newspaper, the *State Tribune*, with urgent editorials that it must be carried out to the letter.

And what now ? Delegates, credential holders, audience, and the Reverend Mr. Crane draw long breaths of heated carbon dioxide. Postmaster Burrows of Edmundton, in rounded periods, is putting in nomination his distinguished neighbour and fellow-citizen, the Honourable Adam B. Hunt, who can subscribe and say *amen* to every plank in that platform. He believes it, he has proclaimed it in public, and he embodies it. Mr. Burrows indulges in slight but effective sarcasm of sham reformers and so-called business men who perform the arduous task of cutting coupons and live in rarefied regions where they can only be seen by the common people when the light is turned on. (Cheers from two partisan bodies and groans and hisses from another. General Doby, with a pained face, pounding with the gavel. This isn't a circumstance to what's coming, General.)

After General Doby has succeeded in abating the noise in honour of the Honourable Adam, there is a hush of expectancy. Humphrey Crewe, who has made all this trouble and enthusiasm, is to be nominated next, and the Honourable Timothy Watling of Newcastle arises to make that celebrated oration which the cynical have called the "thousand-dollar speech." And even if they had named it well (which is not for a moment to be admitted !), it is cheap for the price. How Mr. Crewe's ears must tingle as he paces his headquarters in the Pelican ! Almost would it be sacrilege to set down cold, on paper, the words that come, burning, out of the Honourable Timothy's loyal heart. Here, gentlemen, is a man at last, not a mere puppet who signs his name when a citizen of New York pulls the string ; one who is prepared to make any sacrifice, — to spend his life, if need be, in their service. (A barely audible voice, before the cheering commences, " I guess that's so.") Humphrey Crewe needs no defence — the Honourable Timothy avers — at his hands, or any one's. Not merely an idealist, but a practical man who has studied the needs of the State ; unselfish to the core ; longing, like Washington, the Father of his Country, to remain in a beautiful country home, where he dispenses hospitality with a flowing hand to poor and rich alike, yet harking to the call of duty. Leaving, like the noble Roman of old, his plough in the furrow — (Same voice

2 G

as before, " I wish he'd left his automo'bil' thar ! " Hisses
and laughter.) The Honourable Timothy, undaunted,
snatches his hand from the breast of his Prince Albert
and flings it, with a superb gesture, towards the Pelican.
" Gentlemen, I have the honour to nominate to this convention that peerless leader for the right, the Honourable
Humphrey Crewe of Leith — our next governor."

General Andrew Jackson himself, had he been alive
and on this historic ground and chairman of that convention, could scarce have quelled the tumult aroused by
this name and this speech — much less General Doby.
Although a man of presence, measurable by scales with
weights enough, our general has no more ponderosity
now than a leaf in a mountain storm at Hale — and no
more control over the hurricane. Behold him now, pounding with his gavel on something which should give forth
a sound, but doesn't. Who is he (to change the speech's
figure — not the general's), who is he to drive a wild
eight-horse team, who is fit only to conduct Mr. Flint's
oxen in years gone by ?

It is a memorable scene, sketched to life for the
metropolitan press. The man on the chair, his face
lighted by a fanatic enthusiasm, is the Honourable
Hamilton Tooting, coatless and collarless, leading the
cheers that shake the building, that must have struck
terror to the soul of Augustus P. Flint himself — fifty
miles away. But the endurance of the human throat is
limited.

Why, in the name of political strategy, has United
States Senator Greene been chosen to nominate the Honourable Giles Henderson of Kingston ? Some say that
it is the will of highest authority, others that the senator is a close friend of the Honourable Giles — buys his
coal from him, wholesale. Both surmises are true. The
senator's figure is not impressive, his voice less so, and
he reads from manuscript, to the accompaniment of continual cries of " Louder ! " A hook for Leviathan ! " A great
deal of dribble," said the senator, for little rocks sometimes
strike fire, " has been heard about the ' will of the people.'

The Honourable Giles Henderson is beholden to no man and to no corporation, and will go into office prepared to do justice impartially to all."

But — *copia verborum* — let us to the main business !

To an hundred newspapers, to Mr. Flint at Fairview, and other important personages ticks out the momentous news that the balloting has begun. No use trying to hold your breath until the first ballot is announced; it takes time to obtain the votes of one thousand men — especially when neither General Doby nor any one else knows who they are! The only way is to march up on the stage by counties and file past the ballot-box. Putnam, with their glitter-eyed duke, Mr. Bascom, at their head — presumably solid for Adam B. Hunt; Baron Burrows, who farms out the post-office at Edmundton, leads Edmunds County; Earl Elisha Jane, consul at some hot place where he spends the inclement months, drops the first ticket for Haines County, ostensibly solid for home-made virtue and the Honourable Giles.

An hour and a quarter of suspense and torture passes, while collars wilt and coats come off, and fans in the gallery wave incessantly, and excited conversation buzzes in every quarter. And now, see! there is whispering on the stage among the big-bugs. Mr. Chairman Doby rises with a paper in his hand, and the buzzing dies down to silence.

The Honourable Giles Henderson of Kingston has . . 398
The Honourable Humphrey Crewe of Leith has . . . 353
The Honourable Adam B. Hunt of Edmundton has. . 249
And a majority being required, there is no choice !

Are the supporters of the People's Champion crest-fallen, think you? Mr. Tooting is not leading them for the moment, but is pressing through the crowd outside the hall and flying up the street to the Pelican and the bridal suite, where he is first with the news. Note for an unabridged biography: the great man is discovered sitting quietly by the window, poring over a book on the modern science of road-building, some notes from which he is making for his first message. And instead of the reek of tobacco smoke, the room is filled with the scent of the floral tributes brought down by the Ladies' Auxiliary from Leith. In Mr. Crewe's right-hand pocket, neatly typewritten, is his speech of acceptance. He is never caught unprepared. Unkind, now, to remind him of that prediction made last night about the first ballot to the newspapers — and useless.

"I told you last night they were buyin' 'em right under our noses," cried Mr. Tooting, in a paroxysm of indignation, "and you wouldn't believe me. They got over one hundred and sixty away from us."

"It strikes me, Mr. Tooting," said Mr. Crewe, "that it was your business to prevent that."

There will no doubt be a discussion, when the biographer reaches this juncture, concerning the congruity of reform delegates who can be bought. It is too knotty a point of ethics to be dwelt upon here.

"Prevent it!" echoed Mr. Tooting, and in the strong light of the righteousness of that eye reproaches failed him. "But there's a whole lot of 'em can be seen, right now, while the ballots are being taken. It won't be decided on the next ballot."

"Mr. Tooting," said Mr. Crewe, indubitably proving that he had the qualities of a leader — if such proof were necessary, "go back to the convention. I have no doubt of the outcome, but that doesn't mean you are to relax your efforts. Do you understand?"

"I guess I do," replied Mr. Tooting, and was gone. "He still has his flag up," he whispered into the Honourable Timothy Watling's ear, when he reached the hall. "He'll stand a little more yet."

Mr. Tooting, at times, speaks a language unknown to us — and the second ballot is going on. And during its progress the two principal lieutenants of the People's Champion were observed going about the hall apparently exchanging the time of day with various holders of credentials. Mr. Jane, too, is going about the hall, and Postmaster Burrows, and Postmaster Bill Fleming of

Brampton, and the Honourable Nat Billings, and Messrs.
Bascom and Botcher, and Mr. Manning, division superintendent, and the Honourable Orrin Young, railroad
commissioner and candidate for reappointment — all are
embracing the opportunity to greet humble friends or to
make new acquaintances. Another hour and a quarter,
with the temperature steadily rising and the carbon
dioxide increasing — and the second ballot is announced.

The Honourable Giles Henderson of Kingston has . .   440
The Honourable Humphrey Crewe of Leith has . . .   336
The Honourable Adam B. Hunt of Edmundton has. .   255

And there are three votes besides improperly made out!
What the newspapers call indescribable excitement
ensues. The three votes improperly made out are said
to be trip passes accidentally dropped into the box by the
supporters of the Honourable Elisha Jane. And add up
the sum total of the votes! *Thirty-one votes more than
there are credentials in the hall!* Mystery of mysteries —
how can it be? The ballot, announces General Doby,
after endless rapping, is a blank. Cheers, recriminations,
exultation, disgust of decent citizens, attempts by twenty
men to get the eye of the president (which is too watery
to see any of them), and rushes for the platform to suggest remedies or ask what is going to be done about such
palpable fraud. What can be done? Call the roll! How
in blazes can you call the roll when you don't know
who's here? Messrs. Jane, Botcher, Bascom, and Fleming
are not disturbed, and improve their time. Watling and
Tooting rush to the bridal suite, and rush back again to
demand justice. General Doby mingles his tears with
theirs, and somebody calls him a jellyfish. He does not
resent it. Friction makes the air hotter and hotter —
Shadrach, Meshach, and Abednego would scarce enter into
this furnace, — and General Doby has a large damp spot
on his back as he pounds and pounds and pounds until
we are off again on the third ballot. No dinner, and
three-thirty P.M.! Two delegates have fainted, but the
essential parts of them — the credentials — are left behind.

Four-forty, whispering again, and the gavel drops.

The Honourable Giles Henderson of Kingston has . .   412
The Honourable Humphrey Crewe of Leith has . . .   325
The Honourable Adam B. Hunt of Edmundton has. .   250
And there is no choice on the third ballot!

Thirteen delegates are actually missing this time. Scour
the town ! And now even the newspaper adjectives de-
scribing the scene have given out.   A persistent and ter-
rifying rumour goes the rounds,— where's Tom Gaylord?
Somebody said he was in the hall a moment ago, on a
Ripton credential.   If so, he's gone out again— gone out
to consult the dark horse, who is in town, somewhere.
Another ominous sign: Mr. Redbrook, Mr. Widgeon of
Hull, and the other rural delegates who have been voting
for the People's Champion, and who have not been
observed in friendly conversation with anybody at all,
now have their heads together.   Mr. Billings goes saun-
tering by, but cannot hear what they are saying. Something must be done, and right away, and the knowing
metropolitan reporters are winking at each other and
declaring darkly that a sensation is about to turn up.
Where is Hilary Vane?   Doesn't he realize the danger?
Or—traitorous thought!—doesn't he care?   To see his
son nominated would be a singular revenge for the indig-
nities which are said to have been heaped upon him.
Does Hilary Vane, the strong man of the State, merely
sit at the keyboard, powerless, while the tempest itself
shakes from the organ a new and terrible music?   Nearly
six hours he has sat at the basswood table, while senators,
congressmen, feudal chiefs, and even Chairman Doby himself flit in and out, whisper in his ear, set papers before
him, and figures and problems, and telegrams from highest authority.   He merely nods his head, says a word now
and then, or holds his peace.   Does he know what he's
about?   If they had not heard things concerning his
health, — and other things, — they would still feel safe.
He seems the only calm man to be found in the hall —
but is the calm aberration?

A conference in the corner of the platform, while the fourth ballot is progressing, is held between Senators Whitredge and Greene, Mr. Ridout and Mr. Manning. So far the Honourable Hilary has apparently done nothing but let the storm take its course; a wing-footed messenger has returned who has seen Mr. Thomas Gaylord walking rapidly up Maple Street, and Austen Vane (most astute and reprehensible of politicians) is said to be at the Widow Peasley's, quietly awaiting the call. The name of Austen Vane — another messenger says — is running like wildfire through the hall, from row to row. Mr. Crewe has no chance — so rumour goes. A reformer (to pervert the saying of a celebrated contemporary humorist) must fight Marquis of Queensberry to win; and the People's Champion, it is averred, has not. Shrewd country delegates who had listened to the Champion's speeches and had come to the capital prepared to vote for purity, had been observing the movements since yesterday of Mr. Tooting and Mr. Watling with no inconsiderable interest. Now was the psychological moment for Austen Vane, but who was to beard Hilary?

No champion was found, and the Empire, the fate of which was in the hands of a madman, was cracking. Let an individual of character and known anti-railroad convictions (such as the gentleman said to be at the Widow Peasley's) be presented to the convention, and they would nominate him. Were Messrs. Bascom and Botcher going to act the part of Samsons? Were they working for revenge and a new régime? Mr. Whitredge started for the Pelican, not at his ordinary senatorial gait, to get Mr. Flint on the telephone.

The result of the fourth ballot was announced, and bedlam broke loose.

The Honourable Giles Henderson of Kingston has . . 419
The Honourable Humphrey Crewe of Leith has . . . 337
The Honourable Adam B. Hunt of Edmundton has . 256

Total, one thousand and eleven out of a thousand! Two delegates abstained from voting, and proclaimed the fact, but were heard only a few feet away. Other delegates, whose flesh and blood could stand the atmosphere no longer, were known to have left the hall! Aha! the secret is out, if anybody could hear it. At the end of every ballot several individuals emerge and mix with the crowd in the street. Astute men sometimes make mistakes, and the following conversation occurs between one of the individuals in question and Mr. Crewe's chauffeur.

Individual: Do you want to come in and see the convention and vote?

Chauffeur: I am Frenchman.

Individual: That doesn't cut any ice. I'll make out the ballot, and all you'll have to do is to drop it in the box.

Chauffeur: All right; I vote for Meester Crewe.

Sudden disappearance of the individual.

Nor is this all. The Duke of Putnam, for example, knows how many credentials there are in his county — say, seventy-six. He counts the men present and voting, and his result is sixty-one. Fifteen are absent, getting food or — something else. Fifteen vote over again. But, as the human brain is prone to error, and there are men in the street, the Duke miscalculates; the Earl of Haines miscalculates, too. Result — eleven over a thousand votes, and some nine hundred men in the hall!

How are you going to stop it? Mr. Watling climbs up on the platform and shakes his fist in General Doby's face, and General Doby tearfully appeals for an honest ballot — to the winds.

In the meantime the Honourable Elisha Jane, spurred on by desperation and thoughts of a *dolce far niente* gone forever, has sought and cornered Mr. Bascom.

"For God's sake, Brush," cries the Honourable Elisha, "hasn't this thing gone far enough? A little of it is all right — the boys understand that; but have you thought what it means to you and me if these blanked reformers get in, — if a feller like Austen Vane is nominated?"

That cold, hard glitter which we have seen was in Mr. Bascom's eyes.

" You fellers have got the colic," was the remark of the arch-rebel. " Do you think old Hilary doesn't know what he's about ? "

" It looks that way to me," said Mr. Jane.

" It looks that way to Doby too, I guess," said Mr. Bascom, with a glance of contempt at the general ; " he's lost about fifteen pounds to-day. Did Hilary send you down here ? " he demanded.

" No," Mr. Jane confessed.

" Then go back and chase yourself around the platform some more," was Mr. Bascom's unfeeling advice, " and don't have a fit here. All the brains in this hall are in Hilary's room. When he's ready to talk business with me in behalf of the Honourable Giles Henderson, I guess he'll do so."

But fear had entered the heart of the Honourable Elisha, and there was a sickly feeling in the region of his stomach which even the strong medicine administered by the Honourable Brush failed to alleviate. He perceived Senator Whitredge, returned from the Pelican. But the advice — if any — the president of the Northeastern has given the senator is not forthcoming in practice. Mr. Flint, any more than Ulysses himself, cannot recall the tempests when his own followers have slit the bags — and in sight of Ithaca ! Another conference at the back of the stage, out of which emerges State Senator Nat Billings and gets the ear of General Doby.

" Let 'em yell," says Mr. Billings — as though the general, by raising one adipose hand, could quell the storm. Eyes are straining, scouts are watching at the back of the hall and in the street, for the first glimpse of the dreaded figure of Mr. Thomas Gaylord. " Let 'em yell," counsels Mr. Billings, " and if they do nominate anybody nobody 'll hear 'em. And send word to Putnam County to come along on their fifth ballot."

It is Mr. Billings himself who sends word to Putnam County, in the name of the convention's chairman. Before the messenger can reach Putnam County another arrives on the stage, with wide pupils — " Tom Gaylord is coming!" This momentous news, Marconi-like, penetrates the storm, and is already on the floor. Mr. Widgeon and Mr. Redbrook are pushing their way towards the door. The conference, emboldened by terror, marches in a body into the little room, and surrounds the calmly insane Lieutenant-general of the forces; it would be ill-natured to say that visions of lost railroad commissionerships, lost consulships, lost postmasterships, — yes, of lost senatorships, were in these loyal heads at this crucial time.

It was all very well (so said the first spokesman) to pluck a few feathers from a bird so bountifully endowed as the Honourable Adam, but were not two gentlemen who should be nameless carrying the joke a little too far? Mr. Vane unquestionably realized what he was doing, but — was it not almost time to call in the two gentlemen and — and come to some understanding?

"Gentlemen," said the Honourable Hilary, apparently unmoved, "I have not seen Mr. Bascom or Mr. Botcher since the sixteenth day of August, and I do not intend to."

Some clearing of throats followed this ominous declaration, — and a painful silence. The thing must be said — and who would say it? Senator Whitredge was the hero.

Mr. Thomas Gaylord has just entered the convention hall, and is said to be about to nominate — a dark horse. The moment was favourable, the convention demoralized, and at least one hundred delegates had left the hall. (How about the last ballot, Senator, which showed 1011?)

The Honourable Hilary rose abruptly, closed the door to shut out the noise, and turned and looked Mr. Whitredge in the eye.

"Who is the 'dark horse'?" he demanded.

The members of the conference coughed again, looked at each other, and there was a silence. For some inexplicable reason, nobody cared to mention the name of Austen Vane.

The Honourable Hilary pointed at the basswood table.

"Senator," he said, "I understand you have been telephoning Mr. Flint. Have you got orders to sit down there?"

"My dear sir," said the Senator, "you misunderstand me."

"Have you got orders to sit down there?" Mr. Vane repeated.

"No," answered the Senator; "Mr. Flint's confidence in you — "

The Honourable Hilary sat down again, and at that instant the door was suddenly flung open by Postmaster Bill Fleming of Brampton, his genial face aflame with excitement and streaming with perspiration. Forgotten, in this moment, is senatorial courtesy and respect for the powers of the feudal system.

"Say, boys," he cried, "Putnam County's voting, and there's be'n no nomination and ain't likely to be. Jim Scudder, the station-master at Wye, is here on credentials, and he says for sure the thing's fizzled out, and Tom Gaylord's left the hall!"

Again a silence, save for the high hum let in through the open doorway. The members of the conference stared at the Honourable Hilary, who seemed to have forgotten their presence; for he had moved his chair to the window, and was gazing out over the roofs at the fast-fading red in the western sky.

An hour later, when the room was in darkness save for the bar of light that streamed in from the platform chandelier, Senator Whitredge entered.

"Hilary!" he said.

There was no answer. Mr. Whitredge felt in his pocket for a match, struck it, and lighted the single jet over the basswood table. Mr. Vane still sat by the window. The senator turned and closed the door, and read from a paper in his hand; so used was he to formality that he read it formally, yet with a feeling of intense relief, of deference, of apology.

"Fifth ballot: —

The Honourable Giles Henderson of Kingston has . . 587
The Honourable Adam B. Hunt of Edmundton has. . 230
The Honourable Humphrey Crewe of Leith has . . . 154

And Giles Henderson is nominated — Hilary?"

"Yes," said Mr. Vane.

"I don't think any of us were — quite ourselves to-day. It wasn't that we didn't believe in you — but we didn't have all the threads in our hands, and — for reasons which I think I can understand — you didn't take us into your confidence. I want to — "

The words died on the senator's lips. So absorbed had he been in his momentous news, and solicitous over the result of his explanation, that his eye looked outward for the first time, and even then accidentally.

"Hilary!" he cried; "for God's sake, what's the matter? Are you sick?"

"Yes, Whitredge," said Mr. Vane, slowly, "sick at heart."

It was but natural that these extraordinary and incomprehensible words should have puzzled and frightened the senator more than ever.

"Your heart!" he repeated.

"Yes, my heart," said Hilary.

The senator reached for the ice-water on the table.

"Here," he cried, pouring out a glass, "it's only the heat — it's been a hard day — drink this."

But Hilary did not raise his arm. The door opened — others coming to congratulate Hilary Vane on the greatest victory he had ever won. Offices were secure once more, the feudal system intact, and rebels justly punished; others coming to make their peace with the commander whom, senseless as they were, they had dared to doubt.

They crowded past each other on the threshold, and stood grouped beyond the basswood table, staring — staring — men suddenly come upon a tragedy instead of a feast, the senator still holding the glass of water in a hand that trembled and spilled it. And it was the senator, after all, who first recovered his presence of mind. He set down the water, pushed his way through the group into the hall, where the tumult and the shouting die. Mr. Giles Henderson, escorted, is timidly making his way towards the platform to read his speech of acceptance of a willing bondage, when a voice rings out : —

"If there is a physician in the house, will he please come forward?"

And then a hush, — and then the buzz of comment. Back to the little room once more, where they are gathered speechless about Hilary Vane. And the doctor comes — young Dr. Tredway of Ripton, who is before all others.

"I expected this to happen, gentlemen," he said, "and I have been here all day, at the request of Mr. Vane's son, for this purpose."

"Austen!"

It was Hilary who spoke.

"I have sent for him," said the doctor. "And now, gentlemen, if you will kindly —"

They withdrew and the doctor shut the door. Outside, the Honourable Giles is telling them how seriously he regards the responsibility of the honour thrust upon him by a great party. But nobody hears him in the wild rumours that fly from mouth to mouth as the hall empties. Rushing in against the tide outpouring, tall, stern, vigorous, is a young man whom many recognize, whose name is on many lips as they make way for him, who might have saved them if he would. The door of the little room opens, and he stands before his father, looking down at him. And the stern expression is gone from his face.

"Austen!" said Mr. Vane.

"Yes, Judge."

"Take me away from here. Take me home — now — to-night."

Austen glanced at Dr. Tredway.

"It is best," said the doctor; "we will take him home — to-night."

CHAPTER XXVIII

THE VOICE OF AN ERA

THEY took him home, in the stateroom of the sleeper attached to the night express from the south, although Mr. Flint, by telephone, had put a special train at his disposal. The long service of Hilary Vane was over; he had won his last fight for the man he had chosen to call his master; and those who had fought behind him, whose places, whose very luminary existences, had depended on his skill, knew that the end had come; nay, were already speculating, manœuvring, and taking sides. Who would be the new Captain-general? Who would be strong enough to suppress the straining ambitions of the many that the Empire might continue to flourish in its integrity and gather tribute? It is the world-old cry around the palace walls : Long live the new ruler — if you can find him among the curdling factions.

They carried Hilary home that September night, when Sawanec was like a gray ghost-mountain facing the waning moon, back to the home of those strange, Renaissance Austens which he had reclaimed for a grim puritanism, and laid him in the carved and canopied bedstead Channing Austen had brought from Spain. Euphrasia had met them at the door, but a trained nurse from the Ripton hospital was likewise in waiting; and a New York specialist had been summoned to prolong, if possible, the life of one from whom all desire for life had passed.

Before sunrise a wind came from the northern spruces; the dawn was cloudless, fiery red, and the air had an autumn sharpness. At ten o'clock Dr. Harmon arrived, was met at the station by Austen, and spent half an hour with Dr. Tredway. At noon the examination was complete. Thanks to generations of self-denial by the Vanes of Camden Street, Mr. Hilary Vane might live indefinitely, might even recover, partially; but at present he was condemned to remain, with his memories, in the great canopied bed.

The Honourable Hilary had had another caller that morning besides Dr. Harmon, — no less a personage than the president of the Northeastern Railroads himself, who had driven down from Fairview immediately after breakfast. Austen having gone to the station, Dr. Tredway had received Mr. Flint in the darkened hall, and had promised to telephone to Fairview the verdict of the specialist. At present Dr. Tredway did not think it wise to inform Hilary of Mr. Flint's visit—not, at least, until after the examination.

Mr. Vane exhibited the same silent stoicism on receiving the verdict of Dr. Harmon as he had shown from the first. With the clew to Hilary's life which Dr. Tredway had given him, the New York physician understood the case; one common enough in his practice in a great city where the fittest survive — sometimes only to succumb to unexpected and irreparable blows in the evening of life.

On his return from seeing Dr. Harmon off Austen was met on the porch by Dr. Tredway.

" Your father has something on his mind," said the doctor, "and perhaps it is just as well that he should be relieved. He is asking for you, and I merely wished to advise you to make the conversation as short as possible."

Austen climbed the stairs in obedience to this summons, and stood before his father at the bedside. Hilary lay back among the pillows, and the brightness of that autumn noonday only served to accentuate the pallor of his face, the ravages of age which had come with such incredible swiftness, and the outline of a once vigorous frame. The eyes alone shone with a strange ne⸗ light, and Austen found it unexpectedly difficult to spea⸗. He sat down on the bed and laid his hand on the helpless one that rested on the coverlet.

"Austen," said Mr. Vane, "I want you to go to Fairview."

His son's hand tightened over his own.

"Yes, Judge."

"I want you to go now."

"Yes, Judge."

"You know the combination of my safe at the office. It's never been changed since — since you were there. Open it. You will find two tin boxes, containing papers labelled Augustus P. Flint. I want you to take them to Fairview and put them into the hands of Mr. Flint himself. I — I cannot trust any one else. I promised to take them myself, but — Flint will understand."

"I'll go right away," said Austen, rising, and trying to speak cheerfully. "Mr. Flint was here early this morning — inquiring for you."

Hilary Vane's lips trembled, and another expression came into his eyes.

"Rode down to look at the scrap-heap, — did he?"

Austen strove to conceal his surprise at his father's words and change of manner.

"Tredway saw him," he said. "I'm pretty sure Mr. Flint doesn't feel that way, Judge. He has taken your illness very much to heart, I know, and he left some fruit and flowers for you."

"I guess his daughter sent those," said Hilary.

"His daughter!" Austen repeated.

"If I didn't think so," Mr. Vane continued, "I'd send 'em back. I never knew what she was until she picked me up and drove me down here. I've always done Victoria an injustice."

Austen walked to the door, and turned slowly.

"I'll go at once, Judge," he said.

In the kitchen he was confronted by Euphrasia.

"When is that woman going away?" she demanded. "I've took care of Hilary Vane nigh on to forty years, and I guess I know as much about nursing, and more about Hilary, than that young thing with her cap and apron. I told Dr. Tredway so. She even came down here to let me know what to cook for him, and I sent her about her business."

Austen smiled. It was the first sign, since his return the night before, Euphrasia had given that an affection for Hilary Vane lurked beneath the burr of that strange nature.

"She won't stay long, Phrasie," he answered, and added mischievously, "for a very good reason."

"And what's that?" asked Euphrasia.

"Because you won't allow her to. I have a notion that she'll pack up and leave in about three days, and that all the doctors in Ripton couldn't keep her here."

"Get along with you," said Euphrasia, who could not for the life of her help looking a little pleased.

"I'm going off for a few hours," he said more seriously. "Dr. Tredway tells me they do not look for any developments — for the worse."

"Where are you going?" asked Euphrasia, sharply.

"To Fairview," he said.

Euphrasia moved the kettle to another part of the stove.

"You'll see *her?*" she said.

"Who?" Austen asked. But his voice must have betrayed him a little, for Euphrasia turned and seized him by the elbows and looked up into his face.

"Victoria," she said.

He felt himself tremble at the name, — at the strangeness of its sound on Euphrasia's lips.

"I do not expect to see Miss Flint," he answered, controlling himself as well as he was able. "I have an errand for the Judge with Mr. Flint himself."

Euphrasia had guessed his secret! But how?

"Hadn't you better see her?" said Euphrasia, in a curious monotone.

"But I have no errand with her," he objected, mystified yet excited by Euphrasia's manner.

"She fetched Hilary home," said Euphrasia.

"Yes."

"She couldn't have be'n kinder if she was his own daughter."

2 H

" I know —" he began, but Euphrasia interrupted.

" She sent that Englishman for the doctor, and waited to take the news to her father, and she came out in this kitchen and talked to me."

Austen started. Euphrasia was not looking at him now, and suddenly she dropped his arms and went to the window overlooking the garden.

" She wouldn't go in the parlour, but come right out here in her fine clothes. I told her I didn't think she belonged in a kitchen — but I guess I did her an injustice," said Euphrasia, slowly.

" I think you did," he said, and wondered.

" She looked at that garden," Euphrasia went on, " and cried out. I didn't callate she was like that. And the first thing I knew I was talking about your mother, and I'd forgot who I was talking to. She wahn't like a stranger — it was just as if I'd known her always. I haven't understood it yet. And after a while I told her about that verse, and she wanted to see it — the verse about the skylark, you know —"

" Yes," said Austen.

" Well, the way she read it made me cry, it brought back Sarah Austen so. Somehow, I can't account for it, she puts me in mind of your mother."

Austen did not speak.

" In more ways than one," said Euphrasia. " I didn't look to find her so natural — and so gentle. And then she has a way of scolding you, just as Sarah Austen had, that you'd never suspect."

" Did she scold you — Phrasie ? " asked Austen. And the irresistible humour that is so near to sorrow made him smile again.

" Indeed she did! And it surprised me some — coming right out of a summer sky. I told her what I thought about Hilary, and how he'd driven you out of your own mother's house. She said you'd ought to be sent for, and I said you oughtn't to set foot in this house until Hilary sent for you. She said I'd no right to take such a revenge — that you'd come right away if you knew Hilary'd had a stroke, and that Hilary'd never send for you — because he couldn't.   She said he was like a man on a desert island."

" She was right," answered Austen.

" I don't know about that," said Euphrasia; "she hadn't put up with Hilary for forty years, as I had, and seen what he'd done to your mother and you.   But that's what she said.   And she went for you herself, when she found the doctor couldn't go.   Austen, ain't you going to see her? "

Austen shook his head gently, and smiled at her.

" I'm afraid it's no use, Phrasie," he said.   " Just be-cause she has been — kind, we mustn't be deceived.   It's her nature to be kind."

Euphrasia crossed the room swiftly, and seized his arm again.

" She loves you, Austen," she cried; "she loves *you*. Do you think that I'd love *her*, that I'd plead for her, if she didn't ? "

Austen's breath came deeply.   He disengaged himself, and went to the window.

" No," he said, "you don't know.   You can't know.   I have only seen her — a few times.   She lives a different life — and with other people.   She will marry a man who can give her more."

" Do you think I could be deceived?" exclaimed Euphrasia, almost fiercely.   "It's as true as the sun shining on that mountain.   You believe she loves the Englishman, but I tell you she loves you — you."

He turned towards her.

" How do you know? " he asked, as though he were merely curious.

" Because I'm a woman, and she's a woman," said Eu-phrasia.   " Oh, she didn't confess it. If she had, I shouldn't think so much of her.   But she told me as plain as though she had spoken it in words, before she left this room."

Austen shook his head again.

" Phrasie," he said, " I'm afraid you've been building castles in Spain."   And he went out, and across to the stable to harness Pepper.

Austen did not believe Euphrasia.   On that eventful

evening when Victoria had called at Jabe Jenney's, the
world's aspect had suddenly changed for him ; old values
had faded, — values which, after all, had been but tints and
glows, — and sterner but truer colours took their places.
He saw Victoria's life in a new perspective, — one in which
his was but a small place in the background of her numerous beneficences; which was, after all, the perspective
in which he had first viewed it. But, by degrees, the
hope that she loved him had grown and grown until it
had become unconsciously the supreme element of his
existence, — the hope that stole sweetly into his mind with
the morning light, and stayed him through the day, and
blended into the dreams of darkness.

By inheritance, by tradition, by habits of thought, Austen
Vane was an American, — an American as differentiated
from the citizen of any other nation upon the earth. The
French have an expressive phrase in speaking of a person
as belonging to this or that world, meaning the circle by
which the life of an individual is bounded; the true American recognizes these circles — but with complacency, and
with a sure knowledge of his destiny eventually to find
himself within the one for which he is best fitted by his
talents and his tastes. The mere fact that Victoria
had been brought up amongst people with whom he had
nothing in common would not have deterred Austen Vane
from pressing his suit; considerations of honour had stood
in the way, and hope had begun to whisper that these
might, in the end, be surmounted. Once they had disap-
peared, and she loved him, that were excuse and reason
enough.

And suddenly the sight of Victoria with a probable suitor
— who at once had become magnified into an accepted suitor
— had dispelled hope. Euphrasia! Euphrasia had been
deceived as he had, by a loving kindness and a charity that
were natural. But what so natural (to one who had lived
the life of Austen Vane) as that she should marry amongst
those whose ways of life were her ways ? In the brief time
in which he had seen her and this other man, Austen's
quickened perceptions had detected tacit understanding,

community of interest, a habit of thought and manner, — in short, a common language, unknown to him, between the two. And, more than these, the Victoria of the blissful excursions he had known was changed as she had spoken to him — constrained, distant, apart; although still dispensing kindness, going out of her way to bring Hilary home, and to tell him of Hilary's accident. Rumour, which cannot be confined in casks or bottles, had since informed Austen Vane that Mr. Rangely had spent the day with Victoria, and had remained at Fairview far into the evening; rumour went farther (thanks to Mrs. Pomfret) and declared the engagement already an accomplished fact. And to Austen, in the twilight in front of Jabe Jenney's, the affair might well have assumed the proportions of an intimacy of long standing rather than that of the chance acquaintance of an hour. Friends in common, modes of life in common, and incidents in common are apt to sweep away preliminaries.

Such were Austen's thoughts as he drove to Fairview that September afternoon when the leaves were turning their white backs to the northwest breeze. The sun was still high, and the distant hills and mountains were as yet scarce stained with blue, and stood out in startling clearness against the sky. Would he see her? That were a pain he scarce dared contemplate.

He reached the arched entrance, was on the drive. Here was the path again by which she had come down the hillside; here was the very stone on which she had stood —awaiting him. Why? Why had she done that? Well-remembered figure amidst the yellow leaves dancing in the sunlight! Here he had stopped, perforce, and here she had looked up into his face and smiled and spoken!

At length he gained the plateau across which the driveway ran, between round young maples, straight to Fairview House, and he remembered the stares from the tea-tables, and how she had come out to his rescue. Now the lawn was deserted, save for a gardener among the shrubs. He rang the stable-bell, and as he waited for an answer to his summons, the sense of his remoteness from these surroundings of hers deepened, and with a touch of inevitable humour he recalled the low-ceiled bedroom at Mr. Jenney's and the kitchen in Hanover Street; the annual cost of the care of that lawn and driveway might well have maintained one of these households.

He told the stable-boy to wait. It is to be remarked as curious that the name of the owner of the house on Austen's lips brought the first thought of him to Austen's mind. He was going to see and speak with Mr. Flint,— a man who had been his enemy ever since the day he had come here and laid down his pass on the president's desk; the man who—so he believed until three days ago—had stood between him and happiness. Well, it did not matter now.

Austen followed the silent-moving servant through the hall. Those were the stairs which knew her feet, these the rooms—so subtly flower-scented—she lived in; then came the narrow passage to the sterner apartment of the master himself. Mr. Flint was alone, and seated upright behind the massive oak desk, from which bulwark the president of the Northeastern was wont to meet his opponents and his enemies ; and few visitors came into his presence, here or elsewhere, who were not to be got the better of, if possible. A life-long habit had accustomed Mr. Flint to treat all men as adversaries until they were proved otherwise. His square, close-cropped head, his large features, his alert eyes, were those of a fighter.

He did not rise, but nodded. Suddenly Austen was enveloped in a flame of wrath that rose without warning and blinded him, and it was with a supreme effort to control himself that he stopped in the doorway. He was frightened, for he had felt this before, and he knew it for the anger that demands physical violence.

" Come in, Mr. Vane," said the president.

Austen advanced to the desk, and laid the boxes before Mr. Flint.

" Mr. Vane told me to say that he would have brought these himself, had it been possible. Here is the list, and I shall be much obliged if you will verify it before I go back."

"Sit down," said Mr. Flint.

Austen sat down, with the corner of the desk between them, while Mr. Flint opened the boxes and began checking off the papers on the list.

"How is your father this afternoon?" he asked, without looking up.

"As well as can be expected," said Austen.

"Of course nobody knew his condition but himself," Mr. Flint continued; "but it was a great shock to me when he resigned as my counsel three days ago."

Austen laid his forearm on the desk, and his hand closed.

"He resigned three days ago?" he exclaimed.

Mr. Flint was surprised, but concealed it.

"I can understand, under the circumstances, how he has overlooked telling you. His resignation takes effect to-day."

Austen was silent a moment, while he strove to apply this fact to his father's actions.

"He waited until after the convention."

"Exactly," said Mr. Flint, catching the implied accusation in Austen's tone; "and needless to say, if I had been able to prevent his going, in view of what happened on Monday night, I should have done so. As you know, after his — accident, he went to the capital without informing any one."

"As a matter of honour," said Austen.

Mr. Flint looked up from the papers, and regarded him narrowly, for the tone in which this was spoken did not escape the president of the Northeastern. He saw, in fact, that at the outset he had put a weapon into Austen's hands. Hilary's resignation was a vindication of Austen's attitude, an acknowledgment that the business and political practices of his life had been wrong.

What Austen really felt, when he had grasped the significance of that fact, was relief — gratitude. A wave of renewed affection for his father swept over him, of affection and pity and admiration, and for the instant he forgot Mr. Flint.

"As a matter of honour," Mr. Flint repeated. "Knowing he was ill, Mr. Vane insisted upon going to that convention, even at the risk of his life. It is a fitting close to a splendid career, and one that will not soon be forgotten."

Austen merely looked at Mr. Flint, who may have found the glance a trifle disconcerting, for he turned to the papers again.

"I repeat," he went on presently, "that this illness of Mr. Vane's is not only a great loss to the Northeastern system, but a great blow to me personally. I have been associated with him closely for more than a quarter of a century, and I have never seen a lawyer of greater integrity, clear-headedness, and sanity of view. He saw things as they were, and he did as much to build up the business interests and the prosperity of this State as any man I know of. He was true to his word, and true to his friends."

Still Austen did not reply. He continued to look at Mr. Flint, and Mr. Flint continued to check the papers — only more slowly. He had nearly finished the first box.

"A wave of political insanity, to put it mildly, seems to be sweeping over this country," said the president of the Northeastern. "Men who would paralyze and destroy the initiative of private enterprise, men who themselves are ambitious, and either incapable or unsuccessful, have sprung up; writers who have no conscience, whose one idea is to make money out of a passing craze against honest capital, have aided them. Disappointed and dangerous politicians who merely desire office and power have lifted their voices in the hue and cry to fool the honest voter. I am glad to say I believe that the worst of this madness and rascality is over; that the common sense of the people of this country is too great to be swept away by the methods of these self-seekers; that the ordinary man is beginning to see that his bread and butter depends on the brain of the officers who are trying honestly to conduct great enterprises for the benefit of the average citizen.

"We did not expect to escape in this State," Mr. Flint went on, raising his head and meeting Austen's look;

" the disease was too prevalent and too catching for the weak-minded. We had our self-seekers who attempted to bring ruin upon an institution which has done more for our population than any other. I do not hesitate to speak of the Northeastern Railroads as an institution, and as an institution which has been as conscientiously and conservatively conducted as any in the country, and with as scrupulous a regard for the welfare of all. Hilary Vane, as you doubtless know, was largely responsible for this. My attention, as president of all the roads, has been divided. Hilary Vane guarded the interests in this State, and no man could have guarded them better. He well deserves the thanks of future generations for the uncompromising fight he made against such men and such methods. It has broken him down at a time of life when he has earned repose, but he has the satisfaction of knowing that he has won the battle for conservative American principles, and that he has nominated a governor worthy of the traditions of the State."

And Mr. Flint started checking off the papers again. Had the occasion been less serious, Austen could have smiled at Mr. Flint's ruse — so characteristic of the tactics of the president of the Northeastern — of putting him into a position where criticism of the Northeastern and its practices would be criticism of his own father. As it was, he only set his jaw more firmly, an expression indicative of contempt for such tactics. He had not come there to be lectured out of the "Book of Arguments" on the divine right of railroads to govern, but to see that certain papers were delivered in safety.

Had his purpose been deliberately to enter into a contest with Mr. Flint, Austen could not have planned the early part of it any better than by pursuing this policy of silence. To a man of Mr. Flint's temperament and training, it was impossible to have such an opponent within reach without attempting to hector him into an acknowledgment of the weakness of his position. Further than this, Austen had touched him too often on the quick merely to be considered in the light of a young man who held opposite and unfortunate views — although it was Mr. Flint's endeavour to put him in this light. The list of injuries was too fresh in Mr. Flint's mind — even that last conversation with Victoria, in which she had made it plain that her sympathies were with Austen.

But with an opponent who would not be led into ambush, who had the strength to hold his fire under provocation, it was no easy matter to maintain a height of conscious, matter-of-fact rectitude and implied reproof. Austen's silence, Austen's attitude, declared louder than words the contempt for such manœuvres of a man who knows he is in the right — and knows that his adversary knows it. It was this silence and this attitude which proclaimed itself that angered Mr. Flint, yet made him warily conceal his anger and change his attack.

"It is some years since we met, Mr. Vane," he remarked presently.

Austen's face relaxed into something of a smile.

"Four, I think," he answered.

"You hadn't long been back from that Western experience. Well, your father has one decided consolation; you have fulfilled his hope that you would settle down here and practise in the State. And I hear that you are fast forging to the front. You are counsel for the Gaylord Company, I believe."

"The result of an unfortunate accident," said Austen; "Mr. Hammer died."

"And on the occasion when you did me the honour to call on me," said Mr. Flint, "if I remember rightly, you expressed some rather radical views — for the son of Hilary Vane."

"For the son of Hilary Vane," Austen agreed, with a smile.

Mr. Flint ignored the implication in the repetition.

"Thinking as much as I do of Mr. Vane, I confess that your views at that time rather disturbed me. It is a matter of relief to learn that you have refused to lend yourself to the schemes of men like our neighbour, Mr. Humphrey Crewe, of Leith."

"Honesty compels me to admit," answered Austen, "that I did not refrain on Mr. Crewe's account."

"Although," said Mr. Flint, drumming on the table, "there was some talk that you were to be brought forward as a dark horse in the convention, and as a candidate unfriendly to the interests of the Northeastern Railroads, I am glad you did not consent to be put in any such position. I perceive that a young man of your ability and — popularity, a Vane of Camden Street, must inevitably become a force in this State. And as a force, you must retain the conservatism of the Vanes — the traditional conservatism of the State. The Northeastern Railroads will continue to be a very large factor in the life of the people after you and I are gone, Mr. Vane. You will have to live, as it were, with that corporation, and help to preserve it. We shall have to work together, perhaps, to that end — who can say? I repeat, I am glad that your good sense led you to refrain from coming as a candidate before that Convention. There is time enough in the future, and you could not have been nominated."

"On the contrary," answered Austen, quietly, "I could have been nominated."

Mr. Flint smiled knowingly — but with an effort. What a relief it would have been to him to charge horse and foot, to forget that he was a railroad president dealing with a potential power.

"Do you honestly believe that?" he asked.

"I am not accustomed to dissemble my beliefs," said Austen, gravely. "The fact that my father had faith enough in me to count with certainty on my refusal to go before the convention enabled him to win the nomination for the candidate of your railroads."

Mr. Flint continued to smile, but into his eyes had crept a gleam of anger.

"It is easy to say such things — after the convention," he remarked.

"And it would have been impossible to say them before," Austen responded instantly, with a light in his own eyes. "My nomination was the only disturbing factor in the situation for you and the politicians who had your interests in hand, and it was as inevitable as night and day that the forces of the candidates who represented the two wings of the machine of the Northeastern Railroads should have united against Mr. Crewe. I want to say to you frankly that if my father had not been the counsel for your corporation, and responsible for its political success, or if he could have resigned with honour before the convention, I should not have refused to let my name go in. After all," he added, in a lower tone, and with a slight gesture characteristic of him when a subject was distasteful, "it doesn't matter who is elected governor this autumn."

"What?" cried Mr. Flint, surprised out of his attitude as much by Austen's manner as by Austen's words.

"It doesn't matter," said Austen, "whether the Northeastern Railroads have succeeded this time in nominating and electing a governor to whom they can dictate, and who will reappoint railroad commissioners and other State officials in their interests. The practices by which you have controlled this State, Mr. Flint, and elected governors and councillors and State and national senators are doomed. However necessary these practices may have been from your point of view, they violated every principle of free government, and were they to continue, the nation to which we belong would inevitably decay and become the scorn of the world. Those practices depended for their success on one condition, — which in itself is the most serious of ills in a republic, — the ignorance and disregard of the voter. You have but to read the signs of the times to see clearly that the day of such conditions is past, to see that the citizens of this State and this country are thinking for themselves, as they should; are alive to the danger, and determined to avert it. You may succeed in electing one more governor and one more senate, or two, before the people are able to destroy the machinery you have built up and repeal the laws you have made to sustain it. I repeat, it doesn't matter in the long run.

The era of political domination by a corporation, and mainly for the benefit of a corporation, is over."

Mr. Flint had been drumming on the desk, his face growing a darker red as Austen proceeded. Never, since he had become president of the Northeastern Railroads, had any man said such things to his face. And the fact that Austen Vane had seemingly not spoken in wrath, although forcefully enough to compel him to listen, had increased Mr. Flint's anger. Austen apparently cared very little for him or his opinions in comparison with his own estimate of right and wrong.

"It seems," said Mr. Flint, "that you have grown more radical since your last visit."

"If it be radical to refuse to accept a pass from a railroad to bind my liberty of action as an attorney and a citizen, then I am radical," replied Austen. "If it be radical to maintain that the elected representatives of the people should not receive passes, or be beholden to any man or any corporation, I acknowledge the term. If it be radical to declare that these representatives should be elected without interference, and while in office should do exact justice to the body of citizens on the one hand and the corporations on the other, I declare myself a radical. But my radicalism goes back behind the establishment of railroads, Mr. Flint, back to the foundation of this government, to the idea from which it sprang."

Mr. Flint smiled again.

"We have changed materially since then," he said. "I am afraid such a utopian state of affairs, beautiful as it is, will not work in the twentieth century. It is a commercial age, and the interests which are the bulwark of the country's strength must be protected."

"Yes," said Austen, "we have changed *materially*. The mistake you make, and men like you, is the stress which you lay on that word *material*. Are there no such things as *moral* interests, Mr. Flint? And are they not quite as important in government, if not more important, than material interests? Surely, we cannot have commercial and political stability without commercial and political honour! If, as a nation, we lose sight of the ideals which have carried us so far, which have so greatly modified the conditions of other peoples than ourselves, we shall perish as a force in the world. And if this government proves a failure, how long do you think the material interests of which you are so solicitous will endure? Or do you care whether they endure beyond your lifetime? Perhaps not. But it is a matter of importance, not only to the nation, but to the world, whether or not the moral idea of the United States of America is perpetuated, I assure you."

"I begin to fear, Mr. Vane," said the president of the Northeastern, "that you have missed your vocation. Suppose I were to grant you, for the sake of argument, that the Northeastern Railroads, being the largest taxpayers in this State, have taken an interest in seeing that conservative men fill responsible offices. Suppose such to be the case, and we abruptly cease—to take such an interest. What then? Are we not at the mercy of any and all unscrupulous men who build up a power of their own, and start again the blackmail of the old days?"

"You have put the case mildly," said Austen, "and ingeniously. As a matter of fact, Mr. Flint, you know as well as I do that for years you have governed this State absolutely, for the purpose of keeping down your taxes, avoiding unnecessary improvements for safety and comfort, and paying high dividends—"

"Perhaps you realize that in depicting these criminal operations so graphically," cried Mr. Flint, interrupting, "you are involving the reputation of one of the best citizens the State ever had—your own father."

Austen Vane leaned forward across the desk, and even Mr. Flint (if the truth were known) recoiled a little before the anger he had aroused. It shot forth from Austen's eyes, proclaimed itself in the squareness of the face, and vibrated in every word he spoke.

"Mr. Flint," he said, "I refrain from comment upon your methods of argument. There were many years in which my father believed the practices which he followed in behalf of your railroad to be necessary — and hence justified. And I have given you the credit of holding the same belief. Public opinion would not, perhaps, at that time have protected your property from political blackmail. I merely wished you to know, Mr. Flint, that there is no use in attempting to deceive me in regard to the true colour of those practices. It is perhaps useless for me to add that in my opinion you understand as well as I do the real reason for Mr. Vane's resignation and illness. Once he became convinced that the practices were wrong, he could no longer continue them without violating his conscience. He kept his word to you — at the risk of his life, and, as his son, I take a greater pride in him to-day than I ever have before."

Austen got to his feet. He was formidable even to Mr. Flint, who had met many formidable and angry men in his time — although not of this type. Perhaps — who can say? — he was the unconscious embodiment in the mind of the president of the Northeastern of the new forces which had arisen against him, — forces which he knew in his secret soul he could not combat, because they were the irresistible forces of things not material. All his life he had met and successfully conquered forces of another kind, and put down with a strong hand merely physical encroachments.

Mr. Flint's nature was not an introspective one, and if he had tried, he could not have accounted for his feelings. He was angry — that was certain. But he measured the six feet and more of Austen Vane with his eye, and in spite of himself experienced the compelled admiration of one fighting man for another. A thought, which had made itself vaguely felt at intervals in the past half hour, shot suddenly and poignantly through Mr. Flint's mind : what if this young man, who dared in spite of every interest to oppose him, should in the apparently inevitable trend of things, become . . . ?

Mr. Flint rose and went to the window, where he stood silent for a space, looking out, played upon by unwonted conflicting thoughts and emotions. At length, with a characteristic snap of the fingers, he turned abruptly. Austen Vane was still standing beside the desk. His face was still square, determined, but Mr. Flint noted curiously that the anger was gone from his eyes, and that another — although equally human — expression had taken its place, — a more disturbing expression, to Mr. Flint.

"It appears, Mr. Vane," he said, gathering up the papers and placing them in the boxes, " it appears that we are able to agree upon one point, at least — Hilary Vane."

"Mr. Flint," said Austen, "I did not come up here with any thought of arguing with you, of intruding any ideas I may hold, but you have yourself asked me one question which I feel bound to answer to the best of my ability before I go. You have asked me what, in my opinion, would happen if you ceased — as you express it — to take an interest in the political affairs of this State.

"I believe, as firmly as I stand here, that the public opinion which exists to-day would protect your property, and I base that belief on the good sense of the average American voter. The public would protect you not only in its own interests, but from an inherent sense of fair play. On the other hand, if you persist in a course of political manipulation which is not only obsolete but wrong, you will magnify the just charges against you, and the just wrath; you will put ammunition into the hands of the agitators you rightly condemn. The stockholders of your corporation, perhaps, are bound to suffer some from the fact that you have taken its life-blood to pay dividends, and the public will demand that it be built up into a normal and healthy condition. On the other hand, it could not have gone on as it was. But the corporation will suffer much more if a delayed justice is turned into vengeance.

"You ask me what I could do. I should recognize, frankly, the new conditions, and declare as frankly what the old ones were, and why such methods of defence as you adopted were necessary and justified. I should announce, openly, that from this day onward the Northeastern Railroads depended for fair play on an enlightened public — and I think your trust would be well founded, and your course vindicated. I should declare, from this day onward, that the issue of political passes, newspaper passes, and all other subterfuges would be stopped, and that all political hirelings would be dismissed. I should appeal to the people of this State to raise up political leaders who would say to the corporations, 'We will protect you from injustice if you will come before the elected representatives of the people, openly, and say what you want and why you want it.' By such a course you would have, in a day, the affection of the people instead of their distrust. They would rally to your defence. And, more than that, you would have done a service for American government the value of which cannot well be estimated."

Mr. Flint rang the bell on his desk, and his secretary appeared.

"Put these in my private safe, Mr. Freeman," he said.

Mr. Freeman took the boxes, glanced curiously at Austen, and went out. It was the same secretary, Austen recalled, who had congratulated him four years before. Then Mr. Flint laid his hand deliberately on the desk, and smiled slightly as he turned to Austen.

"If you had run a railroad as long as I have, Mr. Vane," he said, "I do you the credit of thinking that you would have intelligence enough to grasp other factors which your present opportunities for observation have not permitted you to perceive. Nevertheless, I am much obliged to you for your opinion, and I value the — frankness in which it was given. And I shall hope to hear good news of your father. Remember me to him, and tell him how deeply I feel his affliction. I shall call again in a day or two."

Austen took up his hat.

"Good day, Mr. Flint," he said; "I will tell him."

By the time he had reached the door, Mr. Flint had gone back to the window once more, and appeared to have forgotten his presence.

2 I

CHAPTER XXIX

THE VALE OF THE BLUE

AUSTEN himself could not well have defined his mental
state as he made his way through the big rooms towards
the door, but he was aware of one main desire — to escape
from Fairview. With the odours of the flowers in the
tall silver vases on the piano — her piano ! — the spirit of
desire which had so long possessed him, waking and sleeping, returned, — returned to torture him now with greater
skill amidst these her possessions; her volume of Chopin
on the rack, bound in red leather and stamped with her
initials, which compelled his glance as he passed, and
brought vivid to his memory the night he had stood in
the snow and heard her playing. So, he told himself,
it must always be, for him to stand in the snow —
listening.

He reached the hall, with a vast relief perceived that it
was empty, and opened the door and went out. Strange
that he should note, first of all, as he paused a moment at
the top of the steps, that the very day had changed! The
wind had fallen; the sun, well on his course towards the
rim of western hills, poured the golden light of autumn
over field and forest, while Sawanec was already in the
blue shadow; the expectant stillness of autumn reigned,
and all unconsciously Austen's blood was quickened —
though a quickening of pain.

The surprise of the instant over, he noticed that his
horse was gone, — had evidently been taken to the
stables. And rather than ring the bell and wait in the
mood in which he found himself, he took the path through
the shrubbery from which he had seen the groom emerge.

It turned beyond the corner of the house, descended a flight of stone steps, and turned again.

*   *   *   *   *   *   *

They stood gazing each at the other for a space of time not to be computed before either spoke, and the sense of unreality which comes with a sudden fulfilment of intense desire — or dread — was upon Austen.   Could this indeed be her figure, and this her face on which he watched the colour rise (so he remembered afterwards) like the slow flood of day ?   Were there so many Victorias, that a new one — and a strange one — should confront him at every meeting ?   And, even while he looked, this Victoria, too, — one who had been near him and departed, — was surveying him now from an unapproachable height of self-possession and calm.   She held out her hand, and he took it, scarce knowing that it was hers.

"How do you do, Mr. Vane?" she said; "I did not expect to meet you here."

"I was searching for the stable, to get my horse," he answered lamely.

"And your father ? " she asked quickly; "I hope he is not — worse."

It was thus she supplied him, quite naturally, with an excuse for being at Fairview.   And yet her solicitude for Hilary was wholly unaffected.

"Dr. Harmon, who came from New York, has been more encouraging than I had dared to hope," said Austen. "And, by the way, Mr. Vane believes that you had a share in the fruit and flowers which Mr. Flint so kindly brought. If — he had known that I were to see you, I am sure he would have wished me to thank you."

Victoria turned, and tore a leaf from the spiræa.

"I will show you where the stables are," she said; "the path divides a little farther on — and you might find yourself in the kitchen."

Austen smiled, and as she went on slowly, he followed her, the path not being wide enough for them to walk abreast, his eyes caressing the stray hairs that clustered about her neck and caught the light. It seemed so real, and yet so unrealizable, that he should be here with her.

"I am afraid," he said, "that I did not express my gratitude as I should have done the evening you were good enough to come up to Jabe Jenney's."

He saw her colour rise again, but she did not pause.

"Please don't say anything about it, Mr. Vane. Of course I understand how you felt," she cried.

"Neither my father nor myself will forget that service," said Austen.

"It was nothing," answered Victoria, in a low voice. "Or, rather, it was something I shall always be glad that I did not miss. I have seen Mr. Vane all my life, but I never — never really knew him until that day. I have come to the conclusion," she added, in a lighter tone, "that the young are not always the best judges of the old. There," she added, "is the path that goes to the kitchen, which you probably would have taken."

He laughed. Past and future were blotted out, and he lived only in the present. He could think of nothing but that she was here beside him. Afterwards, cataclysms might come and welcome.

"Isn't there another place," he asked, "where I might lose my way?"

She turned and gave him one of the swift, searching looks he recalled so well: a look the meaning of which he could not declare, save that she seemed vainly striving to fathom something in him — as though he were not fathomable! He thought she smiled a little as she took the left-hand path.

"You will remember me to your father?" she said. "I hope he is not suffering."

"He is not suffering," Austen replied. "Perhaps — if it were not too much to ask — perhaps you might come to see him, sometime? I can think of nothing that would give him greater pleasure."

"I will come — sometime," she answered. "I am going away to-morrow, but —"

"Away?" he repeated, in dismay. Now that he was

beside her, all unconsciously the dominating male spirit which was so strong in him, and which moves not woman alone, but the world, was asserting itself. For the moment he was the only man, and she the only woman, in the universe.

"I am going on a promised visit to a friend of mine."

"For how long?" he demanded.

"I don't know," said Victoria, calmly; "probably until she gets tired of me. And there," she added, "are the stables, where no doubt you will find your faithful Pepper."

They had come out upon an elevation above the hard service drive, and across it, below them, was the coach house with its clock-tower and weather-vane, and its two wings, enclosing a paved court where a whistling stable-boy was washing a carriage. Austen regarded this scene an instant, and glanced back at her profile. It was expressionless.

"Might I not linger — a few minutes?" he asked.

Her lips parted slightly in a smile, and she turned her head. How wonderfully, he thought, it was poised upon her shoulders.

"I haven't been very hospitable, have I?" she said. "But then, you seemed in such a hurry to go, didn't you? You were walking so fast when I met you that you quite frightened me."

"Was I?" asked Austen, in surprise.

She laughed.

"You looked as if you were ready to charge somebody. But this isn't a very nice place — to linger, and if you really will stay awhile," said Victoria, "we might walk over to the dairy, where that model protégé of yours, Eben Fitch, whom you once threatened with corporal chastisement if he fell from grace, is engaged. I know he will be glad to see you."

Austen laughed as he caught up with her. She was already halfway across the road.

"Do you always beat people if they do wrong?" she asked.

"It was Eben who requested it, if I remember rightly,"

he said. "Fortunately, the trial has not yet arrived. Your methods," he added, "seem to be more successful with Eben."

They went down the grassy slope with its groups of half-grown trees; through an orchard shot with slanting, yellow sunlight, — the golden fruit, harvested by the morning winds, littering the ground; and then by a gate into a dimpled, emerald pasture slope where the Guernseys were feeding along a water run.   They spoke of trivial things that found no place in Austen's memory, and at times, upon one pretext or another, he fell behind a little that he might feast his eyes upon her.

Eben was not at the dairy, and Austen betraying no undue curiosity as to his whereabouts, they walked on : up the slopes, and still upward towards the crest of the range of hills that marked the course of the Blue.   He did not allow his mind to dwell upon this new footing they were on, but clung to it.   Before, in those delicious moments with her, seemingly pilfered from the angry gods, the sense of intimacy had been deep; deep, because robbing the gods together, they had shared the feeling of guilt, had known that retribution would come.   And now the gods had locked their treasure-chest, although themselves powerless to redeem from him the memory of what he had gained.   Nor could they, apparently, deprive him of the vision of her in the fields and woods beside him, though transformed by their magic into a new Victoria, keeping him lightly and easily at a distance.

Scattering the sheep that flecked the velvet turf of the uplands, they stood at length on the granite crown of the crest itself.   Far below them wound the Blue into its vale of sapphire shadows, with its hillsides of the mystic fabric of the backgrounds of the masters of the Renaissance. For a while they stood in silence under the spell of the scene's enchantment, and then Victoria seated herself on the rock, and he dropped to a place at her side.

"I thought you would like the view," she said; "but perhaps you have been here, perhaps I am taking you to one of your own possessions."

He had flung his hat upon the rock, and she glanced at his serious, sunburned face. His eyes were still fixed, contemplatively, on the Vale of the Blue, but he turned to her with a smile.

" It has become yours by right of conquest," he answered.

She did not reply to that. The immobility of her face, save for the one look she had flashed upon him, surprised and puzzled him more and more — the world-old, indefinable, eternal feminine quality of the Sphinx.

" So you refused to be governor?" she said presently, — surprising him again.

" It scarcely came to that," he replied.

" What did it come to?" she demanded.

He hesitated.

" I had to go down to the capital, on my father's account, but I did not go to the convention. I stayed," he said slowly, " at the little cottage across from the Duncan house where — you were last winter." He paused, but she gave no sign. " Tom Gaylord came up there late in the afternoon, and wanted me to be a candidate."

" And you refused?"

" Yes."

" But you could have been nominated!"

" Yes," he admitted; " it is probable. The conditions were chaotic."

" Are you sure you have done right?" she asked. " It has always seemed to me from what I know and have heard of you that you were made for positions of trust. You would have been a better governor than the man they have nominated."

His expression became set.

" I am sure I have done right," he answered deliberately. " It doesn't make any difference who is governor this time."

" Doesn't make any difference!" she exclaimed.

" No," he said. " Things have changed — the people have changed. The old method of politics, which was wrong, although it had some justification in conditions, has gone out. A new and more desirable state of affairs has come. I am at liberty to say this much to you now," he added, fixing his glance upon her, " because my father has resigned as counsel for the Northeastern, and I have just had a talk with — Mr. Flint."

" You have seen my father ? " she asked, in a low voice, and her face was averted.

" Yes," he answered.

" You — did not agree," she said quickly.

His blood beat higher at the question and the manner of her asking it, but he felt that he must answer it honestly, unequivocally, whatever the cost.

" No, we did not agree. It is only fair to tell you that we differed — vitally. On the other hand, it is just that you should know that we did not part in anger, but, I think, with a mutual respect."

She drew breath.

" I knew," she said, " I knew if he could but talk to you he would understand that you were sincere — and you have proved it. I am glad — I am glad that you saw him."

The quality of the sunlight changed, the very hills leaped, and the river sparkled. Could she care ? Why did she wish her father to know that he was sincere ?

" You are glad that I saw him ! " he repeated.

But she met his glance steadily.

" My father has so little faith in human nature," she answered. " He has a faculty of doubting the honesty of his opponents — I suppose because so many of them have been dishonest. And — I believe in my friends," she added, smiling. " Isn't it natural that I should wish to have my judgment vindicated ? "

He got to his feet and walked slowly to the far edge of the rock, where he stood for a while, seemingly gazing off across the spaces to Sawanec. It was like him, thus to question the immutable. Victoria sat motionless, but her eyes followed irresistibly the lines of power in the tall figure against the sky — the breadth of shoulder and slimness of hip and length of limb typical of the men who had conquered and held this land for their descendants. Suddenly, with a characteristic movement of determination, he swung about and came towards her, and at the same instant she rose.

" Don't you think we should be going back ? " she said. But he seemed not to hear her.

" May I ask you something ? " he said.

" That depends," she answered.

" Are you going to marry Mr. Rangely ? "

" No," she said, and turned away. " Why did you think that ? "

He quivered.

" Victoria ! "

She looked up at him, swiftly, half revealed, her eyes like stars surprised by the flush of dawn in her cheeks. Hope quickened at the vision of hope, the seats of judgment themselves were filled with radiance, and rumour cowered and fled like the spirit of night. He could only gaze, enraptured.

" Yes ? " she answered.

His voice was firm but low, yet vibrant with sincerity, with the vast store of feeling, of compelling magnetism that was in the man and moved in spite of themselves those who knew him. His words Victoria remembered afterwards — all of them ; but it was to the call of the voice she responded. His was the fibre which grows stronger in times of crisis. Sure of himself, proud of the love which he declared, he spoke as a man who has earned that for which he prays, — simply and with dignity.

" I love you," he said ; " I have known it since I have known you, but you must see why I could not tell you so. It was very hard, for there were times when I led myself to believe that you might come to love me. There were times when I should have gone away if I hadn't made a promise to stay in Ripton. I ask you to marry me, because I know that I shall love you as long as I live. I can give you this, at least, and I can promise to protect and cherish you. I cannot give you that to which you have been accustomed all your life, that which you have here at Fairview, but I shouldn't say this to you if I believed that you cared for them above — other things."

" Oh, Austen ! " she cried, " I do not — I do not ! They would be hateful to me — without you. I would rather live with you — at Jabe Jenney's," and her voice caught in an exquisite note between laughter and tears. " I love you, do you understand, *you!* Oh, how could you ever have doubted it ? How could you ? What you believe, I believe. And, Austen, I have been so unhappy for three days."

He never knew whether, as the most precious of graces ever conferred upon man, with a womanly gesture she had raised her arms and laid her hands upon his shoulders before he drew her to him and kissed her face, that vied in colour with the coming glow in the western sky. Above the prying eyes of men, above the world itself, he held her, striving to realize some little of the vast joy of this possession, and failing. And at last she drew away from him, gently, that she might look searchingly into his face again, and shook her head slowly.

" And you were going away," she said, " without a word ! I thought — you didn't care. How could I have known that you were just — stupid ? "

His eyes lighted with humour and tenderness.

" How long have you cared, Victoria ? " he asked.

She became thoughtful.

" Always, I think," she answered ; " only I didn't know it. I think I loved you even before I saw you."

" Before you saw me ! "

" I think it began," said Victoria, " when I learned that you had shot Mr. Blodgett — only I hope you will never do such a thing again. And you will please try to re-member," she added, after a moment, " that I am neither Eben Fitch nor your friend, Tom Gaylord."

*   *   *   *   *   *   *

Sunset found them seated on the rock, with the waters of the river turned to wine at the miracle in the sky — their miracle. At times their eyes wandered to the mountain, which seemed to regard them — from a discreet distance — with a kindly and protecting majesty.

"And you promised," said Victoria, "to take me up there. When will you do it?"

"I thought you were going away," he replied.

"Unforeseen circumstances," she answered, "have compelled me to change my plans."

"Then we will go to-morrow," he said.

"To the Delectable Land," said Victoria, dreamily; "your land, where we shall be — benevolent despots. Austen?"

"Yes?" He had not ceased to thrill at the sound of his name upon her lips.

"Do you think," she asked, glancing at him, "do you think you have money enough to go abroad — just for a little while?"

He laughed joyously.

"I don't know," he said, "but I shall make it a point to examine my bank-account to-night. I haven't done so — for some time."

"We will go to Venice, and drift about in a gondola on one of those gray days when the haze comes in from the Adriatic and touches the city with the magic of the past. Sometimes I like the gray days best — when I am happy. And then," she added, regarding him critically, "although you are very near perfection, there are some things you ought to see and learn to make your education complete. I will take you to all the queer places I love. When you are ambassador to France, you know, it would be humiliating to have to have an interpreter, wouldn't it?"

"What's the use of both of us knowing the language?" he demanded.

"I'm afraid we shall be — too happy," she sighed, presently.

"Too happy!" he repeated.

"I sometimes wonder," she said, "whether happiness and achievement go together. And yet — I feel sure that you will achieve."

"To please you, Victoria," he answered, "I think I should almost be willing to try."

CHAPTER XXX

By request of one who has read thus far, and is still curious.

Yes, and another who, in spite of himself, has fallen in love with Victoria and would like to linger a while longer, even though it were with the paltry excuse of discussing that world-old question of hers — Can sublime happiness and achievement go together? Novels on the problem of sex nowadays often begin with marriages, but rarely discuss the happy ones; and many a woman is forced to sit wistfully at home while her companion soars.

> " Yet may I look with heart unshook
> On blow brought home or missed—
> Yet may I hear with equal ear
> The clarions down the List;
> Yet set my lance above mischance
> And ride the barriere —
> Oh, hit or miss, how little 'tis,
> My Lady is not there ! "

A verse, in this connection, which may be a perversion of Mr. Kipling's meaning, but not so far from it, after all. And yet, would the eagle attempt the great flights if contentment were on the plain? Find the mainspring of achievement, and you hold in your hand the secret of the world's mechanism. Some aver that it is woman.

Do the gods ever confer the rarest of gifts upon him to whom they have given pinions? Do they mate him, ever, with another who soars as high as he, who circles higher that he may circle higher still? Who can answer? Must

those who soar be condemned to eternal loneliness, and
was it a longing they did not comprehend which bade
them stretch their wings toward the sun? Who can say?

Alas, we cannot write of the future of Austen and
Victoria Vane! We can only surmise, and hope, and pray,
—yes, and believe. Romance walks with parted lips and
head raised to the sky; and let us follow her, because
thereby our eyes are raised with hers. We must believe,
or perish.

Postscripts are not fashionable. The satiated theatre-
goer leaves before the end of the play, and has worked
out the problem for himself long before the end of the last
act. Sentiment is not supposed to exist in the orchestra
seats. But above (in many senses) is the gallery, from
whence an excited voice cries out when the sleeper returns
to life, "It's Rip Van Winkle!" The gallery, where are
the human passions which make this world our world;
the gallery, played upon by anger, vengeance, derision,
triumph, hate, and love; the gallery, which lingers and
applauds long after the fifth curtain, and then goes reluctantly home— to dream. And he who scorns the gallery
is no artist, for there lives the soul of art. We raise our
eyes to it, and to it we dedicate this our play; and for it
we lift the curtain once more after those in the orchestra
have departed.

It is obviously impossible, in a few words, to depict
the excitement in Ripton, in Leith, in the State at large,
when it became known that the daughter of Mr. Flint
was to marry Austen Vane,—a fitting if unexpected
climax to a drama. How would Mr. Flint take it? Mr.
Flint, it may be said, took it philosophically; and when
Austen went up to see him upon this matter, he shook
hands with his future son-in-law, —and they agreed to
disagree. And beyond this it is safe to say that Mr.
Flint was relieved; for in his secret soul he had for
many years entertained a dread that Victoria might marry
a foreigner. He had this consolation at any rate.

His wife denied herself for a day to her most intimate
friends,— for it was she who had entertained visions of a

title; and it was characteristic of the Rose of Sharon that she knew nothing of the Vanes beyond the name. The discovery that the Austens were the oldest family in the State was in the nature of a balm; and henceforth, in speaking of Austen, she never failed to mention the fact that his great-grandfather was Minister to Spain in the '30's, — a period when her own was engaged in a far different calling.

And Hilary Vane received the news with a grim satisfaction, Dr. Tredway believing that it had done more for him than any medicine or specialists. And when, one warm October day, Victoria herself came and sat beside the canopied bed, her conquest was complete: he surrendered to her as he had never before surrendered to man or woman or child, and the desire to live surged back into his heart, — the desire to live for Austen and Victoria. It became her custom to drive to Ripton in the autumn mornings and to sit by the hour reading to Hilary in the mellow sunlight in the lee of the house, near Sarah Austen's little garden. Yes, Victoria believed she had developed in him a taste for reading; although he would have listened to Emerson from her lips.

And sometimes, when she paused after one of his long silences to glance at him, she would see his eyes fixed, with a strange rapt look, on the garden or the dim lavender form of Sawanec through the haze, and knew that he was thinking of a priceless thing which he had once possessed, and missed. Then Victoria would close the volume, and fall to dreaming, too.

What was happiness? Was it contentment? If it were, it might endure, — contentment being passive. But could active, aggressive, exultant joy exist for a lifetime, jealous of its least prerogative, perpetually watchful for its least abatement, singing unending anthems on its conquest of the world? The very intensity of her feelings at such times sobered Victoria — alarmed her. Was not perfection at war with the world's scheme, and did not achievement spring from a void?

But when Austen appeared, with Pepper, to drive her

home to Fairview, his presence never failed to revive the
fierce faith that it was his destiny to make the world better,
and hers to help him. Wondrous afternoons they spent
together in that stillest and most mysterious of seasons
in the hill country — autumn! Autumn and happiness!
Happiness as shameless as the flaunting scarlet maples on
the slopes, defiant of the dying year of the future, shadowy
and unreal as the hills before them in the haze. Once,
after a long silence, she started from a revery with the
sudden consciousness of his look intent upon her, and
turned with parted lips and eyes which smiled at him out
of troubled depths.

"Dreaming, Victoria?" he said.

"Yes," she answered simply, and was silent once more.
He loved these silences of hers, — hinting, as they did, of
unexplored chambers in an inexhaustible treasure-house
which by some strange stroke of destiny was his. And
yet he felt at times the vague sadness of them, like the
sadness of the autumn, and longed to dispel it.

"It is so wonderful," she went on presently, in a low
voice, "it is so wonderful I sometimes think that it must
be like — like this; that it cannot last. I have been
wondering whether we shall be as happy when the world
discovers that you are great."

He shook his head at her slowly, in mild reproof.

"Isn't that borrowing trouble, Victoria?" he said. "I
think you need have no fear of finding the world as discerning as yourself."

She searched his face.

"Will you ever change?" she asked.

"Yes," he said. "No man can stand such flattery as
that without deteriorating, I warn you. I shall become
consequential, and pompous, and altogether insupportable,
and then you will leave me and never realize that it has
been all your fault."

Victoria laughed. But there was a little tremor in her
voice, and her eyes still rested on his face.

"But I am serious, Austen," she said. "I sometimes
feel that, in the future, we shall not always have many

such days as these. It's selfish, but I can't help it. There
are so many things you will have to do without me. Don't
you ever think of that?"

His eyes grew grave, and he reached out and took her
hand in his.

" I think, rather, of the trials life may bring, Victoria,"
he answered, " of the hours when judgment halts, when
the way is not clear. Do you remember the last night
you came to Jabe Jenney's? I stood in the road long after
you had gone, and a desolation such as I had never known
came over me. I went in at last, and opened a book to
some verses I had been reading, which I shall never forget.
Shall I tell you what they were?"

" Yes," she whispered.

" They contain my answer to your question," he said.

> " What became of all the hopes,
> Words and song and lute as well?
> Say, this struck you — ' When life gropes
> Feebly for the path where fell
> Light last on the evening slopes,
>
> " ' One friend in that path shall be,
> To secure my step from wrong;
> One to count night day for me,
> Patient through the watches long,
> Serving most with none to see.'

Victoria, can you guess who that friend is?"

She pressed his hand and smiled at him, but her eyes
were wet.

"I have thought of it in that way, too, dear. But—
but I did not know that you had. I do not think that
many men have that point of view, Austen."

" Many men," he answered, " have not the same reason
to be thankful as I."

*   *   *   *   *   *   *

There is a time, when the first sharp winds which fill
the air with flying leaves have come and gone, when the
stillness has come again, and the sunlight is tinged with a

yellower gold, and the pastures are still a vivid green, and
the mountain stained with a deeper blue than any gem,
called Indian summer. And it was in this season that
Victoria and Austen were married, in a little church at
Tunbridge, near Fairview, by the bishop of the diocese,
who was one of Victoria's dearest friends. Mr. Thomas
Gaylord (for whose benefit there were many rehearsals)
was best man, Miss Beatrice Chillingham maid of honour;
and it was unanimously declared by Victoria's bridesmaids,
who came up from New York, that they had fallen in love
with the groom.

How describe the wedding breakfast and festivities at
Fairview House, on a November day when young ladies
could walk about the lawns in the filmiest of gowns! how
recount the guests and leave out no friends — for none
were left out! Mr. Jabe Jenney and Mrs. Jenney, who
wept as she embraced both bride and groom; and Euphrasia, in a new steel-coloured silk and a state of absolute subjection and incredulous happiness. Would that
there were time to chronicle that most amazing of con-
quests of Victoria over Euphrasia! And Mrs. Pomfret,
who, remarkable as it may seem, not only recognized
Austen without her lorgnette, but quite overwhelmed him
with an unexpected cordiality, and declared her intention
of giving them a dinner in New York.

"My dear," she said, after kissing Victoria twice, "he
is *most* distinguished-looking — I had no idea — and a
person who grows upon one. And I am told he is descended from Channing Austen, of whom I have often
heard my grandfather speak. Victoria, I always had the
greatest confidence in your judgment."

Although Victoria had a memory (what woman worth
her salt has not?), she was far too happy to remind Mrs.
Pomfret of certain former occasions, and merely smiled in
a manner which that lady declared to be enigmatic. She
maintained that she had never understood Victoria, and it
was characteristic of Mrs. Pomfret that her respect increased in direct proportion to her lack of understanding.

Mr. Thomas Gaylord, in a waistcoat which was the

2 K

admiration of all who beheld it, proposed the health of
the bride, and proved indubitably that the best of oratory
has its origin in the heart and not in the mind, — for Tom
had never been regarded by his friends as a Demosthenes.
He was interrupted from time to time by shouts of laughter; certain episodes in the early career of Mr. Austen
Vane (in which, if Tom was to be believed, he was an
unwilling participant) were particularly appreciated. And
shortly after that, amidst a shower of miscellaneous articles and rice, Mr. and Mrs. Vane took their departure.

They drove through the yellow sunlight to Ripton, with
lingering looks at the hills which brought back memories
of joys and sorrows, and in Hanover Street bade good-by
to Hilary Vane. A new and strange contentment shone
in his face as he took Victoria's hands in his, and they sat
with him until Euphrasia came. It was not until they
were well on their way to New York that they opened the
letter he had given them, and discovered that it contained
something which would have enabled them to remain in
Europe the rest of their lives — had they so chosen.

We must leave them amongst the sunny ruins of Italy
and Greece and southern France, on a marvellous journey
that was personally conducted by Victoria.

*   *   *   *   *   *   *

Mr. Crewe was unable to go to the wedding, having to
attend a directors' meeting of some importance in the
West. He is still in politics, and still hopeful; and he
was married, not long afterwards, to Miss Alice Pomfret.